PUFFIN CLASSICS

TWENTY THOUSAND LEAGUES UNDER THE SEA

When Professor Aronnax announces to his faithful Conseil that he is about to embark on 'one of those voyages from which people do not always come back' he little realizes how close he is to the truth. His hazardous mission to rid the seas of the huge monster which has puzzled the entire scientific world has astonishing consequences. For the creature is no living beast, but a phenomenon of man's making – a spectacular submarine vessel. And the Professor, Conseil and the Canadian harpooner Ned Land find themselves the helpless captives of Captain Nemo. So begins the most incredible underwater journey ever undertaken. From Atlantis to the South Pole, the three men discover the dangers, the delights and unsurpassed magnificence of the marine world.

Jules Verne is considered the 'Father of Science Fiction'. He was born in Nantes in 1828, and studied for the bar in Paris. In 1862 he published *Five Weeks in a Balloon* and then published at least one novel every year, including *Journey to the Centre of the Earth* (1864), also published in Puffin Classics. Verne's novels were translated into many languages and were tremendously well received, particularly in England. He died in Amiens in 1905.

This edition of *Twenty Thousand Leagues under the Sea* has been specially abridged for Puffin.

Another book by Jules Verne

JOURNEY TO THE CENTRE OF THE EARTH

Jules Verne

TWENTY THOUSAND LEAGUES UNDER THE SEA

PUFFIN BOOKS

PUFFIN BOOKS

Published by the Penguin Group
27 Wrights Lane, London W8 5TZ, England
Viking Penguin Inc., 375 Hudson Street, New York, New York 10014, USA
Penguin Books Australia Ltd, Ringwood, Victoria, Australia
Penguin Books Canada Ltd, 2801 John Street, Markham, Ontario, Canada L3R 1B4
Penguin Books (NZ) Ltd, 182–190 Wairau Road, Auckland 10, New Zealand

Penguin Books Ltd, Registered Offices: Harmondsworth, Middlesex, England

First published in 1870
Published in Puffin Books 1986
5 7 9 10 8 6

This abridgement, by Robin Waterfield copyright © Penguin Books, 1986
All rights reserved

Printed in England by Clays Ltd, St Ives plc
Typeset in Palatino

CONTENTS

PART ONE

PART TWO

PART ONE

1

A FLOATING REEF

In the year 1866 the whole maritime population of Europe and America was excited by a mysterious and inexplicable phenomenon. This excitement was not confined to merchants, common sailors, sea-captains, shippers, and naval officers of all countries, but the governments of many states on the two continents were deeply interested.

The excitement was caused by an enormous 'something' that ships were often meeting. It was a long, spindle-shaped, and sometimes phosphorescent object, much larger and more rapid than a whale.

The different accounts that were written of this object in various log-books agreed generally as to its structure, wonderful speed, and the peculiar life with which it appeared endowed. If it was a cetacean it surpassed in bulk all those that had hitherto been classified. Moreover, reliable sightings many leagues apart, yet close in time, showed that the monster could move at tremendous speed, and was at home in warm water or in cold.

In all the great centres the monster became the fashion; it was sung about in the cafés, scoffed at in the newspapers, and represented at all the theatres. It gave opportunity for hoaxes of every description. In all newspapers short of copy imaginary beings reappeared, from the white whale, the terrible 'Moby Dick' of the northern regions, to the inordinate 'kraken', whose tentacles could fold round a vessel of 500 tons burden and drag it down to the depths of the ocean.

Then broke out the interminable polemics of believers and disbelievers in learned societies and scientific journals. The 'question of the monster' inflamed all minds. The journalists who professed to be scientific, at strife with those who professed to be witty, poured out streams of ink during this memorable controversy.

In the year of 1867 some fresh facts changed it from a scientific problem to be solved to a real and serious danger to be avoided. On 5 March, the *Moravian*, of the Montreal Ocean Company, sailing in the north-west Atlantic, struck her starboard quarter on a rock which no chart gave in that point. She was then going at the rate of thirteen knots under the combined efforts of the wind and her 400 horse power. Had it not been for the more than ordinary strength of the hull in the *Moravian* she would have been broken by the shock, and have gone down with the 237 passengers she was bringing from Canada.

This fact, extremely grave in itself, would perhaps have been forgotten, like so many others, if a few weeks afterwards it had not happened again under identical circumstances, only, thanks to the nationality of the ship that was this time victim of the shock, and the reputation of the company to which the vessel belonged, the circumstance was immensely commented upon.

On 13 April, by a smooth sea and favourable breeze, the Cunard steamer *Scotia* was in the north-east Atlantic. She was going at the rate of thirteen knots under the pressure of her 1,000 horse power.

At 4.17 p.m., as the passengers were assembled at dinner in the great saloon, a slight shock was felt on the hull of the *Scotia*, on her quarter a little aft of the paddle.

The *Scotia* had not struck anything, but had been struck by some sharp and penetrating rather than blunt surface. The shock was so slight that no one on board would have been uneasy at it had it not been for the carpenter's watch, who rushed upon deck, calling out 'She is sinking! She is sinking!'

At first the passengers were much alarmed, but Captain Anderson hastened to reassure them by telling them the danger could not be imminent, as the ship was divided into seven compartments by strong divisions, and could with impunity brave any leak.

Captain Anderson went down immediately into the hold and found that a leak had sprung in the fifth compartment, and the sea was rushing in rapidly. Happily there were no boilers in this compartment, or the fires would have been at once put out. Captain Anderson ordered the engines to be immediately stopped, and one of the sailors dived to ascertain the extent of the damage. Some minutes after it was ascertained that there was a large hole about two yards in diameter in the ship's bottom. Such a leak could not be stopped, and the *Scotia*, with her paddles half submerged, was obliged to continue her voyage. She was then 300 miles from Cape Clear, and after three days' delay, which caused great anxiety in Liverpool, she entered the company's docks.

The engineers then proceeded to examine her in the dry dock, where she had been placed. They could scarcely believe their eyes; at two yards and a half below water-mark was a regular rent in the shape of an isosceles triangle. The place where the piece had been taken out of the iron plates was so sharply defined that it could not have been done more neatly by a punch. The perforating instrument that had done the work was of no common stamp, for after having been driven with prodigious force, and piercing an iron plate one and three-eighths of an inch thick, it had been withdrawn by some wonderful backward movement.

Such was the last fact, and it again awakened public opinion on the subject. After that all maritime disasters which could not be satisfactorily accounted for were put down to the account of the monster. All the responsibility of the numerous wrecks annually recorded at Lloyd's was laid to the charge of this fantastic animal, and they usually amount to 3,000, of which 200 are lost by unknown causes.

Thanks to the 'monster', communication between the two continents became more and more difficult; the public loudly demanded that the seas should be rid of the formidable cetacean at any price.

2

FOR AND AGAINST

At the period when these events were happening I was returning from a scientific expedition into Nebraska, in the United States. In my position as Professor in the Paris Museum of Natural History, the French Government had attached me to that expedition. I arrived at New York, loaded with precious collections made during six months in Nebraska, at the end of March. My departure for France was fixed for the beginning of May. Whilst I waited and was occupying myself with classifying my mineralogical, botanical, and zoological riches, the incident happened to the *Scotia*.

I was perfectly acquainted with the subject which was the question of the day, and it would have been strange had I not been. I had repeatedly read all the American and European papers without being any the wiser as to the cause. The mystery puzzled me, and I hesitated to form any conclusion.

When I arrived at New York the subject was hot. The hypothesis of a floating island or reef, which was supported by incompetent opinion, was quite abandoned, for unless the shoal had a machine in its stomach, how could it change its position with such marvellous rapidity? For the same reason the idea of a floating hull or gigantic wreck was given up.

There remained, therefore, two possible solutions of the enigma which created two distinct parties; one was that the object was a colossal monster, the other that it was a submarine vessel of enormous motive power. This last hypothesis, which, after all, was admissible, could not stand against inquiries made in the two hemispheres. It was hardly probable that a private individual should possess such a machine. Where and when had he caused it to be built, and how could he have kept its construction secret? Certainly a government might possess such a destructive engine, and it was possible in these disastrous times, when the power of weapons of war has been multiplied, that, without the knowledge of others, a state might possess so formidable a weapon.

But the hypothesis of a war machine fell before the declaration of different governments.

On my arrival at New York, several persons did me the honour of consulting me about the phenomenon in question. I had published in France a work in two volumes, called *The Mysteries of the Great Submarine Grounds*. This book made some sensation in the scientific world, and gained me a special reputation in this rather obscure branch of Natural History. As long as I could deny the reality of the fact I kept to a decided negative, but I was soon driven into a corner, and was obliged to explain myself categorically. The Honourable Pierre Aronnax, Professor in the Paris Museum, was asked by the *New York Herald* to give his opinion on the matter. I subjoin an extract from the article which I published on 30 April:

After having examined the different hypotheses one by one, and all other suppositions being rejected, the existence of a marine animal of excessive strength must be admitted.

The greatest depths of the ocean are totally unknown to us. What happens there? What beings can live twelve or fifteen miles below the surface of the sea? We can scarcely conjecture what the organization of these animals is. We either know all the varieties of beings that people our planet or we do not. If we do not know them all, nothing is more reasonable than to admit the existence of fishes or cetaceans of an organization suitable to the strata inaccessible to soundings, which for some reason or other come up to the surface at intervals.

If, on the contrary, we do know all living species, we must of course look for the animal in question amongst the already classified marine animals, and in that case I should be disposed to admit the existence of a gigantic narwhal.

The common narwhal, or sea-unicorn, is often sixty feet long. This size increased five to tenfold, and a strength in proportion to its size being given to the cetacean, and its offensive arms being increased in the same proportion, you obtain the animal required.

The narwhal is armed with a kind of ivory sword or halberd, as some naturalists call it. It is the principal tusk, and is as hard as steel. Some of these tusks have been found embedded in the bodies of whales, which the narwhal always attacks with success. Others have been with difficulty taken out of ships' bottoms, which they pierced through and through like a gimlet in a barrel. The Museum of the Paris Faculty of Medicine contains one of these weapons, two and a quarter yards in length and fifteen inches in diameter at the base.

Now suppose this weapon to be ten times stronger, and its possessor ten times more powerful, hurl it at the rate of twenty miles an hour, and you obtain a shock that might produce the catastrophe required. Therefore, until I get fuller information, I shall suppose it to be a sea-unicorn of colossal dimensions.

My article was well received, and provoked much discussion amongst the public. It rallied a certain number of partisans. Opinion was soon made up as to the nature of the phenomenon, and the public admitted without argument the existence of the prodigious animal which had nothing in common with the fabulous sea serpents.

But if some people saw in this nothing but a purely scientific problem to solve, others more positive, especially in America and England, were of opinion to purge the ocean of this formidable monster, in order to reassure transmarine communications. The United States were first in the field, and preparations for an expedition to pursue the narwhal were at once begun in New York. A very fast frigate, the *Abraham Lincoln*, was put in commission, and the arsenals were opened to Captain Farragut, who actively hastened the arming of his frigate.

But, as generally happens, from the moment it was decided to pursue the monster, the monster was not heard of for two months. So when the frigate had been prepared for a long campaign, and furnished with formidable fishing apparatus, they did not know where to send her to. Impatience was increasing with the delay, when on 2 July it was reported that a steamer of the San Francisco line, from California to Shanghai, had met with the animal three weeks before in the north Pacific Ocean.

The emotion caused by the news was extreme, and twenty-four hours only were granted to Captain Farragut before he sailed. The ship was already victualled and well stocked with coal. The crew were there to a man, and there was nothing to do but to light the fires.

Three hours before the *Abraham Lincoln* left Brooklyn Pier I received the following letter:

To M. ARONNAX, Professor of the Paris Museum,
     Fifth Avenue Hotel,
      New York.

SIR, If you would like to join the expedition of the *Abraham Lincoln*, the United States Government will have great pleasure in seeing France represented by you in the enterprise. Captain Farragut has a cabin at your disposition.

               Faithfully yours,
                  J. B. HOBSON,
                   Secretary of Marine.

3

AS MONSIEUR PLEASES

Three seconds before the arrival of J. B. Hobson's letter I had no more idea of pursuing the unicorn than of attempting the North-west Passage. Three seconds after having read the secretary's letter I had made up my mind that ridding the world of this monster was my veritable vocation and the single aim of my life.

'Conseil!' I called in an impatient tone. 'Conseil!'

Conseil was my servant, a faithful fellow who accompanied me in all my journeys, a brave Dutchman I had great confidence in; he was placid by nature, regular from principle, zealous from habit, showing little astonishment at the varied surprises of life, very skilful with his hands, apt at any service, and, in spite of his name, never giving any counsel, even when not asked for it.

By dint of contact with the world of *savants* in our Jardin des Plantes, Conseil had succeeded in knowing something. He was a specialist, well up in the classification of Natural History, but his science stopped there. As far as practice was concerned, I do not think he could have distinguished a cachalot from a whale. And yet what a brave fellow he was!

Conseil had followed me during the last ten years

wherever science had directed my steps. He never complained of the length or fatigue of a journey, or of having to pack his trunk for any country, however remote, whether China or Congo.

But Conseil had one fault. He was intensely formal, and would never speak to me except in the third person, which was sometimes irritating.

'Conseil!' I repeated, beginning my preparations for departure with a feverish hand.

Certainly, I was certain of this faithful fellow. Usually I did not ask him if it was or was not convenient for him to accompany me on my travels; but this time an expedition was in question which might be a very long and hazardous one, in pursuit of an animal capable of sinking a frigate like a nutshell. There was matter for reflection even to the most impassive man in the world. What would Conseil say?

'Conseil!' I called for the third time.

Conseil appeared.

'Did monsieur call me?' said he on entering.

'Yes, my boy. Get yourself and me ready to start in two hours.'

'As it pleases monsieur,' answered Conseil calmly.

'There is not a minute to lose. Pack up all my travelling utensils, as many coats, shirts and socks as you can get in. Make haste!'

'And monsieur's collections?' asked Conseil.

'We will see to them presently. I will give orders to have our menagerie forwarded to France.'

'We are not going back to Paris, then?' asked Conseil.

'You know about the monster, Conseil – the famous narwhal. We are going to rid the seas of it. The author of the *Great Submarine Grounds* cannot do otherwise than embark with Commander Farragut. A glorious mission, but dangerous too. We don't know where we are going to. Those animals may be very capricious! But we will go, whether or no! We have a captain who will keep his eyes open.'

'As monsieur does I will do,' answered Conseil.

'But think, for I will hide nothing from you. It is one of those voyages from which people do not always come back.'

'As monsieur pleases.'

A quarter of an hour afterwards our trunks were ready.

When we arrived at the *Abraham Lincoln*, our luggage was at once sent on board, and we soon followed it. I asked for Captain Farragut. One of the sailors conducted me to the poop, where I found myself in the presence of a pleasant-looking officer, who held out his hand to me.

'Monsieur Pierre Aronnax?' he said.

'Himself,' replied I. 'Do I see Captain Farragut?'

'In person. You are welcome, professor. Your cabin is ready for you.'

I bowed, and leaving the commander to his duties, went down to the cabin which had been prepared for me.

4

NED LAND

Captain Farragut was a good seaman, worthy of the frigate he was commanding. His ship and he were one. He was the soul of it. No doubt arose in his mind on the question of the cetacean, and he did not allow the existence of the animal to be disputed on board. The monster existed, and he had sworn to deliver the seas from it.

The officers on board shared the opinion of their chief. It was amusing to hear them talking, arguing, disputing and calculating the different chances of meeting whilst they kept a sharp look-out over the vast extent of ocean. More than one took up his position on the crosstrees who would have cursed the duty as a nuisance at any other time. And nevertheless the *Abraham Lincoln* was not yet ploughing with her stern the suspected waters of the Pacific.

As to the crew, all they wanted was to meet the unicorn, harpoon it, haul it on board, and cut it up. Captain Farragut had offered a reward of 2,000 dollars to the first cabin-boy, sailor, or officer who should signal the animal. I have already said that Captain Farragut had carefully provided all the tackle necessary for taking the gigantic cetacean. A whaler would not have been better furnished. We had every known engine, from the hand harpoon to the barbed arrow of the blunderbuss and the explosive bullets of the deck-gun. On the forecastle lay a breechloader. This weapon could throw with ease a conical projectile, weighing nine pounds, to a mean distance of ten miles. Thus the *Abraham Lincoln* not only possessed every means of destruction, but, better still, she had on board Ned Land, the king of harpooners.

Ned Land was a Canadian of uncommon skill, who had no equal in his perilous employment. He possessed ability, sang-froid, audacity, and subtleness to a remarkable degree, and it would have taken a sharp whale or a singularly wily cachalot to escape his harpoon. He was about forty years of age, tall, strongly built, grave, and taciturn, sometimes violent, and very passionate when put out. His person, and especially the power of his glance, which gave a singular expression to his face, attracted attention.

I believe that Captain Farragut had done wisely in engaging this man. He was worth all the rest of the ship's company as far as his eye and arm went. I could not compare him to anything better than a powerful telescope which would be a cannon always ready to fire as well.

However, Ned Land hardly believed in the narwhal, and he was the only one on board who did not share the universal conviction.

One magnificent evening, three weeks after our departure, on 30 July, the frigate was abreast of Cape Blanc, thirty miles to leeward of the Patagonian coast. We had crossed the tropic of Capricorn, and the Straits of Magellan lay less than 700 miles to the south. Another week and the *Abraham Lincoln* would be ploughing the waters of the Pacific.

Seated on the poop, Ned Land and I were talking on all

sorts of subjects, looking at that mysterious sea whose greatest depths have remained till now inaccessible to the eye of man. I brought the conversation naturally to the subject of the giant unicorn, and discussed the different chances of success in our expedition. Then seeing that Ned Land let me go on talking without saying anything himself, I pressed him more closely.

'Well, Ned,' I said to him, 'are you not yet convinced of the existence of the cetacean we are pursuing? Have you any particular reasons for being so incredulous?'

The harpooner looked at me for some minutes before replying, struck his forehead with a gesture habitual to him, shut his eyes as if to collect himself, and said at last:

'Perhaps I have, M. Aronnax.'

'Yet you, Ned, are a whaler by profession. You are familiar with the great marine mammalia, and your imagination ought easily to accept the hypothesis of enormous cetaceans. You ought to be the last to doubt in such circumstances.'

Ned replied, 'I have pursued many cetaceans, harpooned a great number, and killed some few; but however powerful or well armed they were, neither their tails nor their defences could ever have made an incision in the iron plates of a steamer.'

'Yet, Ned, it is said that ships have been bored through by the tusk of a narwhal.'

'Wooden ships, perhaps,' answered the Canadian, 'though I have never seen it, and until I get proof to the contrary I deny that whales, cachalots, or sea-unicorns could produce such an effect.'

'Listen to me, Ned.'

'No, sir, no; anything you like but that – a gigantic squid perhaps?'

'No, that can't be. The squid is only a mollusc; its flesh is too soft.'

'Then you really do believe in this cetacean, sir?' said Ned.

'Yes, Ned. I repeat it with a conviction resting on the logic of facts. I believe in the existence of a mammal, powerfully organized, belonging to the branch of vertebrata, like whales, cachalots, and dolphins, and furnished with a horn tusk, of which the force of penetration is extreme.'

'Hum!' said the harpooner, shaking his head like a man who will not let himself be convinced.

'Remark, my worthy Canadian,' I continued, 'if such an animal exists and inhabits the depths of the ocean, it necessarily possesses an organization the strength of which would defy all comparison.'

'Why must it have such an organization?' asked Ned.

'Because it requires an incalculable strength to keep in such deep water and resist its pressure. If vertebrata can maintain themselves in such depths, especially those whose surface is represented by millions of square inches, it is by hundreds of millions of pounds we must estimate the pressure they bear. Calculate, then, what must be the resistance of their bony structure and the strength of their organization to withstand such a pressure.'

'They must be made of iron plate eight inches thick!' said Ned.

'Yes, and think what destruction such a mass could cause if hurled with the speed of an express against the hull of a ship.'

Ned would not give in.

'Have I not convinced you?' I said.

'You have convinced me of one thing, sir, which is that if such animals do exist at the bottom of the sea they must be as strong as you say.'

'But if they do not exist, Mr Obstinate, how do you account for the *Scotia*'s accident?'

'Because it is –' began Ned hesitatingly.

'Go on!'

'Because it is not true!' answered the Canadian.

This answer proved the obstinacy of the harpooner and nothing else.

5

AT RANDOM

By 20 July we had reached the north Pacific. We were at last on the scene of the last frolics of the monster. For three months – three months, each day of which lasted a century – the *Abraham Lincoln* ploughed all the waters of the north Pacific, running down all the whales signalled, making sharp deviations from her route, veering suddenly from one tack to another, and not leaving one point of the Chinese or Japanese coast unexplored. And yet nothing was seen but the immense waste of waters – nothing that resembled a gigantic narwhal, nor a wreck, nor a floating reef, nor anything at all supernatural.

Discouragement took possession of all minds, and opened a breach for incredulity. A new sentiment was experienced on board, composed of three-tenths of shame and seven-tenths of rage. They called themselves fools for being taken in by an illusion, and were still more furious at it. The mountains of arguments piled up for a year fell down all at once, and all every one thought of was to make up the hours of meals and sleep which they had so foolishly sacrificed.

This useless search could be no further prolonged. The *Abraham Lincoln* had nothing to reproach herself with, having done all she could to succeed. No crew of the American navy had ever shown more patience or zeal; its want of success could not be imputed to it. There was nothing left to do but to return.

A representation in this sense was made to the commander. The commander kept his ground. The sailors did not hide their dissatisfaction, and the service suffered from it. I do not mean that there was revolt on board, but after a reasonable period of obstinacy Captain Farragut asked for three days' patience. If in the delay of three days the monster had not reappeared, the man at the helm should give three turns of the wheel and the *Abraham Lincoln* should make for the European seas.

This promise was made on 2 November. Its first effect was to rally the spirits of the ship's company. The ocean was observed with renewed attention.

Two days passed. The next day, 5 November, was the last of the delay. Japan lay less than 200 miles to leeward. Eight bells had just struck as I was leaning over the starboard side. Conseil, standing near me, was looking straight in front of him. The crew, perched in the ratlins, were keeping a sharp look-out in the approaching darkness. Officers with their night-glasses swept the horizon.

Looking at Conseil, I saw that the brave fellow was feeling slightly the general influence – at least it seemed to me so. Perhaps for the first time, his nerves were vibrating under the action of a sentiment of curiosity.

'Well, Conseil,' said I, 'this is your last chance of pocketing 2,000 dollars.'

'Will monsieur allow me to tell him that I never counted upon the reward, and if the Union had promised a hundred thousand dollars it would never be any the poorer.'

'You are right, Conseil. It has been a stupid affair, after all. We have lost time and patience, and might just as well have been in France six months ago; and besides that, we shall get laughed at.'

'Certainly,' said Conseil tranquilly. 'I think they will laugh at monsieur. And I must say –'

'What, Conseil?'

'That it will serve monsieur right! When one has the honour to be a *savant* like monsieur, one does not expose –'

Conseil did not finish his compliment. In the midst of general silence Ned Land's voice was heard calling out –

'Look out there! The thing we are looking for on our weather beam!'

6

WITH ALL STEAM ON

At this cry the entire crew rushed towards the harpooner.

At two cables' length from the *Abraham Lincoln* on her starboard quarter, the sea seemed to be illuminated below the surface. The monster lay some fathoms below the sea, and threw out the very intense but inexplicable light mentioned in the reports of several captains. This light described an immense and much elongated oval, in the centre of which was condensed a focus the over-powering brilliancy of which died out by successive gradations.

'It is only an agglomeration of phosphoric particles,' cried one of the officers.

'No, sir,' I replied with conviction. 'Never did pholas or salpae produce such a light as that. That light is essentially electric. Besides – see! Look out! It moves – forward – on to us!'

A general cry rose from the frigate.

'Silence!' called out the captain. 'Up with the helm! Reverse the engines!'

The frigate thus tried to escape, but the supernatural animal approached her with a speed double her own.

Stupefaction, more than fear, kept us mute and

motionless. The animal gained upon us. It made the round of the frigate, which was then going at the rate of fourteen knots, and enveloped her with its electric ring like luminous dust. Then it went two or three miles off, leaving a phosphoric trail like the steam of an express locomotive. All at once, from the dark limits of the horizon, where it went to gain its momentum, the monster rushed towards the frigate with frightful rapidity, stopped suddenly at a distance of twenty feet, and then went out, not diving, for its brilliancy did not die out by degrees, but all at once as it turned off. Then it reappeared on the other side of the ship; either going round her or gliding under her hull. A collision might have occurred at any moment, which might have been fatal to us.

All the crew remained up that night. No one thought of going to sleep. The *Abraham Lincoln*, not being able to compete in speed, was kept under half-steam. On its side the narwhal imitated the frigate, let the waves rock it at will, and seemed determined not to leave the scene of combat.

Towards midnight, however, it disappeared, dying out like a large glow-worm. At seven minutes to one in the morning a deafening whistle was heard, like that produced by a column of water driven out with extreme violence.

The captain, Ned Land, and I were then on the poop, peering with eagerness through the profound darkness.

'Ned Land,' asked the commander, 'have you often heard whales roar?'

'Yes, captain, often; but never such a whale as I earned two thousand dollars by sighting.'

'True, you have a right to the prize; but tell me, is it the same noise they make?'

'Yes, sir; but this one is incomparably louder. It is not to be mistaken. It is certainly a cetacean there in our seas. With your permission, sir, we will have a few words with him at daybreak.'

'If he is in a humour to hear them, Mr Land,' said I, in an unconvinced tone.

'Let me get within a length of four harpoons,' answered the Canadian, 'and he will be obliged to listen to me.'

'But in order to approach him,' continued the captain, 'I shall have to put a whaler at your disposition.'

'Certainly, sir.'

'But that will be risking the lives of my men.'

'And mine too,' answered the harpooner simply.

About 2 a.m. the luminous focus reappeared, no less intense, about five miles to the windward of the frigate. Notwithstanding the distance and the noise of the wind and sea, the loud strokes of the animal's tail were distinctly heard, and even its panting breathing.

Until daylight we were all on the alert, and then the fishing-tackle was prepared. The first mate loaded the blunderbusses, which throw harpoons the distance of a mile, and long duck-guns with explosive bullets, which inflict mortal wounds even upon the most powerful animals. Ned Land contented himself with sharpening his harpoon – a terrible weapon in his hands.

At 6 a.m. day began to break, and with the first glimmer of dawn the electric light of the narwhal disappeared. At 7 a.m. a very thick sea-fog obscured the atmosphere, and the best glasses could not pierce it.

I climbed the mizenmast and found some officers already perched on the mast-heads.

At 8 a.m. the mist began to clear away. Suddenly, like the night before, Ned Land's voice was heard calling –

'The thing in question on the port quarter!'

All eyes were turned towards the point indicated. There, a mile and a half from the frigate, a large black body emerged more than a yard above the waves. Its tail, violently agitated, produced a considerable eddy. An immense track, dazzlingly white, marked the passage of the animal, and described a long curve.

The frigate approached the cetacean, and I could see it well. I estimated its length at 150 feet. As to its other dimensions, I could only conceive them to be in proportion.

Whilst I was observing it, two jets of vapour and water sprang from its vent-holes and ascended to a height of fifty yards, thus fixing my opinion as to its way of breathing.

The crew were waiting impatiently for their captain's orders. Farragut, after attentively examining the animal, had the chief engineer called.

'Is your steam up, sir?' asked the captain.

'Yes, captain,' answered the engineer.

'Then make up your fires and put on all steam.'

Three cheers greeted this order. The hour of combat had struck. Some minutes afterwards the funnels of the frigate were giving out torrents of black smoke, and the deck shook under the trembling of the boilers.

The *Abraham Lincoln*, propelled by her powerful screw, went straight at the animal, who let her approach to within half a cable's length, and then, as if disdaining to dive, made a little attempt at flight, and contented itself with keeping its distance.

This pursuit lasted about three-quarters of an hour, without the frigate gaining four yards on the cetacean. It was quite evident she would never reach it at that rate.

The captain twisted his beard impatiently.

'Ned Land!' called the captain. 'Do you think I had better have the boats lowered?'

'No, sir,' answered Ned Land, 'for that animal won't be caught unless it chooses.'

'What must be done, then?'

'Force steam if you can, captain, and I, with your permission, will post myself under the bowsprit, and if we get within a harpoon length I shall hurl one.'

'Very well, Ned,' said the captain. 'Engineer, put on more pressure.'

Ned Land went to his post, the fires were increased, the screw revolved forty-three times a minute, and the steam poured out of the valves. The frigate was going eighteen miles and five-tenths an hour. But the animal went eighteen and five-tenths an hour too.

For another hour the frigate kept up that speed without gaining a yard. It was humiliating for one of the quickest vessels in the American navy. The crew began to get very angry. The sailors swore at the animal, who did not deign to answer them. The captain not only twisted his beard, he began to gnaw it too. The engineer was called once more.

'Have you reached your maximum of pressure?' asked the captain.

'Yes, sir.'

The captain ordered him to do all he could without absolutely blowing up the vessel, and coal was at once piled up on the fires. The speed of the frigate increased. Her masts shook again. This time she was making nineteen miles and three-tenths. But the cetacean did the nineteen miles and three-tenths as easily as the eighteen and five-tenths.

What a chase! I cannot describe the emotion that made my whole being vibrate again. Ned Land kept at his post, harpoon in hand. The animal allowed itself to be approached several times. Sometimes it was so near that the Canadian raised his hand to hurl the harpoon, when the animal rushed away at a speed of at least thirty miles an hour, and even during our maximum of speed it bullied the frigate, going round and round it.

A cry of fury burst from all lips. We were not further advanced at twelve o'clock than we had been at eight. Captain Farragut then made up his mind to employ more direct means.

'Ah!' said he. 'So that animal goes faster than my ship! Well, we'll see if he'll go faster than a conical bullet. Master, send your men to the forecastle.'

The forecastle gun was immediately loaded and pointed. It was fired, but the ball passed some feet above the cetacean, which kept about half a mile off.

'Let someone else have a try!' called out the captain. 'Five hundred dollars to whomsoever will hit the beast!'

An old gunner with a grey beard – I think I see now his calm face as he approached the gun – put it into position and took a long aim. A loud report followed and mingled with the cheers of the crew.

The bullet reached its destination; it struck the animal, but, gliding off the rounded surface, fell into the sea two miles off.

'Malediction!' cried the captain. 'That animal must be clad in six-inch iron plates. But I'll catch it, if I have to blow up my frigate!'

It was to be hoped that the animal would be exhausted, and that it would not be indifferent to fatigue like a steam-engine. But the hours went on, and it showed no signs of exhaustion.

It must be said, in praise of the *Abraham Lincoln*, that she struggled on indefatigably. I cannot reckon the distance we made during this unfortunate day at less than 300 miles. But night came on and closed round the heaving ocean.

At that minute I believed our expedition to be at

an end, and that we should see the fantastic animal no more.

I was mistaken, for at 10.50 p.m. the electric light reappeared, three miles windward to the frigate, as clear and intense as on the night before.

The narwhal seemed motionless. Perhaps, fatigued with its day's work, it was sleeping in its billowy cradle. That was a chance by which the captain resolved to profit.

He gave his orders. The *Abraham Lincoln* was kept up at half-steam, and advanced cautiously so as not to awaken her adversary. It is not rare to meet in open sea with whales fast asleep, and Ned Land had harpooned many a one in that condition. The Canadian went back to his post under the bowsprit.

The frigate noiselessly approached, and stopped at two cables' length from the animal. No one breathed. A profound silence reigned on deck. We were not 1,000 feet from the burning focus, the light of which increased and dazzled our eyes.

At that minute, leaning on the forecastle bulwark, I saw Ned Land below me, holding the martingale with one hand and with the other brandishing his terrible harpoon, scarcely twenty feet from the motionless animal.

All at once he threw the harpoon, and I heard the sonorous stroke of the weapon, which seemed to have struck a hard body.

The electric light suddenly went out, and two enormous waterspouts fell on the deck of the frigate, running like a torrent from fore to aft, upsetting men, and breaking the lashing of the spars.

A frightful shock followed. I was thrown over the rail before I had time to stop myself, and fell into the sea.

7

A WHALE OF AN UNKNOWN SPECIES

Although I was surprised by my unexpected fall, I still kept a very distinct impression of my sensations. I was at first dragged down to a depth of about twenty feet. I was a good swimmer and this plunge did not make me lose my presence of mind. Two vigorous kicks brought me back to the surface.

My first care was to look for the frigate. Had the crew seen me disappear? Had the *Abraham Lincoln* veered round? Would the captain have a boat lowered? Might I hope to be saved?

The darkness was profound. I perceived a black mass disappearing in the east, the beacon lights of which were dying out in the distance. It was the frigate. I gave myself up.

'Help! Help!' cried I, swimming towards the frigate with desperate strokes.

My clothes embarrassed me. The water glued them to my body. They paralysed my movements. I was sinking.

'Help!' rang out again in the darkness.

This was the last cry I uttered. My mouth filled with water. I struggled not to be sucked into the abyss.

Suddenly my clothes were seized by a vigorous hand,

and I felt myself brought back violently to the surface of the water, and I heard – yes, I heard these words uttered in my ear:

'If monsieur will have the goodness to lean on my shoulder, monsieur will swim much better.'

I seized the arm of my faithful Conseil.

'You!' I cried. 'You!'

'Myself,' answered Conseil, 'at monsieur's service.'

'Did the shock throw you into the sea too?'

'No; but being in the service of monsieur, I followed him.'

The worthy fellow thought that quite natural.

'What about the frigate?' I asked.

'The frigate!' answered Conseil, turning on his back. 'I think monsieur will do well not to count upon the frigate.'

'Why?'

'Because, as I jumped into the sea, I heard the man at the helm call out, "The screw and the rudder are broken."'

'Broken?'

'Yes, by the monster's tusk. It is the only damage she has sustained, I think; but without a helm she can't do anything for us.'

'Then we are lost!'

'Perhaps,' answered Conseil tranquilly. 'In the meantime we have still several hours before us, and in several hours many things may happen.'

The imperturbable sang-froid of Conseil did me good. I swam more vigorously, but, encumbered by my garments, which dragged me down like a leaden weight, I found it extremely difficult to keep up. Conseil perceived it.

'Will monsieur allow me to make a slit?' said he. And, slipping an open knife under my clothes, he slit them rapidly from top to bottom. I rendered him the same service, and we went on swimming near each other.

In the meantime our situation was none the less terrible. Perhaps our disappearance had not been remarked, and even if it had the frigate could not tack without her helm. Our only chance of safety was in the event of the boats being lowered.

The collision had happened about 11 p.m. About 1 a.m. I was taken with extreme fatigue, and all my limbs became stiff with cramp. Conseil was obliged to keep me up, and the care of our preservation depended upon him alone. I heard the poor fellow breathing hard, and knew he could not keep up much longer.

'Let me go! Leave me!' I cried.

'Leave monsieur? Never!' he answered. 'I shall drown with him.'

Just then the moon appeared through the fringe of a large cloud that the wind was driving eastward. The surface of the sea shone under her rays. I lifted my head and saw the frigate. She was five miles from us, and only looked like a dark mass, scarcely distinguishable. I saw no boats.

I tried to call out, but it was useless at that distance. My swollen lips would not utter a sound. Conseil could still speak, and I heard him call out 'Help!' several times.

We suspended our movements for an instant and listened. It might be only a singing in our ears, but it seemed to me that a cry answered Conseil's.

'Did you hear?' I murmured.

'Yes, yes!'

At that moment I hit against something hard, and I clung to it in desperation. Then I felt myself lifted up out of the water, and I fainted – I soon came to, thanks to the vigorous friction that was being applied to my body, and I half-opened my eyes.

I perceived a face that was not Conseil's, but which I immediately recognized.

'Ned!' I cried.

'The same, sir, looking after his prize,' replied the Canadian.

'Were you thrown into the sea when the frigate was struck?'

'Yes, sir, but, luckier than you, I soon got upon a floating island.'

'An island?'

'Yes, or if you like better, on our giant narwhal.'

'What do you mean, Ned?'

'I mean that I understand now why my harpoon did not stick into the skin, but was blunted.'

'Why, Ned, why?'

'Because the beast is made of sheet-iron plates.'

I wriggled myself quickly to the top of the half-submerged being or object on which we had found refuge. I struck my foot against it. It was evidently a hard and impenetrable body, and not the soft substance which forms the mass of great marine mammalia.

The blow produced a metallic sound. Doubt was no longer possible. The animal, monster, natural phenomenon that had puzzled the entire scientific world, and misled the imagination of sailors in the two hemispheres, was, it must be acknowledged, a still more astonishing phenomenon, a phenomenon of man's making. The discovery of the existence of the most fabulous and mythological being would not have astonished me in the same degree. It seems quite simple that anything prodigious should come from the hand of the Creator, but to find the impossible realized by the hand of man was enough to confound the imagination.

'But then,' said I, 'this apparatus must have a locomotive machine, and a crew inside of it to work it.'

'Evidently,' replied the harpooner, 'and yet for the three hours that I have inhabited this floating island it has not given a sign of life.'

'We know, without the slightest doubt, however, that it is endowed with great speed, and as a machine is necessary to produce the speed, and a mechanician to guide it, I conclude from that that we are saved.'

'Hum,' said Ned Land in a reserved tone of voice.

At that moment, and as if to support my arguments, a boiling was heard at the back of the strange apparatus, the propeller of which was evidently a screw, and it began to move. We only had time to hold on to its upper part, which emerged about a yard out of the water. Happily its speed was not excessive.

'As long as it moves horizontally,' murmured Ned Land, 'I have nothing to say. But if it takes it into its head to plunge, I would not give two dollars for my skin!'

The Canadian might have said less still. It therefore became urgent to communicate with whatever beings were shut up in the machine. I looked on its surface for an opening, a panel; but the lines of bolts, solidly fastened down on the joints of the plates, were clear and uniform.

Besides, the moon then disappeared and left us in profound obscurity. We were obliged to wait till daybreak to decide upon the means of penetrating to the interior of this submarine boat.

About 4 a.m. the rapidity of the apparatus increased. We resisted with difficulty this vertiginous impulsion, when the waves beat upon us in all their fury. Happily Ned touched with his hand a wide balustrade fastened on to the upper part of the iron top, and we succeeded in holding on to it solidly.

At last this long night slipped away. When daylight appeared the morning mists enveloped us, but they soon rose, and I proceeded to make an attentive examination of the sort of horizontal platform we were on, when I felt myself gradually sinking.

'*Mille diables!*' cried Land, kicking against the sonorous metal. 'Open, inhospitable creatures!'

But it was difficult to make oneself heard amidst the deafening noise made by the screw. Happily the sinking ceased.

Suddenly a noise like iron bolts violently withdrawn was heard from the interior of the boat. One of the iron plates was raised, a man appeared, uttered a strange cry, and disappeared immediately.

Some moments later eight strong fellows, with veiled faces, silently appeared, and dragged us down into their formidable machine.

8

MOBILIS IN MOBILI

This abduction, so brutally executed, took place with the rapidity of lightning. I do not know what my companions felt at being introduced into this floating prison; but, for my own part, a rapid shudder froze my very veins. With whom had we to do? Doubtless with a new species of pirates, who made use of the sea in a way of their own.

The narrow panel had scarcely closed upon me when I was enveloped by profound darkness. My eyes, dazzled by the light outside, could distinguish nothing. I felt my naked feet touch the steps of an iron ladder. Ned Land and Conseil, firmly held, followed me. At the bottom of the ladder a door opened and closed again immediately with a sonorous bang.

We were alone. Where? I neither knew nor could I imagine. All was darkness, and such absolute darkness that after some minutes I had not been able to make out even those faint glimmers of light which float in the darkest nights.

Meanwhile, Ned Land, furious at this manner of proceeding, gave free course to his indignation.

'Calm yourself, friend Ned; calm yourself,' said

Conseil tranquilly. 'Don't get into a rage beforehand. We aren't on the spit yet.'

'No, but we're in the oven. This hole's as dark as one. Happily my knife is still on me, and I shall see well enough to use it. The first of these rascals that lays his hand on me –'

'Don't get irritated, Ned,' then said I to the harpooner, 'and do not compromise yourself by useless violence. Who knows that we are not overheard? Let us rather try to make out where we are.'

I groped my way about. When I had gone about five steps I came to an iron wall made of riveted plates. Then turning, I knocked against a wooden table, near which were several stools. The flooring of this prison was hidden under thick matting, which deadened the noise of our footsteps. The walls revealed no traces of either door or window. Conseil, going round the reverse way, met me, and we returned to the centre of the room, which measured about twenty feet by ten. As to its height, Ned Land, notwithstanding his tall stature, could not measure it.

Half an hour passed away without bringing any change in our position, when from the extreme of obscurity our eyes passed suddenly to the most violent light. Our prison was lighted up all at once. It was the same electric light that shone around the submarine boat like a magnificent phosphoric phenomenon. After having involuntarily closed my eyes I opened them again, and saw that the luminous agent was escaping from a polished half-globe, which was shining in the top part of the room.

'Well, we can see at last!' cried Ned Land, who, with his knife in hand, held himself on the defensive.

'Yes,' answered I, 'but the situation is none the less obscure.'

'Let monsieur have patience,' said the imperturbable Conseil.

The sudden lighting of the cabin had allowed me to examine its least details. It only contained the table and five stools. The invisible door seemed hermetically closed. No noise reached our ears. All seemed dead in the interior of this machine. Was it moving, or was it motionless on the surface of the ocean, or deep in its depths? I could not guess.

However, the luminous globe was not lighted without a reason. I hoped that the men of the crew would soon show themselves, and my hope was well founded. A noise of bolts and bars being withdrawn was heard, the door opened, and two men appeared. One was short in stature, vigorously muscular, with broad shoulders, robust limbs, large head, abundant black hair, thick moustache.

The second deserves a more detailed description. I read at once his dominant qualities on his open face – self-confidence, because his head was firmly set on his shoulders, and his black eyes looked round with cold assurance – calmness, for his pale complexion announced the tranquillity of his blood – energy, demonstrated by the rapid contraction of his eyebrows; and lastly, courage, for his deep breathing denoted vast vital expansion. I felt involuntarily reassured in his presence, and augured good from it. He might be of any age from thirty-five to fifty. His tall stature, wide forehead, straight nose, clear-cut mouth, magnificent teeth, tapered hands, indicated a highly nervous temperament. This man formed certainly the most admirable type I had ever met with. One strange detail was that his eyes, rather far from each other, could take in nearly a quarter of the horizon at once. This faculty – I verified it later on – was added to a power of vision superior even to that of

Ned Land. When the unknown fixed on an object he frowned, and his large eyelids closed round so as to contract the range of his vision, and the result was a look that penetrated your very soul. With it he pierced the liquid waves that looked so opaque to us as if he read to the very depths of the sea.

The two strangers had on caps made from the fur of the sea-otter, sealskin boots, and clothes of a peculiar texture, which allowed them great liberty of movement.

The taller of the two – evidently the chief on board – examined us with extreme attention without speaking a word. Then he turned towards his companion, and spoke to him in a language I could not understand. It was a sonorous, harmonious, and flexible idiom, of which the vowels seemed very variously accented.

The other answered by shaking his head and pronouncing two or three perfectly incomprehensible words. Then, from his looks, he seemed to be questioning me directly.

I answered in good French that I did not understand his language; but he did not seem to know French, and the situation became very embarrassing.

'If monsieur would relate his story,' said Conseil, 'these gentlemen may understand some words of it.'

I began the recital of my adventures, articulating clearly all my syllables, without leaving out a single detail. I gave our names and positions. The man with the soft, calm eyes listened to me calmly, and even politely, with remarkable attention. But nothing in his face indicated that he understood me. When I had done he did not speak a single word.

We next tried English, German – even schoolboy Latin.

After this last attempt the strangers exchanged a few words in their incomprehensible language, and went away without a gesture that could reassure us. The door closed upon them.

'It is infamous!' cried Ned Land, who broke out again for the twentieth time. 'French, English, German, and Latin are spoken to those rascals, and not one of them has the politeness to answer.'

'Calm yourself, Ned,' said I to the enraged harpooner; 'anger will do no good.'

'But do you know, professor,' continued our irascible companion, 'that it is quite possible to die of hunger in this iron cage? Do you not see that those fellows have a language of their own – a language invented to make honest men who want their dinners despair?'

As he was saying these words the door opened, and a steward entered. He brought us clothes similar to those worn by the two strangers, which we hastened to don.

Meanwhile the servant – dumb and deaf too in all appearance – had laid the cloth for three.

'This is something like,' said Conseil, 'and promises well.'

'I'll bet anything there's nothing here fit to eat,' said the harpooner. 'Tortoise liver, fillets of shark, or beefsteak from a sea-dog, perhaps!'

'We shall soon see,' said Conseil.

The dishes with their silver covers were symmetrically placed on the table. We had certainly civilized people to deal with, and had it not been for the electric light which inundated us I might have imagined myself in some grand hotel. Amongst the dishes that were placed before us I recognized several kinds of fish delicately cooked; but there were some that I knew nothing about, though they were delicious. The dinner service was elegant and in perfect taste; each piece was engraved with a letter and motto:

Mobilis in Mobili.
N.

Mobile in a mobile element! The letter N was doubtless the initial of the enigmatical person who commanded at the bottom of the sea.

But at last even our appetite was satisfied, and we felt overcome with sleep. A natural reaction after the fatigue of the interminable night during which we had struggled with death.

My two companions lay down on the carpet, and were soon fast asleep. I did not go so soon, for too many thoughts filled my brain; too many insoluble questions asked me for a solution; too many images kept my eyes open. Then my brain grew calmer, my imagination melted into dreaminess, and I fell into a deep sleep.

9

NED LAND'S ANGER

I do not know how long our sleep lasted, but it must have been a long time, for it rested us completely from our fatigues. I awoke first. My companions had not yet moved.

Nothing was changed in the room. The prison was still a prison, and the prisoners prisoners. The steward, profiting by our sleep, had cleared the supper-things away. Nothing indicated an approaching change in our position, and I asked myself seriously if we were destined to live indefinitely in that cage.

This prospect seemed to me the more painful because, though my head was clear, my chest was oppressed. The heavy air weighed upon my lungs. We had evidently consumed the larger part of the oxygen the cell contained, although it was large.

I was reduced to multiplying my respirations to extract from our cell the small quantity of oxygen it contained, when, suddenly, I was refreshed by a sea breeze. I opened my mouth wide, and my lungs became saturated with fresh particles. At the same time I felt the boat roll, and the iron-plated monster had evidently just ascended to the surface of the ocean to breathe like the whales.

When I had breathed fully, I looked for the ventilator which had brought us the beneficent breeze, and before long, found it.

I was making these observations when my two companions awoke nearly at the same time, doubtless through the influence of the reviving air. They rubbed their eyes, stretched themselves, and were on foot instantly.

'Did monsieur sleep well?' Conseil asked me with his usual politeness.

'Very well, old fellow. And you, Mr Land?'

'Profoundly, Mr Professor. But if I am not mistaken, I am breathing a sea breeze.'

A seaman could not be mistaken in that, and I told the Canadian what had happened while he was asleep.

'That accounts for the roarings we heard when the supposed narwhal was in sight of the *Abraham Lincoln*.'

'Yes, Mr Land, that is its breathing.'

'I have not the least idea what time it can be, M. Aronnax, unless it be dinner time.'

'Dinner time, Ned? Say breakfast time at least, for we have certainly slept something like twenty-four hours.'

'Anyway,' said the harpooner, 'I am devilishly hungry, and, dinner or breakfast, the meal does not arrive!'

'What is the use of complaining?' asked Conseil.

'It does one good to complain! It is something. And if these pirates think that they are going to keep me in this cage where I am stifled without hearing how I can swear, they are mistaken. Come, M. Aronnax, speak frankly. Do you think they will keep us long in this iron box?'

'To tell you the truth I know no more about it than you, friend Land.'

'But what do you think about it?'

'I think that hazard has made us masters of an important secret. If it is the interest of the crew of this submarine vessel to keep it, and if this interest is of more consequence than the life of three men, I believe our existence to be in great danger. In the contrary case, on the first opportunity, the monster who has swallowed us will send us back to the world inhabited by our fellow men.'

'Unless he enrols us among his crew,' said Conseil, 'and he keeps us thus –'

'Until some frigate,' replied Ned Land, 'more rapid or more skilful than the *Abraham Lincoln*, masters this nest of plunderers, and sends its crew and us to breathe our last.'

'Well reasoned, Mr Land,' I replied. 'But I believe no proposition of the sort has yet been made to us, so it is useless to discuss what we should do in that case. I repeat, we must wait, take counsel of circumstances, and do nothing, as there is nothing to do.'

'On the contrary, Mr Professor,' answered the harpooner, who would not give up his point, 'we must do something.'

'What, then?'

'Escape.'

'To escape from a terrestrial prison is often difficult, but from a submarine prison, that seems to me quite impracticable.'

'Then, M. Aronnax,' he said, after some minutes' reflection, 'you do not guess what men ought to do who cannot escape from prison?'

'No, my friend.'

'It is very simple; they must make their arrangements to stop in it.'

'I should think so,' said Conseil; 'it is much better to be inside than on the top or underneath.'

'But after you have thrown your gaolers and keepers out?' added Ned Land.

'What, Ned? You seriously think of seizing this vessel?'

'Quite seriously,' answered the Canadian.

'It is impossible.'

'How so, sir? A favourable chance may occur, and I do not see what could prevent us profiting by it. If there are twenty men on board this machine they will not frighten two Frenchmen and a Canadian, I suppose.'

It was better to admit the proposition of the harpooner than to discuss it. So I contented myself with answering:

'Let such circumstances come, Mr Land, and we will see. But until they do I beg of you to contain your impatience. We can only act by stratagem, and you will not make yourself master of favourable chances by getting in a rage. Promise me, therefore, that you will accept the situation without too much anger.'

'I promise you, professor,' answered Ned Land in a not very assuring tone; 'not a violent word shall leave my mouth, not an angry movement shall betray me, not even if we are not waited upon at table with desirable regularity.'

'I have your word, Ned,' I answered.

Two more hours rolled on, and Ned's anger increased; he cried and called at the top of his voice, but in vain. The iron walls were deaf. The boat seemed quite still. The silence became quite oppressive.

I dared no longer think how long our abandonment and isolation in this cell might last. The hopes that I had conceived after our interview with the commander of the vessel vanished one by one. The gentle look of this man, the generous expression of his face, the nobility of his carriage, all disappeared from my memory. I again saw this enigmatical personage such as he must necessarily be, pitiless and cruel. I felt him to be outside the pale of humanity, inaccessible to all sentiment of pity, the implacable enemy of his fellow men, to whom he had vowed imperishable hatred.

But was the man going, then, to let us perish from starvation, shut up in this narrow prison, given up to the horrible temptations to which ferocious famine leads? This frightful thought took a terrible intensity in my mind, and imagination helping, I felt myself invaded by reasoning fear. Conseil remained calm. Ned was roaring. At that moment a noise was heard outside. Steps clanged on the metal slabs. The bolts were withdrawn, the door opened, the steward appeared.

Before I could make a movement to prevent him, the Canadian had rushed upon the unfortunate fellow, knocked him down, and fastened on his throat. The steward was choking under his powerful hand.

Conseil was trying to rescue his half-suffocated victim from the hands of the harpooner, and I was going to join my efforts to his, when, suddenly, I was riveted to my place by these words spoken in French:

'Calm yourself, Mr Land, and you, professor, please to listen to me.'

10

NEMO

The man who spoke thus was the commander of the vessel.

When Ned Land heard these words he rose suddenly. The almost strangled steward went tottering out on a sign from his master; but such was the power of the commander on his vessel that not a gesture betrayed the resentment the man must have felt towards the Canadian. Conseil, interested in spite of himself, and I stupefied, awaited the result of this scene in silence.

The commander, leaning against the angle of the table, with his arms folded, looked at us with profound attention. After some minutes of a silence which none of us thought of interrupting, he said in a calm and penetrating voice:

'Gentlemen, I speak French, English, German and Latin equally well. I might, therefore, have answered you at our last interview, but I wished to know you first, and afterwards to ponder on what you said. The stories told by each of you agreed in the main, and assured me of your identity. I know now that accident has brought me into the presence of M. Pierre Aronnax, Professor of

Natural History in the Paris Museum, charged with a foreign scientific mission, his servant Conseil, and Ned Land, of Canadian origin, harpooner on board the frigate *Abraham Lincoln* of the United States navy.'

I bent my head in sign of assent. There was no answer necessary. This man expressed himself with perfect ease, and without the least foreign accent. And yet I felt that he was not one of my countrymen. He continued the conversation in these terms:

'I dare say you thought me a long time in coming to pay you this second visit. It was because, after once knowing your identity, I wished to ponder upon what to do with you. I hesitated long. The most unfortunate circumstances have brought you into the presence of a man who has broken all ties that bound him to humanity. You came here to trouble my existence –'

'Unintentionally,' said I.

'Unintentionally?' he repeated, raising his voice a little. 'Is it unintentionally that the *Abraham Lincoln* pursues me in every sea? Was it unintentionally that you took passage on board her? Was it unintentionally that your bullets struck my vessel? Did Mr Land throw his harpoon unintentionally?'

'You are doubtless unaware,' I answered, 'of the commotion you have caused in Europe and America. When the *Abraham Lincoln* pursued you on the high seas everyone on board believed they were pursuing a marine monster.'

A slight smile curled round the commander's lips, then he went on in a calmer tone:

'Dare you affirm, M. Aronnax, that your frigate would not have pursued a submarine vessel as well as a marine monster?'

This question embarrassed me, for it was certain that Captain Farragut would not have hesitated. He would have thought it as much his duty to destroy such a machine as the gigantic narwhal he took it to be.

'You see, sir,' continued the commander, 'I have the right to treat you as enemies. Nothing obliges me to give you hospitality. I could place you upon the platform of this vessel, upon which you took refuge; I might sink it beneath the waters and forget that you ever existed. I should only be using my right.'

'The right of a savage, perhaps,' I answered, 'but not that of a civilized man.'

'Professor,' quickly answered the commander, 'I am not what is called a civilized man. I have done with society entirely for reasons that seem to me good; therefore I do not obey its laws, and I desire you never to allude to them before me again.'

This was uttered clearly. A flash of anger and contempt had kindled in the man's eyes, and I had a glimpse of a terrible past in his life. He had not only put himself out of the pale of human laws, but he had made himself independent of them, free, in the most rigorous sense of the word, entirely out of their reach. No man could ask him for an account of his works. God, if he believed in Him, his conscience, if he had one, were the only judges he could depend upon.

After a rather long silence the commander went on speaking.

'I have hesitated, therefore,' said he, 'but I thought that my interest might be reconciled with that natural pity to which every human being has a right. You may remain on my vessel, since fate has brought you to it. You will be free, and in exchange for this liberty, which after all will be relative, I shall only impose one condition upon you. Your word of honour to submit to it will be sufficient.'

'Speak, sir,' I answered. 'I suppose this condition is one that an honest man can accept?'

'Yes. It is this. It is possible that certain unforeseen events may force me to consign you to your cabin for some hours, or even days. As I do not wish to use violence, I expect from you, in such a case, more than from all others, passive obedience. By acting thus I take all the responsibility; I acquit you entirely, by making it impossible for you to see what ought not to be seen. Do you accept the condition?'

So things took place on board which were, at least, singular and not to be seen by people who were not placed beyond the pale of social laws.

'We accept,' I replied. 'Only I ask your permission to address to you one question – only one. What degree of liberty do you intend giving us?'

'The liberty to move about freely and observe even all that passes here – except under rare circumstances – in short, the liberty that my companions and I enjoy ourselves.'

It was evident that we did not understand each other.

'Pardon me, sir,' I continued, 'but this liberty is only that of every prisoner to pace his prison. It is not enough for us.'

'You must make it enough.'

'Do you mean to say we must for ever renounce the idea of seeing country, friends, and relations again?'

'Yes, sir. But to renounce the unendurable worldly yoke that men call liberty is not perhaps so painful as you think.'

'I declare,' said Ned Land, 'I'll never give my word of honour not to try to escape.'

'I did not ask for your word of honour, Mr Land,' answered the commander coldly.

'Sir,' I replied, carried away in spite of myself, 'you take advantage of your position towards us. It is cruel!'

'No, sir, it is kind. You are my prisoners of war. I keep

you when I could, by a word, plunge you into the depths of the ocean. You attacked me. You came and surprised a secret that I mean no man inhabiting the world to penetrate – the secret of my whole existence. And you think that I am going to send you back to that world? Never! In retaining you it is not you I guard, it is myself!'

These words indicated that the commander's mind was made up, and that argument was useless.

'Then, sir,' I answered, 'you give us the simple choice between life and death?'

'As you say.'

'My friends,' said I, 'to a question thus put there is nothing to answer. But no word of honour binds us to the master of this vessel.'

'None, sir,' answered the unknown.

Then in a gentler voice he went on:

'Now allow me to finish what I have to say to you. I know you, M. Aronnax. You, if not your companions, will not have so much to complain of in the chance that has bound you to my lot. You will find amongst the books which are my favourite study the work you have published on the *Great Submarine Grounds*. I have often read it. You have carried your investigations as far as terrestrial science allowed you. But on board my vessel you will have an opportunity of seeing what no man has seen before. Thanks to me, our planet will give up her last secrets.'

I cannot deny that these words had a great effect upon me. My weak point was touched, and I forgot for a moment that the contemplation of these divine things was not worth the loss of liberty. Besides, I counted upon the future to decide that grave question, and so contented myself with saying:

'What name am I to call you by, sir?'

'Captain Nemo,' answered the commander. 'That is all

I am to you, and you and your companions are nothing to me but the passengers of the *Nautilus*.'

The captain called, and a steward appeared. The captain gave him his orders in that foreign tongue which I could not understand. Then turning to the Canadian and Conseil:

'Your meal is prepared in your cabin,' he said to them. 'Be so good as to follow that man.'

My two companions in misfortune left the cell where they had been confined for more than thirty hours.

'And now, M. Aronnax, our breakfast is ready. Allow me to lead the way.'

I followed Captain Nemo into a sort of corridor lighted by electricity, similar to the waist of a ship. After going about a dozen yards a second door opened before me into a kind of dining-room, decorated and furnished with severe taste. High oaken sideboards, inlaid with ebony ornaments, stood at either end of the room, and on their shelves glittered china, porcelain and glass of inestimable value. The plate that was on them sparkled in the light which shone from the ceiling, tempered and softened by fine painting. In the centre of the room was a table richly spread. Captain Nemo pointed to my seat.

'Sit down,' said he, 'and eat like a man who must be dying of hunger.'

While I ate, Captain Nemo explained to me, in passionate tones, how all the food, clothing and furniture on board were the produce of the sea.

'You love the sea, captain?' I asked.

'Yes, I love it. The sea is everything. It covers seven-tenths of the terrestrial globe. Its breath is pure and healthy. It is an immense desert where man is never alone, for he feels life quivering around him on every side. The sea does not belong to despots. On its surface iniquitous rights can still be exercised, men can fight there, devour each other there, and transport all terrestrial horrors there. But at thirty feet below its level their power ceases, their influence dies out, their might disappears. Ah, sir, live in the bosom of the waters! There alone is independence! There I recognize no masters! There I am free!'

Captain Nemo stopped suddenly in the midst of this burst of enthusiasm which overflowed in him. Had he let himself be carried out of his habitual reserve? Had he said too much? For some moments he walked about much agitated. Then his nerves became calmer, his face regained its usual calm expression, and turning towards me:

'Now, professor,' said he, 'if you wish to visit the *Nautilus*, I am at your service.'

11

THE *NAUTILUS*

Captain Nemo rose, and I followed him. A folding door, contrived at the back of the room, opened, and I entered a room about the same size as the one I had just left.

It was a library. High bookcases of black rosewood supported on their shelves a great number of books in uniform binding. They went round the room, terminating at their lower part in large divans, covered with brown leather, curved so as to afford the greatest comfort. Light movable desks, made to slide in and out at will, were there to rest one's book while reading. In the centre was a vast table, covered with pamphlets, amongst which appeared some newspapers, already old.

'Captain Nemo,' said I to my host, who had just thrown himself on one of the divans, 'you have a library here that would do honour to more than one continental palace, and I am lost in wonder when I think that it can follow you to the greatest depths of the ocean.'

'Where could there be more solitude or more silence, professor?' answered Captain Nemo. 'Did your study in the museum offer you as complete quiet?'

'No, and I must acknowledge it is a very poor one

compared with yours. You must have from six to seven thousand volumes here.'

'Twelve thousand, M. Aronnax. These are the only ties between me and the earth. But the day that my *Nautilus* plunged for the first time beneath the waters the world was at an end for me. That day I bought my last books, my last pamphlets, and my last newspapers; and since then I wish to believe that men no longer think nor write. These books, professor, are at your disposition, and you can use them freely.'

I thanked Captain Nemo, and went up to the library shelves. Books of science, ethics, and literature – written in every language – were there in quantities; but I did not see a single work on political economy amongst them; they seemed to be severely prohibited on board.

The most recent volume had been published in 1865. It was, therefore, three years, at the most, since Captain Nemo began his submarine existence.

He then opened the opposite door to the one by which we had entered the library, and I passed into an immense and brilliantly lighted saloon. It was a vast four-sided room, with panelled walls, measuring thirty feet by eighteen, and about fifteen feet high. It was, in fact, a museum in which an intelligent and prodigal hand had gathered together all the treasures of nature and art with the artistic confusion of a painter's studio.

About thirty pictures by the best artists, uniformly framed and separated by brilliant drapery, were hung on tapestry of severe design. I saw there works of great value, most of which I had admired in the special collections of Europe, and in exhibitions of paintings. The amazement which the captain of the *Nautilus* had predicted had already begun to take possession of me.

'Professor,' then said this strange man, 'you must

excuse the unceremonious way in which I receive you, and the disorder of this room.'

'Sir,' I answered, 'without seeking to know who you are, may I be allowed to recognize in you an artist?'

'Only an amateur, sir. Formerly I liked to collect these works of art. I was a greedy collector and an indefatigable antiquary, and have been able to get together some objects of great value. These are my last gatherings from that world which is now dead to me. In my eyes your modern artists are already old; they have two or three thousand years of existence, and all masters are of the same age in my mind.'

'And these musicians?' said I, pointing to the works of eminent composers scattered over a large piano organ fixed in one of the panels of the room.

'These musicians,' answered Captain Nemo, 'are contemporaries of Orpheus, for all chronological differences are effaced in the memory of the dead; and I am dead, as much dead as those of your friends who are resting six feet under the earth!'

Captain Nemo ceased talking, and seemed lost in a profound reverie. I looked at him with great interest, analysing in silence the strange expressions of his face.

Leaning on the corner of a costly mosaic table, he no longer saw me, and forgot my presence.

I respected his meditation, and went on passing in review the curiosities that enriched the saloon. They consisted principally of marine plants, shells, and other productions of the ocean, which must have been found by Captain Nemo himself. In the centre of the saloon rose a jet of water lighted up by electricity, and falling into a basin formed of a single clam shell, measuring about seven yards in circumference.

All round this basin were elegant glass cases, fastened by copper rivets, in which were classed and labelled the most precious productions of the sea that had ever been presented to the eye of a naturalist. My delight as a professor may be imagined.

It was impossible to estimate the worth of this collection of corals, shells, fish and pearls. Captain Nemo must have spent millions in acquiring these various specimens, and I was asking myself from whence he had drawn the money to gratify his fancy for collecting, when I was interrupted by these words:

'You are examining my shells, professor. They certainly must be interesting to a naturalist, but for me they have a greater charm, for I have collected them all myself, and there is not a sea on the face of the globe that has escaped my search.'

'I understand, captain – I understand the delight of moving amongst such riches. You are one of those people who lay up treasures for themselves. There is not a museum in Europe that possesses such a collection of marine products. But if I exhaust all my admiration upon it, I shall have none left for the vessel that carries it. I do not wish to penetrate into your secrets, but I must confess that this *Nautilus*, with the motive power she contains, the contrivances by which she is worked, the powerful agent which propels her, all excite my utmost curiosity. I see hung on the walls of this room instruments the use of which I ignore.'

'When I told you that you were free on board my vessel, I meant that every portion of the *Nautilus* was open to your inspection. The instruments you will see in my room, professor, where I shall have much pleasure in explaining their use to you. But come and look at your own cabin.'

I followed Captain Nemo, who, by one of the doors opening from each panel of the drawing-room, regained the waist of the vessel. He conducted me aft, and there I found, not a cabin, but an elegant room with a bed, toilette-table, and several other articles of furniture. I could only thank my host.

'Your room is next to mine,' said he, opening a door; 'and mine opens into the saloon we have just left.'

I entered the captain's room; it had a severe, almost monkish aspect. A small iron bedstead, an office desk, some articles of toilet – all lighted by a strong light. There were no comforts, only the strictest necessaries.

Captain Nemo pointed to a seat.

'Pray sit down,' he said.

Captain Nemo showed me the full range of his vessel's instruments, from thermometer to manometer, or depth-gauge, and explained to me the locomotive power of the *Nautilus.* It was gained by electricity, but Captain Nemo had not only discovered the secret of extracting electricity from the chemical elements of the sea, but had found a way of harnessing the potency of electricity to drive his vast submarine vehicle, to light the vessel, to run chronometers with marvellous accuracy, and even to communicate by wire with the ship's boat, which could be released to the surface of the water.

He went on to explain how the strength of the *Nautilus* was due to its having two hulls, fitted one inside the other in a cellular arrangement, so that they resisted as if they were a single, immensely thick hull. Not only were these hulls capable of resisting projectiles, but also the unimaginable pressures of the depths to which the vessel could sink by filling its reservoirs. Electricity again drove the pumps which expelled the water and allowed the vessel to rise again. The jets of water, which we had earlier mistaken for the exhalations of some giant cetacean, were the final expulsion of water when the vessel reached the surface.

'But how,' I ventured to ask, 'is the *Nautilus* steered?'

'In order to steer my vessel horizontally,' Captain Nemo replied, 'I use an ordinary rudder, worked by a wheel and tackle. But I can also move the *Nautilus* by a vertical movement, by means of two inclined planes fastened to the sides and at the centre of flotation, planes that can move in every direction, and are worked from the interior by means of powerful levers. When these planes are kept parallel with the boat it moves horizontally; when slanted, the *Nautilus*, according to their inclination, and under the influence of the screw, either sinks according to an elongated diagonal, or rises diagonally as it suits me. And when I wish to rise even more quickly to the surface I engage the screw, and the pressure of the water causes the *Nautilus* to rise vertically like a balloon into the air.'

'Bravo, captain!' I cried. 'But how can the helmsman follow the route you give him in the midst of the waters?'

'The helmsman is placed in a glass cage jutting from the top of the *Nautilus* and furnished with lenses.'

'Capable of resisting such pressure?'

'Perfectly. Glass, which a blow can break, offers, nevertheless, considerable resistance. During some fishing experiments we made in 1864 we saw plates less than a third of an inch thick resist a pressure of sixteen atmospheres. Now the glass that I use is not less than thirty times thicker.'

'I see now. But after all, it is dark under water; how do you see where you are going?'

'There is a powerful electric reflector placed behind the helmsman's cage, the rays from which light up the sea for half a mile in front.'

'Ah, now I can account for the phosphorescence in the supposed narwhal that puzzled me so. May I now ask you if the damage you did to the *Scotia* was due to an accident?'

'Yes, it was quite accidental. I was sailing only one fathom below the surface when the shock came. Had it any bad result?'

'None, sir. But how about the shock you gave the *Abraham Lincoln*?'

'Professor, it was a great pity for one of the best ships in the American navy; but they attacked me and I had to defend myself! Besides, I contented myself with putting it out of the power of the frigate to harm me; there will be no difficulty in getting her repaired at the nearest port.'

'Ah, commander!' I cried with conviction. 'Your *Nautilus* is certainly a marvellous boat.'

'Yes, professor,' answered Captain Nemo with real emotion, 'and I love it as if it were flesh of my flesh! Though all is danger on one of your ships in subjection to the hazards of the ocean, below and on board the *Nautilus* the heart of man has nothing to dread. There is no deformation to fear, for the double hull of this vessel is as rigid as iron; no rigging to be injured by rolling and pitching; no sails for the wind to carry away; no boilers for steam to blow up; no fire to dread, as the apparatus is made of iron and not of wood; no coal to get exhausted, as electricity is its mechanical agent; no collision to fear, as it is the only vessel in deep waters; no tempests to set at defiance, as there is perfect tranquillity at some yards before the surface of the sea! The *Nautilus* is the ship of ships, sir. And if it is true that the engineer has more confidence in the vessel than the constructor, and the constructor more than the captain himself, you will understand with what confidence I trust to my *Nautilus*, as I am at the same time captain, constructor, and engineer.'

Captain Nemo spoke with captivating eloquence. His fiery look and passionate gestures transfigured him. Yes! He did love his vessel like a father loves his child!

But a question, perhaps an indiscreet one, came up naturally, and I could not help putting it.

'Then you are an engineer, Captain Nemo?'

'Yes, professor, I studied in London, Paris and New York when I was still an inhabitant of the world's continents.'

'But how could you construct this admirable *Nautilus* in secret?'

'I had each separate portion made in different parts of the globe, and it reached me through a disguised address. And all the manufacturers had my orders under different names.'

'But how did you get all the parts put together?'

'I set up a workshop upon a desert island in the ocean. There, my workmen – that is to say, my brave companions whom I instructed – and I put together our *Nautilus*. When the work was ended, fire destroyed all trace of our proceedings on the island, which I should have blown up if I could.'

'One last question, Captain Nemo.'

'Ask it, professor.'

'You must be rich?'

'Immensely rich, sir; and I could, without missing it, pay the English National Debt.'

I stared at the singular person who spoke thus. Was he taking advantage of my credulity? The future alone could decide.

12

AN INVITATION

'Now, professor,' said Captain Nemo, 'we will, if you please, take our bearings and fix the starting-point of this voyage. It wants a quarter to twelve. I am going up to the surface of the water.'

The captain pressed an electric bell three times. The pumps began to drive the water out of the reservoirs; the needle of the manometer marked by the different pressures the upward movement of the *Nautilus*, then it stopped.

'We have arrived,' said the captain.

We went to the central staircase which led up to the platform, climbed the iron steps, and found ourselves on the top of the *Nautilus*.

The platform was only three feet out of the water. I noticed that the iron plates of the *Nautilus* slightly over-laid each other, like the scales on the body of our large terrestrial reptiles. I well understood how, in spite of the best glasses, this boat should have been taken for a marine animal.

Towards the middle of the platform, the boat, half sunk in the vessel, formed a slight excrescence. Fore and aft rose two cages of medium height, with inclined sides, and partly enclosed by thick lenticular glasses. In the one was the helmsman who directed the *Nautilus*; in the other a powerful electric lantern that lighted up his course.

The sea was beautiful, the sky pure. The long vessel could hardly feel the broad undulations of the ocean. A slight breeze from the east rippled the surface of the water. The horizon was quite clear, making observation easy. There was nothing in sight – not a rock nor an island, no *Abraham Lincoln*, nothing but a waste of waters.

Captain Nemo took the altitude of the sun with his sextant to get his latitude. He waited some minutes till the planet came on a level with the edge of the horizon. Whilst he was observing not one of his muscles moved, and the instrument would not have been more motionless in a hand of marble.

'It is noon. Professor, when you are ready –'

I cast a last look at the sea, slightly yellowed by the Japanese coast, and went down again to the saloon.

There the captain made his point, and calculated his longitude. Then he said to me:

'M. Aronnax, we are about three hundred miles from the coasts of Japan. Today, 8 November, at noon, our voyage of exploration under the waters begins.'

'God preserve us!' I answered.

'And now, professor,' added the captain, 'I leave you to your studies. I have given ENE as our route at a depth of fifty yards. Here are maps on a large scale on which you can follow it. The saloon is at your disposition, and I ask your permission to withdraw.'

Captain Nemo bowed to me. I remained alone, absorbed in my thoughts. All of them referred to the commander of the *Nautilus*. Should I ever know to what nation belonged the strange man who boasted of belonging to none? This hatred which he had vowed to humanity – this hatred which perhaps sought terrible means of revenge – what had provoked it? I could not yet say. I, whom hazard had just cast upon his vessel – I, whose life he held in his hands – he had received me coldly, but with hospitality. Only he had never taken the hand I had held out to him. He had never held out his to me.

For a whole hour I remained buried in these reflections, seeking to pierce the mystery that interested me so greatly. Then my eyes fell upon the vast planisphere on the table, and I placed my finger on the very spot where we presently lay.

Just then Ned Land and Conseil appeared at the door of the saloon.

My two companions were petrified at the sight of the marvels spread out before their eyes.

'Where are we – where are we?' cried the Canadian. 'At Quebec Museum?'

'If monsieur allows me to say so,' replied Conseil, 'it is more like the Hôtel du Sommerard.'

'My friends,' said I, making them a sign to enter, 'you are neither in Canada nor France, but on board the *Nautilus*, and at more than twenty-five fathoms below the sea level.'

'We must believe what monsieur says,' replied Conseil, 'but really this saloon is enough to astonish even a Dutchman like me.'

'Marvel and look, Conseil, for there is enough for such a good classifier as you to do here.'

There was no need for me to encourage Conseil. The worthy fellow, leaning over the cases, was already muttering words in the language of naturalists.

During this time Ned Land, who was not much interested in conchology, questioned me about my interview with Captain Nemo. Had I discovered who he was, from whence he came, whither he was going, to what depths he was dragging us? – in short, a thousand questions, to which I had not time to answer.

I told him all I knew, or rather all I did not know, and I asked him what he had heard or seen on his side.

'I have seen nothing, heard nothing,' answered the Canadian. 'I have not even perceived the ship's crew. But you, M. Aronnax, can you tell me how many men there are on board? Are there ten, twenty, fifty, a hundred?'

'I know no more than you, Mr Land; it is better to abandon at present all idea of either taking possession of the *Nautilus* or escaping from it. This vessel is a master-piece of modern industry, and I should regret not to have seen it. Many people would accept our position only to move amidst such marvels. The only thing to do is to keep quiet and watch what passes around us.'

'Watch!' exclaimed the harpooner. 'But there's nothing to watch; we can't see anything in this iron prison. We are moving along blindfolded.'

Ned Land had scarcely uttered these words when it became suddenly dark. The light in the ceiling went out, and so rapidly that my eyes ached with the change, in the same way as they do after passage from profound darkness to the most brilliant light.

We remained mute and did not stir, not knowing what surprise, agreeable or disagreeable, awaited us. But a sliding noise was heard. It was as if panels were being drawn back in the sides of the *Nautilus*.

'It is the end of all things!' said Ned Land.

Suddenly light appeared on either side of the saloon, through two oblong openings. The liquid mass appeared vividly lighted up by the electric effluence.

Two crystal panes separated us from the sea. At first I shuddered at the thought that this feeble partition might break, but strong copper bands bound it, giving an almost infinite power of resistance.

The sea was distinctly visible for a mile round the *Nautilus*. What a spectacle! What pen could describe it? Who could paint the effect of the light through those transparent sheets of water, and the softness of its successive gradations from the lower to the upper beds of the ocean?

The *Nautilus* did not seem to be moving. It was because there were no landmarks. Sometimes, however, the lines of water, furrowed by her prow, flowed before our eyes with excessive speed.

Lost in wonder we stood before these windows, and none of us had broken this silence of astonishment when Conseil said:

'Well, friend Ned, you wanted to look; well, now you see!'

'It is curious!' exclaimed the Canadian, who, forgetting his anger and projects of flight, was under the influence of irresistible attraction. 'Who wouldn't come for the sake of such a sight?'

'Now I understand the man's life,' I exclaimed. 'He has made a world of marvels for himself!'

'But I don't see any fish,' said the Canadian.

'What does it matter to you, friend Ned,' answered Conseil, 'since you know nothing about them?'

'I! A fisherman!' cried Ned Land.

And thereupon a dispute arose between the two friends, for each had some knowledge of fish, though in a very different way.

'Well, friend Conseil,' said the harpooner eventually, leaning against the glass of the panel, 'there are some varieties passing now.'

'Yes; some fish,' cried Conseil. 'It is like being at an aquarium.'

'No,' I answered, 'for an aquarium is only a cage, and those fish are as free as birds in the air.'

'Well, now, Conseil, tell me their names! Tell me their names!' said Ned Land.

'I?' answered Conseil. 'I could not do it; that is my master's business.'

And, in fact, the worthy fellow, though an enthusiastic classifier, was not a naturalist, and I do not know if he could have distinguished a tunny-fish from a bonito. The Canadian, on the contrary, named them all without hesitation.

'A balister,' said I.

'And a Chinese balister too!' answered Ned Land.

'Genus of the balisters, family of the scleroderms; order of the plectognaths,' muttered Conseil.

Decidedly, between them, Ned Land and Conseil would have made a distinguished naturalist.

For two hours a whole aquatic army escorted the *Nautilus*. Our admiration was excited to the highest pitch. Ned named the fish, Conseil classified them, and I was delighted with their vivacity and the beauty of their forms. It had never been my lot to see these animals living and free in their natural element. I shall not cite all the varieties that passed before our dazzled eyes, all that collection from the Japanese and Chinese seas. More numerous than the birds of the air, these fish swam round us, doubtless attracted by the electric light.

Suddenly light again appeared in the saloon. The iron panels were again closed. The enchanting vision disappeared. But long after that I was dreaming still.

I expected Captain Nemo, but he did not appear. The clock was on the stroke of five. Ned Land and Conseil returned to their cabin, and I regained my room.

I passed the evening reading, writing, and thinking. Then sleep overpowered me, and I stretched myself on my zostera couch and slept profoundly, whilst the *Nautilus* glided rapidly along.

The next day, 9 November, I awoke after a long sleep that had lasted twelve hours. Conseil came, as was his custom, to ask 'how monsieur had passed the night,' and to offer his services. He had left his friend the Canadian sleeping like a man who had never done anything else in his life.

I let the brave fellow chatter on in his own fashion, without troubling to answer him much. I was anxious about the absence of Captain Nemo during our spectacle of the evening before, and hoped to see him again that day.

I was soon clothed in my byssus garments. Their nature provoked many reflections from Conseil. I told him they were manufactured with the lustrous and silky filaments which fasten a sort of shell, very abundant on the shores of the Mediterranean, to the rocks.

When I was dressed I went into the saloon. It was deserted.

I plunged into the study of the conchological treasures piled up in the cases. I ransacked in great herbals filled with the rarest marine plants, which, though dried up, retained their lovely colours.

The whole day passed without my being honoured with a visit from Captain Nemo. The panels of the saloon were not opened. Perhaps they did not wish us to get tired of such beautiful things.

The next day, 10 November, the same desertion, the same solitude. I did not see one of the ship's crew. Ned and Conseil passed the greater part of the day with me. They were astonished at the inexplicable absence of the captain. Was the singular man ill? Did he mean to alter his plans about us?

After all, as Conseil said, we enjoyed complete liberty; we were delicately and abundantly fed. Our host kept to the terms of his treaty. We could not complain, and, besides, the singularity of our destiny reserved us such great compensations that we had no right to accuse it.

That day I began the account of these adventures, which allowed me to relate them with the most scrupulous exactness, and, curious detail, I wrote it on paper made with marine zostera.

Early in the morning of 11 November, the fresh air spread over the interior of the *Nautilus* told me that we were again on the surface of the ocean to renew our supply of oxygen. I went to the central staircase and ascended it to the platform. It was 6 a.m. The weather was cloudy, the sea grey, but calm. There was scarcely any swell. I hoped to meet Captain Nemo there. Would he come? I only saw the helmsman in his glass cage. Seated on the upper portion of the hull, I drank in the sea breeze with delight.

Little by little the clouds disappeared under the action of the sun's rays. The clouds announced wind for all that day. But the wind was no concern to the *Nautilus*. I was admiring this joyful sunrise, so gay and reviving, when I heard someone coming up to the platform. I prepared to address Captain Nemo, but it was his mate – whom I had already seen during the captain's first visit – who appeared. He did not seem to perceive my presence, and with his powerful glass he swept the horizon, after which he approached the stair-head and called out some words which I reproduce exactly, for every morning they were uttered under the same conditions. They were the following:

'Nautron respoc lorni virch.'

What those words meant I know not.

After pronouncing them the mate went below again, and I supposed that the *Nautilus* was going to continue her submarine course. I therefore followed the mate and regained my room.

Five days passed thus and altered nothing in our position. Each morning I ascended to the platform. The same sentence was pronounced by the same individual. Captain Nemo did not appear.

I had made up my mind that I was not going to see him again, when on 16 November, on entering my room with Ned Land and Conseil, I found a note directed to me upon the table.

I opened it with impatient fingers. It was written in a bold, clear hand:

To Professor ARONNAX, on board the *Nautilus*.

November 16th, 1867.

Captain Nemo invites Professor Aronnax to a hunt which will take place tomorrow morning in the forest of the island of Crespo. He hopes nothing will prevent the professor joining it, and he will have much pleasure in seeing his companions also.

The Commander of the *Nautilus*,

CAPTAIN NEMO

'A hunt!' cried Ned.

'And in the forests of Crespo Island,' added Conseil.

'Then that fellow does land sometimes,' said Ned Land.

'It looks like it,' said I, reading the letter again.

'Well, we must accept,' replied the Canadian. 'Once on land we can decide what to do. Besides, I shall not be sorry to eat some fresh meat.'

I consulted the planisphere as to the whereabouts of the island of Crespo and pointed out to my companions the little rock lost in the midst of the north Pacific.

'If Captain Nemo does land sometimes,' I said, 'he at least chooses quite desert islands.'

Ned Land shrugged his shoulders without speaking, and he and Conseil left me. After supper, which was served by the mute steward, I went to bed, not without some anxiety.

The next day, 17 November, when I awoke, I felt that the *Nautilus* was perfectly still. I dressed quickly and went to the saloon.

Captain Nemo was there waiting for me. He rose, bowed and asked me if it was convenient for me to accompany him.

As he made no allusion to his eight days' absence I abstained from speaking of it, and answered simply that my companions and I were ready to follow him.

'May I ask you, captain,' I said, 'how it is that, having broken all ties with earth, you possess forests in Crespo Island?'

'Professor,' answered the captain, 'my forests are not terrestrial forests but submarine forests.'

'Submarine forests!' I exclaimed.

'Yes, professor.'

'And you offer to take me to them?'

'Precisely.'

'On foot?'

'Yes, and dry-footed too.'

'But how shall we hunt? With a gun?'

'Yes, with a gun.'

I thought the captain was gone mad, and the idea was expressed on my face, but he only invited me to follow him like a man resigned to anything. We entered the dining-room, where breakfast was laid.

'M. Aronnax,' said the captain, 'will you share my breakfast without ceremony? We will talk as we eat. You will not find a restaurant in our walk though you will a forest. Breakfast like a man who will probably dine very late.'

I did honour to the meal. Captain Nemo went on eating at first without saying a word. Then he said to me:

'When I invited you to hunt in my submarine forests, professor, you thought I was mad. You judged me too lightly. You know as well as I do that man can live under water, providing he takes with him a provision of air to breathe. When submarine work has to be done, the workman, clad in an impervious dress, with his head in a metal helmet, receives air from above by means of pumps and regulators.'

'Then it is a diving apparatus?'

'Yes. I have adapted current inventions to construct a diving suit, equipped with enough compressed air for nine or ten hours and with a source of illumination for the dark places of the ocean floor. Thus provided, I breathe and see.'

'But, Captain Nemo, what sort of gun do you use?'

'It is not a gun for powder, but an air-gun.'

'But it seems to me that in the half-light, and amidst a liquid so much more dense than the atmosphere, bodies cannot be projected far, and are not easily mortal.'

'Sir, with these guns every shot is mortal, and as soon as the animal is touched, however slightly, it falls crushed.'

'Why?'

'Because they are not ordinary bullets. We use little glass percussion-caps, of which I have a considerable provision. These glass caps, covered with steel, and weighted with a leaden bottom, are really little bulbs in which electricity is forced to a very high tension. At the slightest shock they go off, and the animal, however powerful it may be, falls dead.'

'I will argue no longer,' I replied, rising from the table. 'The only thing left me is to take my gun. Besides, where you go I will follow.'

Captain Nemo then led me aft of the *Nautilus*, and whilst passing the cabin of Ned and Conseil, I called my

two companions, who followed me immediately. Then
we came to a kind of cell, situated near the engine-room,
in which we were to put on our walking dress.

13

AT THE BOTTOM OF THE SEA

This cell was, properly speaking, the arsenal and wardrobe of the *Nautilus*. A dozen diving apparatus, hung from the wall, awaited our use.

Ned Land, seeing them, manifested evident repugnance to put one on.

'But, my worthy Ned,' I said, 'the forests of Crespo Island are only submarine forests!'

The disappointed harpooner saw his dreams of fresh meat fade away.

'And you, M. Aronnax, are you going to put on one of those things?'

'I must, Master Ned.'

'You can do as you please, sir,' replied the harpooner shrugging his shoulders, 'but as for me, unless I am forced, I will never get into one.'

'No one will force you, Ned,' said Captain Nemo.

'Does Conseil mean to risk it?' said Ned.

'I shall follow monsieur wherever he goes,' answered Conseil.

Two of the ship's crew came to help us on the call of the captain and we donned the heavy and impervious clothes made of seamless indiarubber, and constructed expressly to resist considerable pressure. They looked like a suit of armour, both supple and resisting, and formed trousers and coat; the trousers were finished off with thick boots, furnished with heavy leaden soles. The texture of the coat was held together by bands of copper, which crossed the chest, protecting it from the pressure of the water, and leaving the lungs free to act; the sleeves ended in the form of supple gloves, which in no way restrained the movements of the hands.

Captain Nemo and one of his companions – a sort of Hercules, who must have been of prodigious strength – Conseil, and myself, were soon enveloped in these dresses. There was nothing left but to put our heads into the metallic globes. But before proceeding with this operation I asked the captain's permission to examine the guns we were to take.

One of the crew gave me a simple gun, the butt-end of which, made of steel and hollowed in the interior, was rather large; it served as a reservoir for compressed air, which a valve, worked by a spring, allowed to escape into a metal tube. A box of projectiles, fixed in a groove in the thickness of the butt-end, contained about twenty electric bullets, which, by means of a spring, were forced into the barrel of the gun. As soon as one shot was fired another was ready.

'Captain Nemo,' said I, 'this arm is perfect and easily managed; all I ask now is to try it. But how shall we gain the bottom of the sea?'

'At this moment, professor, the *Nautilus* is stranded in five fathoms of water, and we have only to start.'

'But how shall we get out?'

'You will soon see.'

Captain Nemo put on his helmet. Conseil and I did the same, not without hearing an ironical 'Good sport' from the Canadian. The upper part of our coat was terminated by a copper collar, upon which the metal helmet was screwed. As soon as it was in position the apparatus on our backs began to act, and for my part, I could breathe with ease.

I found when I was ready, lamp and all, that I could not move a step. But this was foreseen. I felt myself pushed along a little room contiguous to the wardrobe-room. My companions, tugged along in the same way, followed me. I heard a door close behind us, and we were wrapped in profound darkness.

After some minutes I heard a loud whistling, and felt the cold mount from my feet to my chest. It was evident that they had filled the room in which we were with sea-water by means of a tap. A second door in the side of the *Nautilus* opened then. A faint light appeared. A moment after, our feet were treading the bottom of the sea.

And now, how could I retrace the impression made upon me by that walk under the sea? Words are powerless to describe such marvels. When the brush itself is powerless to depict the particular effects of the liquid element, how can the pen reproduce them?

Captain Nemo walked on in front, and his companion followed us some steps behind. Conseil and I remained near one another, as if any exchange of words had been possible through our metallic covering. I no longer felt the weight of my clothes, shoes, air-reservoir, nor of that thick globe in the midst of which my head shook like an almond in its shell.

The light which lighted up the ground at thirty feet below the surface of the ocean astonished me by its power. The solar rays easily pierced this watery mass and dissipated its colour. One easily distinguished objects 120 yards off. Beyond that the tints faded into fine gradations of ultramarine, and became effaced in a vague obscurity. The water around me only appeared a sort of air, denser than the terrestrial atmosphere, but nearly as transparent. Above me I perceived the calm surface of the sea.

We were walking on fine even sand, not wrinkled, as it is on a flat shore which keeps the imprint of the billows. This dazzling carpet reflected the rays of the sun with surprising intensity.

Many wonders I saw in the space of a quarter of a mile. Soon the nature of the soil changed; to the sandy plains succeeded an extent of slimy mud. Then we travelled over meadows of seaweed so soft to the foot that they would rival the softest carpet made by man.

We had left the *Nautilus* about an hour and a half.

The ground gradually sloped downwards, and the light took a uniform tint. We were at a depth of more than a hundred yards, and bearing a pressure of ten atmospheres. But my diving apparatus was so small that I suffered nothing from this pressure. I merely felt a slight discomfort in my finger-joints, and even that soon disappeared. As to the fatigue that this walk in such unusual harness might be expected to produce, it was nothing. My movements, helped by the water, were made with surprising facility.

At this depth of three hundred feet I could still see the rays of the sun, but feebly. To their intense brilliancy had succeeded a reddish twilight, middle term between day and night. Still we saw sufficiently to guide ourselves, and it was not yet necessary to light our lamps.

At that moment Captain Nemo stopped. He waited for me to come up to him, and with his finger pointed to some obscure masses which stood out of the shade at some little distance.

'It is the forest of Crespo Island,' I thought, and I was not mistaken.

14

A SUBMARINE FOREST

We had at last arrived on the borders of this forest, doubtless one of the most beautiful in the immense domain of Captain Nemo. He looked upon it as his own, and who was there to dispute his right? This forest was composed of arborescent plants, and as soon as we had penetrated under its vast arcades, I was struck at first by the singular disposition of their branches, which I had not observed before.

None of those herbs which carpeted the ground, and none of the branches of the larger plants, were either bent, drooped, or extended horizontally. There was not a single filament, however thin, that did not keep as upright as a rod of iron. When I bent them with my hand these plants immediately resumed their first position. It was the reign of perpendicularity.

I soon accustomed myself to this fantastic disposition of things, as well as to the relative obscurity which enveloped us.

Amongst these different shrubs, as large as the trees of temperate zones, and under their humid shade, were massed veritable bushes of living flowers, and, to complete the illusion, the fish-flies flew from branch to branch like a swarm of humming-birds.

About one o'clock Captain Nemo gave the signal to halt. I, for my part, was not sorry, and we stretched ourselves under a thicket of alariae, the long thin blades of which shot up like arrows.

This short rest seemed delicious to me. Nothing was wanting but the charm of conversation, but it was impossible to speak – I could only approach my large copper head to that of Conseil. I saw the eyes of the worthy fellow shine with contentment, and he moved about in his covering in the most comical way in the world.

After this four hours' walk I was much astonished not to find myself violently hungry, and I cannot tell why, but instead I was intolerably sleepy, as all divers are. My eyes closed behind their thick glass, and I fell into an unavoidable slumber, which the movement of walking had alone prevented up till then. Captain Nemo and his robust companion, lying down in the clear crystal, set us the example.

How long I remained asleep I cannot tell, but when I awoke the sun seemed sinking towards the horizon. Captain Nemo was already on his feet, and I was stretching myself when an unexpected apparition brought me quickly to my feet.

A few steps off an enormous sea-spider, more than a yard high, was looking at me with his squinting eyes ready to spring upon me. Although my dress was thick enough to defend me against the bite of this animal, I could not restrain a movement of horror. Conseil and the sailor of the *Nautilus* awoke at that moment. Captain Nemo showed his companions the hideous crustacean, and a blow from the butt-end of a gun killed it, and I saw its horrible claws writhe in horrible convulsions.

This accident reminded me that other animals, more to

be feared, might haunt these obscure depths, and that my diver's dress would not protect me against their attacks. I had not thought of that before, and resolved to be on my guard. I supposed that this halt marked the limit of our excursion, but I was mistaken, and instead of returning to the *Nautilus*, Captain Nemo went on.

The ground still inclined and took us to greater depths. It must have been about three o'clock when we reached a narrow valley between two high cliffs, situated about seventy-five fathoms deep. Thanks to the perfection of our apparatus, we were forty-five fathoms below the limit which Nature seems to have imposed on the submarine excursions of man.

I knew how deep we were because the obscurity became so profound – not an object was visible at ten paces. I walked along groping when I suddenly saw a white light shine out. Captain Nemo had just lighted his lamp. His companion imitated him. Conseil and I followed their example. The sea, lighted up by our four lanterns, was illuminated in a radius of twenty-five yards.

Captain Nemo still kept on plunging into the dark depths of the forest, the trees of which were getting rarer and rarer.

As we walked I thought that our lights could not fail to draw some inhabitants from these sombre depths. But if they did approach us they at least kept a respectful distance from the hunters. Several times I saw Captain Nemo stop and take aim; then, after some minutes' observation, he rose and went on walking.

At last, about four o'clock, this wonderful excursion was ended. A wall of superb rocks rose up before us, enormous granite cliffs impossible to climb. It was the island of Crespo. Captain Nemo stopped suddenly. We stopped at a sign from him. Here ended the domains of the captain.

The return began. Captain Nemo again kept at the head of his little band, and directed his steps without hesitation. I thought I perceived that we were not returning to the *Nautilus* by the road we had come. This new one was very steep, and consequently very painful. We approached the surface of the sea rapidly. But this return to the upper beds was not so sudden as to produce the internal injuries so fatal to divers. Very soon light reappeared and increased, and as the sun was already low on the horizon refraction edged the different objects with a spectral ring.

At a depth of ten yards we were walking in a swarm of little fish of every sort, more numerous than birds in the air, and more agile too. But no aquatic game worthy of a shot had as yet met our gaze.

At that moment I saw the captain put his gun to his shoulder and follow a moving object into the shrubs. He fired, I heard a feeble hissing, and an animal fell a few steps from us.

It was a magnificent sea-otter. This otter was five feet long, and must have been very valuable. Its skin, chestnut brown above and silvery underneath, would have made one of those beautiful furs so sought after in the Russian and Chinese markets. Captain Nemo's companion took up the animal and threw it over his shoulders, and we continued our route.

During the next hour a plain of sand lay stretched before us. Sometimes it rose within two yards and some inches of the surface of the water. I then saw the reflection of our images above us, like us in every point, except that they walked with their heads downwards and their feet in the air.

The thick waves above us looked like clouds above our heads – clouds which were no sooner formed than they vanished rapidly. I even perceived the shadows of the large birds as they floated on the surface of the water.

On this occasion I was witness to one of the finest gun-shots which ever made a hunter's nerve thrill. A large bird, with great breadth of wing, hovered over us. Captain Nemo's companion shouldered his gun and fired when it was only a few yards above the waves. The bird fell dead, and the fall brought it in reach of the skilful hunter's grasp. It was an albatross of the finest kind.

Our march was not interrupted by this incident. I was worn out by fatigue when we at last perceived a faint light half a mile off. Before twenty minutes were over we should be on board and able to breathe with ease, for it seemed to me that my reservoir of air was getting very deficient in oxygen, but I did not reckon upon a meeting which delayed our arrival.

I was about twenty steps behind Captain Nemo when he suddenly turned towards me. With his vigorous hand he threw me to the ground, whilst his companion did the same to Conseil. At first I did not know what to think of this sudden attack, but I was reassured when I saw that the captain lay down beside me and remained perfectly motionless.

I was stretched on the ground just under the shelter of a bush of algae, when, on raising my head, I perceived enormous masses throwing phosphorescent gleams pass blusteringly by.

My blood froze in my veins. I saw two formidable dogfish threatening us; they were terrible creatures, with enormous tails and a dull and glassy stare, who threw out phosphorescent beams from holes pierced round their muzzles. Monstrous brutes which would crush a whole man in their jaws! I do not know if Conseil stayed to classify them. For my part, I noticed their silver stomachs and their formidable mouths bristling with teeth from a very unscientific point of view – more as a possible victim than as a naturalist.

Happily, these voracious animals see badly. They passed without perceiving us, brushing us with their brownish fins, and we escaped, as if by a miracle, this danger, certainly greater than the meeting of a tiger in a forest.

Half an hour after, guided by the electric light, we reached the *Nautilus*. The outside door had remained open, and Captain Nemo closed it as soon as we had entered the first cell. Then he pressed a knob. I heard the pumps worked inside the vessel. I felt the water lower around me, and in a few moments the cell was entirely empty. The inner door then opened, and we entered the wardrobe-room.

There our diving dresses were taken off, and, quite worn out from want of food and sleep, I returned to my room, lost in wonder at this surprising excursion under the sea.

15

FOUR THOUSAND LEAGUES
UNDER THE PACIFIC

The next morning, 18 November, I was perfectly recovered from my fatigue of the day before, and I went up on to the platform at the very moment that the mate was pronouncing his daily sentence. It then came into my mind that it had to do with the state of the sea, and that it signified, 'There is nothing in sight.'

And, in fact, the ocean was quite clear. There was not a sail on the horizon. The heights of Crespo Island had disappeared during the night. The sea, absorbing the colours of the solar prism, with the exception of the blue rays, reflected them in every direction, and was of an admirable indigo shade. A large wave was regularly undulating its surface.

I was admiring this magnificent aspect of the sea when Captain Nemo appeared. He did not seem to perceive my presence, and began a series of astronomical observations. Then, when he had ended his operation, he went and leaned against the cage of the watch-light and watched the surface of the ocean.

In the meantime about twenty sailors from the *Nautilus*, strong and well-built men, ascended upon the platform. They came to draw in the nets which had been out all night. These sailors evidently belonged to different nations, although they were all of the European type. They spoke very little, and only used the strange idiom of which I could not even guess the origin, so that I could not question them.

The nets were hauled in. They were like those used on the Normandy coast, vast pockets which a floating yard and a chain marled into the lower stitches keep half open. These pockets, thus dragged along in their iron gauntlets, swept the bottom of the ocean, and took in all its products on their way.

I reckoned that the haul that day had brought in more than nine hundredweight of fish. We should not want for food.

These different products of the sea were immediately lowered down by the panel leading to the storerooms, some to be eaten fresh, others to be preserved.

The fishing ended and the provision of air renewed, I thought that the *Nautilus* was going to continue its submarine excursion, and I was preparing to return to my room, when, without further preamble, the captain turned to me and said:

'Is not the ocean gifted with real life, professor? It is sometimes gentle, at other times tempestuous. Yesterday it slept as we did, and now it has awaked after a peaceful night.'

Neither 'Good morning' nor 'Good evening'! It was as though this strange personage was continuing a conversation already commenced with me.

'See now,' he said, 'it wakes under the sun's influence. It will now renew its diurnal existence. It is deeply interesting to watch the play of its organization. It possesses a pulse and arteries, it has its spasms, and I agree with the view that it has a circulation as real as the circulation of blood in animals.'

It was certain that Captain Nemo expected no answer from me, and it appeared to me useless to keep saying 'Evidently,' or 'You are right,' or 'It must be so.' He spoke rather to himself, taking some time between each sentence. It was a meditation aloud.

'True existence is there,' added he, 'and I could conceive the foundation of nautical towns, agglomeration of submarine houses, which, like the *Nautilus*, would go up every morning to breathe on the surface of the water – free towns, if ever there were any, independent cities! And yet who knows if some despot –'

Captain Nemo finished his sentence by a violent gesture. Then, addressing himself directly to me as if to drive away some gloomy thought, he said:

'M. Aronnax, do you know how deep the ocean is?'

'I know at least, captain, what the principal soundings have taught us. If I am not mistaken they have found an average depth of 8,200 metres in the north Atlantic, and 2,500 metres in the Mediterranean. The most remarkable soundings have been taken in the south Atlantic; and they have given 12,000 metres, 14,081 metres, and 15,149 metres – in short, it is estimated that if the bottom of the sea was levelled its average depth would be about five miles.'

'Well, professor,' answered Captain Nemo, 'we shall show you better than that, I hope. As to the average depth of this part of the Pacific, I can tell you that it is only 4,000 metres.'

That said, Captain Nemo went towards the panel and disappeared down the ladder. I followed him, and went into the saloon. The screw then began to work, and the log gave twenty miles an hour.

For days and weeks Captain Nemo was very sparing of his visits. I only saw him at rare intervals. His mate pricked the ship's course regularly on the chart, and I could always tell the exact route of the *Nautilus*.

Conseil and Land passed long hours with me. Conseil had related to his friend the marvels of our excursion, and the Canadian regretted not having accompanied us.

Almost every day, during some hours, the panels of the saloon were opened, and our eyes were never tired of penetrating the mysteries of the submarine world.

During the day of 11 December, I was reading in the saloon, when Conseil interrupted me.

'Will monsieur come here for a moment?' said he in a singular voice.

I rose, went to the window, and looked out. Full in the electric light an enormous black mass, immovable, was suspended in the midst of the waters. I looked at it attentively, trying to make out the nature of this gigantic cetacean. But an idea suddenly came into my mind.

'A vessel!' I cried.

'Yes,' replied the Canadian, 'a disabled ship sunk perpendicularly.'

Ned Land was right. We were close to a vessel of which the tattered shrouds still hung from their chains. The hull seemed to be in good order, and it could not have been wrecked more than a few hours; the vessel had had to sacrifice its mast. It lay on its side, had filled, and was heeling over to port. This skeleton of what it had once been was a sad spectacle under the waves, but sadder still was the sight of the deck, where corpses, bound with rope, were still lying. I counted five; one man was at the helm, and a woman stood by the poop holding an infant in her arms; she was quite young. I could clearly see her features by the light of the *Nautilus* – features which the water had not yet decomposed. In a last effort she had raised the child above her head, and the arms of the little one were round his mother's neck. The sailors looked frightful, and seemed to be making a last effort to free themselves from the cords that bound them to the vessel. The helmsman alone, calm, with a clear, grave face and iron-grey hair glued to his forehead, was clutching the wheel of the helm, and seemed, even then, to be guiding the vessel through the depths of the ocean!

What a scene! It struck us numb, and our hearts beat faster at the sight of this wreck, photographed at the last moment, and I already saw, advancing towards it with hungry eyes, enormous sharks attracted by the human flesh!

The *Nautilus* just then turned round the submerged vessel, and I read on the stern 'Florida, Sunderland'.

16

TORRES STRAITS

This phase of the expedition lasted from 26 November to 27 December. We passed the Sandwich Islands, the Marquesas, the archipelago of Pomotou, Tahiti, the New Hebrides and Vanikoro. On Christmas Day, Ned Land seemed to me to regret that it could not be celebrated as the family occasion dear to Protestant hearts.

While we were by Pomotou, I reflected that, as the islands which form this archipelago are made of coral and are still growing, they will one day form a new island, and thence a new continent, when joined to neighbouring lands. The day that I developed this theory before Captain Nemo, he assured me coldly:

'The earth does not want new continents, but new men!'

During the night between 27 and 28 December the *Nautilus* left the neighbourhood of Vanikoro with excessive speed. Its direction was south-west, and in three days it cleared the 750 leagues that separated the archipelago from the south-east point of Papua. Early on the morning of 1 January 1868, Conseil joined me on the platform.

'Monsieur,' said the brave fellow, 'will monsieur allow me to wish him a happy New Year?'

'Why, anyone would think, Conseil, that I was in Paris in my Jardin des Plantes study. Thank you for your good wishes, only I should like to ask you what you mean by a "happy year" in our present circumstances? Will this year bring the end of our imprisonment, or will it see us continue this strange voyage?'

'I do not know quite what to say to monsieur,' answered Conseil. 'It is certain that we see curious things, and the last two months we have not had time to be dull. The last marvel is always the most astonishing, and if this rate of progress is maintained I do not know how it will end. My opinion is that we shall never find such another occasion.'

'Never, Conseil.'

'Besides, M. Nemo, who well justifies his Latin name, is not more troublesome than if he did not exist. I therefore think a happy year would be a year which would allow us to see everything.'

'To see everything, Conseil? That would perhaps take too long. But what does Ned Land think about it?'

'Ned thinks exactly the contrary to what I do,' answered Conseil. 'I think as much of remaining as Land does of taking flight. Therefore, if the year that is beginning is not a happy one for me it will be for him; or vice versa. By that means someone will be satisfied. In short, to conclude, I wish monsieur anything that would please him.'

'Thank you, Conseil; only I must ask you to put off the question of a New Year's present, and to accept provisionally a shake of the hand. That is all I have upon me.'

'Monsieur has never been so generous.'

And thereupon the worthy fellow went away.

On 4 January we sighted the Papuan coasts. On this occasion Captain Nemo informed me that it was his intention to get into the Indian Ocean by Torres Straits. His communication ended there. Ned Land saw with pleasure that this route would take him nearer to the European seas.

The *Nautilus* then entered the most dangerous straits on the globe.

The Torres Straits are about thirty-four leagues wide, but are obstructed by an innumerable quantity of islands, reefs and rocks, which made its navigation almost impracticable. Captain Nemo consequently took every precaution to cross it. The *Nautilus*, on a level with the surface of the water, moved slowly along. Its screw, like the tail of a cetacean, slowly beat the billows.

Profiting by this situation, my two companions and I took our places on the constantly deserted platform. Before us rose the helmsman's cage, and I am very much mistaken if Captain Nemo was not there directing his *Nautilus* himself.

Around the *Nautilus* the sea was furiously rough. The current of the waves, which was bearing from SE to NW with a speed of two and a half knots, broke over the coral reefs that emerged here and there.

'An ugly sea!' said Ned Land to me.

'Detestable indeed,' I answered, 'and one that is not suitable to such a vessel as the *Nautilus*.'

'That confounded captain must be very certain of his route,' answered the Canadian, 'for I see coral reefs which would break its keel in a thousand pieces if it only just touched them!'

Suddenly a shock overthrew me. The *Nautilus* had just touched on a reef, and was quite still, lying lightly to port side.

When I rose I saw Captain Nemo and his second on the

platform. They were examining the situation of the vessel, and talking in their incomprehensible dialect.

The situation was the following. Two miles on the starboard appeared the Island of Gilboa, the coast of which was rounded from N to W; like an immense arm towards the S and E some heads of coral rocks were jutting, which the ebb tide left uncovered. We had run aground, and in one of the seas where the tides are very slight, an unfortunate circumstance in the floating of the *Nautilus*; however, the vessel had in no wise suffered, its keel was so solidly joined; but although it could neither sink nor split, it ran the risk of being for ever fastened on to these reefs, and then Captain Nemo's submarine apparatus would be done for.

I was reflecting thus, when the captain, cool and calm, always master of himself, appearing neither vexed nor moved, came up.

'An accident?' I asked.

'No, an incident,' he answered.

'But an incident,' I replied, 'which will perhaps again force you to become an inhabitant of the land from which you flee.'

Captain Nemo looked at me in a curious manner, and made a negative gesture. It was as much as to say to me that nothing would ever force him to set foot on land again. Then he said:

'Besides, M. Aronnax, the *Nautilus* is not lost. It will yet carry you amid the marvels of the ocean. Our voyage is only just begun, and I do not wish to deprive myself so soon of the honour of your company.'

'But, Captain Nemo,' I replied, without noticing the irony of his sentence, 'the *Nautilus* ran aground at high tide. Now tides are not strong in the Pacific, and if you cannot lighten the *Nautilus* I do not see how it can be floated again.'

'Tides are not strong in the Pacific – you are right, professor,' answered Captain Nemo; 'but in Torres Straits there is a difference of five feet between the level of high and low tide. Today is the fourth of January, and in five days the moon will be at the full. Now I shall be very much astonished if this complaisant satellite does not sufficiently raise these masses of water, and render me a service which I wish to owe to her alone.'

This said, Captain Nemo, followed by his second, went down again into the interior of the *Nautilus*. The vessel remained as immovable as if the coral polypi had already walled it up in their indestructible cement.

'Well, sir?' said Ned Land, who came to me after the departure of the captain.

'Well, friend Ned, we must wait patiently for high tide on the ninth. It appears that the moon will be kind enough to set us afloat again.'

'Really?'

'Really.'

'And this captain is not going to weigh anchor, to set his machine to work, or to do anything to get the vessel off?'

'Since the tide will súffice,' answered Conseil simply.

The Canadian looked at Conseil, then shrugged his shoulders. It was the seaman who spoke in him.

'Sir,' he replied, 'you may believe me when I tell you that this piece of iron will never be navigated again, either on or under the seas. It is only fit to be sold by weight. I think, then, that the moment is come to part company with Captain Nemo.'

'Friend Ned,' I answered, 'I do not despair, like you, of this valiant *Nautilus*, and in four days we shall know what to think of these tides on the Pacific. Besides, the advice to fly might be opportune if we were in sight of the coasts of England or Provence, but in the Papuan regions it is another thing, and it will be quite time to resort to that extremity if the *Nautilus* does not succeed in getting off, which I should look upon as a grave event.'

'But still we might have a taste of land,' replied Ned Land. 'There is an island; on that island there are trees; under those trees are terrestrial animals, bearers of cutlets and roast beef, which I should like to be able to taste.'

'There friend Ned is right,' said Conseil, 'and I am of his opinion. Could not monsieur obtain from his friend Captain Nemo the permission to be transported to land, if it was only not to lose the habit of treading the solid parts of our planet?'

'I can ask him,' I answered, 'but he will refuse.'

'Let monsieur risk it,' said Conseil, 'and then we shall know what to think about the captain's amiability.'

To my great surprise Captain Nemo gave the permission I asked for, and he gave it me very courteously, without even exacting from me a promise to come back on board. But a flight across the lands of New Guinea would have been very perilous, and I should not have advised Ned Land to attempt it. It was better to be a prisoner on board the *Nautilus* than to fall into the hands of the natives of Papua.

At eight o'clock next morning, armed with guns and hatchets, we descended the sides of the *Nautilus* into the longboat. The sea was pretty calm. A slight breeze was blowing from land. Conseil and I rowed vigorously, and Ned steered in the narrow passages between the breakers. The boat was easily managed, and fled along rapidly.

Ned Land could not contain his joy. He was a prisoner escaped from prison, and did not think of the necessity of going back to it again.

'Meat!' he repeated. 'We are going to eat meat, and what meat! Real game! I don't say that fish is not a good thing, but you can have too much of it, and a piece of fresh venison, grilled over burning coals, would be an agreeable variation to our ordinary fare.'

17

SOME DAYS ON LAND

Touching land again made a great impression on me. Ned Land struck the ground with his foot as if to take possession of it. Yet we had only been, according to Captain Nemo's expression, the 'passengers of the *Nautilus*' for two months – that is to say, in reality, we had only been the captain's prisoners for two months.

In a very short time we were within a gunshot of the coast. All the horizon was hidden by a curtain of admirable forests. Ned perceived a coconut tree, brought down some nuts, broke them, and we drank their milk and ate their kernel with a relish that protested against the ordinary fare of the *Nautilus*.

'Excellent!' said Ned Land.

'Exquisite!' answered Conseil.

'Let us go on with our excursion,' I replied, 'and keep a sharp look-out. Although the island appears to be uninhabited, it might contain individuals who would be easier to please than we on the nature of the game.'

We penetrated the sombre vaults of the forest, and for two hours walked about in every direction. We found that the bread-tree was abundant on this island. Ned

Land knew this fruit well; he had eaten it before in his numerous voyages, and he knew how to prepare its edible substance. The sight of it excited his appetite, and he could contain himself no longer.

'Sir,' he said to me, 'may I die if I don't taste a little of that bread-fruit!'

'Taste, friend Ned – taste as much as you like. We are here to make experiments; let us make them.'

'It will not take long,' answered the Canadian; and with a burning-glass he lighted a fire of dead wood which crackled joyously.

Conseil took a dozen of the fruit to Ned Land, who placed them on a fire of cinders, after having cut them into thin slices, during which he kept saying:

'You will see, sir, how good this bread is!'

'Especially when one has been deprived of it for so long, Conseil.'

'It is better than bread,' added the Canadian; 'it is like delicate pastry. Have you never eaten any, sir?'

'No, Ned.'

'Well, then, prepare for something very good. If you don't return I am no longer the king of harpooners.'

In a short time the side exposed to the fire was quite black. In the interior appeared a white paste and a sort of tender crumb, with a taste something like that of an artichoke.

It must be acknowledged this bread was excellent, and I ate it with great pleasure.

Later we gathered bananas, mangoes and pineapples. But Ned was still not satisfied.

'All these vegetables cannot constitute a meal,' he said; 'they are only good for dessert. There is the soup and the roast.'

'Yes,' said I. 'You had promised us cutlets, which seemed to me very problematic.'

'Sir,' answered the Canadian, 'our sport is not only not ended, but is not even begun. Patience! We shall end by meeting with some animal or bird, and if it is not in this place it will be in another.'

'And if it is not today it will be tomorrow,' added Conseil, 'for we must not go too far away. I vote to go back to the boat now.'

'What, already?' cried Ned.

'We must come back before night,' I said.

'What time is it?' asked the Canadian.

'Two o'clock at least,' answered Conseil.

'How the time does go on dry land!' cried Ned Land with a sigh of regret.

At last, at five o'clock in the evening, loaded with our riches, we left the shores of the island, and half an hour later reached the *Nautilus*. No one appeared on our arrival. The enormous iron cylinders seemed deserted. When the provisions were embarked I went down to my room. There I found my supper ready. I ate it, and then went to sleep.

The next day, 6 January, there was nothing new on board. No noise in the interior, not a sign of life. The canoe had remained alongside, in the very place where we had left it. We resolved to return to the Island of Gilboa. Ned Land hoped to be more fortunate than before from a hunting point of view, and wished to visit another part of the forest.

We set out at sunrise. The boat, carried away by the waves, which were flowing inland, reached the island in a few minutes. We landed, and thinking it was better to trust to the instinct of the Canadian, we followed Ned Land, whose long legs threatened to outdistance us. Ned Land went up the coast westward, and fording some beds of streams, he reached the high plain, bordered by the admirable forests. Some kingfishers were on the banks of the stream, but they would not let themselves be approached; their circumspection proved to me that these fowl knew what to think of bipeds of our sort, and I therefore concluded that, if the island were not inhabited, it was at least frequented by human beings. After having crossed some rich meadow land we reached the borders of a little wood, animated by the song and flight of a great number of birds.

'There are only birds yet,' said Conseil.

'But some of them are good to eat,' answered the harpooner.

'No, friend Ned,' replied Conseil, 'for I see nothing but simple parrots.'

'Friend Conseil,' answered Ned gravely, 'a parrot is the friend of those who have nothing else to eat.'

'And I may add,' I said, 'that this bird, well prepared, is quite worth eating.'

About 11 a.m. we had traversed the first range of mountains that form the centre of the island, and we had killed nothing. Hunger drove us on. The hunters had relied on the products of the chase, and they had done wrong. Fortunately, Conseil, to his great surprise, made a double shot, and secured breakfast. He brought down a white and a wood pigeon, which, quickly plucked and suspended to a skewer, were roasted before a flaming fire of dead wood. Whilst these interesting animals were cooking, Ned had prepared some bread-fruit, then the pigeons were devoured to the bones, and pronounced excellent. Nutmegs, with which they are in the habit of stuffing their crops, flavours their flesh, and makes it delicious.

'And now, Ned, what is there wanting?' I asked the Canadian.

'Some four-footed game, M. Aronnax,' answered Ned Land. 'All these pigeons are only side-dishes and mouthfuls, and until I have killed an animal with cutlets I shall not be content.'

Happily, about two o'clock Ned Land killed a magnificent hog. The animal came in time to give us real quadruped meat, and it was well received. Ned Land was very proud of his shot. The hog, struck by the electric bullet, had fallen stone dead.

The Canadian soon skinned and prepared it after having cut out half a dozen cutlets to furnish us with grilled meat for our evening meal. Then we went on with the chase that was again to be marked by Ned and Conseil's exploits.

The two friends, by beating the bushes, roused a herd of kangaroos that fled away bounding on their elastic paws. But these animals did not take flight too rapidly for the electric capsule to stop them in their course.

'Ah, professor,' cried Ned Land, excited by the pleasure of hunting, 'what excellent game, especially stewed! What provisions for the *Nautilus*! Two, three, five down! And when I think that we shall eat all that meat, and that those imbeciles on board will not have a mouthful!'

These animals were small. They belong to a species of kangaroo 'rabbits' that live habitually in the hollow of trees, and that are of extraordinary speed; but although they are of middling size, they, at least, furnish excellent meat.

We were very much satisfied with the result of our hunt. The delighted Ned proposed to return the next day to this enchanted island, which he wanted to clear of all its edible quadrupeds. But he reckoned without circumstances.

At 6 p.m. we returned to the shore. Our boat was stranded in its place. The *Nautilus*, like a long rock, emerged from the waves two miles from the island.

Ned Land, without more delay, began to prepare the dinner.

'Suppose we do not return to the *Nautilus* this evening,' said Conseil.

'Suppose we never return,' added Ned Land.

Just then a stone fell at our feet and cut short the harpooner's proposition.

18

CAPTAIN NEMO'S THUNDERBOLT

We looked towards the forest without rising, my hand stopping in its movement towards my mouth, Ned Land's completing its office.

'A stone does not fall from the sky,' said Conseil.

A second stone, carefully rounded, which struck out of Conseil's hand a savoury pigeon's leg, gave still more weight to his observations.

'The boat,' said I, making for the sea. In fact, we were obliged to beat a retreat, for about twenty natives, armed with bows and slings, appeared on the skirts of the thicket that hid the horizon one hundred steps off.

Our boat was anchored at about sixty feet from us.

The savages approached us, not running, making most hostile demonstrations. It rained stones and arrows.

Ned Land did not wish to leave his provisions, notwithstanding the imminence of the danger. He went on tolerably fast with his pig on one side and his kangaroos on the other.

In two minutes we were on shore. It was the affair of an instant to land the boat with the provisions and arms, to push it into the sea, and to take the two oars. We had not gone two cables' length when a hundred savages, howling and gesticulating, entered the water up to their waists. I watched to see if their appearance would not attract some men from the *Nautilus* on to the platform.

But no. The enormous machine, lying off, seemed absolutely deserted. Twenty minutes later we ascended the sides; the panels were open. After we had made the boat fast we re-entered the interior of the *Nautilus*.

I went to the saloon, from whence I heard some chords. Captain Nemo was there, bending over his organ, and plunged into a musical ecstasy.

'Captain,' I said to him.

He did not hear me.

'Captain,' I repeated, touching his hand.

He shuddered and turned.

'Ha, it is you, professor?' he said to me. 'Well, have you had good sport?'

'Yes, captain,' answered I, 'but we have, unfortunately, brought back a troop of bipeds, whose neighbourhood appears to me dangerous.'

'What bipeds?'

'Savages.'

'Savages?' answered Captain Nemo in an ironical tone. 'And you are astonished, professor, that having set foot on one of the lands of this globe, you find savages there? Where are there no savages? Besides, those you call savages, are they worse than others?'

'But, captain –'

'For my part, sir, I have met with some everywhere.'

'Well,' I answered, 'if you do not wish to receive any on board the *Nautilus*, you will do well to take some precautions.'

'Make yourself easy, professor; there is nothing worth troubling about.'

'But these natives are numerous.'

'How many did you count?'

'A hundred at least.'

'M. Aronnax,' answered Captain Nemo, who had again placed his fingers on the organ keys, 'if all the natives of Papua were gathered together on that shore, the *Nautilus* would have nothing to fear from their attacks.'

I went up again on to the platform. Night had already come, for in this low latitude the sun sets rapidly, and there is no twilight. I could only see the island indistinctly. But the numerous fires lighted on the beach showed that the natives did not dream of leaving it.

I remained thus alone for several hours, sometimes thinking about the natives, but not otherwise anxious about them, for the imperturbable confidence of the captain gained upon me, sometimes forgetting them to admire the splendours of the tropical night. About midnight, seeing that all was tranquil on the dark waves, as well as under the trees on the shore, I went down to my cabin and went peacefully to sleep.

The night passed without misadventure. The Papuans were, doubtless, frightened by the very sight of the monster stranded in the bay, for the open panels would have given them easy access to the interior of the *Nautilus*.

At 6 a.m., on 8 January, I went up on the platform. The morning was breaking. The island soon appeared through the rising mists, its shores first, then its summits.

The natives were still there, more numerous than the day before, perhaps five or six hundred strong. Some of them, taking advantage of the low tide, had come on to the coral heads at less than two cables' length from the *Nautilus*.

During the whole time of low water these natives

roamed about near the *Nautilus*, but they were not noisy. I heard them frequently repeat the word 'Assai', and from their gestures I understood that they invited me to land, an invitation that I thought it better to decline.

The savages returned to land about 11 a.m., as soon as the heads of coral began to disappear under the waves of the rising tide. But I saw their number considerably increase on the shore. It was probable that they came from the neighbouring islands.

Within two hours they had assembled about twenty pirogues and then surrounded the *Nautilus*. These pirogues, hollowed trunks of trees, long, narrow, and well calculated for speed, were kept in equilibrium by means of double balances of bamboo, which floated on the surface of the water. They were worked by skilful paddlers, half-naked, and their approach made me uneasy. It was evident that these Papuans had already had some relations with Europeans, and knew their ships. But what must they have thought of this long iron cylinder, without either masts or funnel? Nothing good, but they kept first at a respectful distance. However, seeing it did not move, they regained confidence by degrees and tried to familiarize themselves with it. Now it was precisely this familiarity which it was necessary to prevent. Our arms, which made no noise, could only produce an indifferent effect on these natives, who only respect noisy weapons. A thunderbolt without the rolling of thunder would not much frighten men, although the danger exists in the lightning and not in the noise.

At that moment the pirogues approached nearer the *Nautilus*, and a shower of arrows fell upon it.

'Why, it hails,' said Conseil, 'and perhaps poisoned hail.'

'I must tell Captain Nemo,' said I, going through the panel.

I went down to the saloon. I found no one there. I ventured to knock at the door of the captain's room.

A 'Come in!' answered me.

I entered, and found Captain Nemo occupied with a calculation where x and other algebraical signs were plentiful.

'I fear I am disturbing you,' said I.

'Yes, M. Aronnax,' answered the captain, 'but I think you must have serious reasons for seeing me.'

'Very serious; we are surrounded by the pirogues of the natives, and in a few minutes we shall certainly be assailed by several hundreds of savages.'

'Ah,' said Captain Nemo, tranquilly, 'so they are here with their pirogues?'

'Yes.'

'Well, all we have to do is to shut the panels.'

'Precisely, and I came to tell you.'

'Nothing is easier,' said Captain Nemo.

Pressing an electric bell he transmitted an order to the crew's quarters.

'That's done, sir,' said he after a few minutes; 'the boat is in its place, and the panels are shut. You do not fear, I imagine, that these gentlemen can break in walls which the bails from your frigate could not touch?'

'No, captain, but there exists another danger.'

'What is that, sir?'

'It is that tomorrow, at the same time, you will be obliged to open the panels to renew the air of the *Nautilus*.'

'Certainly, sir, as our vessel breathes like the cetaceans do.'

'Now, if at that moment the Papuans occupied the platform, I do not know how you could prevent them entering.'

'Then you believe they will get up on the vessel?'

'I am certain of it.'

'Well, let them. I see no reason for preventing them. These Papuans are poor devils, and I will not let my visit to Gilboa cost the life of one poor wretch.'

I was left alone. I went to bed, but slept badly. I heard the savages stamping about on the platform making a deafening noise. The night passed thus without the crew seeming to come out of their habitual inertia. They were not more anxious about the presence of these cannibals than the soldiers of an ironclad fortress would be about the ants that crawl over the iron.

I rose at 6 a.m. The panels had not been opened. The air, therefore, had not been renewed in the interior, but the reservoirs, filled ready for any event, sent some cubic yards of oxygen into the impoverished atmosphere of the *Nautilus*.

I worked in my room till noon without seeing Captain Nemo, even for an instant. There seemed to be no preparation for departure made on board.

I waited for some time longer, and then went into the saloon. The clock was at half-past two. In ten minutes the tide would be at its maximum, and if Captain Nemo had not made a boasting promise the *Nautilus* would be immediately set free. If not, many months would pass before it would leave its coral bed.

In the meantime several shocks were felt in the hull of the vessel. I heard its sides grate against the coral.

At 2.35 p.m. Captain Nemo appeared in the saloon.

'We are going to start,' said he.

'Ah!' I said.

'I have given orders to have the panels opened.'

'What about the Papuans?'

'The Papuans?' answered Captain Nemo, slightly raising his shoulders.

'Will they not penetrate into the interior of the *Nautilus*?'

'How can they?'

'Through the panels you have had opened.'

'M. Aronnax,' answered Captain Nemo tranquilly, 'it is not so easy to enter the *Nautilus* through its panels, even when they are opened.'

I looked at the captain.

'You do not understand?' he asked.

'Not at all.'

'Well, come, and you will see.'

I went towards the central staircase. There Ned Land and Conseil, much puzzled, were looking at some of the crew, who were opening the panels, whilst cries of rage and fearful vociferations resounded outside.

The lids were opened on the outside. Seventy horrible faces appeared. But the first of the natives who put his hand on the balustrade, thrown backwards by some invisible force, fled, howling and making extraordinary gambols.

Ten of his companions succeeded him. Ten had the same fate.

Conseil was in ecstasies. Ned Land, carried away by his violent instincts, sprang up the staircase. But as soon as he had seized the hand-rail with both hands he was overthrown in his turn.

'Malediction!' he cried. 'I am thunderstruck.'

That word explained it all to me. It was no longer a hand-rail but a metal cable, charged with electricity. Whoever touched it felt a formidable shock, and that shock would have been mortal if Captain Nemo had thrown all the current of his apparatus into this conductor. It may be truly said that between his assailants and himself he had hung an electric barrier that no one could cross with impunity.

In the meantime the frightened Papuans had beaten a retreat, maddened with terror. We, half-laughing, consoled the unfortunate Ned Land, who was swearing like one possessed.

But at that moment the *Nautilus*, raised by the last tidal waves, left its coral bed. Its screw beat the waves with majestic slowness. Its speed increased by degrees, and navigating on the surface of the ocean, it left safe and sound the dangerous passages of Torres Straits.

19

MORBID SLUMBER

The following day, 10 January, the *Nautilus* resumed its course under the water, but at a remarkable speed, which I could not estimate at less than thirty-five miles an hour.

We headed west for several days. The days fled rapidly away, and I counted them no longer. Ned, according to his custom, tried to vary the fare on board. Veritable snails, we had become accustomed to our shell, and I affirmed that it is easy to become a perfect snail. This existence, then, appeared to us easy and natural, and we no longer thought of the different life that existed on the surface of the terrestrial globe, when an event happened to recall to us the strangeness of our situation.

On 18 January, the weather was threatening, the sea rough. The wind was blowing a strong gale from the east. The barometer, which had been going down for some days, announced an approaching war of the elements.

I had gone up on to the platform at the moment the first officer was taking his bearings. I expected as usual to hear the daily sentence pronounced. But that day it was replaced by another phrase not less incomprehensible. Almost immediately I saw Captain Nemo appear and sweep the horizon with a telescope.

For some minutes the captain remained immovable, without leaving the point enclosed in the field of his object-glass. Then he lowered his telescope and exchanged about ten words with his officer, who seemed to be a prey to an emotion that he tried in vain to suppress.

I looked carefully in the direction they were observing without perceiving anything. Sky and water mixed in a perfectly clear horizon.

In the meantime Captain Nemo walked up and down the platform without looking at me, perhaps without seeing me. His step was assured, but less regular than usual. Sometimes he stopped, folded his arms, and looked at the sea. What was he seeking in that immense space? The *Nautilus* was then some hundreds of miles from the nearest coast.

The first officer had taken up his telescope again, and was obstinately interrogating the horizon, going and coming, stamping, and contrasting with his chief by his nervous excitement.

This mystery must necessarily be soon cleared up, for, obeying an order of Captain Nemo's, the machine, increasing its propelling power, gave a more rapid rotatory movement to the screw.

At that moment the officer again attracted the captain's attention, who stopped his walk and directed his telescope towards the point indicated. He observed it for a long time. I, feeling very curious about it, went down to the saloon and brought up an excellent telescope that I generally used. Then leaning it against the lantern-cage that jutted in front of the platform, I prepared to sweep all the line of sky and sea. But I had not placed my eye to it when the instrument was quickly snatched out of my hands.

I turned. Captain Nemo was before me, but I hardly knew him. His eyes shone with sombre fire under his frowning eyebrows. His teeth glittered between his firm-set lips. His stiffened body, closed fists, and head set hard on his shoulders, showed the violent hatred breathed by his whole appearance. He did not move. My telescope, fallen from his hand, had rolled to his feet.

Had I, then, unintentionally provoked this angry attitude? Did the incomprehensible personage imagine that I had surprised some secret interdicted to the guests of the *Nautilus*?

No! I was not the object of this hatred, for he was not looking at me; his eyes remained fixed on the impenetrable point of the horizon.

At last Captain Nemo recovered his self-possession. His face, so profoundly excited, resumed its habitual calmness. He addressed some words in a foreign tongue to his officer, and then turned towards me again.

'M. Aronnax,' said he in a rather imperious tone, 'I require from you the fulfilment of one of the engagements that bind me to you.'

'What is that, captain?'

'To let yourself be shut up – you and your companions – until I shall think proper to set you at liberty again.'

'You are master here,' I answered, looking at him fixedly. 'But may I ask you one question?'

'No, sir, not one!'

After that I had nothing to do but obey, as all resistance would have been impossible.

I went down to the cabin occupied by Ned Land and Conseil, and I told them of the captain's determination. I leave it to be imagined how that communication was received by the Canadian. Besides, there was no time for any explanation. Four of the crew were waiting at the door, and they conducted us to the cell where we had passed our first night on board the *Nautilus*.

Ned Land wanted to expostulate, but for all answer the door was shut upon him.

'Will monsieur tell me what this means?' asked Conseil.

I related what had happened to my companions. They were as astonished as I, and not more enlightened.

I was overwhelmed with reflections, and the strange look on Captain Nemo's face would not go out of my head. I was incapable of putting two logical ideas together, and was losing myself in the most absurd hypotheses, when I was aroused by these words of Ned Land:

'Why, they have laid dinner for us!'

In fact, the table was laid. It was evident that Captain Nemo had given this order at the same time that he caused the speed of the *Nautilus* to be hastened.

'Will monsieur allow me to recommend something to him?' asked Conseil.

'Yes, my boy,' I replied.

'It is that monsieur should breakfast. It would be prudent, for we do not know what may happen.'

'You are right, Conseil.'

'Unfortunately,' said Ned Land, 'they have only given us the usual fare on board.'

'Friend Ned,' replied Conseil, 'what should you say if you had had no dinner at all?'

That observation cut short the harpooner's grumbling.

We sat down to dinner. The meal was eaten in silence. I ate little. Conseil forced himself to eat for prudence sake, and Ned Land ate as usual. Then, breakfast over, we each made ourselves comfortable in a corner.

At that moment the luminous globe that had been lighting us went out and left us in profound darkness. Ned Land soon went to sleep, and, what astonished me, Conseil went off into a heavy slumber. I was asking myself what could have provoked in him so imperious a need of sleep, when I felt heaviness creep over my own brain. My eyes, which I wished to keep open, closed in spite of my efforts. I became a prey to painful hallucinations. It was evident that soporific substances had been mixed with the food we had just eaten. Imprisonment, then, was not enough to conceal Captain Nemo's projects from us; we must have sleep as well.

I heard the panels closed. The undulations of the sea, that of a slight rolling motion, ceased. Had the *Nautilus*, then, left the surface of the ocean? Had it again sunk to the motionless depth?

I wished to resist sleep. It was impossible. My breathing became weaker. I felt a deathlike coldness freeze and paralyse my limbs. My eyelids fell like leaden coverings over my eyes. I could not raise them. A morbid slumber, full of hallucinations, took possession of my whole being. Then the visions disappeared and left me in complete insensibility.

20

THE CORAL KINGDOM

The next day I awoke with my faculties singularly clear. To my great surprise I was in my own room. My companions had doubtless been carried to their cabin without being more aware of it than I. They knew no more what had happened during the night than I, and to unveil the mystery I only depended on the hazards of the future.

I then thought of leaving my room. Was I once more free or a prisoner? Entirely free. I opened the door, went through the waist, and climbed the central staircase. The panels, closed the night before, were opened. I stepped on to the platform.

Ned Land and Conseil were awaiting me there. I questioned them; they knew nothing. They had slept a dreamless sleep, and had been much surprised to find themselves in their cabin on awaking.

As to the *Nautilus*, it appeared to us tranquil and mysterious as usual. It was floating on the surface of the waves at a moderate speed. Nothing on board seemed changed.

Ned Land watched the sea with his penetrating eyes. It was deserted. The Canadian signalled nothing fresh on the horizon – neither sail nor land. There was a stiff west breeze blowing, and the vessel was rolling under the influence of long waves raised by the wind.

Captain Nemo did not appear. Of the men on board I only saw the emotionless steward, who served me with his usual exactitude and speechlessness.

About 2 p.m. I was in the saloon, occupied in classifying my notes, when the captain opened the door and appeared. I bowed to him. He returned it almost imperceptibly, without uttering a word. I went on with my work, hoping he would perhaps give me some explanation of the events that had occurred the previous night. He did nothing of the kind. I looked at him. His face appeared to me fatigued; his reddened eyelids showed they had not been refreshed by sleep; his physiognomy expressed profound and real grief. He walked about, sat down, rose up, took a book at random, abandoned it immediately, consulted his instruments without making his usual notes, and did not seem able to keep an instant in peace.

At last he came towards me and said:

'Are you a doctor, M. Aronnax?'

I so little expected such a question that I looked at him for some time without answering.

'Are you a doctor?' he repeated.

'Yes,' I said; 'I am doctor and surgeon. I was in practice for several years before entering the museum.'

'That is well.'

My answer had evidently satisfied Captain Nemo, but not knowing what he wanted, I awaited fresh questions, meaning to answer according to circumstances.

'M. Aronnax,' said the captain, 'will you consent to prescribe for a sick man?'

'There is someone ill on board?'

'Yes.'

'I am ready to follow you.'

'Come.'

I must acknowledge that my heart beat faster. I do not know why I saw some connection between the illness of this man of the crew and the events of the night before, and this mystery preoccupied me at least as much as the sick man.

Captain Nemo conducted me aft of the *Nautilus*, and made me enter a cabin situated in the crew's quarters.

There, upon a bed, a man of some forty years, with an energetic face and true Anglo-Saxon type, was reposing.

I bent over him. He was not only a sick man but a wounded one too. His head, wrapped in bandages, was resting on a double pillow. I undid the bandages, and the wounded man, looking with his large fixed eyes, let me do it without uttering a single complaint.

The wound was horrible. The skull, crushed by some blunt instrument, showed the brain. Clots of blood had formed in the wound the colour of wine-dregs. The breathing of the sick man was slow, and spasmodic movements of the muscles agitated his face.

I felt the pulse; it was intermittent. The extremities were already growing cold, and I saw that death was approaching without any possibility of my preventing it. After dressing the wound I bandaged it again, and turned towards Captain Nemo.

'How was this wound caused?' I asked.

'What does it matter?' answered the captain evasively. 'A shock of the *Nautilus* broke one of the levers of the machine, which struck this man. But what do you think of his condition?'

I hesitated to reply.

'You may speak,' said the captain; 'this man does not understand French.'

I looked a last time at the wounded man, then I answered:

'He will be dead in two hours.'

'Can nothing save him?'

'Nothing.'

Captain Nemo clenched his hand, and his eyes, which I did not think made for weeping, filled with tears.

For some time I still watched the dying man, whose life seemed gradually ebbing. He looked still paler under the electric light that bathed his deathbed. I looked at his intelligent head, furrowed with premature lines which misfortune, misery perhaps, had long ago placed there. I tried to learn the secret of his life in the last words that escaped from his mouth.

'You can go now, M. Aronnax,' said Captain Nemo.

I left the captain in the room of the dying man, and went back to my room much moved by this scene. During the whole day I was agitated by sinister presentiments. I slept badly that night, and, amidst my frequently interrupted dreams, I thought I heard distant sighs and a sound like funeral chants. Was it the prayer for the dead murmured in that language which I could not understand?

The next morning I went up on deck. Captain Nemo had preceded me there. As soon as he perceived me he came to me.

'Professor,' said he, 'would it suit you to make a submarine excursion today?'

'With my companions?' I asked.

'If they like.'

'We are at your disposition, captain.'

'Then please put on your diving dresses.'

I went to Ned Land and Conseil and told them of Captain Nemo's proposal. Conseil accepted it immediately, and this time the Canadian seemed quite ready to go with us.

It was 8 a.m. At half-past we were clothed for our walk,

and furnished with our breathing and lighting apparatus. The double door was opened and, accompanied by Captain Nemo, who was followed by a dozen men of the crew, we set foot at a depth of ten yards on the firm ground where the *Nautilus* was stationed.

A slight incline brought us to an undulated stretch of ground at about fifteen fathoms depth. This ground differed completely from any I saw during my first excursion under the waters of the Pacific Ocean. Here there was no fine sand, no submarine meadows, no seaweed forests. I immediately recognized this region of which Captain Nemo was doing the honours. It was the kingdom of coral.

We switched on our lamps and followed a coral bank in process of formation, which, helped by time, would one day close in that portion of the Indian Ocean. The route was bordered by inextricable bushes formed by the entanglement of shrubs that the little white-starred flowers covered.

But soon the bushes contracted. Real petrified thickets and long galleries of fantastic architecture opened before our steps. Captain Nemo entered a dark gallery, the inclined plane of which led us down a depth of 100 yards. The light of our lamps sometimes produced magical effects by following the rough outlines of the natural arches and pendants, like bushes, which it pricked with points of fire.

At last, after two hours' walking, we reached a depth of about 150 fathoms – that is to say, the extreme limit that coral begins to form itself. But there it was no longer the isolated shrub nor the modest thicket of low brushwood. It was the immense forest, the great mineral vegetations, the enormous petrified trees. We passed freely under their high branches lost in the depths of the water above.

It was an indescribable spectacle! Ah, why could we

not communicate our sensations? Why were we imprisoned under these masks of metal and glass? Why were words between us forbidden? Why did we not at least live the life of the fish that people the liquid element, or rather that of the amphibians who can traverse as they like the double domain of land and water?

In the meantime Captain Nemo had stopped. My companions and I imitated him, and, turning round, I saw that his men had formed a semicircle round their chief. Looking with more attention, I noticed that four of them were carrying an object of oblong form on their shoulders.

We were then in the centre of a vast open space surrounded by the submarine forest. Our lamps lighted up the space with a sort of twilight which immoderately lengthened the shadows on the ground. At the limit of the open space darkness again became profound, and was only 'made visible' by little sparks reflected in the projections of the coral.

Ned Land and Conseil were near me. We looked on, and the thought that I was going to assist at a strange scene came into my mind. As I looked at the ground I saw that it was raised in certain places by slight mounds encrusted with calcareous deposits, and laid out with a regularity that betrayed the hand of man.

In the centre of the open space, on a pedestal of rocks roughly piled together, rose a coral cross, which extended its long arms, that one might have said were made of petrified blood.

Upon a sign from Captain Nemo one of his men came forward, and at some feet distance from the cross began to dig a hole with a pickaxe that he took from his belt.

I then understood it all! This space was a cemetery; this hole a grave; this oblong object the body of the man who had died during the night! Captain Nemo and his men came to inter their companion in this common resting-place in the depths of the inaccessible ocean!

My mind was never so much excited before. More impressionable ideas had never invaded my brain! I would not see what my eyes were looking at!

In the meantime the tomb was being slowly dug. Fish fled hither and thither as their retreat was troubled. I heard on the calcareous soil the ring of the iron pickaxe that sparkled when it struck some flint lost at the bottom of the sea. The hole grew larger and wider, and was soon deep enough to receive the body.

Then the bearers approached. The body, wrapped in a tissue of white byssus, was lowered into its watery tomb. Captain Nemo, with his arms crossed on his chest, and all the friends of the man who had loved them, knelt in the attitude of prayer. My two companions and I bent religiously.

The tomb was then filled with the matter dug from the soil, and formed a slight mound.

When this was done Captain Nemo and his men rose; then, collecting round the tomb, all knelt again, and extended their hands in sign of supreme adieu.

Then the funeral procession set out for the *Nautilus* again, repassing under the arcades of the forest, amidst the thickets by the side of the coral-bushes, going uphill all the way.

At last the lights on board appeared. Their luminous track guided us to the *Nautilus*. We were back at one o'clock.

As soon as I had changed my clothes I went up on to the platform, and, a prey to a terrible conflict of emotions, I went and seated myself near the lantern-cage.

Captain Nemo joined me there. I rose and said:

'Then, as I foresaw, that man died in the night?'

'Yes, M. Aronnax,' answered Captain Nemo.

'And now he is resting by the side of his companions in the coral cemetery?'

'Yes, forgotten by everyone but us! We dig the grave, and the polypi take the trouble of sealing our dead therein for eternity.'

And hiding his face in his hands with a brusque gesture, the captain tried in vain to suppress a sob. Then he added:

'That is our peaceful cemetery, at some hundreds of feet below the surface of the waves!'

'Your dead sleep, at least, tranquil, captain, out of reach of the sharks!'

'Yes, sir,' answered Captain Nemo gravely, 'of sharks and men!'

PART TWO

1

THE INDIAN OCEAN

Here begins the second part of this voyage under the sea. The first ended with the painful scene at the coral cemetery, which has left a profound impression on my mind. Thus, then, in the bosom of the immense ocean Captain Nemo's entire life was passed, and he had even prepared his grave in the most impenetrable of its depths. There not one of the ocean monsters would trouble the last slumber of the inhabitants of the *Nautilus* – of these men, riveted to each other in death as in life! 'Nor man either!' Captain Nemo had added. There was always in him the same implacable and ferocious defiance towards all human society.

I no longer contented myself with the hypotheses that satisfied Conseil. The worthy fellow persisted in only seeing in the commander of the *Nautilus* one of the unappreciated *savants* who give back to humanity disdain for indifference. He was still for him a misunderstood genius, who, tired of the deceptions of the world, had sought refuge in the inaccessible medium where he could freely exercise his instincts. But, in my opinion, that hypothesis only explained one of Captain Nemo's aspects.

In fact, the mystery of that last night during which we had been enchained in prison and sleep, the precaution so violently taken by the captain of snatching from my eyes the telescope ready to sweep the horizon, the mortal wound of that man due to an inexplicable shock of the *Nautilus* – all that inclined me in a fresh direction. No! Captain Nemo did not content himself with flying from mankind! His formidable apparatus not only served his instincts of liberty, but was perhaps also the instrument of terrible revenge.

Nothing really binds us to Captain Nemo. He knows that to escape from the *Nautilus* is impossible. We are not even prisoners of honour. We are only captives, prisoners disguised under the name of guests by an appearance of courtesy. Nevertheless, Ned Land has not renounced the hope of recovering his liberty. It is certain that he will profit by the first occasion chance offers him. I shall, doubtless, do the same, and yet it will not be without a sort of regret that I shall take away what the captain's generosity has allowed us to penetrate of the mysteries of the *Nautilus*. For, after all, is the man to be hated or admired? Is he a victim or an executioner? And, to speak frankly, I should like before leaving him for ever to have accomplished the submarine tour round the world of which the beginning has been so magnificent. I should like to have observed the complete series of marvels piled under the seas of the globe. I should like to have seen what no man has seen before, even if I should pay with my life for this insatiable desire to learn. What have I yet discovered? Nothing, or nearly nothing, since we have only yet been over 6,000 leagues of the Pacific.

However I know that the *Nautilus* is approaching inhabited lands, and that, if some chance of salvation was offered to us, it would be cruel to sacrifice my companions to my passion for the unknown. I must follow them, perhaps guide them. But will this occasion ever present itself? The man deprived by force of his freedom may desire it, but the *savant*, the learner, dreads it.

That day, 21 January 1868, at noon, the first officer came to take the height of the sun. I went up on to the platform and followed the operation. It appeared evident to me that this man did not understand French for several reasons. I made reflections aloud which must have drawn from him some involuntary sign of attention if he had understood them, but he remained expressionless and mute.

When the *Nautilus* was prepared to continue her submarine journey, I went down to the saloon. The panels were closed, our course was directly west, and so it continued for several days.

On the morning of the 24th, we sighted Keeling Island, planted with magnificent cocoas. The *Nautilus* kept along the shores of this desert island for some little distance.

Soon Keeling Island disappeared from the horizon, and we directed our course to the north-west, towards the Indian peninsula.

'Civilized land,' said Ned Land to me that day. 'That is better than the islands of Papua, where you meet with more savages than venison! On that Indian ground, professor, there are roads, railways, English, French, or Hindu towns. One would not go five miles without meeting with a countryman. Well, is it not the moment to take French leave of Captain Nemo?'

'No, Ned, no,' I answered in a very determined tone. 'Let us see what comes of it. The *Nautilus* is getting nearer the inhabited continents. It is going back towards Europe; let it take us there. Once in our own seas, we shall see what prudence advises us to attempt. Besides, I do not suppose that Captain Nemo would allow us to go

and shoot on the coasts of Malabar or Coromandel, like
he did in the forests of New Guinea.'

'Well, sir, can't we do without his permission?'

I did not answer the Canadian, for I did not wish to
argue. At the bottom of my heart I wished to exhaust to
the end the chances of destiny that had thrown me on
board the *Nautilus*.

2

A FRESH PROPOSITION OF CAPTAIN NEMO'S

By 28 January we were near the island of Ceylon. I went to look in the library for a book giving an account of this island, one of the most fertile on the globe. At this moment Captain Nemo and the mate appeared. The captain glanced at the map, then turned towards me.

'The island of Ceylon,' said he, 'is very celebrated for its pearl fisheries. Would you like to see one of them, M. Aronnax?'

'I should indeed, captain.'

'Then, professor,' said the captain, 'you and your companions shall see the oyster-bank of Manaar, and if by chance some early diver should be found there, we shall see him at work.'

'Agreed, captain.'

'But, M. Aronnax, you are not afraid of sharks?'

'Sharks?' cried I.

This question appeared to me at least a very idle one.

'Well?' continued Captain Nemo.

'I confess, captain, that I am not yet quite at home with that kind of fish.'

'We are used to them,' answered Captain Nemo, 'and

in time you will be so also. However, we shall be armed, and on the road we may have a shark-hunt. So good-bye till tomorrow, sir, and early in the morning.'

This said in a careless tone, Captain Nemo left the saloon.

Now if you were invited to hunt the bear in the Swiss mountains you would say, 'Very well, we'll go and hunt the bear tomorrow.' If you were invited to hunt the lion in the plains of the Atlas, or the tiger in the jungles of India, you would say, 'Ah, ah! It seems we are going to hunt lions and tigers!' But if you were invited to hunt the shark in its native element, you would, perhaps, ask time for reflection before accepting the invitation.

As to me, I passed my hand over my forehead, where stood several drops of cold sweat.

'I must reflect and take time,' I said to myself. 'To hunt otters in submarine forests, as we did in the forests of Crespo Island, is one thing, but to walk along the bottom of the sea when you are pretty sure of meeting with sharks is another!'

And I began to dream of sharks, thinking of their vast jaws armed with multiplied rows of teeth, capable of cutting a man in two. I already felt a sharp pain in my loins. And then I could not digest the cool way in which the captain had made this deplorable invitation. Any one would have thought it was only to follow some inoffensive fox!

'Good!' thought I. 'Conseil will never come, and that will dispense me from accompanying the captain.'

As to Ned Land, I must acknowledge I did not feel so sure of his prudence – a peril, however great, had always some attraction for his warlike nature.

I went on reading my book on Ceylon, but I turned over the leaves mechanically. I saw formidably opened jaws between the lines. At that moment Conseil and the

Canadian entered, looking calm, and even gay. They did not know what was awaiting them.

'Faith, sir,' said Ned Land, 'your Captain Nemo – whom the devil take! – has just made us a very amiable offer.'

'Ah!' I said. 'So you know –'

'Yes,' interrupted Conseil, 'the commander of the *Nautilus* has invited us to visit tomorrow, in company with monsieur, the magnificent fisheries of Ceylon. He did it handsomely, and like a real gentleman.'

'Did he not tell you anything more?'

'No, sir,' answered the Canadian, 'except that he had mentioned the little excursion to you.'

'So he did,' I said. 'And he gave you no detail about –'

'Nothing, Mr Naturalist. You will go with us, won't you?'

'I? Oh, of course! I see it is to your taste, Ned.'

'Yes, it will be very curious.'

'Dangerous too, perhaps,' I said in an insinuating tone.

'Dangerous?' answered Ned Land. 'A simple excursion on an oyster-bank dangerous?'

It was evident that Captain Nemo had not thought proper to awake the idea of sharks in the mind of my companions. I looked at them with a troubled eye as if some limb were wanting to them already. Ought I to warn them? Yes, certainly, but I hardly knew how to set about it.

'Are many pearls found in the same oyster?' asked Conseil.

'Yes,' I answered, 'mention has been made of an oyster, but I cannot help doubting it, which contained no less than a hundred and fifty sharks.'

'A hundred and fifty sharks!' cried Ned Land.

'Did I say sharks?' I cried quickly. 'I mean a hundred and fifty pearls. Sharks would be nonsense.'

'I have heard tell,' said the Canadian, 'that a certain lady of ancient times drank pearls in her vinegar.'

'Cleopatra,' suggested Conseil.

'It must have been nasty,' added Ned Land.

'Detestable, friend Ned,' answered Conseil; 'but a little glass of vinegar that costs £60,000; it is a nice price.'

'I am sorry I did not marry that lady,' said the Canadian, moving about his arms in no very reassuring manner.

'But,' said I, 'to return to pearls of great value, I do not think any sovereign has ever possessed one better than that of Captain Nemo.'

'This one you mean,' said Conseil, pointing to a magnificent jewel under its glass case.

'Certainly I am not mistaken in assigning it a value of two millions of –'

'Francs!' said Conseil quickly.

'Yes,' said I, 'two millions of francs, and I dare say it only cost the captain the trouble of picking it up.'

'Eh!' cried Ned Land. 'Who says that during our excursion tomorrow we shall not meet with its fellow?'

'Bah!' said Conseil.

'And why not?'

'What use would millions be to us on board the *Nautilus*?'

'On board, no,' said Ned Land; 'but – elsewhere.'

'Oh, elsewhere!' said Conseil, shaking his head.

'In point of fact,' said I, 'Ned Land is right. And if we ever take back to Europe or America a pearl worth millions, that at least will give great authenticity, and at the same time a great value, to the account of our adventures.'

'I should think so,' said the Canadian.

'But,' said Conseil, who always returned to the instructive side of things, 'is this diving for pearls dangerous?'

'No,' answered I, 'especially if one takes certain precautions.'

'What risk can there be,' said Ned Land, 'except that of swallowing a few mouthfuls of sea-water?'

'You are right, Ned,' said I; then trying to assume Captain Nemo's careless tone, 'Are you afraid of sharks, Ned?'

'I?' answered the Canadian. 'A harpooner by profession? It is my business to laugh at them.'

'But,' said I, 'there is no question of fishing them with a merlin, drawing them up on to the deck of a ship, and cutting off their tails with hatchets, of cutting them open, taking out their hearts, and throwing them back into the sea!'

'Then it means –'

'Yes, precisely.'

'In the water?'

'In the water.'

'Faith, with a good harpoon! You know, sir, these sharks are awkward fellows and badly put together. They must turn on their stomachs to nab you, and during that time –'

Ned Land had a way of saying the word 'nab' that made my blood run cold.

'Well, and you, Conseil, what do you think of sharks?'

'I?' said Conseil. 'I will tell monsieur frankly.'

'There is some hope,' thought I.

'If monsieur means to face the sharks,' said Conseil, 'I do not see why his faithful servant should not face them with him!'

3

A PEARL WORTH TEN MILLIONS

Night came. I went to bed and slept badly. Sharks played an important part in my dreams.

The next day, at 4 a.m., I was awakened by the steward, whom Captain Nemo had specially placed at my service. I rose rapidly, dressed, and went into the saloon. Captain Nemo was waiting for me there.

'Are you ready to start, M. Aronnax?'

'I am ready.'

'Then follow me, please.'

'And my companions, captain?'

'They are waiting for us.'

'Are we to put on our diving dresses?'

'Not yet. I have not allowed the *Nautilus* to come too near this coast, and we are still some way off Manaar Bank; but I have ordered the boat to be got ready, and it will take us to the exact point for landing, which will save us a rather long journey. It will have on board our diving dresses, and we shall put them on as soon as our submarine exploration begins.'

Captain Nemo accompanied me to the central staircase, which led to the platform. Ned and Conseil were there, delighted at the notion of the pleasure party which was being prepared. Five sailors from the *Nautilus*, oars in hand, awaited us in the boat, which had been made fast against the side.

The night was yet dark. Heavy clouds covered the sky, and scarcely allowed a star to be seen. I looked towards the land, but saw nothing but a faint line enclosing three-quarters of the horizon from south-west to north-west. The *Nautilus* having moved up the western coast of Ceylon during the night, was now on the west of the bay, or rather gulf, formed by the land and the island of Manaar.

There under the dark waters stretched the oyster-bank, an inexhaustible field of pearls, the length of which is more than twenty miles.

Captain Nemo, Conseil, Ned Land, and I took our places in the stern of the boat, and we moved off.

Our course was in a southerly direction. The rowers did not hurry themselves. We were silent. What was Captain Nemo thinking of? Perhaps of the land that we were approaching, and which he found too near him, contrary to the opinion of the Canadian, who thought it too far off.

About half-past five the first streaks of daylight showed more clearly the upper line of the coast. Flat enough in the east, it rose a little towards the south. Five miles still separated us from it, and the shore was indistinct, owing to the mist on the water. There was not a boat or a diver to be seen.

At 6 a.m. it became daylight suddenly, with that rapidity peculiar to the tropical regions, which have neither dawn nor twilight. I saw the land distinctly, with a few trees scattered here and there. The boat neared Manaar Island; Captain Nemo rose from his seat and watched the sea.

At a sign from him the anchor was dropped, but it had

but a little distance to fall, for it was scarcely more than a yard to the bottom, and this was one of the highest points of the oyster-bank.

'Now, M. Aronnax,' said Captain Nemo, 'here we are. In a month numerous boats will be assembled here, and these are the waters that the divers explore so boldly. This bay is well placed for the purpose; it is sheltered from the high winds, the sea is never very rough here, which is highly favourable for divers' work. We will now put on our diving dresses and begin our investigations.'

Aided by the sailors, I began to put on my heavy dress. Captain Nemo and my two companions also dressed themselves. None of the sailors from the *Nautilus* were to accompany us.

We were soon imprisoned to the throat in our india-rubber dresses, and the air apparatus was fixed to our backs by means of braces. There was no need for lamps. Before putting on the copper cap I had asked Captain Nemo about them.

'We shall not require them,' said he. 'We shall not go to any great depth, and the solar rays will give us light enough. Besides, it would be very imprudent to use an electric lantern under these waters; its brilliancy might unexpectedly attract some of the dangerous inhabitants of these shores.'

As Captain Nemo uttered these words I turned towards Conseil and Ned Land. But my two friends had already encased their heads in their metal caps, and could neither hear nor reply.

I had one more question to ask Captain Nemo.

'Our weapons?' I asked. 'Our guns?'

'Guns? What for? Do not the mountaineers attack the bear dagger in hand, and is not steel surer than lead? Here is a stout blade; put it in your belt, and we will start.'

I looked at my companions. They were armed like us, and more than this, Ned Land brandished an enormous harpoon which he had put into the boat before leaving the *Nautilus*.

Then, following the example of the captain, I let them put on my heavy copper helmet, and the air reservoirs were at once put in activity. Directly afterwards we were landed in about five feet of water upon a firm sand. Captain Nemo gave us a sign with his hand. We followed him, and going down a gentle slope, we disappeared under the waves.

Captain Nemo pressed on determinedly through the oyster-bank. We left it behind and descended into deeper water. After a short time there opened before us a vast grotto, hollowed in a picturesque cluster of rocks, and carpeted with seaweed. At first this grotto appeared very dark to me. The solar rays seemed to die out there in successive gradations. The clear light became drowned light.

Captain Nemo entered. We followed him. My eyes soon became accustomed to the relative darkness. Why did our incomprehensible guide lead us into the depths of this submarine crypt! I should soon know.

After descending a rather steep incline we were at the bottom of a sort of circular well. There Captain Nemo stopped and pointed to an object we had not perceived before.

It was an oyster of extraordinary dimensions, a font that would have contained a lake of holy water, a vase more than two yards across, and consequently larger than the one in the saloon of the *Nautilus*.

Captain Nemo evidently knew of the existence of this bivalve. It was not the first visit he had paid to it, and I thought that in conducting us to that place he merely wished to show us a natural curiosity. I was mistaken.

Captain Nemo had an interest in seeing the actual condition of this oyster.

The two valves of the mollusc were half-open. The captain went up to them and put his dagger between them to prevent them shutting, then with his hand he raised the membranous tunic, fringed at the border, that formed the animal's mantle.

There, amidst its foliated pleats, I saw a pearl as large as a coconut. Its globular form, perfect limpidity, and admirable water made it a jewel of inestimable price. Carried away by curiosity, I stretched out my hand to take it, weigh it, feel it. But the captain stopped me, made a sign in the negative, and drawing back his dagger by a rapid movement, he let the two valves fall together.

I then understood the purpose of Captain Nemo. By leaving this pearl wrapped up in the mantle of the oyster he allowed it to grow insensibly. With each year the secretion of the mollusc added fresh concentric layers to it. The captain alone knew of this grotto where this admirable fruit of Nature was ripening; he alone was raising it, thus to speak, in order one day to transport it to his precious museum.

I estimated its value at ten million francs at least. It was a superb natural curiosity, and not a jewel *de luxe*, for I do not know what feminine ears could have supported it.

The visit was over. Captain Nemo left the grotto, and we went up on to the bank of oysters again, amidst the clear waters that were not yet troubled by the work of the divers.

We walked separately, stopping or going on according to our pleasure. For my own part I had forgotten the dangers that my imagination had so ridiculously exaggerated. The bottom of the sea sensibly approached its surface, and soon my head passed above the oceanic level. Conseil joined me, and placing his glass plate next to mine, gave me a friendly salutation with his eyes. But this elevated plateau was only some yards long, and we were soon back again in our own element. I think I have now the right of calling it thus.

Ten minutes afterwards Captain Nemo suddenly stopped. I thought he was making a halt before going back. But no; with a gesture he ordered us to squat down near him. He was pointing to a point of the liquid mass, and I looked attentively.

At five yards from me a shade appeared and bent to the ground. The uneasy idea of sharks came into my mind. But I was mistaken, and this time we had not to do with any oceanic monster. It was a man, a living man, a black Indian, a diver, a poor fellow, no doubt, come to glean before the harvest. I perceived the bottom of his canoe anchored at some feet above his head. He plunged and went up again successively. A stone cut in the form of a sugar-loaf which he had tied to his foot, whilst a cord fastened him to the boat, made him descend more rapidly to the bottom. That was all his stock-in-trade. Arrived on the ground by about three fathoms' depth he threw himself on his knees and filled his bag with oysters picked up at random. Then he went up again, emptied his bag, put on his stone again, and recommenced the operation that only lasted thirty seconds.

The diver did not see us. The shadow of the rock hid us from him. And, besides, how could a poor Indian ever suppose that men, beings like him, were there under the water, watching his movements, and losing no detail of his work?

He went up and plunged again several times. He did not bring up more than ten oysters at each plunge, for he was obliged to tear them from the bank to which they were fastened by their strong byssus. And how many of these oysters for which he risked his life were destitute of pearls!

I watched him with profound attention. His work was done regularly, and for half an hour no danger seemed to threaten him. I was, therefore, getting familiar with the spectacle of this interesting fishery, when, all at once, at the moment the Indian was kneeling on the ground, I saw him make a movement of terror, get up, and spring to remount to the surface of the waves.

I understood his fear. A gigantic shadow appeared above the unfortunate plunger. It was an enormous shark advancing diagonally, with eyes on fire and open jaws. I was mute with terror, incapable of making a movement.

The voracious animal, with a vigorous stroke of his fin, was springing towards the Indian, who threw himself on one side and avoided the bite of the shark, but not the stroke of his tail, for that tail, striking him on the chest, stretched him on the ground.

This scene had hardly lasted some seconds. The shark returned to the charge, and turning on his back, it was prepared to cut the Indian in two, when I felt Captain Nemo, who was near me, suddenly rise. Then, his dagger in hand, he walked straight up to the monster, ready for a hand-to-hand struggle with him.

The shark, at the moment he was going to nab the unfortunate diver, perceived his fresh adversary, and going over on to its stomach again, directed itself rapidly towards him.

I still see the attitude of Captain Nemo. Thrown backwards, he was waiting with admirable sang-froid the formidable shark; when it threw itself upon him he threw himself on one side with prodigious agility, avoided the shock, and thrust his dagger into its stomach. But that was not the end. A terrible combat took place.

The shark reddened, thus to speak. The blood flowed in streams from its wounds. The sea was dyed red, and across this opaque liquid I saw no more until it cleared a little, and I perceived the audacious captain holding on to one of the animal's fins, struggling hand-to-hand with the monster, belabouring its body with dagger thrusts without being able to reach the heart, where blows are mortal. The shark in the struggle made such a commotion in the water that the eddies threatened to overthrow me.

I wanted to run to the captain's aid. But, nailed down by horror, I could not move.

I looked on with haggard eyes. I saw the phases of the struggle change. The captain fell on the ground, over-thrown by the enormous mass that was bearing him down. Then the jaws of the shark opened inordinately, and all would have been over for the captain, if, prompt as thought, harpoon in hand, Ned Land, rushing towards the shark, had not struck it with its terrible point. The waves became impregnated with a mass of blood. They were agitated by the movements of the shark that beat them with indescribable fury. Ned Land had not missed his aim. It was the death-rattle of the monster. Struck in the heart, it struggled in fearful spasms, the rebound of which knocked over Conseil.

In the meantime Ned Land had set free the captain, who rose unhurt, went straight to the Indian, quickly cut the cord which fastened him to the stone, took him in his arms, and with a vigorous kick, he went up to the surface of the sea. We all three followed him, and in a short time, miraculously saved, we reached the diver's boat.

Captain Nemo's first care was to recall the unfortunate man to life. I did not know if he would succeed. I hoped so, for the immersion of the poor fellow had not been long. But the blow from the shark's tail might have killed him. Happily, under the vigorous friction of Conseil and the captain, I saw the drowned man gradually recover his senses. He opened his eyes. What must have been his surprise, terror even, at seeing four large brass heads leaning over him! And, above all, what must he have thought when Captain Nemo, drawing from a pocket in his garment a bag of pearls, put it into his hand! This magnificent gift from the man of the sea to the poor Indian of Ceylon was accepted by him with a trembling hand. His frightened eyes showed that he did not know to what superhuman beings he owed at the same time his fortune and his life.

At a sign from the captain we went back to the bank of oysters, and following the road we had already come along, half-an-hour's walking brought us to the anchor that fastened the boat of the *Nautilus* to the ground.

Once embarked, we each, with the help of the sailors, took off our heavy brass carapaces.

Captain Nemo's first word was for the Canadian.

'Thank you, Land,' he said.

'It was by way of retaliation, captain,' answered Ned Land. 'I owed it you.'

A pale smile glided over the captain's lips, and that was all.

At half-past eight we were back on board the *Nautilus*.

Then I began to reflect on the incidents of our excursion to the Manaar Bank. Two observations naturally resulted from it. One was upon the unparalleled audacity of Captain Nemo, the other was his devóting his own life to saving a human being, one of the representatives of that race he was flying from under the seas. Whatever he might say, that man had not succeeded in entirely killing his own heart.

When I said as much to him, he answered me in a slightly moved tone:

'That Indian, professor, is an inhabitant of an oppressed country, and I am, and until my last breath shall be, the same.'

4

THE RED SEA

During the day of 29 January the island of Ceylon disappeared upon the horizon, and the *Nautilus*, at a speed of twenty miles an hour, glided amongst that labyrinth of canals that separate the Maldives from the Laccadives.

We had then made 16,220 miles since our starting-point in the seas of Japan.

The next day, when the *Nautilus* went up to the surface of the ocean, there was no longer any land in sight. It was going NNW, and directing its course towards that Sea of Oman, situated between Arabia and the Indian peninsula, into which the Persian Gulf flows.

It was evidently without egress. Where was Captain Nemo taking us? I could not tell. That did not satisfy the Canadian. He asked me that day where we were going.

'We are going where the captain pleases, Ned.'

'That can't be far,' answered the Canadian. 'The Persian Gulf has no outlet, and if we enter it we shall soon have to come back.'

'Well, we must, Mr Land; and if, after the Persian Gulf, the *Nautilus* wishes to visit the Red Sea, the straits of Bab-el-Mandeb are there for it to go through.'

'I need not inform you, sir,' answered Ned Land, 'that

the Red Sea is as much shut up as the gulf, seeing the Isthmus of Suez has not yet been pierced; and even if it were, a vessel as mysterious as ours would not venture into its canals cut up with locks. So the Red Sea is not yet the road to Europe.'

'I did not say that we were going to Europe.'

'What do you suppose, then?'

'I suppose that after visiting the curious shores of Egypt and Arabia, the *Nautilus* will go down the Indian Ocean again, perhaps through the Mozambique Channel, perhaps by the Comoro Islands, so as to reach the Cape of Good Hope.'

'And once at the Cape of Good Hope, what then?' asked the Canadian, singularly persistent.

'Well, we shall then go into the Atlantic, which we don't know yet. Why, Ned, are you tired, then, of your voyage under the sea? Are you wearied of the incessantly varied spectacle of submarine marvels? For my own part I should be extremely sorry to see the end of this voyage it is given to so few men to make.'

'But do you know, M. Aronnax, that we shall soon have been three months imprisoned on board this *Nautilus*?'

'No, Ned, I don't know, I don't want to know, and I neither count the days nor hours.'

'But how is it to end?'

'The end will come in its own good time. Besides, we can't do anything, and we are arguing uselessly. If you came to me and said, "There is now a chance of escape," I would discuss it with you. But such is not the case, and to tell you the truth, I do not believe Captain Nemo ever ventures into European seas.'

By this short dialogue it will be seen that I was so fond of the *Nautilus* that I rowed in the same boat as its commander.

As to Ned Land, he ended the conversation by these words in a sort of monologue:

'All that is very well, but in my opinion where discomfort begins pleasure ends.'

The *Nautilus* did indeed enter the Red Sea, and many were the marvels to be seen there.

On 11 February, the *Nautilus* was floating in that wide part of the Red Sea that is comprised between Souakin on the west coast and Guonfodah on the east coast, on a diameter of one hundred and ninety miles.

That day, at noon, after the position was taken, Captain Nemo came up on to the platform where I happened to be. I promised myself not to let him go down again without having at least made an attempt to ascertain his ulterior projects. He came to me as soon as he saw me, gracefully offered me a cigar, and said:

'Well, professor, does this Red Sea please you? Have you sufficiently observed the marvels it covers, its fish, zoophytes, beds of sponge, and forests of coral? Have you caught sight of the towns on its shores?'

'Yes, captain,' I answered, 'and the *Nautilus* has helped much in the study. Ah, it is an intelligent vessel!'

'Yes, sir, intelligent, audacious, and invulnerable! It neither dreads the terrible tempests of the Red Sea, nor its currents, nor its reefs.'

'That is true,' I answered; 'our vessel is a century, perhaps several, in advance of its epoch. What a misfortune it is that such a secret must die with its inventor!'

Captain Nemo did not answer. After a short silence:

'Unfortunately,' he resumed, 'I cannot take you through the Suez Canal, but you will be able to see the long piers of Port Saïd the day after tomorrow when we shall be in the Mediterranean.'

'In the Mediterranean?' I cried.

'Yes, professor. Does that astonish you?'

'What astonishes me is that we shall be there the day after tomorrow.'

'Really?'

'Yes, captain, although I ought to be accustomed to being astonished at nothing on board your vessel.'

'But why are you surprised now?'

'At the frightful speed your *Nautilus* must reach to find itself tomorrow in full Mediterranean, having made the tour of Africa and doubled the Cape of Good Hope.'

'And who told you it would make the tour of Africa, professor? Who spoke of doubling the Cape of Good Hope?'

'Unless the *Nautilus* can move along *terra firma* and passes over the isthmus —'

'Or underneath, M. Aronnax.'

'Underneath?'

'Certainly,' answered Captain Nemo tranquilly. 'It is a long time since Nature has done under that tongue of land what men are now doing on its surface.'

'What? There exists a passage?'

'Yes, a subterranean passage that I have named Abraham Tunnel. It begins above Suez and ends in the Gulf of Pelusium.'

'But the isthmus is only formed of moving sand.'

'To a certain depth. But at a depth of fifty yards only there is a stratum of rock.'

'And did you discover that passage by accident?' I asked, more and more surprised.

'By accident and reasoning, professor, and by reasoning more than by accident.'

'Captain, I hear you, but my ear resists what it hears.'

'Ah, sir! Not only does this passage exist, but I have passed by it several times. But for that I should not have adventured today into the impassable Red Sea.'

'Would it be indiscreet to ask you how you discovered this tunnel?'

'Sir,' answered the captain, 'there can be no secret between people who are never to leave each other again.'

I paid no attention to the insinuation, and awaited Captain Nemo's communication.

'Professor,' said he, 'it was a naturalist's reasoning that led me to discover this passage, which I alone know about. I had noticed that in the Red Sea and the Mediterranean there existed a certain number of fish of absolutely identical species. Certain of this fact, I asked myself if there existed no communication between the two seas. If one did exist, the subterranean current must necessarily flow from the Red Sea to the Mediterranean on account of the different levels. I therefore took a great number of fish in the neighbourhood of Suez. I put a brass ring on their tails, and threw them back into the sea. A few months later, on the coast of Syria, I again took some specimens of my fish with their tell-tale ornaments. The communication between the two seas was then demonstrated. I looked for it with my *Nautilus*, discovered it, ventured into it, and before long, professor, you too will have been through my Arabic tunnel.'

That day I repeated to Conseil and Ned Land the part of this conversation in which they were directly interested. When I told them that in two days' time we should be in the midst of the waters of the Mediterranean, Conseil clapped his hands, but the Canadian shrugged his shoulders.

'A submarine tunnel!' he cried. 'A communication between the two seas! Whoever heard of such a thing?'

'Friend Ned,' answered Conseil, 'had you ever heard of such a thing as the *Nautilus*? No. Yet it exists. So don't shrug your shoulders so easily, and laugh at things because you have never heard of them before.'

'We shall see,' answered Ned Land, shaking his head. 'After all, I want to believe in this captain's passage, and Heaven grant that it may take us into the Mediterranean!'

Late that night, while Conseil and Ned were asleep, I was privileged to observe Captain Nemo himself steer his vessel through the narrow tunnel and into the Mediterranean.

5

THE MEDITERRANEAN

The next day, 12 February, at daybreak, the *Nautilus* went up to the surface of the sea. I rushed up to the platform.

About seven o'clock Ned and Conseil joined me. These two inseparable companions had slept tranquilly, thinking no more of the *Nautilus'* feat.

'Well, Mr Naturalist,' asked the Canadian in a slightly jeering tone, 'what about the Mediterranean?'

'We are on its surface, friend Ned.'

'What?' said Conseil, 'last night –'

'Yes, last night itself, in a few minutes, we cleared the insuperable isthmus.'

'I don't believe it,' said the Canadian.

'And you are wrong, Land,' I resumed. 'The low coast rounding off towards the south is the Egyptian coast.'

'You won't take me in,' said the obstinate Canadian.

'But it must be true,' said Conseil, 'or monsieur would not say so.'

'Besides, Ned, Captain Nemo did the honours of his tunnel, and I was near him in the helmsman's cage whilst he guided the *Nautilus* through the narrow passage himself.'

'You hear, Ned?' said Conseil.

'And you who have such good eyes,' I added, 'you, Ned, can see the piers of Port Saïd stretching out into the sea.'

The Canadian looked attentively.

'Yes,' said he, 'you are right, professor, and your captain is a clever man. We are in the Mediterranean. Good. Well, now let us talk, if you please, about our own concerns, but so that no one can hear.'

I saw very well what the Canadian was coming to. In any case I thought it better to talk about it, as he desired, and we all three went and sat down near the lantern-house, where we were less exposed to be wet by the spray from the waves.

'Now, Ned, we are ready to hear you,' said I. 'What have you to tell us?'

'What I have to tell you is very simple,' answered the Canadian. 'We are in Europe, and before Captain Nemo's caprice drags us to the bottom of the Polar Seas, or takes us back to Oceania, I want to leave the *Nautilus*.'

I must acknowledge that a discussion with the Canadian on the subject always embarrassed me.

I did not wish to trammel the liberty of my companions in any way, and yet I felt no desire to leave Captain Nemo. Thanks to him and his apparatus, I was each day completing my submarine studies, and I was writing my book on submarine depths again in the very midst of its element. Should I ever again meet with such an opportunity of observing the marvels of the ocean? No, certainly. I could not, therefore, reconcile myself to the idea of leaving the *Nautilus* before our cycle of investigations was accomplished.

'Friend Ned,' I said, 'answer me frankly. Are you dull here? Do you regret the destiny that has thrown you into the hands of Captain Nemo?'

The Canadian remained for some moments without answering. Then crossing his arms:

'Frankly,' he said, 'I do not regret this voyage under the seas. I shall be glad to have made it; but to have made it, it must come to an end. That is my opinion.'

'It will come to an end, Ned.'

'Where and when?'

'I do not know where, and I can't say when, or rather I suppose it will end when these seas have nothing further to teach us. All that begins has necessarily an end in this world.'

'I think like monsieur,' answered Conseil, 'and it is quite possible that after going over all the seas of the globe Captain Nemo will give us our discharge.'

'We have nothing to fear from the captain,' I resumed, 'but I am not of Conseil's opinion either. We are acquainted with the secrets of the *Nautilus*, and I have no hope that its commander, in order to set us at liberty, will resign himself to the idea of our taking them about the world with us.'

'Then what do you hope?' asked the Canadian.

'That circumstances will happen of which we can and ought to take advantage, as well in six months' time as now.'

'Phew!' said Ned Land. 'And where shall we be in six months, if you please, Mr Naturalist?'

'Perhaps here, perhaps in China. You know that the *Nautilus* is a quick sailer. It crosses oceans like a swallow the air, or an express a continent. It does not fear frequented seas. How do we know that it will not rally round the coasts of France, England, or America, where we can attempt to escape as advantageously as here?'

'M. Aronnax,' answered the Canadian, 'your premisses are bad. You speak in the future tense: "We shall be there! we shall be here!" I speak in the present: "We are here, and we must take advantage of it." '

I was closely hemmed in by Ned Land's logic, and felt myself beaten on that ground. I no longer knew what arguments to use.

'Sir,' Ned went on, 'let us suppose, for the sake of argument, that Captain Nemo were to offer you your liberty today, should you accept it?'

'I do not know,' I replied.

'And if he were to add that the offer he makes today he would not renew later on, should you accept?'

I did not answer.

'And what do you think about it, friend Conseil?' asked Ned Land.

'I have nothing to say. I am absolutely disinterested in the question. Like my master, I am a bachelor. No wife, relations, nor children expect my return. I am at monsieur's service. I think like monsieur, I say what monsieur says, and you must not depend upon me to make a majority. Two persons only are concerned; monsieur on one side, Ned Land on the other. That said, I listen, and am ready to count for either.'

I could not help smiling at seeing Conseil annihilate his personality so completely. The Canadian must have been enchanted not to have him against him.

'Then, sir,' said Ned Land, 'as Conseil does not exist, we have only to speak to each other. I have spoken, you have heard me. What have you to answer?'

It was evident that I must sum up, and subterfuges were repugnant to me.

'Friend Ned,' I said, 'this is my answer. You are right and I am wrong. We must not depend upon Captain Nemo's goodwill. The commonest prudence forbids him to set us at liberty. On the other hand, prudence tells us that we must profit by the first opportunity of leaving the *Nautilus*.'

'Very well, M. Aronnax, that is wisely spoken.'

'Only,' I said, 'I have but one observation to make – the occasion must be serious. Our first attempt must succeed, for if it fail we shall not find another opportunity of attempting it again, and Captain Nemo would not forgive us.'

'That's true enough,' answered the Canadian. 'But your observation applies to every attempt at flight, whether it be made in two years' or two days' time. Therefore the question is still the same; if a favourable opportunity occurs, we must seize it.'

'Agreed. And now, friend Ned, will you tell me what you mean by a favourable opportunity?'

'For instance, a dark night when the *Nautilus* would be only a short distance from some European coast.'

'Then you would attempt to escape by swimming?'

'Yes, if we were sufficiently near the coast, and the vessel were on the surface; but if we were far off, or if the vessel were under water –'

'And in that case?'

'In that case I should try to take possession of the boat. I know how it is worked. We would get into the interior of it, undo the bolts, and get up to the surface without even the helmsman seeing us.'

'Well, Ned, look out for that opportunity; but do not forget that a failure would be fatal to us.'

'I will not forget it, sir.'

'And now, Ned, should you like to know what I think of your plan?'

'Yes, M. Aronnax.'

'Well, I think – I do not say I hope – that so favourable an opportunity will not occur.'

'Why?'

'Because Captain Nemo cannot be unaware that we have not renounced the hope of recovering our liberty, and will keep watch above all in European seas.'

'I am of monsieur's opinion,' said Conseil.

'We shall see,' answered Ned Land, shaking his head in a determined manner.

'And now, Ned Land,' I added, 'we must leave it there. Not another word on this subject. The day you are ready you will inform us and we shall follow you. I leave it entirely to you.'

This conversation, that was destined to have such grave consequences later on, ended thus. I ought now to say that facts seemed to confirm my suspicions, to the Canadian's great despair. Did Captain Nemo distrust us in these frequented seas, or did he merely wish to keep out of sight of the numerous ships of all nations that plough the Mediterranean? I do not know, but he generally kept under water and a good distance from land. When the *Nautilus* rose to the surface nothing but the helmsman's cage emerged, and it went to great depths, for between the Grecian Archipelago and Asia Minor the sea is more than 2,000 yards deep.

On 14 February I resolved to spend some hours in studying the fish of the archipelago; but for some motive or other the panels remained hermetically closed. By taking the direction of the *Nautilus* I saw that it was making towards the island of Crete. At the epoch I had embarked on board the *Abraham Lincoln*, that island had just revolted against Turkish despotism. But what had become of the insurrection since I knew nothing, and Captain Nemo, cut off as he was from all communication with land, could not inform me.

I therefore made no allusion to this event when in the evening I was alone with him in the saloon. Besides, he seemed taciturn and preoccupied. Then, contrary to his custom, he ordered the panels of the saloon to be opened, and going from one to another he attentively observed the mass of water, for what purpose I could not guess, and on my side I employed my time in studying the fish that passed before my eyes.

I could not take my eyes off these wonders of the sea, when they were suddenly struck with an unexpected apparition. In the midst of the waters a man appeared, a diver, wearing in his belt a leather purse. It was a living man, swimming vigorously, occasionally disappearing to take breath on the surface, then plunging again immediately. I turned to Captain Nemo, and exclaimed in an agitated voice:

'A man! A shipwrecked man! He must be saved at any price!'

The captain did not answer, but came and leaned against the window.

The man had approached, and with his face flattened against the glass, he was looking at us.

To my profound stupefaction Captain Nemo made a sign to him. The diver answered him with his hand, immediately went up again to the surface of the sea, and did not appear again.

'Don't be uneasy,' said the captain to me. 'It is Nicholas of Cape Matapan, surnamed the Pesce. He is well known in all the Cyclades. A bold diver! Water is his element, and he lives in it more than on land, going constantly from one island to another, and even as far as Crete.'

'Do you know him, captain?'

'Why not, M. Aronnax?'

That said, Captain Nemo went towards a piece of furniture placed near the left panel of the saloon. Near this piece of furniture I saw an iron safe, on the lid of which was a brass plate with the initials of the *Nautilus*, and its motto, '*Mobilis in Mobili*,' upon it.

At that moment the captain, without taking further notice of my presence, opened the piece of furniture, which contained a great number of ingots.

They were ingots of gold. From whence came this precious metal that represented an enormous sum? Where did the captain get this gold, and what was he going to do with it?

I did not speak a word. I looked. Captain Nemo took these ingots, one by one, and arranged them methodically in the safe, which he entirely filled.

The safe was securely fastened, and the captain wrote an address on the lid in what must have been modern Greek characters.

This done, Captain Nemo pressed a knob, the wire of which communicated with the quarters of the crew. Four men appeared, and, not without some trouble, pushed the safe out of the saloon. Then I heard them pulling it up the iron staircase with pulleys.

Then Captain Nemo turned to me.

'Did you speak, professor?'

'No, captain.'

'Then, sir, if you allow me, I will wish you good-night.'

Upon which Captain Nemo left the saloon.

I went back to my room very curious, as may be believed. I tried in vain to sleep. I tried to find what connection there could be between the diver and the safe filled with gold. I soon felt by its pitching and tossing that the *Nautilus* was back on the surface of the water.

Then I heard a noise of steps on the platform. I understood that they were unloosening the boat and launching it on the sea. It struck for an instant against the sides of the *Nautilus*, and then the noise ceased.

Two hours afterwards the same noise, the same movements, were repeated. The boat, hoisted on board, was replaced in its socket, and the *Nautilus* sank again under the waves.

Thus, then, the gold had been sent to its address. To what point of the continent? Who was Captain Nemo's correspondent?

The next day I related to Conseil and the Canadian the events of the preceding night, which had excited my curiosity to the highest pitch. My companions were no less surprised than I.

'But where does he find all that gold?' asked Ned Land.

To that there was no answer possible. I went to the saloon after breakfast and began to work. Until 5 p.m. I wrote out my notes. At that moment I felt extremely hot, and I was obliged to take off my garment of byssus – an incomprehensible fact, for we were not in high latitudes, and besides, when the *Nautilus* was submerged, it ought to experience no elevation of temperature. I looked at the manometer. It indicated a depth of sixty feet, to which atmospheric heat cannot reach.

I went on with my work, but the heat became intolerable.

'Can the vessel be on fire?' I asked myself.

I was going to leave the saloon when Captain Nemo entered. He approached the thermometer, corrected it, and said:

'Forty-two degrees.'

'I feel it, captain,' I answered, 'and if the heat augments we cannot bear it.'

'The heat will not augment unless we choose.'

'Then you can moderate it as you please?'

'No, but I can get away from the focus that produces it.'

'Then it is exterior?'

'Certainly. We are floating in boiling water.'

'Is it possible?' I cried.

'Look!'

The panels opened, and I saw the sea entirely white round the *Nautilus*. A sulphurous smoke was curling amongst the waves that boiled like water in a copper. I placed my hand on one of the panes of glass, but the heat was so great that I was obliged to withdraw it.

'Where are we?' I asked.

'Near the island of Santorin, professor,' replied the captain, 'and precisely in the channel that separates Nea-Kamenni from Pali-Kamenni. I wished to show you the curious spectacle of a submarine eruption.'

I returned to the window. The *Nautilus* was no longer moving. The heat was growing intolerable. Notwithstanding the saloon's being hermetically closed, an unbearable sulphurous smell pervaded it, and I perceived scarlet flames the brilliancy of which killed the electric light.

I was in a bath of perspiration, choking, and nearly broiled.

'We cannot remain any longer in this boiling water,' I said to the captain.

'No, that would not be prudent,' answered the unmoved Nemo.

An order was given. The *Nautilus* tacked about, and left the furnace it could not with impunity set at defiance. A quarter of an hour later we were breathing on the surface of the waves.

The thought then occurred to me that if Ned Land had chosen that part of the sea for our flight we should not have come out of it alive.

The next day, 16 February, we left this basin and we had cleared the Straits of Gibraltar by sunrise on the 18th.

It was evident to me that this Mediterranean, enclosed by the countries which he wished to avoid, was distasteful to Captain Nemo. Its waves and breezes recalled too many memories, if not too many regrets. He had not here that liberty of movement, that independence of manoeuvre, that he had in the ocean, and his *Nautilus* was cramped between the shores of Africa and Europe.

Our speed was now twenty-five miles an hour. It is useless to say that Ned Land, notwithstanding his great wish, was obliged to renounce his projects of flight. He could not use a boat that was being dragged along at the rate of thirteen yards a second. To leave the *Nautilus* then would be like jumping out of a train going at the same speed, as imprudent a thing as could possibly be attempted. Besides, our apparatus only went up to the surface at night in order to renew its provision of air, and it was guided entirely by the compass and log.

I therefore only saw of the Mediterranean what passengers by an express see of the country that is flying before their eyes – that is to say, the distant horizon, and not the nearer objects which pass like a flash of lightning. However, Conseil and I could notice some of the Mediterranean fish, the power of whose fins would keep them for some moments in sight of the *Nautilus*. We lay in wait for them before the windows of the saloon.

During the night between 16 and 17 February we entered the second Mediterranean basin, the greatest depths of which are found at 1,500 fathoms. The *Nautilus*, under the action of its screw, gliding over its inclined planes, sank into the lowest depths of the sea.

There, instead of natural marvels, the mass of waters offered me many touching and terrible scenes. In fact, we were then crossing all that part of the Mediterranean so fertile in disasters.

In that rapid course across the great depths what wrecks I saw lying on the ground! Some already encrusted with coral, others simply covered with a layer of rust, anchors, cannons, bullets, iron tackle, screws, pieces of engines, broken cylinders, crushed boilers, and hulls floating in mid-water, some upright, some overturned.

Amongst these wrecks some had been caused by collision, others had struck upon some granite rock. I saw some that had sunk straight down with upright masts, and rigging stiffened by the water. They seemed to be at anchor in an immense roadway, only awaiting the time of starting. When the *Nautilus* passed amongst them, and enveloped them with its electric light, it seemed as if they would salute our vessel with their colours, and give the orders. But no; nothing but the silence of death reigned in the field of catastrophes!

I observed that the bottom of the Mediterranean was more encumbered with these wrecks as the *Nautilus* approached the Straits of Gibraltar. The coasts of Africa and Europe are then nearer each other, and in the narrow space collisions are frequent. I saw there numerous iron keels, the fantastic ruins of steamers, some lying down, others upright, like formidable animals. One of these boats with open sides, bent funnel, wheels of which only the mounting remained, the helm separated from the sternpost, and still held by an iron chain, its stern eaten away by marine salts, presented a terrible spectacle! How many existences did this shipwreck destroy! How many victims swallowed up by the waves! Had any sailor on board survived to relate the terrible disaster, or did the waves still keep the fatal secret? Ah, what a fatal history would be that of these Mediterranean depths, this vast charnel-house where so many riches have been lost, and so many victims have met with their death!

In the meantime the *Nautilus*, indifferent and rapid, journeyed at full speed amidst these ruins. On 18 February, about 3 a.m., it was at the entrance to the

Straits of Gibraltar. It rushed rapidly through the narrow passage, and a few minutes later we were afloat on the waves of the Atlantic.

6

VIGO BAY

The Atlantic! A magnificent plain, incessantly ploughed by ships of all nations, sheltered under the flags of every nation, and terminated by the two terrible points, dreaded by navigators, Cape Horn and the Cape of Tempests.

The *Nautilus* was culling its waters under her sharp prow after having accomplished nearly ten thousand leagues in three months and a half, a distance greater than one of the great circles of the earth. Where were we going now, and what had the future in store for us?

The *Nautilus* once out of the Straits of Gibraltar came up to the surface again, and our daily walks on the platform were thus restored to us.

I immediately went up there, accompanied by Ned Land and Conseil. At a distance of twelve miles, Cape Vincent, which forms the SW point of the Spanish peninsula, was dimly to be seen. It was blowing a rather strong gale. The sea was rough. It made the *Nautilus* rock violently. It was almost impossible to keep on the platform, which enormous seas washed at every moment. We therefore went down again after taking in some mouthfuls of fresh air.

I went back to my room, and Conseil returned to his cabin, but the Canadian, with a preoccupied air, followed me. Our rapid passage across the Mediterranean had prevented him putting his projects into execution, and he did not hide his disappointment.

When the door of my cabin was shut, he sat down and looked at me in silence.

'Friend Ned,' I said, 'I understand you, but you have nothing to reproach yourself with. To have attempted to leave the *Nautilus* while it was going at that rate would have been madness.'

Ned Land answered nothing. His compressed lips and frowning brow indicated the violent possession this fixed idea had taken of his mind.

'Well,' said I, 'we need not despair yet. We are going up the coast of Portugal. France and England are not far off, where we should easily find a refuge. If the *Nautilus*, once out of the Straits of Gibraltar, had gone southward, if it had carried us towards those regions where land is wanting, I should share your uneasiness. But now we know that Captain Nemo does not avoid civilized seas, and in a few days I think we can act with some security.'

Ned Land looked at me more fixedly still, and at length he opened his lips.

'It is for tonight,' said he.

I started. I must acknowledge I was little prepared for this communication. I wanted to answer the Canadian, but words would not come.

'We agreed to wait for an opportunity,' said Ned Land. 'I have that opportunity. This night we shall only be a few miles off the Spanish coast. The night will be dark. I have your word, M. Aronnax, and I depend upon you.'

As I still was silent, the Canadian rose, and coming nearer to me said:

'This evening, at 9 o'clock. I have told Conseil. At that

time Captain Nemo will be shut up in his room, and probably in bed. Neither the engineers nor any of the crew can see us. Conseil and I will go to the central staircase. You, M. Aronnax, must remain in the library not far off, and await our signal. The oars, mast, and sail are in the boat, and I have even succeeded in putting some provisions into it. I procured a wrench to unscrew the bolts that fasten the boat to the hull of the *Nautilus*. Thus everything is ready for tonight.'

'The sea is bad.'

'That I allow,' answered the Canadian, 'but we must risk that. Liberty is worth paying for. Besides, the boat is solid, and a few miles with the wind in our favour are not of any consequence. Who knows if tomorrow we shall not be a hundred leagues out? If circumstances favour us we shall land, living or dead, on some point of solid ground between 10 and 11 o'clock. Then tonight, by the grace of God!'

Thereupon the Canadian withdrew, leaving me almost stunned. I had imagined that when the matter turned up I should have time to reflect and discuss it. My stubborn companion had not allowed me to do that. And, after all, what could I have said to him? Ned Land was quite right. It was almost an occasion, and he took advantage of it. Could I take back my word, and assume the responsibility of compromising, by personal interest, the future of my companion? Tomorrow Captain Nemo might carry us far away from any land.

At that moment a rather strong hissing sound informed me that the reservoirs were being filled, and then the *Nautilus* sank under the waves of the Atlantic.

I remained in my room. I wished to avoid the captain in order to hide from his eyes the emotion I was labouring under. It was a sad day I passed thus between the desire of being free again and the regret of abandoning the marvellous *Nautilus*, leaving my submarine studies unfinished! To leave my ocean, 'my Atlantic', as I liked to call it, thus, without having observed its lowest strata, or learnt from it those secrets that the Indian seas and the Pacific had taught me! My romance had fallen from my hand while I was yet at the first volume, my dream was interrupted at its most delightful moment! What wretched hours passed thus, sometimes seeing myself safely on board with my companions, sometimes wishing, in spite of my reason, that some unforeseen circumstance would prevent the realization of Ned Land's projects!

Twice I went into the saloon. I wished to consult the compass, and to see if the *Nautilus* was approaching or going farther away from the coast. But no. The *Nautilus* kept constantly in the Portuguese waters. It was making for the north along the shores of the ocean.

I was, therefore, obliged to make up my mind to it, and prepare for flight. My baggage was not heavy, and consisted of my notes, nothing more. I asked myself what Captain Nemo would think of our flight, what uneasiness it might cause him, what harm it might do him, and what he would do in case it was discovered or it failed. Certainly I had no fault to find with him – on the contrary. Hospitality was never given more freely than his. In leaving him I could not be accused of ingratitude. No oath bound us to him. He counted upon the force of circumstances alone, and not upon our word, to keep us with him for ever. But his intention, openly avowed, of keeping us eternally prisoners on board his vessel justified our attempts.

I had not seen the captain again since our visit to the island of Santorin. Would chance bring me into his presence before our departure? I both desired and feared it might. I listened if I could hear him walking in the room next to mine. No noise reached my ear. There could be no one in the room.

Then I asked myself if the strange personage was on board at all. Since the night during which the boat had left the *Nautilus* on a mysterious mission, my ideas about him were slightly modified. I thought, whatever he might say about it, that Captain Nemo must have kept up some sort of communication with land. Did he never leave the *Nautilus*? Entire weeks had passed without my having seen him. What was he doing during that time? Was he not far off accomplishing some secret act the nature of which had thus far escaped me?

All these ideas, and a thousand more, assailed me at once. The field of conjectures could not be but infinite in our strange situation. I felt an insupportable discomfort. That day of waiting seemed to me eternal. The hours struck too slowly for my impatience.

My dinner was served as usual in my room. I ate little, being too much preoccupied. I left the table at seven o'clock. A hundred and twenty minutes – I counted them – still separated me from the time when I was to join Ned Land. My agitation redoubled. My pulse beat violently. I could not remain immovable. I walked about, hoping to calm the trouble of my mind by movement. The idea of failing in our bold enterprise was the least painful of my thoughts; but at the idea of seeing our project discovered before leaving the *Nautilus*, and of being brought before Captain Nemo, irritated, or, what would have been worse, saddened by my leaving him, my heart palpitated.

I wished to see the saloon for the last time. I went by the waist, and entered that museum where I had passed so many useful and agreeable hours. I looked at all these riches and treasures like a man on the eve of eternal exile, and who is going away never to return. These marvels of

nature, these masterpieces of art, amongst which for so
many days my life had been concentrated, I was going to
leave them for ever. I should have liked to look through
the windows across the waters of the Atlantic; but
the panels were hermetically shut, and an iron sheet
separated me from that ocean which I did not know as
yet.

As I moved thus about the saloon I reached the door,
let into the angle, which opened into the captain's room.
To my great astonishment this door was ajar. I drew back
involuntarily. If Captain Nemo was in his room he could
see me. However, hearing no noise, I drew near it. The
room was empty. I pushed open the door and entered.
Still the same severe monk-like aspect.

At that moment some prints, hung up, that I had not
noticed during my first visit, struck me. They were
portraits, portraits of great historical men whose existence was but a perpetual devotion to one great humane
idea.

What tie could exist between these heroic souls and the
soul of Captain Nemo? Could I at last, from that assem-
blage of portraits, find out the mystery of his existence?
Was he the champion of oppressed nations, the liberator
of slaves? Had he figured in the social or political com-
motions of this century? Had he been one of the heroes of
the terrible American war – a war lamentable, but for ever
glorious?

Suddenly the clock struck eight. The first stroke awoke
me to reality. I trembled as if some invisible eye could see
to the bottom of my thoughts, and I rushed out of the
room.

There I glanced at the compass. Our course was still
north. The log indicated moderate speed, the manometer
a depth of about sixty feet. Circumstances, therefore,
were favouring the Canadian's project.

I went back to my room and clothed myself warmly in my sea-boots, sealskin cap, and vest of byssus lined with sealskin. I was ready. I waited. The vibration of the screw alone disturbed the profound silence that reigned on board. I listened attentively. Would not a shout tell me all at once that Ned Land had been caught in his effort to escape? A mortal dread took possession of me. I tried in vain to regain my sang-froid.

At a few minutes to nine o'clock I put my ear against the captain's door. No sound. I left my room and went back to the saloon, which was insufficiently lighted, but empty.

I opened the door communicating with the library. The same insufficient light, the same solitude. I went and placed myself near the door that opened into the cage of the central staircase, and awaited Ned Land's signal.

At that moment the vibration from the screw sensibly diminished, then ceased altogether. Why was this change made in the working of the *Nautilus*? Whether this halt would be favourable to or against Ned Land's plans I could not tell.

The silence was only broken by the beatings of my heart.

Suddenly I felt a slight shock. I understood that the *Nautilus* had just stopped on the bottom of the ocean. My anxiety increased. The Canadian's signal did not reach me. I wanted to go to Ned Land and beg him to put off his attempt. I felt that something was changed in our usual navigation.

At that moment the saloon door opened, and Captain Nemo appeared. He perceived me, and said without further preamble, in an amiable tone:

'Ah, professor, I was looking for you. Do you know your Spanish history?'

Anyone knowing the history of his own country

thoroughly under the same conditions of mental worry and anxiety, would not be able to quote a single word of it.

'Well,' continued Captain Nemo, 'you heard my question. Do you know the history of Spain?'

'Very badly,' I replied.

'That is like *savants*,' said the captain, 'they know nothing. Well, sit down,' added he, 'and I will relate a curious episode of that history to you.'

The captain stretched himself upon a divan, and I mechanically took a place beside him, with my back to the light.

'Professor,' he said, 'give me all your attention. This history will interest you in some sort, for it will answer a question that doubtless you have not been able to solve.'

'I hear, captain,' said I, not knowing what my interlocutor was driving at, and wondering whether it had anything to do with our projects of flight.

'Professor,' resumed the captain, 'if you have no objection we will go as far back as 1702. As you know, your king, Louis XIV, thinking that the gesture of a potentate was sufficient to make the Pyrenees sink into the ground, had imposed his grandson, the Duke of Anjou, on the Spaniards. This prince, who reigned more or less badly under the name of Philip V, had a strong party against him from without.

'In fact, the year before, the Royal houses of Holland, Austria and England had concluded a treaty of alliance at the Hague, for the aim of taking the crown of Spain from Philip V and placing it on the head of an archduke, to whom they gave the premature title of Charles III.

'Spain had this coalition to resist. But she was nearly destitute of soldiers and sailors. However, money would not be wanting, provided that their galleons, loaded with gold and silver from America, could enter her ports. Now, towards the end of 1702 she was expecting a rich convoy that France had sent, a fleet of twenty-three vessels, commanded by the Admiral Château-Renaud to escort, for the combined fleets were then scouring the Atlantic.

'This convoy was bound for Cadiz; but the admiral, having learnt that the English fleet was cruising in the neighbourhood, resolved to make for a French port.

'The Spanish commanders of the convoy protested against this decision. They wished to be accompanied to a Spanish port, and if not to Cadiz, to Vigo Bay, situated on the NW coast of Spain, which was not blockaded.

'The Admiral Château-Renaud was weak enough to obey this injunction, and the galleons entered Vigo Bay.

'Unfortunately, this bay is an open roadstead that cannot be in the least defended. They were, therefore, obliged to hasten the unloading of the galleons before the arrival of the combined fleets, and there would have been plenty of time to do it in, but for a miserable question of rivalry that arose suddenly.

'You are following the links of these facts?' said the captain.

'Perfectly,' said I, not knowing why I was receiving this lesson in history.

'Then I continue. This is what happened. The merchants of Cadiz had a privilege by which they were to receive all the merchandise that came from the East Indies, and the landing of the ingots from the galleons at the port of Vigo was a contravention of their rights. They made complaints at Madrid, and obtained from the feeble Philip V the order to make the convoy remain without unloading in the roadstead of Vigo until the enemy's fleets should be out of the road.

'Now whilst this decision was being arrived at, on 22 October 1702, the English ships arrived in Vigo Bay. The Admiral Château-Renaud, notwithstanding his inferior forces, fought courageously. But when he saw that the riches of the convoy were about to fall into the hands of enemies, he burnt and scuttled the galleons that went to the bottom with their immense treasures.'

Captain Nemo stopped. I acknowledged that I did not perceive as yet how his story could interest me.

'Well?' I asked him.

'Well, M. Aronnax,' answered Captain Nemo, 'we are in Vigo Bay, and it rests with yourself whether you will penetrate into its mysteries.'

The captain rose and begged me to follow him. I had had time to recover myself. I obeyed. The saloon was dark, but across the transparent panes glittered the sea. I looked.

For a radius of half a mile round the *Nautilus* the waters seemed impregnated with electric light, the sandy bottom clear and distinct. Some of the crew, clothed in their bathing dresses, were at work emptying half-rotten casks, splintered cases, amidst still blackened spars. From these cases and casks escaped ingots of gold and silver, cascades of piastres and jewels. The sand was strewed with them. Then, loaded with their precious booty, these men returned to the *Nautilus*, deposited their load, and went back to continue their inexhaustible gold and silver fishery.

I understood. It was the battlefield of 22 October 1702. In this very place the galleons laden for the Spanish government had sunk. Here Captain Nemo came, according to his needs, to encase the millions with which he ballasted his *Nautilus*. It was for him, and for him alone, that America had given up her precious metals. He was the direct heir, without any one to share, of these treasures taken from the Incas and Ferdinand Cortez' conquered people.

'Did you know, professor,' he asked me, smiling, 'that the sea contained such riches? I have only to pick up what men have lost, not only in this Vigo Bay, but in a thousand other scenes of shipwreck, all marked on my marine chart. Now do you understand why I am so many times a millionaire?'

'Yes, captain. But allow me to tell you that in your work in Vigo Bay you have only been beforehand with a rival company.'

'What company, pray?'

'A company that has received from the Spanish government the privilege of seeking the shipwrecked galleons. The shareholders are tempted by the bait of an enormous profit, for they estimate the value of these shipwrecked treasures at five hundred millions of francs.'

'Five hundred millions!' answered Captain Nemo. 'They were that much once, but are so no longer.'

'Just so,' said I, 'and a warning to the shareholders would be an act of charity. Who knows, however, if it would be well received? What speculators regret, above all, generally, is less the loss of money than that of their insane hopes. I pity them, after all, less than the thousands of unfortunates to whom so much wealth, well distributed, would have been profitable, whilst it is for ever lost to them.'

I had no sooner expressed this regret than I felt it must have wounded Captain Nemo.

'Lost to them!' he answered, getting animated. 'Do you think, then, that this wealth is lost when it is I that gather it? Do you think I give myself the trouble to pick up these treasures for myself? Who says that I do not make a good use of them? Do you believe that I ignore the existence of suffering beings, of races oppressed in this world, of miserable creatures to solace, of victims to revenge? Do you not understand –'

Captain Nemo stopped, regretting, perhaps, having said so much. But I had guessed. Whatever might be the motives that had forced him to seek independence under the seas, he was still a man! His heart still beat for the sufferings of humanity, and his immense charity was given to oppressed races, as well as to individuals.

And I then understood to whom the millions were sent by Captain Nemo, while the *Nautilus* was cruising in the waters of revolted Crete.

7

A VANISHED CONTINENT

On the morning of the next day, 19 February, I saw the Canadian enter my room. I was expecting his visit. He looked much disappointed.

'Well, sir,' he said to me.

'Well, Ned, luck was against us yesterday.'

'Yes, that captain must stop at the very time we were going to escape from his vessel.'

'Yes, Ned, he had business with his banker.'

'His banker?'

'Yes, or rather his bank. I mean by that this ocean, where his wealth is in greater safety than it would be in the coffers of a state.'

I then related to the Canadian the incident of the preceding evening, in the secret hope of making him wish not to leave the captain; but the only result of my account was an energetic regret expressed by Ned at not being able to take a walk on the Vigo battlefield on his own account.

'But all is not over,' he said. 'It is only one harpoon-throw lost. Another time we shall succeed, and this very evening, if necessary —'

'What is the direction of the *Nautilus*?' I asked.

'I do not know,' answered Ned.

'Well, at noon we shall find our bearings.'

The Canadian returned to Conseil. As soon as I was dressed I went into the saloon. The compass was not reassuring. The direction of the *Nautilus* was SSW. We were turning our backs on Europe.

I waited impatiently for our bearings to be taken. About 11.30 a.m. the reservoirs were emptied, and our apparatus went up to the surface of the ocean. I sprang upon the platform. Ned Land preceded me there.

There was no land in sight. Nothing but the immense sea. A few sails on the horizon, doubtless those that go as far as San Roque in search of favourable winds for doubling the Cape of Good Hope. The weather was cloudy. A gale was spreading up.

Ned, in a rage, tried to pierce the misty horizon. He still hoped that behind the mist stretched the land so much desired.

At noon the sun appeared for an instant. The first officer took advantage of the gleam to take the altitude. Then, the sea becoming rougher, we went down again, and the panel was closed.

It was no use to dream of escaping now, and I leave Ned Land's anger to be imagined when I informed him of our situation.

On my own account I was not overwhelmed with grief. I felt relieved from a weight that was oppressing me, and I could calmly take up my habitual work again.

That evening, about 11 p.m., I received the very unexpected visit of Captain Nemo. He asked me very graciously if I felt fatigued from sitting up so late the night before. I answered in the negative.

'Then, M. Aronnax, I have a curious excursion to propose to you.'

'What is it, captain?'

'You have as yet only been on the sea-bottom by daylight. Should you like to see it on a dark night?'

'I should like it much.'

'It will be a fatiguing walk, I warn you. You will have to go far, and climb a mountain. The roads are not very well kept in repair.'

'What you tell me makes me doubly curious. I am ready to follow you.'

'Come, then, professor. We will go and put on our diving dresses.'

When we reached the ward-room I saw that neither my companions nor any of the crew were to follow us in our excursion. Captain Nemo had not even asked me to take Ned or Conseil.

In a few minutes we had put on our apparatus. They placed on our backs the reservoirs full of air, but the lamps were not prepared. I said as much to the captain.

'They would be of no use to us,' he answered.

I thought I had not heard aright, but I could not repeat my observation, for the captain's head had already disappeared under its metallic covering. I finished harnessing myself, felt that someone placed an iron spiked stick in my hand, and a few minutes later, after the usual manoeuvre, we set foot on the bottom of the Atlantic, at a depth of 150 fathoms.

Midnight was approaching. The waters were in profound darkness, but Captain Nemo showed me a reddish point in the distance, a sort of large light shining about two miles from the *Nautilus*. What this fire was, with what fed, why and how it burnt in the liquid mass, I could not tell. Anyway it lighted us, dimly it is true, but I soon became accustomed to the peculiar darkness, and I understood, under the circumstances, the uselessness of the lamps.

I caught a glimpse of heaps of stones covered by

thickets of seaweed. My foot often slipped upon this viscous carpet of seaweed, and without my stick I should have fallen several times. Turning, I still saw the white light of the *Nautilus* beginning to gleam in the distance.

The heaps of stones of which I have just spoken were heaped on the bottom of the ocean with a sort of regularity I could not explain to myself. I perceived gigantic furrows which lost themselves in the distant darkness, the length of which escaped all valuation. Other peculiarities presented themselves that I did not know how to account for. It seemed to me that my heavy leaden shoes were crushing a litter of bones that cracked with a dry noise. What, then, was this vast plain I was thus moving across? I should have liked to question the captain, but his language by signs, that allowed him to talk to his companions when they followed him in his submarine excursions, was still incomprehensible to me.

In the meantime the reddish light that guided us increased and inflamed the horizon. The presence of this fire under the seas excited my curiosity to the highest pitch. Was it some electric effluence? Was I going towards a natural phenomenon still unknown to the *savants* of the earth? Or – for this thought crossed my mind – had the hand of man any part in the conflagration? Had it lighted this fire? Was I going to meet in this deep sea companions and friends of Captain Nemo living the same strange life, and whom he was going to see? All these foolish and inadmissible ideas pursued me, and in that state of mind, ceaselessly excited by the series of marvels that passed before my eyes, I should not have been surprised to see, at the bottom of the sea, one of the submarine towns Captain Nemo dreamed of.

Our road grew lighter and lighter. The light shone from the top of a mountain about eight hundred feet high. But what I perceived was only a reflection made by the crystal of the water. The fire, the source of the inexplicable light, was on the opposite side of the mountain.

Amidst the stony paths that furrowed the bottom of the Atlantic Captain Nemo went on without hesitating. He knew the dark route, had doubtless often been along it, and could not lose himself in it. I followed him with unshaken confidence. He appeared, whilst walking before me, like one of the sea genii, and I admired his tall stature like a black shadow on the luminous background of the horizon.

It was one o'clock in the morning. We had reached the first slopes of the mountain. But the way up led through the difficult paths, of a vast thicket.

Yes, a thicket of dead trees, leafless, sapless, mineralized under the action of the water, overtopped here and there by gigantic pines.

The paths were encumbered with seaweed and fucus, amongst which swarmed a world of crustaceans. I went on climbing over the rocks, leaping over the fallen trunks, breaking the sea-creepers that balanced from one tree to another, startling the fish that flew from branch to branch. Pressed onwards, I no longer felt any fatigue. I followed my guide, who was never fatigued.

What a spectacle! How can I depict it? How describe the aspect of the woods and rocks in this liquid element, their lower parts sombre and wild, the upper coloured with red tints in the light which the reverberating power of the water doubled? We were climbing rocks which fell in enormous fragments directly afterwards with the noise of an avalanche. Right and left were deep dark galleries where sight was lost. Here opened vast clearings that seemed made by the hand of man, and I asked myself sometimes if some inhabitant of these submarine regions was not about to appear suddenly.

But Captain Nemo still went on climbing. Two hours after having quitted the *Nautilus* we had passed the trees, and a hundred feet above our heads rose the summit of the mountain, the projection of which made a shadow on the brilliant irradiation of the opposite slope. A few petrified bushes were scattered hither and thither in grimacing zigzags. The fish rose in shoals under our footsteps like birds surprised in tall grass. The rocky mass was hollowed out into deep holes, in which I heard formidable noises. My blood froze in my veins when I perceived some enormous antenna barricading my path, or some frightful claw shutting up with noise in the dark cavities. Thousands of luminous points shone amidst the darkness. They were the eyes of gigantic lobsters setting themselves up like halberdiers, and moving their claws with the clanking sound of metal; titanic crabs pointed like cannon on their carriages, and frightful squid, intertwining their tentacles like a living nest of serpents.

But I could not stop. Captain Nemo, familiar with these terrible animals, paid no attention to them. We had arrived at the first plateau, where other surprises awaited me. There rose picturesque ruins which betrayed the hand of man, and now that of the Creator. They were vast heaps of stones in the vague outlines of castles and temples, clothed with a world of zoophytes in flower, and, instead of ivy, seaweed and fucus clothed them with a vegetable mantle.

But what, then, was this portion of the globe swallowed up by cataclysms? Where was I? Where had Captain Nemo's whim brought me to?

I should have liked to question him. As I could not do that, I stopped him. I seized his arm. But he, shaking his head, and pointing to the last summit, seemed to say to me:

'Higher! Still higher!'

I followed him with a last effort, and in a few minutes I had climbed the peak that overtopped for about thirty feet all the rocky mass.

I looked at the side we had just climbed. The mountain only rose seven or eight hundred feet above the plain; but on the opposite side it commanded from twice that height the depths of this portion of the Atlantic. My eyes wandered over a large space lighted up by a violent flashing. In fact, this mountain was a volcano. At fifty feet below the peak, amidst a rain of stones, a wide crater was vomiting forth torrents of lava which fell in a cascade of fire into the bosom of the liquid mass. Thus placed, the volcano, like an immense torch, lighted up the lower plain to the last limits of the horizon.

There, before my eyes, ruined, destroyed, overturned, appeared a town, its roofs crushed in, its temples thrown down, its arches dislocated, its columns lying on the ground; further on were the remains of a gigantic aqueduct; there, some vestiges of a quay, as if some ancient port had formerly sheltered, on the shores of an extinct ocean, merchant vessels and war triremes; further on still, long lines of ruined walls, wide deserted streets, a second Pompeii buried under the waters, raised up again for me by Captain Nemo.

Where was I? Where was I? I wished to know at any price. I felt I must speak, and tried to take off the globe of brass that imprisoned my head.

But Captain Nemo came to me and stopped me with a gesture. Then picking up a piece of clayey stone he went up to a black rock and traced on it the single word – 'Atlantis'.

Ah, why did time fail me? I should have liked to descend the abrupt sides of this mountain, and go over the whole of the immense continent that doubtless joined

Africa to America, and to visit the great antediluvian cities.

Whilst I was thus dreaming, trying to fix every detail of the grand scene in my memory, Captain Nemo, leaning against a moss-covered fragment of ruin, remained motionless as if petrified in mute ecstasy. Was he dreaming about the long-gone generations and asking them the secret of human destiny? Was it here that this strange man came to refresh his historical memories and live again that ancient existence – he who would have no modern one? What would I not have given to know his thoughts, to share and understand them!

We remained in the same place for a whole hour, contemplating the vast plain in the light of the lava that sometimes was surprisingly intense. The interior bubblings made rapid tremblings pass over the outside of the mountain. Deep noises, clearly transmitted by the liquid medium, were echoed with majestic amplitude.

At that moment the moon appeared for an instant through the mass of waters and threw her pale rays over the engulfed continent. It was only a gleam, but its effect was indescribable. The captain rose, gave a last look at the immense plain, and then, with his hand, signed to me to follow him.

We rapidly descended the mountain. When we had once passed the mineral forest I perceived the lantern of the *Nautilus* shining like a star. The captain walked straight towards it, and we were back on board as the first tints of dawn whitened the surface of the ocean.

8

SARGASSO SEA, CACHALOTS AND WHALES

The next day, 20 February, I awoke very late. The fatigues of the previous night had prolonged my sleep until eleven o'clock. I dressed promptly. I was in a hurry to know the direction of the *Nautilus*. The instruments informed me that it was running southward at a speed of twenty miles an hour and a depth of fifty fathoms.

Conseil entered. I gave him an account of our nocturnal excursion, and the panels being opened, he could still get a glimpse of the submerged continent.

In fact, the *Nautilus* was moving only five fathoms from the soil of the Atlantis plain. It was flying like a balloon before the wind above terrestrial prairies; but it would be more according to fact to say that we were in this saloon like being in a carriage of an express train. In the foreground were fantastically shaped rocks, forests of trees transformed from the vegetable to the mineral kingdom whose immovable outlines appeared under the waves. There were also stony masses, buried under a carpet of axides and anemones, bristling with long vertical hydrophytes; then blocks of lava strangely twisted that attested the fury of the underground expansions.

Whilst these strange sites shone under our electric

light I related the history of the Atlantides to Conseil. I told him all about the wars of these heroic peoples. I discussed the question of the Atlantides as a man who has no doubts left on the subject. But Conseil did not pay much attention to my historical lesson, and I soon saw why.

Numerous fishes were attracting his attention, and when fish were passing Conseil was always lost in an abyss of classification and left the real world. In that case all I had to do was to follow him and go on with our studies.

But whilst I was observing different specimens of marine fauna, I did not grow tired of walking the long plains of Atlantis. Sometimes the capricious undulations of the ground forced the *Nautilus* to slacken speed whilst it glided, with all the skill of a cetacean, amongst the narrow passes between the hills. If the labyrinth proved inextricable the apparatus rose like a balloon, and, once the obstacle cleared, it went on its rapid way some yards above the bottom – admirable and charming navigation that recalled the manoeuvres of a balloon journey.

About 4 p.m. the ground, generally composed of thick mud and mineralized branches, gradually changed and became more rocky. I thought that a mountainous region would soon succeed the long plains, and in fact, during certain evolutions of the *Nautilus*, I perceived the southern horizon bounded by a high wall that seemed to close all issue. Its summit evidently passed above the level of the ocean. It must be a continent, or at least an island – either one of the Canaries or one of the Cape Verd Islands. Our bearings not having been taken – perhaps purposely – I was ignorant of our whereabouts. In any case such a wall appeared to me to mark the end of that Atlantis of which, after all, we had seen so little.

The direction of the *Nautilus* had not been changed. All hope of returning to the European seas must for the present be given up. Captain Nemo kept to the south. Where was he taking us to? I dared not imagine.

Soon the *Nautilus* was crossing a singular part of the Atlantic Ocean. Everyone knows of the existence of that great current of warm water known under the name of the Gulf Stream. One of its arms surrounds with its circles of warm water that portion of the cool, quiet, immovable ocean called the Sargasso Sea.

The Sargasso Sea covers all the submerged part of Atlantis. Certain authors have even stated that the numerous herbs with which it is strewn are torn from the prairies of that ancient continent. It is more probable, however, that these herbs, sea-wrack and fucus, carried away from the shores of Europe and America, are brought to this zone by the Gulf Stream. That was one of the reasons that brought Columbus to suppose the existence of a new world. When the ships of this bold navigator arrived at the Sargasso Sea they sailed with difficulty amidst the herbs that impeded their course to the great terror of their crews, and they lost three long weeks crossing it.

Such was the region the *Nautilus* was now visiting, a veritable prairie, a thick carpet of sea-wrack, fucus, and tropical berries, so thick and compact that the stem of a vessel could hardly tear its way through it. And Captain Nemo, not wishing to entangle his screw in that herby mass, kept at a depth of some yards beneath the surface of the waves.

All the day of 22 February was passed in the Sargasso Sea, where the fish that feed on marine plants and crustaceans find abundant food. The next day the ocean had resumed its accustomed aspect.

From that date, for nineteen days, from 23 February to 12 March, the *Nautilus*, keeping in the midst of the Atlantic, carried us along at a constant speed of one hundred leagues in twenty-four hours. Captain Nemo evidently intended to accomplish his submarine programme, and I had no doubt that after doubling Cape Horn he meant to go back into the South Pacific.

Ned Land had therefore cause to fear. In these wide seas, destitute of islands, leaving the vessel could not be attempted. Neither were there any means of opposing Captain Nemo's will. The only thing to do was to submit; but that which could no longer be expected from force or ruse I liked to think might be obtained by persuasion. This voyage ended, would not Captain Nemo consent to give us liberty if we swore never to reveal his existence – an oath of honour which we should have kept? But that delicate question must be discussed with the captain. But would this request for liberty be well received? Had he not himself declared at the very beginning, in the most formal manner, that the secret of his life required our perpetual imprisonment on board the *Nautilus*? Would not my silence of the last four months appear to him a tacit acceptance of the situation? Would not a return to this subject give rise to suspicions that might be prejudicial to our projects if some favourable circumstance should cause us to renew them? I turned over all these reasons, weighed them in my mind, and submitted them to Conseil, who was no less embarrassed than I. On the whole, although I am not easily discouraged, I understood that the chances of ever seeing my fellows again were diminishing from day to day; above all, now that Captain Nemo was boldly rushing to the very south of the Atlantic.

During the above-mentioned nineteen days no particular incident occurred. I saw little of the captain. He was working. I often found books in the library that he had left open, and especially works of natural history. My book on the submarine depths was covered by him with notes in the margin that sometimes contradicted my theories and systems. But the captain contented himself with thus revising my work, and it was rare that he discussed it with me. Sometimes I heard the melancholy tones of his organ, which he played with much expression, but at night only, amidst the most secret obscurity, when the *Nautilus* was sleeping in the deserts of the ocean.

During this part of the voyage we went along for whole days on the surface of the waves. The sea was abandoned. A few sailing vessels only were to be seen, bound for the Indies, and making for the Cape of Good Hope. One day we were pursued by the boats of a whaler that had doubtless taken us for some enormous whale of great value. But Captain Nemo did not wish the brave fellows to lose their time and trouble, and he ended the pursuit by plunging under the water. This incident seemed greatly to interest Ned Land. I do not think I am mistaken in saying that the Canadian regretted that our iron-plated cetacean could not be struck dead by the harpoon of the fishers.

During the night, from 13 to 14 March, the *Nautilus* resumed her southerly direction. I thought that, once abreast of Cape Horn, the head would be turned westward, so as to make for the seas of the Pacific, and so complete its voyage round the world. Nothing of the kind was done, however, and the vessel kept on its way. Where was it going? To the Pole? That was madness! I began to think that the daring of the captain justified Ned Land's fears.

For some time past the Canadian had not spoken to me about his projects of flight. He had become less communicative, almost silent. I could see how much this prolonged imprisonment was weighing upon him. I felt how his anger was accumulating. When he met the captain his eyes lighted up with sombre fire, and I always feared that his natural violence would lead him into some extreme.

That day, 14 March, Conseil and he came into my room to find me. I asked them the reason for their visit.

'I have a simple question to ask you, sir,' answered the Canadian.

'Speak, Ned.'

'How many men do you think there are on board the *Nautilus*?'

'I cannot say, my friend.'

'It seems to me,' commented Ned Land, 'that it would not take a large crew to work it.'

'Certainly, under existing circumstances, ten men ought to be enough.'

'Well,' said the Canadian, 'why should there be any more?'

'Why?' I replied.

I looked fixedly at Ned Land, whose intentions were easy to guess.

'Because,' I added, 'if my surmises are correct, if I understand the captain's existence rightly, the *Nautilus* is not only a vessel. It must also be a place of refuge for those who, like its commander, have ceased all communication with land. There may be as many as sixty men on board.'

'Too many for three men!' murmured Conseil.

'Therefore, my poor Ned, I can only preach patience to you.'

'And even more than patience,' answered Conseil; 'resignation too.'

Conseil had used the right word.

'After all,' he continued, 'Captain Nemo cannot always go southward! He must stop somewhere, if only before an ice-bank, and afterwards he will return to more civilized seas! It will then be time to return to Ned Land's projects.'

The Canadian shook his head, passed his hand across his forehead, and left the room without answering.

'Will monsieur allow me to make one observation?' said Conseil. 'That poor Ned thinks of everything he cannot have. Everything in his past life comes back to him. Everything we are forbidden seems to him regrettable. His old recollections oppress him and make him heartsick. It is easy to understand. What has he to do here? Nothing. He is not learned like monsieur, and cannot have the same taste for the beauties of the sea as we have. He would risk all to be able once more to enter a tavern in his own country.'

It is certain that the monotonous life on board must appear insupportable to the Canadian, accustomed as he was to a free and active life. The events he could take an interest in were rare. However, that day an event did happen that recalled the bright days of the harpooner.

About 11 a.m. the *Nautilus*, being then on the surface of the ocean, fell in with a troop of whales – an encounter that did not surprise me, for I knew that these animals, hunted to death, had taken refuge in the high latitudes.

We were seated on the platform, with a quiet sea. The month of October in those latitudes gave us some beautiful autumnal days. It was the Canadian – he could not be mistaken – who signalled a whale on the eastern horizon. Looking attentively, we could see its black back rise and fall above the waves at five miles' distance from the *Nautilus*.

'Ah!' cried Ned Land, 'if I was on board a whaler now what pleasure that sight would give me! It is one of large size. Look with what strength its blow-holes throw up columns of air and vapour! Confound it all! Why am I chained to this piece of iron?'

As the whale drew nearer, Ned's eyes discerned a new factor.

'Ah!' cried he. 'It is not one whale, but ten, twenty, a whole troop of them! And I can't do anything! I'm bound hand and foot!'

'But, friend Ned,' said Conseil, 'why not ask the captain's permission to pursue them?'

Conseil had not finished his sentence before Ned Land had lowered himself through the panel, and was running to seek the captain. A short time afterwards both appeared on the platform.

Captain Nemo looked at the troop of cetaceans that were playing on the waters about a mile from the *Nautilus.*

'They are southern whales,' said he. 'There's the fortune of a fleet of whalers there.'

'Well, sir,' asked the Canadian, 'can't I pursue them just to prevent myself forgetting my old trade of harpooner?'

'What is the use?' answered Captain Nemo. 'We have no use for whale-oil on board. It would only be for the pleasure of killing. I know that it is a privilege reserved to man, but I do not approve of such a murderous pastime. Let the unfortunate cetaceans alone. They have quite enough of their natural enemies, the cachalots, sword-fish, and saw-fish, without your interfering.'

I leave the Canadian's face during this moral lecture to be imagined. It was a waste of words to give such reasons to a sportsman. Ned Land looked at Captain Nemo, and evidently did not understand what he meant.

However, Captain Nemo looked at the troop of cetaceans, and addressed me:

'I was right in saying whales had enough natural enemies. They will have plenty to do before long. Do you see those black moving points, M. Aronnax, about eight miles to leeward?'

'Yes, captain,' I replied.

'They are cachalots – terrible animals that I have sometimes met with in troops of two or three hundred. As to those cruel and mischievous creatures, it is right to exterminate them.'

The Canadian turned quickly at these last words.

'Well, captain,' I said; 'in the interest of the whales there is still time.'

'It is useless to expose oneself, professor. The *Nautilus* will suffice to disperse these cachalots. It is armed with a steel spur that I imagine is quite worth Mr Land's harpoon.'

The Canadian did not repress a shrug of the shoulders. Attack cetaceans with a prow! Who had ever heard of such a thing?

'Wait, M. Aronnax,' said Captain Nemo. 'We will show you a hunt you have never seen before. I have no pity for such ferocious cetaceans. They are all mouth and teeth.'

The formidable troop was drawing nearer. They had perceived the whales, and were preparing to attack them. One could prophesy beforehand that the cachalots would be victorious, not only because they were better built for attack than their inoffensive adversaries, but also because they could remain longer under the waves without rising to the surface.

There was only just time to go to the help of the whales when the *Nautilus* came up to them. The *Nautilus* sank; Conseil, Ned, and I took our places at the windows of the saloon. Captain Nemo joined the helmsman in his cage to work his apparatus as an engine of destruction. I soon felt the vibration of the screw increase and our speed become greater.

The combat between the cachalots and whales had already begun when the *Nautilus* reached them. It was worked so as to divide the cachalots, who at first showed no fear at the sight of the new monster joining in the conflict. But they soon had to guard against its blows.

What a struggle! Ned Land himself, soon enthusiastic, ended by clapping his hands. The *Nautilus* was now nothing but a formidable harpoon, brandished by the hand of its captain. It hurled itself against the fleshy mass, cut it through from end to end, leaving behind it two quivering halves of an animal. It did not feel the formidable blows on its sides from the cachalots' tails, nor the shocks it produced itself. One cachalot exterminated, it ran to another, tacked on the spot that it might not miss its prey, going backwards and forwards obedient to its helm, plunging when the cetacean dived into deep water, coming back with it to the surface, striking it in front or sideways, cutting or tearing in all directions and at any pace, piercing it through with its terrible spur.

What carnage! What a noise on the surface of the waves! What sharp hissing and snorting, peculiar to these animals when frightened! Amidst these generally peaceful waters their tails made perfect billows.

For an hour this Homeric massacre went on, which the cachalots could not escape. Ten or twelve of them tried several times to crush the *Nautilus* under their mass. We saw through the window their enormous mouths, paved with teeth, and their formidable eyes. Ned Land, who could no longer contain himself, threatened and stormed at them. We could feel them clinging to our vessel, like dogs worrying a wild boar in a copse. But the *Nautilus*, forcing its screw, carried them hither and thither, or to the upper level of the waters, in spite of their enormous weight or powerful hold.

At last the mass of cachalots was broken up, the waves became quiet again, and I felt that we were rising to the surface of the ocean. The panel was opened, and we rushed on to the platform.

The sea was covered with mutilated bodies. A formidable explosion could not have divided or cut up these fleshy masses more effectually. We were floating amidst gigantic bodies, bluish on the back, whitish underneath, covered with enormous protuberances. Some terrified cachalots were flying away on the horizon. The waves were dyed red for several miles round, and the *Nautilus* was floating in a sea of blood.

Captain Nemo joined us.

'Well, Mr Land?' said he.

'Well, sir,' answered the Canadian, whose enthusiasm had calmed down, 'it is a terrible spectacle, certainly. But I am not a butcher – I am a hunter, and this is only butchery.'

'It is a massacre of mischievous animals,' replied the captain, 'and the *Nautilus* is not a butcher's knife.'

'I like my harpoon better,' answered the Canadian.

'Each to his arm,' replied the captain, looking fixedly at Ned Land.

I feared that the Canadian would give way to some act of violence that would have deplorable consequences. But his anger was averted by the sight of a whale which the *Nautilus* had just come up with.

The animal had not been able to escape the cachalots' teeth. Captain Nemo steamed the *Nautilus* close to the body of the animal. Two of his men mounted on the whale's side, and I saw, not without astonishment, that they were drawing from its udders all the milk they contained – that is to say, about two or three tons.

The captain offered me a cup of this milk, which was still warm. I could not help showing him my repugnance to this drink. He assured me that it was excellent, and not to be distinguished from cow's milk.

I tasted it, and was of his opinion. It was a useful reserve for us, for this milk under the form of butter or cheese would make an agreeable variety to our daily food.

From that day I noticed, with uneasiness, that Ned Land's ill-will for the captain increased, and I resolved to watch the Canadian's doings and gestures very closely.

9

THE ICE-BANK

The *Nautilus* resumed her imperturbable southwardly course. Did it mean, then, to reach the Pole? I did not think so, for hitherto every attempt to reach that point had failed. The season, besides, was far advanced, for in the Antarctic regions 13 March corresponds to 13 September of Arctic regions.

On 14 March I perceived floating ice. Ned Land, who had already fished in the Arctic seas, was familiar with the spectacle of icebergs. Conseil and I were admiring it for the first time.

In the air, towards the southern horizon, stretched a white band of dazzling aspect. English whalers have given it the name of 'ice-blink'. However thick the clouds may be, they cannot hide it; it announces the presence of an ice-pack or bank.

In fact, larger blocks soon appeared, the brilliancy of which was modified according to the caprices of the mist.

The more we went down south the more these floating islands gained in number and importance. The Polar birds rested on them by thousands; petrels, danners, and puffins deafened us with their cries. Some of them took the *Nautilus* for the body of a whale, came upon it to rest, and pecked its sonorous plates with their beaks.

During the navigation amidst the ice Captain Nemo often kept on the platform. He attentively observed these solitary regions. I saw his calm look sometimes change to an animated one. Did he say to himself that in these Polar seas, interdicted to man, he was at home, master of unbounded space? Perhaps – but he did not speak. He remained motionless, only coming to himself when his steersman's instincts were uppermost. Then directing his *Nautilus* with consummate skill, he cleverly avoided the shock of those masses, some of which were several miles long and from 200 to 300 feet high. The horizon often appeared entirely closed up. But Captain Nemo, by careful search, soon found some narrow opening through which he audaciously glided, knowing well, however, that it closed up behind him.

On 15 March, about 8 a.m., the *Nautilus* crossed the Antarctic Polar Circle. Ice surrounded us on every side and closed the horizon. Still Captain Nemo went through one passage after another, and still more southward.

'Where can he be going to?' I asked.

'He is following his nose,' answered Conseil. 'After all, when he cannot go any farther he will stop.'

'I would not swear to that!' I answered. And, to tell the truth, I must acknowledge that this adventurous excursion did not displease me. I cannot express my astonishment at the beauties of these new regions. The ice took most superb forms. Here the grouping formed an Oriental town, with its innumerable minarets and mosques; there an overturned city, looking as if thrown to the earth by some earthquake – aspects incessantly varied by the oblique rays of the sun or lost in the grey mists amidst snowstorms. Detonations and ice-slips were heard on all sides – great overthrows of icebergs that changed the scene like the landscape of a diorama.

When the *Nautilus* was submerged at the moment that these equilibriums were disturbed, the noise was propagated under the water with frightful intensity, and the fall of the masses created fearful eddies as far as the greatest depth of the ocean. The *Nautilus* then pitched and tossed like a ship given up to the fury of the elements.

Often, seeing no issue, I thought we were definitely prisoners; but instinct guided him, and on the slightest indication Captain Nemo discovered new passages. He never made a mistake in observing the slender threads of bluish water that furrowed the ice-fields. I did not doubt that he had already steered his *Nautilus* in the Antarctic seas.

However, on 16 March ice-fields absolutely barricaded the road. It was not yet the ice-bank, but vast ice-fields cemented by the cold. This obstacle could not stop Captain Nemo, and he threw himself against the ice-field with frightful violence. The *Nautilus* entered the brittle mass like a wedge, and split it up with a frightful cracking noise. Pieces of ice, thrown high in the air, fell in hail around us. By its single power of impulsion our apparatus made a canal for itself. Sometimes by the force of its own impetus it fell on the ice-field and crushed it with its weight, or, deeply engaged in the ice, it divided it by a simple pitching movement that opened up wide fissures in it.

At length, on 17 March, after many useless assaults, the *Nautilus* was positively blocked up. It was no longer stopped by either streams, packs, or ice-fields, but an interminable and immovable barrier, formed by icebergs soldered together.

'The ice-bank!' said the Canadian to me.

There was no longer the slightest appearance of sea or liquid surface before our eyes. Under the prow of the *Nautilus* stretched a vast plain covered with confused blocks, looking like the surface of a river some time before the breaking up of the ice, but on a gigantic scale. Here and there sharp peaks and slender needles rising to a height of two hundred feet; farther, a line of cliffs with precipitous sides, covered with greyish tints, vast mirrors that reflected a few rays of the sun, half-drowned in the mist. Then over this desolate scene a savage silence, scarcely broken by the flapping of petrels' or puffins' wings. All was then frozen, even sound.

The *Nautilus* was then obliged to stop in its adventurous course amidst the ice-fields.

'Sir,' said Ned Land to me one day, 'if your captain goes any farther —'

'Well?'

'He will be a clever man.'

'Why, Ned?'

'Because no one can pass the ice-bank. He is powerful, your captain, but confound it, he is not more powerful than Nature, and where it has put limits he must stop whether he likes it or not.'

'That's certain, Ned Land, and yet I should like to know what is behind that ice-bank! A wall; that is what irritates me the most.'

'Monsieur is right,' said Conseil. 'Walls have only been invented to irritate *savants*. There ought to be walls nowhere.'

'Well,' said the Canadian, 'it is well known what is behind the ice-bank.'

'What?' I asked.

'Ice, ice, and nothing but ice!'

In fact, notwithstanding all its efforts, notwithstanding the powerful means employed to break up the ice, the

Nautilus was reduced to immobility. Generally, if you cannot go any farther, all you have to do is to go back. But here going back was as impossible as going on, for the passages had closed up behind us, and if our apparatus remained stationary long it would soon be blocked up. That is what happened about 2 p.m., and the young ice formed on its sides with astonishing rapidity. I was forced to acknowledge that Captain Nemo's conduct was more than imprudent. I was at that moment on the platform. The captain, who had been observing the situation for some minutes, said to me:

'Well, professor, what do you think of it?'

'I think we are caught, captain.'

'Then, M. Aronnax, you do not think the *Nautilus* can be set free?'

'Not easily, captain, for the season is already too far advanced for you to depend upon the breaking up of the ice.'

'Ah, professor!' answered the captain in an ironical tone, 'you are always the same! You only see obstacles and difficulties. But I affirm to you that not only will the *Nautilus* be set free, but it will go farther still!'

'Farther south?' I asked, looking at the captain.

'Yes, sir, it will go to the Pole.'

'To the Pole!' I cried, unable to restrain a movement of incredulity.

It then came into my head to ask Captain Nemo if he had already discovered the Pole, which no human being had set foot upon.

'No, professor,' he answered, 'and we will discover it together. There, where so many have failed, I shall not fail. I had never brought my *Nautilus* so far south; but, I repeat, it shall go farther still.'

'I wish to believe you, captain,' said I in a slightly ironical tone. 'I do believe you! There is no obstacle before us! We will break up that ice-bank, and if it resists, we will give the *Nautilus* wings so that we can pass over it!'

'Over it, professor?' answered Captain Nemo tranquilly. 'No, not over it, but under it.'

'Under it!' I cried.

A sudden revelation of the captain's projects illuminated my mind. I understood. The marvellous qualities of the *Nautilus* would again be of service in this superhuman enterprise.

'It is certain,' said I, carried along by the captain's reasoning, 'that though the surface of the sea is solidified by ice, its depths are free. And if I am not mistaken, the submerged part of this ice-bank is to the emerged part as four is to one.'

'About that, professor. For every foot that icebergs have above the sea they have three below. Now as these mountains of ice are 300 feet high, they are not more than 900 deep. Well, what is 900 feet to the *Nautilus*?'

'Nothing, captain.'

'The only difficulty,' continued Captain Nemo, 'will be to remain submerged for several days without renewing the air.'

'Is that all?' I replied. 'The *Nautilus* contains vast reservoirs; we will fill them, and they will furnish us with all the oxygen we shall want.'

'Well imagined, M. Aronnax,' said the captain, smiling. 'But I did not wish you to accuse me of foolhardiness, so I submit all objections to you beforehand.'

'Have you any more to make?'

'One only. It is possible that if sea exists at the South Pole, that sea may be entirely frozen over, and consequently we cannot go up to the surface.'

'Well, sir, do you forget that the *Nautilus* is armed with a powerful prow, and can we not hurl it diagonally against the ice-fields, which will open at the shock?'

'Ah, professor, you have some good ideas today!' said Captain Nemo. 'I will only observe to you that after uttering so many objections to my scheme, you now crush me with arguments in favour of it.'

The preparations for this audacious attempt were now begun. The powerful pumps of the *Nautilus* were working air into the reservoirs, and storing it at high pressure. About four o'clock Captain Nemo informed me that the panels of the platform were going to be closed. I threw a last look at the thick ice-bank we were going to pass. The weather was clear, the atmosphere pure, and the cold very piercing, twelve degrees below zero; but the wind had lulled, and this temperature did not seem unbearable.

About ten men got up on the sides of the *Nautilus*, and, armed with pickaxes, broke the ice round the hull, which was soon set free. This was a speedy operation, for the young ice was still thin. We all went back into the interior. The usual reservoirs were filled with the liberated water, and the *Nautilus* soon sank.

I had taken my place with Conseil in the saloon. Through the open window we watched the different depths of the Southern Ocean. The thermometer rose. The needle of the manometer deviated on its dial.

At about 900 feet, as Captain Nemo had foreseen, we were floating under the undulated surface of the ice-bank. But the *Nautilus* sank lower still. It reached a depth of four hundred fathoms. The temperature of the water, which gave 12° on the surface, was now only 10°. Two degrees were already gained. Of course the temperature of the *Nautilus*, raised by its heating apparatus, kept up to a much superior degree. All the manoeuvres were accomplished with extraordinary precision.

'We shall pass it, if monsieur will allow me to say so,' said Conseil.

'I count upon it,' I answered in a tone of profound conviction.

The next day, 18 March, at 5 a.m., I went back to my station in the saloon. The electric log indicated that the speed of the *Nautilus* had only been moderate. It was then going up towards the surface, but prudently, by slowly emptying its reservoirs.

My heart beat quickly. Were we going to emerge and find the free atmosphere of the Pole?

No. A shock told me that the *Nautilus* had struck against the bottom of the ice-bank, still very thick, to judge by the dullness of the sound. We had struck at a depth of 1,000 feet. That gave 2,000 feet above us, 1,000 feet of which emerged. The ice-bank, therefore, was higher than it was on its border – a not very reassuring fact.

During that day the *Nautilus* several times recommenced the same experiment, and always struck against the wall that hung above it like a ceiling. At certain moments it met it at a depth of five hundred fathoms. Sometimes it was double the height it was where the *Nautilus* sank.

In the evening no change had occurred in our situation. Still ice between two and three hundred fathoms deep – an evident diminution, but what thickness there still was between us and the surface of the ocean!

It was then 8 p.m. According to the daily custom on board the air ought to have been renewed four hours before. I did not suffer from it much, although Captain Nemo had not yet drawn upon his reservoirs for a supplement of oxygen.

My sleep was restless that night. Hope and fear besieged me by turns. I rose several times. The gropings of the *Nautilus* were still going on. About 3 a.m. I noticed that the lower surface of the ice-bank was met with at a depth of only twenty-five fathoms. A hundred and fifty feet next separated us from the surface of the water. The ice-bank was gradually becoming an ice-field. The mountain was becoming a plain.

My eyes no longer left the manometer. We were still ascending, diagonally following the brilliant surface that shone under the rays of the electric lamp. The ice-bank was getting lower above and below in long slopes. It got thinner from mile to mile.

At last, at 6 a.m. on this memorable 19 March, the door of the saloon opened. Captain Nemo appeared.

'The open sea!' he said.

10

THE SOUTH POLE

I rushed upon the platform. Yes! There lay the open sea. A few pieces of ice and moving icebergs were scattered about; in the distance a long stretch of sea; a world of birds in the air, and myriads of fish in the waters, which, according to their depth, varied from intense blue to olive green. The thermometer marked three degrees centigrade above zero. It was like a relative spring enclosed behind this ice-bank, whose distant masses were outlined on the northern horizon.

'Are we at the Pole?' I asked the captain, with a palpitating heart.

'I do not know yet,' he answered. 'At noon we will take our bearings.'

'But will the sun show itself through these mists?' said I, looking at the grey sky.

'However little it shows, it will be enough for me,' answered the captain.

About ten miles south of the *Nautilus* a solitary island rose to a height of six hundred feet. We were bearing down upon it, but prudently, for the sea might be strewn with reefs.

The *Nautilus*, for fear of being stranded, had stopped at

three cables' length from a beach, over which rose a superb heap of rocks. The boat was launched. The captain, two of his men carrying the instruments, Conseil, and I embarked. It was 10 a.m. I had not seen Ned Land. The Canadian, doubtless, did not wish to acknowledge himself in the wrong in the presence of the South Pole.

A few strokes of the oars brought the boat on to the sand, where it stranded. As Conseil was going to jump out I stopped him.

'Captain Nemo,' said I, 'to you belongs the honour of first setting foot on this land.'

'Yes, professor,' answered the captain, 'and I do not hesitate to do so, because, until now, no human being has left the imprint of his footsteps upon it.'

That said he jumped lightly on to the sand. Keen emotion made his heart beat faster. He climbed a rock which overhung, forming a small promontory, and there, with his arms crossed, mute and motionless, he seemed to take possession with an eager look of these southern regions. After five minutes passed in this rapt contemplation he turned towards us.

'When you are ready, professor,' he called to me.

I disembarked, followed by Conseil, leaving the two men in the boat. I spent the best part of an hour observing the volcanic origin of the place and its wildlife.

In the meantime the mist was not rising, and at 11 a.m. the sun had not yet made its appearance. Its absence made me uneasy. Without it there was no observation possible. How, then, could we settle whether we had reached the Pole?

When I rejoined Captain Nemo I found him silently leaning against a rock, and looking at the sky. He seemed impatient and vexed. But there was no help for it. This powerful and audacious man could not command the sun like he did the sea.

Twelve o'clock came without the sun having showed itself for a single instant. Even the place it occupied behind the curtain of mist could not be distinguished. The mist soon after dissolved in snow.

'We must wait till tomorrow,' said the captain simply, and we went back to the *Nautilus* amidst the snow.

The snow-storm lasted until the next day. It was impossible to keep upon the platform. From the saloon, where I was taking notes of the incidents of this excursion, to the Polar continent, I heard the cries of petrels and albatrosses playing amidst the tempest. The *Nautilus* did not remain motionless and, coasting the continent, it went about ten miles farther south in the sort of twilight that the sun left as it skirted the horizon.

The next day the snow had ceased. It was slightly colder. The thermometer indicated two degrees below zero. The mists rose, and I hoped it would be possible to take an observation that day.

I stood near Captain Nemo and waited without speaking. Twelve o'clock came, and, like the day before, the sun did not appear.

It was like fatality. We still wanted an observation. If it were not taken tomorrow we must definitely renounce taking our position.

In fact, we were at 20 March. The next day, the 21st, was the day of the equinox, and the refraction not counting, the sun would disappear below the horizon for six months, and with its disappearance the long Polar night would begin.

The next day, at 5 a.m., I went up on to the platform and found Captain Nemo there.

'The weather is clearing up a little,' said he; 'I have great hopes of it. After breakfast we will land and choose a post of observation.'

We landed at nine o'clock. The sky was getting clearer;

the clouds were flying south. The mists were rising from the cold surface of the water. Captain Nemo walked towards the peak, of which he doubtless meant to make his observatory.

It took us two hours to get to the summit of this peak. From there the view comprised a vast expanse of sea which on the north distinctly traced its horizon-line on the sky. At our feet lay fields of dazzling whiteness; over our heads, a pale azure free from mist. On the north lay the sun's disc, like a ball of fire, already sinking below the horizon. From the bosom of the waters rose hundreds of sparkling fountains. In the distance lay the *Nautilus*, like a cetacean asleep; behind us, on the south and east, an immense stretch of land, a chaotic heap of rocks and icebergs, the limits of which were not visible.

When Captain Nemo reached the top he carefully took its height by means of the barometer, for he would have to take it into consideration in taking his observation.

At a quarter to twelve the sun, then only seen by refraction, looked like a golden disc, shedding its last rays over these lands and seas which man had never before ploughed.

We took our bearings. We were indeed at the South Pole!

Captain Nemo solemnly enumerated the men whose exploits, however bold, yet failed to bring them to this, their goal. Finally he said:

'I, Captain Nemo, on 21 March 1868, have reached the South Pole, and I take possession of this part of the globe, equal to the sixth part of known continents.'

'In whose name, captain?'

'In my own, sir.'

So saying, Captain Nemo unfurled a black flag, bearing an N in gold, quartered on its bunting. Then, turning towards the sun, whose last rays were lapping the horizon of the sea, he exclaimed:

'Adieu, sun! Disappear, thou radiant star! Rest beneath this free sea, and let a six months' night spread its darkness over my new domain!'

11

ACCIDENT OR INCIDENT?

The next day, 22 March, at 6 a.m., preparations for departure were begun. The last gleams of twilight were melting into night. The cold was intense. The constellations shone with wonderful intensity. In the zenith glittered that wondrous southern cross, the Polar star of Antarctic regions.

The panels of the saloon were closed for prudence sake, for the hull of the *Nautilus* might strike against some submerged block, so I passed that day in writing out my notes. I gave myself up to thoughts about the Pole. We had reached this inaccessible point without fatigue or danger, as if our floating carriage had glided over the rails of a railroad. And now the return had really begun. Did it reserve any fresh surprises for me? I thought it might, so inexhaustible is the series of submarine marvels! During the five months and a half that fate had thrown me on board this vessel, we had come 14,000 leagues, and during this distance, greater in extent than the terrestrial equator, how many curious or terrible incidents had varied our voyage – the hunt in the forests of Crespo, the stranding in the Torres Straits, the coral cemetery, the fisheries of Ceylon, the Arabic tunnel, the fires of

Santorin, the millions of Vigo Bay, Atlantis, the South Pole! During the night all these memories passed like a dream, not letting my brain repose for an instant.

At 3 a.m. I was awakened by a violent shock. I rose up in bed, and was listening amidst the obscurity, when I was roughly thrown into the middle of the room. The *Nautilus* had evidently made a considerable rebound after having struck.

I groped along the partition through the waist to the saloon, which was lighted up by the luminous ceiling. The furniture was all upset. Happily the window-sashes were firmly set, and had stood fast. The pictures on the starboard side, through the vessel being no longer vertical, were sticking to the tapestry, whilst those on the larboard side were hanging a foot from the wall at their lower edge. The *Nautilus* was lying on its starboard side completely motionless.

In the interior I heard a noise of footsteps and confused voices. But Captain Nemo did not appear. At the moment I was going to leave the saloon Ned Land and Conseil entered.

'What is the matter?' said I immediately.

'I came to ask monsieur,' answered Conseil.

'*Mille diables!*' cried the Canadian. 'I know very well what it is. The *Nautilus* has struck, and to judge by the way it is lying, it won't come off quite so easily as in Torres Straits.'

'But at least,' I asked, 'is it on the surface of the sea?'

'We do not know,' answered Conseil.

'It is easy to find out,' said I.

I consulted the manometer. To my great surprise it indicated a depth of one hundred and eighty fathoms.

'What can this mean?' I exclaimed.

'We must ask Captain Nemo,' said Conseil.

'But where shall we find him?' asked Ned Land.

'Follow me,' I said to my two companions.

We left the saloon. There was no one in the library, or on the central staircase, or in the ward-room. I supposed that Captain Nemo must be in the helmsman's cage. The only thing to do was to wait. We all three returned to the saloon.

I shall pass by the Canadian's recriminations in silence. He had now something to be in a rage about. I let him give off his bad humour at his ease without answering him.

We had been thus for twenty minutes listening to the least noise in the interior of the *Nautilus*, when Captain Nemo entered. He did not seem to see us. His countenance, habitually so impassive, revealed a certain anxiety. He looked at the compass and manometer in silence, and put his finger on a point of the planisphere in that part that represented the South Seas.

I did not wish to interrupt him. When, a few instants afterwards, he turned towards me, I said to him, using an expression he had used in Torres Straits:

'An incident, captain?'

'No, professor,' he replied. 'An accident this time.'

'Grave?'

'Perhaps.'

'Is the danger immediate?'

'No.'

'The *Nautilus* has struck upon something?'

'Yes.'

'How?'

'Through a caprice of Nature, not through the incapacity of man. There has not been a fault committed in our manoeuvres. But no one can prevent equilibrium producing its effects. We may resist human laws, but we cannot stand against natural ones.'

Captain Nemo chose a singular moment to utter this

philosophical reflection. On the whole, his answer taught me nothing.

'May I know, sir,' I asked, 'the cause of this accident?'

'An enormous block of ice, a whole mountain, has turned over,' he answered. 'When icebergs are undermined by warmer water or reiterated shocks, their centre of gravity ascends. Then the whole thing turns over. That is what has happened. One of these blocks as it turned over struck the *Nautilus*, which was floating under the waters. Then gliding under its hull, and raising it with irresistible force, it has raised it to less dense waters, and thrown it on its side.'

'But cannot the *Nautilus* be got off by employing the reservoirs so as to restore its equilibrium?'

'That is what they are doing now, sir. You can hear the pump working. Look at the needle of the mano-meter. It indicates that the *Nautilus* is ascending, but the block of ice is ascending with it, and until some obstacle stops its upward movement our position will not be changed.'

The *Nautilus* still kept the same position. It would, doubtless, right itself when the block itself stopped. But at that moment how did we know that we should not strike against the ice-bank and so be frightfully squeezed between the two frozen surfaces?

Suddenly a slight movement was felt in the hull. The *Nautilus* was evidently righting itself a little. The objects hung up in the saloon were insensibly recovering their normal position. The partitions became more vertical. No one spoke. With heightened emotion we watched the vessel right itself. The flooring became horizontal under our feet.

'At last we are straight!' I exclaimed.

'Yes,' said Captain Nemo, going towards the door of the saloon.

'But shall we get afloat again?' I asked him.

'Certainly,' he answered, 'since the reservoirs are not yet empty, and that when they are the *Nautilus* will ascend to the surface of the sea.'

The captain went out, and I soon saw that, following his orders, they had stopped the ascension of the *Nautilus*. In fact, it would soon have struck against the bottom of the ice-bank, and it was better to keep it in the water.

'We have had a narrow escape!' then said Conseil.

'Yes. We might have been crushed between two blocks of ice, or, at least, imprisoned. And then, not being able to renew the air – Yes, we have had a narrow escape!'

'If that is all!' murmured Ned Land.

I did not wish to begin a useless discussion with the Canadian, so did not answer him. Besides, at that moment the panels of the saloon were opened and the electric light shone through the glass panes.

We were in full water, as I have said; but at a distance of thirty feet on each side of the *Nautilus* rose a dazzling wall of ice. Above and below, the same wall. Above, because the bottom of the ice-bank formed an immense ceiling. Below, because the overturned block, gliding down by degrees, had found on the lateral walls two resting-places which kept it in that position. The *Nautilus* was imprisoned in a veritable tunnel of ice, about sixty feet wide, filled with tranquil water. It would, therefore, be easy for it to go out of it by going either backwards or forwards, and finding, at some hundreds of feet lower down, a free passage under the ice-bank.

'Oh, how beautiful! How beautiful!' exclaimed Conseil.

'Yes!' said I. 'It is an admirable sight. Is it not, Ned?'

'Yes, *mille diables!* Yes,' answered Ned Land. 'It is superb. I'm in a rage at being obliged to acknowledge it. No one has ever seen anything like it. But we may have to pay dearly for the sight. And I believe that here we see things God never meant us to see.'

Ned was right. It was too beautiful. All at once a cry from Conseil made me turn round.

'What is the matter?' I asked.

'Let monsieur close his eyes and not look!'

So saying, Conseil quickly carried his hand to his eyes.

'But what has happened, my boy?'

'I am dazzled – blinded.'

My eyes involuntarily turned to the window, but I could not bear the fire that devoured them.

I understood what had happened. The *Nautilus* had just put on full speed. All the tranquil brilliancy of the ice-walls had then changed into flashes of lightning. The fires of these myriads of diamonds were united together.

'When we return to land,' added Conseil, 'blasé with so many marvels of Nature, what shall we think of the miserable continents and little works done by the hand of man? No, the inhabited world is no longer worthy of us.'

Such words from the mouth of an impassive Dutchman showed to what a boiling point our enthusiasm had reached. But the Canadian did not fail to throw cold water on it.

'The inhabited world!' said he, shaking his head. 'Don't be uneasy, friend Conseil, we shall never see that again.'

It was then 5 a.m. At that moment a shock took place in the bows of the *Nautilus*. I knew that its prow had struck against a block of ice. This, I thought, must be a mistaken manoeuvre, for the submarine tunnel, obstructed by the ice-block, was not easily navigated. I therefore imagined that Captain Nemo, changing his direction, woud turn round these obstacles, or follow the windings of the tunnel. In any case our forward journey could not be quite prevented. Still contrary to my expectation, the *Nautilus* began a decided backward movement.

'We are going backwards?' said Conseil.

'Yes,' I answered, 'the tunnel must be without issue on that side.'

'And what will be done then?'

'Then,' I said, 'the manoeuvre is very simple. We shall retrace our steps and get out by the southern orifice, that is all.'

In speaking thus I wished to appear more confident than I really was. In the meantime the backward movement of the *Nautilus* was getting more rapid, and with reversed screw it was carrying us along with great rapidity.

'This will cause a delay,' said Ned.

'What do a few hours more or less matter, so that we get out?'

'Yes,' echoed Ned Land, 'so that we get out.'

I walked backwards and forwards for some minutes between the saloon and the library. My companions also were silent. I soon threw myself upon a divan, and took a book which my eyes ran over mechanically.

A quarter of an hour afterwards Conseil came up to me and said:

'Is what monsieur is reading very interesting?'

'Very interesting,' I replied.

'I thought so. It is monsieur's book that monsieur is reading!'

'My book?'

In fact, I held in my hand the work of the *Submarine Depths*. I had not the least idea of it. I closed the book and resumed my walk. Ned and Conseil rose to go.

'Stay, my friends,' I said, detaining them. 'Let us remain together till we are out of this tunnel.'

'As monsieur pleases,' answered Conseil.

Some hours passed. I often looked at the instruments hung up on the walls of the saloon. The manometer indicated that the *Nautilus* kept at a constant depth of nine hundred feet, the compass that we were going south, the log that our speed was twenty miles an hour – an excessive speed in that narrow space. But Captain Nemo knew that he could not make too much haste, and that now minutes were worth centuries.

At twenty-five minutes past eight a second shock took place, this time at the back. I turned pale. My companions came up to me. I seized Conseil's hand. We questioned each other with a look more directly than if words had interpreted our thoughts.

At that moment the captain entered the saloon. I went to him.

'The route is barricaded on the south?' I asked.

'Yes, sir. As the iceberg turned over it closed all issue.'

'Then we are blocked up?'

'Yes.'

12

WANT OF AIR

Thus there was around the *Nautilus*, above and below, an impenetrable wall of ice. We were imprisoned in the ice-bank. The Canadian struck a formidable blow on the table with his fist. Conseil said nothing. I looked at the captain. His face had regained its usual impassiveness. He had crossed his arms over his breast and was reflecting. The *Nautilus* was quite still.

The captain then spoke.

'Gentlemen,' said he, in a calm voice, 'there are two ways of dying under our present circumstances.'

This inexplicable personage looked like a professor of mathematics stating a problem to his pupils.

'The first,' he continued, 'is to be crushed to death; the second is to be suffocated. I need not speak of the possibility of dying of hunger, for the provisions of the *Nautilus* will certainly outlast us.'

'We cannot be suffocated, captain,' I answered, 'for our reservoirs are full.'

'True,' said Captain Nemo, 'but they will only give us air for two days. Now we have already been six-and-thirty hours under water, and the heavy atmosphere of the *Nautilus* already wants renewing. In forty-eight hours our reserve will be exhausted.'

'Well, captain, we must get out before forty-eight hours.'

'We will try, at all events, by piercing through the wall that surrounds us.'

'On which side?' I asked.

'The bore will tell us that. I am going to run the *Nautilus* on the lower bank, and my men will put on their diving dresses and attack the wall where it is the least thick.'

'Can we have the saloon panels opened?'

'Certainly; we are no longer moving.'

Captain Nemo went out. A hissing sound soon told me that the reservoirs were being filled with water. The *Nautilus* gradually sank, and rested on the ice at a depth of 175 fathoms.

'My friends,' said I, 'the situation is grave, but I count on your courage and energy.'

'Sir,' answered the Canadian, 'it is not the time to worry you with my grumbling. I am ready to do anything for the common safety.'

'That is right, Ned,' said I, holding out my hand to the Canadian.

'I am as handy with the pickaxe as the harpoon,' he added, 'and if I can be useful to the captain he may dispose of me.'

'He will not refuse your aid. Come, Ned.'

I led the Canadian to the room where the men of the *Nautilus* were putting on their diving dresses. I told the captain of Ned's proposition, which was accepted.

When Ned was dressed I went back to the saloon, where the panels were open, and, taking a place beside Conseil, I examined the ambient beds that supported the *Nautilus*.

Some moments later we saw a dozen men of the crew

step out on to the ice with Ned Land amongst them, recognizable from his tall stature. Captain Nemo was with them.

Before beginning to dig through the walls he had them bored to assure a good direction to the work. Long bores were sunk into the lateral walls, but after forty-five feet they were again stopped by a thick wall. It was useless to attack the ice-ceiling, for it was the ice-bank itself, which was more than 1,200 feet high. Captain Nemo then had the lower surface bored. There thirty feet of ice separated us from the water, such was the thickness of this ice-field. It was, therefore, necessary to cut away a part equal in extent to the water-line of the *Nautilus*. There were, therefore, about 7,000 cubic yards to detach in order to dig a hole through which we could sink below the ice-field.

The work was immediately begun and carried on with indefatigable energy. Instead of digging round the *Nautilus*, which would have been exceedingly difficult, Captain Nemo had an immense trench made, about eight yards from its port quarter. Then his men began simultaneously to work at it in different points of its circumference, and large blocks were soon detached from the mass. By a curious effect of specific gravity, these blocks, being lighter than water, fled up to the vault of the tunnel, which thus became thicker at the top as it became thinner at the bottom. But it was of no consequence so long as the bottom ice was so much the less thick.

After two hours of energetic work Ned Land entered exhausted. His companions and he were relieved by fresh workers, whom Conseil and I joined. The first officer of the *Nautilus* directed us.

The water seemed to me singularly cold, but I soon grew warmer with handling the pickaxe. My movements were very free, though made under a pressure of thirty atmospheres.

When I re-entered, after two hours of work, to take food and rest, I found a notable difference between the air the diving apparatus furnished me with and the atmosphere of the *Nautilus*, already loaded with carbonic acid gas. The air had not been renewed for forty-eight hours, and its life-giving qualities were considerably weakened. However, in twelve hours we had broken off a slice of ice a yard thick, or about six hundred cubic yards. Admitting that we could go on at the same rate, it would take still five nights and four days to accomplish our task.

'Five nights and four days!' said I to my companions, 'and we have only air for two days in the reservoirs.'

'Without reckoning,' replied Ned, 'that, once out of this confounded prison, we shall still be imprisoned under the ice-bank without any possible communication with the atmosphere!'

True enough. Who could then foresee the minimum of time necessary for our deliverance? Should we not all be suffocated before the *Nautilus* could reach the surface of the waves? Was it destined to perish in this tomb of ice with all the people it contained? The situation appeared terrible, but each of us looked it in the face, and we were all decided to do our duty to the end.

As I had foreseen, during the night another slice, a yard thick, was dug off the immense pit. But in the morning, when, clothed in my bathing-dress, I walked in the liquid mass in a temperature of from 6° to 7° below zero, I remarked that the lateral walls were gradually approaching each other. The water away from the trench, which was not warmed by the men's work and the play of the tools, showed a tendency to solidify. In the presence of this new and imminent danger what chance of safety had we, and how could we prevent the solidification of this liquid medium that would have crushed the sides of the *Nautilus* like glass?

I did not make known this new danger to my companions. Why risk the damping of that energy which they were employing in their painful toil? But when I went back on board I spoke to Captain Nemo about this grave complication.

'I know it,' he said in his calm tone, which no terrible conjuncture of circumstances could modify. 'It is one danger more, but I see no means of avoiding it. The only chance of safety is to work quicker than the solidification. We must be first, that is all.'

Towards evening the trench had been dug another yard deeper. When I went back on board I was nearly suffocated with the carbonic acid with which the air was filled.

That evening Captain Nemo was obliged to open the taps of his reservoirs and throw some columns of pure air into the interior of the *Nautilus*. Without that precaution we should never have awakened.

The next day, 26 March, I went on with my mining work on the fifth yard. The lateral walls and lower surface of the ice-bank thickened perceptibly. It was evident that they would come together before the *Nautilus* could be extricated. Despair came over me for an instant. My axe nearly dropped from my hands. What was the use of digging if I was to perish suffocated, crushed by the water that was turning to stone – a death that even the ferocity of savages would not have invented? It seemed to me that I was between the formidable jaws of a monster, which were irresistibly closing.

At that moment Captain Nemo, directing the work and working himself, passed close to me. I touched him, and pointed to the walls of our prison. The port wall had advanced to within four yards of the *Nautilus*.

The captain understood me and signed to me to follow him. We re-entered the vessel. Once my diving dress was off, I accompanied him into the saloon.

'M. Aronnax,' said he, 'we must try some heroic means or we shall be sealed up in this freezing water as in cement.'

'Yes,' said I, 'but what can we do?'

'Boiling water!' murmured he.

'Boiling water?' I cried.

'Yes, sir. We are enclosed in a relatively restricted space. Would not some jets of boiling water, constantly injected by the pumps of the *Nautilus*, raise the temperature of this medium, and delay its freezing?'

'It must be tried,' said I resolutely.

'We will try it, professor.'

The thermometer then indicated seven degrees outside. Captain Nemo took me to the kitchens, where vast distilling apparatus was at work, which furnished drinking-water, by evaporation. It was filled with water, and all the electric heat of the piles was put into the pipes, bathed by the liquid. In a few moments the water had attained 100°. It was sent to the pumps, while fresh water constantly supplied its place. The heat given off by the piles was such that the cold water taken from the sea after going through the apparatus arrived boiling in the pump.

The injection began, and three hours later the thermometer outside indicated six degrees below zero. It was one degree gained. Two hours later the thermometer only indicated four.

'We shall succeed,' I said to the captain, after having followed and controlled by numerous remarks the progress of the operation.

'I think we shall,' he answered. 'We shall not be crushed. We have only suffocation to fear now.'

During the night the temperature of the water went up to one degree below zero. The apparatus could not send it up any higher. But as sea-water does not freeze at less than two degrees, I was at last reassured against the danger of solidification.

The next day, 27 March, eighteen feet of ice had been taken from the trench. There still remained twelve. Another forty-eight hours' work. The air could not be renewed in the interior of the *Nautilus*. That day things went from bad to worse.

An intolerable heaviness weighed upon me. About 3 p.m. this feeling of agony became exceedingly violent. I dislocated my jaws with gaping. My lungs panted. A moral torpor took possession of me. I lay down without strength to move, almost without consciousness. My brave Conseil, seized by the same symptoms, suffering the same agony, did not leave my side. He took my hand, encouraged me, and I heard him murmur:

'Ah, if I could but do without breathing in order to leave more air for monsieur!'

Tears came into my eyes at hearing him speak thus.

If our situation was intolerable in the interior, with what haste and pleasure we donned our bathing-dresses to work in our turn! The pickaxes rang on the frozen surface. Our arms were tired, our hands skinned, but what mattered fatigues and wounds? Our lungs had vital air. We breathed! We breathed!

And yet no one thought of prolonging his work under water beyond his allotted time. His task accomplished, each gave to his panting companion the reservoir that was to pour life into him. Captain Nemo set the example, and was the first to submit to this severe discipline. When the time came he gave up his apparatus to another, and re-entered the vitiated atmosphere on board, always calm, unflinching, and uncomplaining.

That day the usual work was accomplished with still more vigour. But six feet of ice remained. Six feet alone separated us from the open sea. But the reservoirs of air were almost empty. The little that remained must be kept for the workers. Not an atom for the *Nautilus*.

When I re-entered the vessel I was half-suffocated. What a night! Such suffering could not be expressed. The next day my breathing was oppressed. Along with pains in my head came dozy vertigo that made a drunken man of me. My companions felt the same symptoms. Some of the crew had rattling in their throats.

On that day, the sixth of our imprisonment, Captain Nemo, finding the pickaxes' work too slow, resolved to crush in the bed of ice that still separated us from the water. This man kept all coolness and energy. He subdued physical pain by moral force. He thought, planned, and acted.

He ordered the vessel to be lightened. When it floated it was towed above the immense trench dug according to its water-line. Then its reservoirs of water were filled; it sank into the hole.

At that moment all the crew came on board, and the double door of communication was shut. The *Nautilus* was then resting on a sheet of ice not three feet thick, which the bores had pierced in a thousand places.

The taps of the reservoirs were then turned full on, and a hundred cubic yards of water rushed in, increasing by 200,000 pounds the *Nautilus*'s weight.

We waited and listened, forgetting our sufferings, hoping still. We had made our last effort.

Notwithstanding the buzzing in my head, I soon felt the vibrations in the hull of the *Nautilus*. A lower level was reached. The ice cracked with a singular noise like paper being torn, and the *Nautilus* sank.

'We have gone through!' murmured Conseil in my ear.

I could not answer him. I seized his hand and pressed it convulsively.

All at once, dragged down by its fearful overweight, the *Nautilus* sank like a cannon-ball!

Then all the electric force was put into the pumps, which immediately began to drive the water out of the reservoirs. After a few minutes our fall was stopped. Soon even the manometer indicated an ascensional movement. The screw, with all speed on, made the iron hull tremble to its very bolts, and dragged us northwards.

But how long would this navigation under the ice-bank last before we reached the open sea? Another day? I should be dead first.

Half lying on a divan in the library, I was suffocating. My face was violet, my lips blue, my faculties suspended. I saw nothing, heard nothing. All idea of time had disappeared from my mind. I could not contract my muscles.

I do not know how long this lasted. But I knew that my death-agony had begun. I saw that I was dying. Suddenly I came to myself. A few whiffs of air penetrated into my lungs. Had we, then, reached the surface of the water? Had we cleared the ice-bank?

No! Ned and Conseil, my two brave friends, were sacrificing themselves to save me. Some atoms of air had remained at the bottom of an apparatus. Instead of breathing it, they had kept it for me; and while they were suffocating, they poured me out life drop by drop! I wished to push the apparatus away. They held my hands, and for some minutes I breathed voluptuously.

My eyes fell on the clock. It was 11 a.m. It must be 28

March. The *Nautilus* was going at a frightful speed of forty miles an hour.

Where was Captain Nemo? Had he succumbed? Had his companions died with him?

At that moment the manometer indicated that we were only twenty feet from the surface. A simple field of ice separated us from the atmosphere. Could we not break it?

Perhaps. Anyway, the *Nautilus* was going to attempt it. I felt that it was taking an oblique position, lowering its stern, and raising its prow. An introduction of water had been sufficient to disturb its equilibrium. Then, propelled by its powerful screw, it attacked the ice-field from below like a powerful battering-ram. It broke it in slightly, then drew back, drove at full speed against the field, which broke up, and at last, by a supreme effort, it sprang upon the frozen surface, which it crushed under its weight.

The panel was opened, I might say torn up, and the pure air rushed in to all parts of the *Nautilus*.

13

SQUIDS

I have no idea how I got to the platform. Perhaps the Canadian carried me there. But I was breathing, inhaling the vivifying air of the sea. My two companions were beside me, intoxicating themselves with the fresh particles.

Our strength promptly returned to us, and when I looked around me I saw that we were alone upon the platform. Not a man of the crew was there, not even Captain Nemo. The strange sailors of the *Nautilus* contented themselves with the air that circulated in the interior. Not one came to take delight in the open air.

The first words I uttered were words of thanks and gratitude to my two companions. Ned and Conseil had prolonged my existence during the last hours of this agony. All my gratitude was not too much for such self-sacrifice.

'Good, professor!' answered Ned Land. 'That is not worth speaking about. What merit had we in doing that? None. It was merely a question in arithmetic. Your existence was worth more than ours, therefore it had to be preserved.'

'My friends,' I answered, much moved, 'we are bound to one another for ever, and I am under an obligation.'

'Which I shall take advantage of,' replied the Canadian.

'What?' said Conseil.

'Yes,' continued Ned Land, 'by taking you with me when I leave this infernal *Nautilus*.'

'That reminds me,' said Conseil, 'are we going the right way?'

'Yes,' I answered, 'for we are going towards the sun, and here the sun is north.'

'Doubtless,' said Ned Land; 'but it remains to be seen if we are making for the Pacific or the Atlantic – that is to say, the frequented or solitary seas.'

That I could not answer, and I feared that Captain Nemo would take us to that vast ocean that bathes the coasts both of Asia and America. He would thus complete his journey round the submarine world, and would return to those seas where the *Nautilus* found the most entire independence. But if we returned to the Pacific, far from all inhabited land, what would become of Ned Land's projects?

We were soon to be apprised of this important fact. The *Nautilus* was going at great speed. The Polar circle was soon passed, and the vessel's head directed towards Cape Horn. We were abreast of the American point on 31 March at 7 p.m.

Then all our past sufferings were forgotten. The remembrance of our imprisonment under the ice faded from our minds. We only thought of the future. Captain Nemo appeared no more either in the saloon or on the platform. The bearings taken each day and marked upon the planisphere by the first officer allowed me to tell the exact direction of the *Nautilus*. That evening it became evident, to my great satisfaction, that we were going up north by the Atlantic route.

I told the result of my observations to the Canadian and Conseil.

'Good news,' said the Canadian; 'but where is the *Nautilus* going to?'

'I cannot tell, Ned.'

'Is its captain going to try the North Pole after the South, and return to the Pacific by the famous North-west Passage?'

'It would not do to defy him to do it,' answered Conseil.

'Well,' said the Canadian, 'we would part company beforehand.'

'In any case,' added Conseil, 'Captain Nemo is a great man, and we shall not regret having known him.'

'Especially when we have left him!' answered Ned Land.

For twelve days the *Nautilus* kept at not too great a distance from the coast of South America, heading north, but on 13 April we veered out to sea again. The captain evidently did not wish to frequent the waters of the Gulf of Mexico, or the seas of the Antilles. However, there would have been plenty of water, for the average depth of these seas is nine hundred fathoms; but probably these regions, strewn with islands and ploughed by steamers, did not suit Captain Nemo.

On 16 April we sighted Martinique and Guadaloupe, at a distance of about thirty miles. I caught a glimpse of their high peaks.

The Canadian, who counted upon putting his schemes into execution in the Gulf, either by reaching some land or hailing one of the numerous boats that coast from one island to another, was much put out. Flight would have been very practicable if Ned Land had been able to take possession of the boat without the knowledge of the captain. But in open ocean it was useless to think of it.

The Canadian, Conseil, and I had a rather long conversation on this subject. We had been prisoners on board the *Nautilus* for six months. We had come 17,000 leagues, and, as Ned Land said, there seemed no end to it. He therefore made a proposal that I did not expect. It was to ask Captain Nemo, once and for all, if he meant to keep us indefinitely in his vessel.

Such a proceeding was very repugnant to me, and I thought it useless. It was useless to expect anything from Captain Nemo, and we could only depend upon ourselves. Besides, for some time past, this man had become graver, more retiring, less sociable. He seemed to avoid me. I only met him at rare intervals. Formerly he took some pleasure in explaining the submarine marvels to me; now he left me to my studies and came no more to the saloon.

What change had come over him? For what cause? I had nothing to reproach myself with. Perhaps our presence on board was a burden to him. However, I did not think he was a man to restore us to liberty.

I therefore begged Ned Land to reflect well before acting. If what he did had no result, it would only excite suspicion and make our situation more painful. I may add that I could in no wise complain of our health. If we except the rude shock it received under the southern ice-bank, we had never been better. The wholesome food, the salubrious atmosphere, the regular life, the uniformity of temperature, prevented illness, and for a man to whom the remembrance of earth left no regret, for a Captain Nemo in his own vessel, I understand such an existence. But we had not broken all ties that bound us to humanity. For my own part, I did not wish my curious and novel studies to be buried with me. I had now the right of writing a true account of the sea, and I wished for that account to appear sooner or later.

On 20 April we rose to an average depth of 700 fathoms. The nearest land was then the archipelago of the Bahamas, scattered like a heap of stones on the surface of the sea. There rose high submarine cliffs, straight walls of corroded blocks, amongst which were black holes that our electric rays did not light up to their depths.

It was about eleven o'clock when Ned Land attracted my attention to a formidable swarming that was going on in the large seaweed.

'Well,' said I, 'there are veritable caverns of squids, and I should not be astonished to see some of those monsters. But friend Land is doubtless mistaken, for I see nothing.'

'I am sorry for that,' replied Conseil. 'I should like to contemplate face to face one of those squids I have heard so much talk about, that can drag ships down to the bottom of the sea. Those animals are called krakens.'

'None will ever make me believe that such animals exist,' said Ned Land.

'Why not?' answered Conseil. 'We all believed in monsieur's narwhal.'

'We were wrong, Conseil,' I pointed out.

'Certainly, but others believe in it still.'

'That is probable, Conseil; but, for my part, I am quite decided only to admit the existence of these monsters after I have dissected one with my own hand.'

'Then,' asked Conseil, 'monsieur does not believe in gigantic squids?'

'Who the dickens does?' cried the Canadian.

'Many people, friend Ned.'

'No fishermen. *Savants* do, perhaps.'

'Excuse me, Ned, both fishers and *savants*.'

'But I myself,' said Conseil seriously, 'I perfectly recollect having seen a large vessel being dragged under the waves by the arms of a cephalopod.'

'You have seen that?' asked the Canadian.

'Yes, Ned.'

'With your own eyes?'

'With my own eyes.'

'And where, pray?'

'At Saint Malo,' replied Conseil coolly.

'In the port?' said Ned Land ironically.

'No, in a church,' answered Conseil.

'In a church!' exclaimed the Canadian.

'Yes, friend Ned. It was a picture that represented the squid in question.'

'Good!' said Ned Land, laughing. 'Conseil is trying to do me.'

'However,' I said, 'in 1861, in the north-east of Teneriffe, nearly in the same latitude as we are in now, the crew of the despatch-boat *Alecton* perceived a monstrous squid swimming in its waters. The commander, Bouguer, approached the animal and attacked it with harpoons and cannon without much success, for cannon-balls and harpoons traversed the soft, fleshlike jelly. After several fruitless attempts the crew succeeded in throwing a running noose round the body of the mollusc; this noose slipped down to the caudal fins and there stopped. They tried to haul the monster on board, but its weight was so great that the cord cut its tail from its body, and, deprived of that ornament, it disappeared under the water.'

'A fact at last,' said Ned Land.

'And an indisputable fact, Ned. They proposed to call it a "Bouguer squid".'

'How long was it?' asked the Canadian.

'Did it not measure about eighteen feet?' said Conseil

who, posted at the window, was again examining the cliff.'

'Precisely,' I replied.

'Was not its head crowned with eight tentacles that moved about in the water like a nest of serpents?'

'Precisely.'

'And were not its eyes prominent and very large?'

'Yes, Conseil.'

'And was not its mouth a veritable parrot's beak, but a formidable beak.'

'Yes, Conseil.'

'Well, then, if monsieur will please to come to the window, he will see, if not the Bouguer squid, at least one of its brethren.'

I looked at Conseil. Ned Land rushed to the window.

'The frightful animal!' he cried. I looked in my turn, and could not restrain a movement of repulsion. Before my eyes was a monster worthy to figure in squid legends.

It was a squid of colossal dimensions, at least thirty-two feet long. It was swimming backwards with extreme velocity in the direction of the *Nautilus*. It was staring with its enormous green eyes; its eight arms, or rather eight feet, starting from its head, were twice as long as its body. We could distinctly see the 250 blowholes on the inner side of the tentacles under the form of semispherical capsules. Sometimes these blowholes fastened themselves on to the pane and made a vacuum. The mouth of the monster – a horned beak made like that of a parrot – opened and shut vertically. Its tongue, a horny substance armed with several rows of sharp teeth, came quivering out of this veritable pair of shears. Its body made a fleshy mass that must have weighed from 40,000 to 50,000 pounds. Its inconstant colour, changing with extreme rapidity according to the irritation of the animal, passed successively from livid grey to reddish brown.

'Perhaps it is the same as the *Alecton* one,' said Conseil.

'No,' answered the Canadian, 'for this one is entire, and the other had lost its tail.'

'That would not be a reason,' I replied. 'The arms and tail of these animals grow again, and in seven years the tail of the Bouguer has had plenty of time to grow.'

'Besides,' replied Ned, 'if it is not this one perhaps it is one of those!'

In fact, other squids had appeared at the port window. I counted seven. They formed a procession after the *Nautilus*, and I heard their beaks grating on the iron hull.

All at once the *Nautilus* stopped. A shock made it tremble in every joint.

'Can we be stranded?' I asked.

'Anyway,' answered the Canadian, 'we must be off again, for we are floating.'

The *Nautilus* was certainly floating, but it was not moving onwards. The branches of its screw were not beating the waves. A minute passed. Captain Nemo, followed by his first officer, came into the saloon.

I had not seen him for some time; he looked to me very gloomy. Without speaking to us, or, perhaps, even seeing us, he went to the panel, looked at the squids, and said a few words to his officer.

The latter went out. Soon the panels were closed. The ceiling was lighted up again.

I went towards the captain.

'A curious collection of squids,' I said in as indifferent a tone as an amateur might take before the crystal of an aquarium.

'Yes, professor,' he replied, 'and we are going to fight them face to face.'

I looked at the captain, thinking I had not rightly heard.

'Face to face?' I echoed.

'Yes, sir. The screw is stopped. I think that the horny mandibles of one of them are caught in its branches. That prevents us moving on.'

'And what are you going to do?'

'Go up to the surface and massacre all that vermin.'

'A difficult enterprise.'

'As you say. The electric bullets are powerless against their soft flesh, and where they do not find enough resistance to make them go off. But we will attack them with axes.'

'And with harpoons, sir,' said the Canadian, 'if you do not refuse my aid.'

'I accept it, Mr Land.'

'We will accompany you,' said I, and, following Captain Nemo, we went to the central staircase.

There about ten men armed with boarding hatchets were standing ready for the attack. Conseil and I took two hatchets. Ned Land seized a harpoon.

The *Nautilus* was then on the surface of the sea. One of the sailors, placed on the lowest steps, was unscrewing the bolts of the panel. But he had hardly finished before the panel was raised with extreme violence, evidently drawn up by a blowhole in the arm of a squid.

Immediately one of these long arms glided like a serpent through the opening, and twenty others were brandishing above it. With a blow of the hatchet Captain Nemo cut off this formidable tentacle, which glided twisting down the steps.

At the moment we were crowding together to get up to the platform, two other arms stretched down to a sailor placed in front of Captain Nemo, and drew him up with irresistible violence.

Captain Nemo uttered a cry and rushed out. We followed.

What a scene! The unhappy man, seized by the tentacle and fastened to its blowholes, was balanced in the air according to the caprice of this enormous trunk. He was choking, and cried out, 'A moi! A moi! – Help! help!' These French words caused me a profound stupor. Then I had a countryman on board, perhaps several! I shall hear that heart-rending cry all my life!

The unfortunate man was lost. Who would rescue him from that powerful grasp? Captain Nemo threw himself on the squid, and with his hatchet cut off another arm. His first officer was fighting with rage against other monsters that were climbing the sides of the *Nautilus*. The crew were fighting with hatchets.

The Canadian, Conseil, and I dug our arms into the fleshy masses. A violent smell of musk pervaded the atmosphere. It was horrible.

For an instant I believed that the unfortunate man, encircled by the squid, would be drawn away from its powerful suction. Seven of its eight arms had been cut off, one only brandishing its victim like a feather twisted about in the air. But at the very moment that Captain Nemo and his officer were rushing upon it, the animal hurled out a column of black liquid, secreted in a bag in its stomach. We were blinded by it. When this cloud was dissipated the squid had disappeared, and with it my unfortunate countryman!

With what rage we then set upon these monsters! Ten or twelve squids had invaded the platform and sides of the *Nautilus*. We rolled pell-mell amongst the serpents' trunks that wriggled about the platform in pools of blood and black ink. Ned Land's harpoon at each stroke plunged into the green eyes of the squid and put them out. But my brave companion was suddenly thrown over by one of the tentacles of a monster which he had not been able to avoid.

Ah, how my heart beat with emotion and horror! The

squid's formidable beak opened over Ned Land. The unfortunate man was about to be cut in two. I rushed to his aid. But Captain Nemo was before me. His hatchet disappeared in the two enormous mandibles, and, miraculously preserved, the Canadian rose and plunged the whole of his harpoon into the squid's triple heart.

'We are quits,' said Captain Nemo to the Canadian.

Ned bowed without answering.

This combat had lasted a quarter of an hour. The monsters, vanquished, mutilated, and death-stricken, left the place clear at last, and disappeared under the waves.

Captain Nemo, covered with blood, stood motionless near the lantern, and looked at the sea that had swallowed one of his companions, whilst tears rolled from his eyes.

14

THE GULF STREAM

We none of us can forget that terrible scene of 20 April. I wrote it under the impression of violent emotion. Since then I have revised it and read it to Conseil and the Canadian. They find it exact as to facts, but insufficient as to effect.

I said that Captain Nemo wept as he looked at the sea. His grief was immense. It was the second companion he had lost since our arrival on board. And what a death! This friend, crushed and stifled by the formidable arm of a squid, ground to pieces by its iron mandibles, was not destined to repose with his companions in the peaceful waters of the coral cemetery.

Amidst the struggle it was the cry of despair uttered by the unfortunate man that had wrung my heart. The poor Frenchman, forgetting his conventional language, had spoken the language of his country and his mother to utter his last appeal! Then I had a countryman amongst the crew of the *Nautilus*, associated body and soul with Captain Nemo, avoiding, like him, contact with men! Was he the only representative of France in this mysterious association, evidently composed of individuals of different nationalities? This was one more of the insoluble problems that ceaselessly came up in my mind.

Captain Nemo went back to his room, and I saw him no more for some time. But how sad, despairing, and irresolute he was, I judged by the vessel of which he was the soul, and which received all his impressions! The *Nautilus* no longer kept any determined direction. It went and came, floating like a lifeless thing on the waves. Its screw was free again, but was little used. It went about at random. But it could not tear itself away from the theatre of its last struggle – from that sea which had devoured one of its children.

On 8 May we were still abreast of Cape Hatteras, at the height of the North Carolinas. The Gulf Stream is seventy-five miles wide there, and one hundred and five fathoms deep. The *Nautilus* continued to move about at random. All supervision seemed banished from the vessel. I acknowledged that under those circumstances an escape might succeed. In fact, the inhabited shores offered easy refuges on all sides. The sea was incessantly ploughed by numerous steamers that run between New York or Boston and the Gulf of Mexico, and night and day by little schooners that do the coasting trade on the different points of the American coast. We might hope to be picked up.

But one vexatious circumstance thwarted the Canadian's schemes. The weather was very bad. We were approaching the regions where tempests are frequent. To tempt such a sea in a fragile boat was to court destruction. Ned Land agreed to that himself, and fretted his life away with nostalgia that nothing but flight could cure.

'Sir,' said he to me that day, 'there must be an end to this. I want to know how things stand. Your Nemo is going away from land, up north. But I declare to you that

I have had enough of the South Pole, and I won't follow him to the North Pole.'

'But what is to be done, Ned, as flight is impracticable just now?'

'I return to my first idea. The captain must be spoken to. You said nothing to him when he was in the seas of your country. I will speak now that we are in the seas of mine. When I think that before many days are over the *Nautilus* will be abreast of Nova Scotia, and that there, near Newfoundland, there is a wide bay, that into this bay the St Lawrence falls, that the St Lawrence is my river, the river of Quebec, my native town; when I think of that I am furious; my hair stands on end. I tell you, sir, I would rather throw myself into the sea! I will not stay here! I am stifled!'

The Canadian had evidently lost all patience. His vigorous nature could not get accustomed to this prolonged imprisonment. His countenance grew daily worse, his temper more sullen. I felt what he must suffer, for nostalgia had seized me too. Nearly seven months had gone by since we had heard any news of earth. What is more, Captain Nemo's isolation, his altered humour, especially since the fight with the squids, his taciturnity, all made me see things in a different light. I no longer felt the enthusiasm of the first days.

'Well, sir?' said Ned, seeing that I did not answer.

'Well, Ned, you want me to ask Captain Nemo what his intentions are concerning us?'

'Yes, sir.'

'Although he has already told them to you?'

'Yes. I want to be certain about it, once and for all. Speak for me only if you like.'

'But I rarely meet him. He even avoids me.'

'A greater reason for going to see him.'

'I will ask him, Ned.'

'When?' asked the Canadian, insisting.

'When I meet him.'

'M. Aronnax, do you want me to go to him?'

'No, leave it to me. Tomorrow –'

'Today,' said Ned Land.

'Very well. I will see him today,' replied I to the Canadian, who would have certainly compromised all by acting on his own account.

I remained alone. Once decided to ask, I resolved to have done with it immediately. I like things better done than about to be done.

I entered my room. There I heard some one walking about in Captain Nemo's. I could not let this occasion of meeting him slip. I knocked at the door. I obtained no answer. I knocked again, and then turned the handle. The door opened.

I entered. The captain was there. Bent over his work-table, he had heard nothing. Resolved not to go out without questioning him, I approached him. He raised his head suddenly, frowned, and said rather rudely:

'You here? What do you want?'

'To speak to you, captain.'

'But I am occupied, sir. I am at work. The liberty I allow you to shut yourself up, may I not enjoy it also?'

My reception was not very encouraging, but I was decided to hear everything in order to answer everything.

'Captain,' said I coldly, 'I have to speak to you on business that I cannot put off.'

'What can that be, sir?' he replied ironically. 'Have you made some discovery that has escaped me? Has the sea given up to you any fresh secret?'

We were far from the subject. Before I could answer, the captain pointed to a manuscript on the table, and said in a grave tone:

'Here is a manuscript written in several languages, M. Aronnax. It contains the account of my studies on the sea, and, if God so please, it shall not perish with me. This manuscript, signed by my own name, completed by the history of my life, will be enclosed in an insubmersible case. The last survivor of us all on board the *Nautilus* will throw this case into the sea, and it will go where the waves will carry it.'

The name of this man! His history written by himself! Then the mystery that surrounds him will be one day revealed? But at that moment I only saw in this communication an opening for me.

'Captain,' I answered, 'I can but approve the idea that influences you. The fruit of your studies must not be lost. But the means you employ seem to me very primitive. Who knows where the winds will carry that case, in what hands it will fall? Could you not find some better means? Could not you or one of yours –'

'Never, sir,' said the captain, interrupting me.

'But I and my companions will preserve your manuscript if you will give us liberty –'

'Liberty, sir?' said Captain Nemo, rising.

'Yes, captain, and that is the subject I wished to ask you about. We have now been seven months on your vessel, and I now ask you, in the name of my companions and myself, if you mean to keep us here always?'

'M. Aronnax,' said Captain Nemo, 'I have only the same answer to give you that I gave you seven months ago. Whoever enters my vessel never leaves it again.'

'But that is slavery!'

'Call it by what name you please.'

'But everywhere a slave keeps the right of recovering his liberty! Whatever means offer he has the right to consider them legitimate.'

'Who has denied you that right?' answered Captain

Nemo. 'Have I ever asked you to bind yourself by an oath?'

The captain looked at me and folded his arms.

'Sir,' I said to him, 'we shall neither of us care to return to this subject. But as we have begun it I must go on. To me study is a help, a powerful diversion, a passion that can make me forget anything. Like you, I could live ignored, obscure, in the hope of bequeathing to the future the result of my work, but there are other aspects of your life surrounded with complications and mysteries in which my companions and I alone have no part. It is this feeling of being strangers to everything that concerns you that makes our position unbearable, even for me, but much more for Ned Land. Every man, because he is man, is worth attention. Have you ever asked yourself what the love of liberty and hatred of slavery might arouse in a nature like that of the Canadian, what he might think or attempt –'

I was silent. Captain Nemo rose.

'It does not matter to me what Ned Land thinks or attempts. I did not take him; I do not keep him on board my vessel for my own pleasure. As to you, M. Aronnax, you are one of the few people who can understand anything, even silence. I have nothing more to answer you. This first time that you come to speak on this subject must also be the last, for I cannot even listen to you again.'

I withdrew. From that day our position was clear. I related our conversation to my two companions.

'We now know,' said Ned Land, 'that there is nothing to expect from that man. The *Nautilus* is approaching Long Island. We will escape, no matter what the weather is.'

But the sky became more and more threatening. Symptoms of a hurricane became manifest.

The tempest broke out on 18 May, just as the *Nautilus* was floating abreast of Long Island, at some miles from the port of New York. We were obliged to sink to twenty-five fathoms to find rest.

15

A HECATOMB

The storm had thrown us eastward once more. All hope of escaping on the shores of New York or the St Lawrence had vanished. Poor Ned, in despair, shut himself up like Captain Nemo. Conseil and I left each other no more.

On 30 May we sighted Land's End, between the extreme point of England and the Scilly Isles, which were left to starboard.

If the vessel was going to enter the Channel it must go direct east. It did not do so.

During the whole of 31 May the *Nautilus* described a series of circles on the water that greatly interested me. It seemed to be seeking a spot there was some difficulty in finding. At noon Captain Nemo came to take the bearings himself. He did not speak to me, and seemed gloomier than ever. What could sadden him thus? Was it his proximity to European shores? Was it some memory of the country he had abandoned? What was it he felt, remorse or regret? For a long time this thought haunted my mind, and I felt a kind of presentiment that before long chance would reveal the captain's secrets.

The next day, 1 June, the *Nautilus* continued the same manoeuvres. It was evidently trying to find a precise point in the ocean. Captain Nemo came to take the sun's altitude like he did the day before. The sea was calm, the sky pure. Eight miles to the east a large steamship appeared on the horizon. No flag fluttered from its mast, and I could not find out its nationality.

Some minutes before the sun passed the meridian Captain Nemo took his sextant and made his obervation with extreme precision. The absolute calm of the waters facilitated the operation. The motionless *Nautilus* neither pitched nor rolled.

At that moment I was upon the platform. When the captain had taken his observation he pronounced these words:

'It is here!'

He went down through the panel. Had he seen the ship that had tacked about, and seemed to be bearing down upon us? I cannot tell.

I returned to the saloon. The panel was shut, and I heard the water hissing into the reservoirs. The *Nautilus* began to sink vertically, its screw was stopped, and communicated no movement to it.

A few minutes later it stopped at a depth of 418 fathoms, and rested on the ground.

The luminous ceiling of the saloon was then extinguished, the panels were opened, and through the windows I saw the sea lighted up within a radius of half a mile by our electric lantern.

I looked through the larboard window and saw nothing but an immensity of tranquil water.

On the starboard appeared a large protuberance which attracted my attention. It looked like a ruin buried under a crust of whitish shells like a mantle of snow. Whilst attentively examining this mass I thought I recognized the swollen outlines of a ship, cleared of her masts, that must have gone down prow foremost. The disaster must have taken place at a distant epoch. This wreck, encrusted with lime, had been lying many years at the bottom of the ocean.

What was this ship? Why did the *Nautilus* come to visit its tomb? Was it only a wreck that had drawn the *Nautilus* under water?

I did not know what to think, when, near me, I heard Captain Nemo say in a slow voice:

'It is 74 years ago today, that in this same place this ship, after an heroic fight, dismasted, the water in her hold, the third of her crew disabled, preferred to sink with her 356 sailors than to surrender, and, nailing her colours to her stern, disappeared under the waves to the cry of "Vive la République!"'

'The *Vengeur*!' I exclaimed.

'Yes, sir. The *Vengeur*! A glorious name!' murmured the captain as he folded his arms.

The unexpectedness of this scene and the way it was spoken of, the account of the patriotic ship, given coldly at first, and then the emotion with which the strange person had uttered his last words, this name of *Vengeur*, the signification of which could not escape me, all struck my imagination profoundly. My eyes no longer left the captain. He, with hands stretched out to the sea, was looking with ardent eyes at the glorious wreck. Perhaps I never was to know who he was, from whence he came, whither he was going, but I saw the man separate himself more and more from the *savant*. It was not a vulgar misanthropy that had enclosed Captain Nemo and his companions in the sides of the *Nautilus*, but a monstrous or sublime hatred that time could not quench.

Did this hatred still seek vengeance? The future was soon to tell me that.

In the meantime the *Nautilus* was slowly ascending to the surface of the sea, and I saw the confused outlines of the *Vengeur* gradually disappear. Soon a slight pitching told me we were floating in the open air.

At that moment a dull detonation was heard. I looked at the captain, but he did not stir.

'Captain?' I said.

He did not answer.

I left him and went up on to the platform. Conseil and the Canadian had preceded me there.

'What was that noise?' I asked.

'A gunshot,' answered Ned Land.

I looked in the direction of the ship I had perceived before. She had neared the *Nautilus*, and was putting on more steam. Six miles separated us from her.

For a quarter of an hour we went on looking at the ship that was bearing down upon us. Still I did not think she had sighted the *Nautilus* at that distance, still less did she know what it was.

The Canadian soon announced that this vessel was a large warship, a two-decker, and an ironclad with a ram.

Thick black smoke was issuing from her two funnels. Her reefed sails could not be distinguished from her yards. She bore no colours. Distance prevented us making out the colour of her pendant, which streamed like a narrow ribbon.

She was rapidly approaching. If Captain Nemo allowed her to come near it would offer us a chance of escape.

'Sir,' said Ned Land to me, 'if that ship passes within a mile of us I shall throw myself into the sea, and I advise you to do the same.'

I did not answer the Canadian's proposition, and went on looking at the ship, which grew gradually larger. Whether she were English, French, American, or Russian, she would certainly take us in if we could reach her.

'Monsieur will please to remember that we have had some experience in swimming. He can leave me the care of towing him towards the ship if it suits him to follow Ned,' said Conseil.

I was going to answer when some white smoke issued from the prow of the vessel. Then, a few seconds afterwards the water aft of the *Nautilus* was thrown up by the fall of some heavy body. In a short time we heard the report.

'Why, they are firing at us!' I exclaimed.

'Good people!' muttered the Canadian. 'Then they do not take us for shipwrecked men on a raft!'

'If monsieur will allow me to say so, that's right,' said Conseil, shaking off the water that another shot had sprinkled him with. 'If monsieur will allow me to say so, they have sighted the narwhal, and are firing at the narwhal.'

'But they must see that they have men to deal with!' I exclaimed.

'Perhaps that is the reason,' answered Ned Land, looking at me.

Quite a revelation was made in my mind. They doubtless knew now what to think about the existence of the pretended monster. Doubtless Captain Farragut had found out that the *Nautilus* was a submarine boat, and more dangerous than a supernatural cetacean when it struck against the *Abraham Lincoln*.

Yes, it must be so, and they were doubtless pursuing the terrible engine of destruction in every sea.

Terrible if, as might be supposed, Captain Nemo was employing the *Nautilus* in a work of vengeance. During that night when he had imprisoned us in the cell, in the Indian Ocean, had he not attacked some ship? The man now interred in the coral cemetery, was he not a victim of the shock provoked by the *Nautilus*? Yes, I repeat, it must be so. A part of the mysterious existence of Captain Nemo was revealed. And if his identity was not found out, at least nations coalesced against him, chasing now no illusory being, but a man who had vowed them implacable hatred!

All the formidable past appeared before my eyes. Instead of meeting with friends on the ship that was approaching, we should only find pitiless enemies.

In the meantime cannon-balls were multiplying round us. Some, meeting the liquid surface, ricocheted to considerable distances. But none reached the *Nautilus*.

The ironclad was then not more than three miles off. Notwithstanding the violent cannonade, Captain Nemo did not make his appearance on the platform. And yet if one of these conical shots had struck the hull of the *Nautilus* in a normal line it would have been fatal to it.

The Canadian then said to me:

'Sir, we ought to attempt anything to get out of this. Let us make signals! *Mille diables!* They will perhaps understand that we are honest men!'

Ned Land took out his handkerchief to wave it in the air. But he had hardly spread it out than, floored by a grasp of iron, notwithstanding his prodigious strength, he fell on the platform.

'Wretch!' cried the captain. 'Do you want me to nail you to the ram of the *Nautilus* before it rushes against that ship?'

Captain Nemo, terrible to hear, was still more terrible to behold. His face had grown pale under the spasms of his heart, which must for an instant have ceased to beat. The pupils of his eyes were fearfully contracted. His voice no longer spoke, it roared. With body bent forward, he shook the Canadian by the shoulders.

Then leaving him, and turning to the ironclad, whose shots rained round him, he said:

'Ah! You know who I am, ship of a cursed nation!' cried he in a powerful voice. 'I do not need to see your colours to recognize you! Look, I will show you mine!'

And Captain Nemo spread out a black flag in the front of the platform like the one he had planted at the South Pole.

At that moment a projectile struck the hull of the *Nautilus* obliquely, and, ricocheting near the captain, fell into the sea.

Captain Nemo shrugged his shoulders. Then, speaking to me:

'Go down,' he said in a curt tone, 'go down, you and your companions.'

'Sir,' I cried, 'are you going to attack that ship?'

'Sir, I am going to sink it!'

'You will not do that.'

'I shall do it!' replied Captain Nemo. 'Do not take upon yourself to judge me, sir. Fate has shown you what you were not to see. The attack has been made. The repulse will be terrible. Go down below.'

'What is that ship?'

'You do not know? Well, so much the better! Its nationality, at least, will remain a secret to you. Go below.'

The Canadian, Conseil and I were obliged to obey. About fifteen of the *Nautilus*'s crew had surrounded the captain, and were looking with an implacable feeling of hatred at the ship that was advancing towards them. We felt that the same feeling of vengeance animated them all.

I went down as another projectile struck the *Nautilus*, and I heard its captain exclaim:

'Strike, mad vessel! Shower your useless shot! You will not escape the ram of the *Nautilus*! But this is not the place you are to perish in! Your ruins shall not mix with those of the *Vengeur*!'

I went to my room. The captain and his officer remained on the platform. The screw was put in movement. The *Nautilus* speedily put itself out of range of the ship. But the pursuit went on, and Captain Nemo contented himself with keeping his distance.

About 4 p.m. I could not contain the impatience and anxiety that devoured me, and returned to the central staircase. The panel was opened. I ventured on to the platform. The captain was walking about it still in agitation. He was looking at the vessel, which was lying five or six miles to leeward. Perhaps he hesitated to attack her.

I wished to intervene once again. But I had hardly spoken to Captain Nemo when he imposed silence on me, saying:

'I represent right and justice here! I am the oppressed, and there is the oppressor! It is through it that all I loved, cherished, and venerated – country, wife, children, father and mother – all perished! All that I hate is there! Be silent!'

I looked for the last time at the ironclad, which was putting on more steam. Then I went back to Ned and Conseil.

'We must fly!' I cried.

'Well,' said Ned, 'what ship is it?'

'I do not know. But whatever it is it will be sunk before night. In any case it is better to perish also than to be the accomplices of a retaliation the justice of which we cannot judge.'

'I think so too,' answered Ned Land coldly. 'We must wait till night.'

Night came. Profound silence reigned on board. The compass indicated that the *Nautilus* had not changed its direction. I heard its screw beating the waves with rapid regularity. It kept on the surface of the water, and a slight rolling sent it from side to side.

My companions and I had resolved to fly when the vessel was near enough either to hear or see us, for the moon, that would be full three days later, shone brightly. Once on board the vessel, if we could not prevent the blow that threatened her, we could at least do all that circumstances would allow us to attempt. I thought several times that the *Nautilus* was preparing for the attack. But it contented itself with allowing its adversary to approach, and a short time afterwards fled away again.

A part of the night passed without incident. We were awaiting an occasion to act. We spoke little, being too much excited. Ned Land wanted to throw himself into the sea. I made him wait. I thought the *Nautilus* would attack the two-decker on the surface of the sea, and then it would not only be possible but easy to escape.

At 3 a.m., being uneasy, I went up on to the platform. Captain Nemo had not left it. He was standing near his flag, which a slight breeze was waving over his head. He did not lose sight of the vessel. His look, of extraordinary intensity, seemed to attract her, fascinate her, and draw her onward more surely than if he had been towing her.

The ship kept at two miles' distance from us. She kept approaching the phosphorescent light that indicated the presence of the *Nautilus*. I could see her green and red lights and white lantern hung from her mainstay. An indistinct reflection lighted up her rigging and showed that the fires were heated to the uttermost. Sparks and flames were escaping from her funnels and starring the atmosphere.

I remained thus till 4 a.m. without Captain Nemo appearing to perceive me. The vessel was a mile and a half off, and with the break of day her cannonade began again. The moment could not be distant when, the *Nautilus* attacking its adversary, my companions and I would for ever leave this man whom I dared not judge.

I was about to go down to tell them about it when the officer came up on the platform. Several sailors accompanied him. Captain Nemo either did not or would not see them. Certain precautions were taken, which might be called the clearing up for the fight. They were very simple. The iron balustrade was lowered. The lantern and pilot-cages were sunk into the hull until they were on a level with the deck. The surface of the long steel-plated cigar no longer offered a single salient point that could hinder its manoeuvres.

I returned to the saloon. The *Nautilus* was still above the water. Some morning beams were filtering through their liquid bed. Under certain undulations of the waves the windows were lighted up with the red beams of the rising sun. The dreadful 2 June had dawned.

At 5 a.m. the log showed me that the speed of the *Nautilus* was slackening. I understood that it was letting the ship approach. Besides, the firing was more distinctly heard, and the projectiles, ploughing up the surrounding water, were extinguished with a strange hissing noise.

'My friends,' said I, 'the time is come. One grasp of the hand, and may God help us!'

Ned Land was resolute, Conseil calm, I nervous, scarcely able to contain myself.

We all passed into the library. As I was opening the door that gave on to the cage of the central staircase I heard the upper panel shut with a bang.

The Canadian sprang up the steps, but I stopped him. A well-known hissing sound told me that they were letting water into the reservoirs. In a few minutes' time the *Nautilus* sank a few yards below the surface of the sea.

I now understood its manoeuvre. It was too late to do

anything. The *Nautilus* did not think of striking the two-decker in her impenetrable armour, but below her water-line, where her metal covering no longer protected her.

We were again imprisoned, unwilling witnesses to the fatal drama that was preparing. We had hardly time to reflect. Taking refuge in my room, we looked at each other without speaking a word. A profound stupor took possession of my mind. My thoughts seemed to stand still. I was in that painful state of expectation that precedes a dreadful crash. I waited and listened. I was all ears.

In the meantime the speed of the *Nautilus* visibly increased. It was taking a spring. All its hull vibrated.

Suddenly I uttered a cry. A shock had taken place, but a relatively slight one. I felt the penetrating force of the steel ram. I heard a grating, scraping sound. But the *Nautilus*, carried along by its force of propulsion, passed through the mass of the ship like a needle through sailcloth.

I could stand it no longer. I rushed like a madman into the saloon.

Captain Nemo was there. Mute, sombre, implacable, he was looking through the port panel.

An enormous mass was sinking through the water, and, in order to lose nothing of its agony, the *Nautilus* was sinking with it. At thirty feet from me I saw the broken hull, into which the water was rushing with a noise like thunder, then the double line of guns and bulwarks. The deck was covered with black moving shades.

The water rose. The unfortunate creatures were crowding in the ratlines, clinging to the masts, struggling in the water. It was a human ant-hill inundated by the sea!

Paralysed, stiffened with anguish, my hair standing on end, eyes wide open, panting, breathless, voiceless, I looked too. An irresistible attraction glued me to the window.

The enormous ship sank slowly. The *Nautilus*, following her, watched all her movements. All at once an explosion took place. The compressed air blew up the decks of the ship as though her magazines had been set fire to. The water was so much disturbed that the *Nautilus* swerved.

Then the unfortunate ship sank more rapidly. Her tops, loaded with victims, appeared; then her spars, bending under the weight of men; then the summit of her mainmast. Then the dark mass disappeared, and with it the dead crew, drawn down by a formidable eddy.

I turned to Captain Nemo. That terrible avenger, a perfect archangel of hatred, was still looking. When all was over he went to the door of his room, opened it, and went in. I followed him with my eyes.

On the end panel, below his heroes, I saw the portrait of a woman still young, and two little children. Captain Nemo looked at them for a few moments, held out his arms to them, and, kneeling down, burst into sobs.

16

CAPTAIN NEMO'S LAST WORDS

The panels were closed on this frightful vision, but light had not been restored to the saloon. In the interior of the *Nautilus* reigned darkness and silence. It was leaving this place of desolation, a hundred feet under the water, at a prodigious speed. Where was it going – north or south? Where was the man flying to after this horrible retaliation?

I went back to my room, where Ned and Conseil had silently stopped. I felt an insurmountable horror of Captain Nemo. Whatever he may have suffered he had no right to punish thus. He had made me, if not his accomplice, at least the witness of his vengeance! That was too much!

At eleven o'clock the electric light reappeared. I went into the saloon and consulted the different instruments. The *Nautilus* was flying north at a speed of twenty-five miles an hour, sometimes on the surface of the sea, sometimes thirty feet below it.

By taking our bearings on the chart I saw that we were passing the entrance to the English Channel, and that we were going to the north seas at a frightful speed.

In the evening we had traversed two hundred leagues

of the Atlantic. Night came, and the sea was dark till the moon rose.

I went to my room, but could not sleep. I was assailed by nightmare. The horrible scene of destruction was repeated in my mind.

From that day who could tell where the *Nautilus* took us in this north Atlantic basin? Always with inappreciable speed. Always amidst the hyperborean mists.

I estimate – but perhaps I am mistaken – that this adventurous course of the *Nautilus* lasted fifteen or twenty days, and I do not know how long it would have lasted but for the catastrophe that ended this voyage. Captain Nemo never appeared, nor his officer. Not a man of the crew was visible for an instant. The *Nautilus* kept below the water almost incessantly. When it went up to the surface to renew the air, the panels opened and shut mechanically. The bearings were no longer reported on the chart. I did not know where we were.

I must say also that the Canadian, out of all patience, did not appear either. Conseil could not get a word out of him, and feared that in an access of delirium, and under the influence of dreadful nostalgia, he might kill himself. He watched over him, therefore, with constant devotion.

It will be understood that under such circumstances the situation was no longer bearable.

One morning – I do not know its date – I had fallen into an uneasy slumber at early dawn. When I woke I saw Ned Land bending over me, and heard him whisper:

'We are going to fly!'

I sat up.

'When?' I asked.

'Tonight. All supervision seems to have disappeared from the *Nautilus*. Stupor seems to reign on board. Shall you be ready, sir?'

'Yes. Where are we?'

'In sight of land that I have just sighted through the mist, twenty miles to the east.'

'What land is it?'

'I do not know, but whatever it is we will seek refuge on it.'

'Yes! Ned – yes, we will go tonight, even should the sea swallow us up!'

'The sea is rough, the wind violent, but twenty miles in that light boat of the *Nautilus* do not frighten me. I have put some provisions and a few bottles of water in it without the knowledge of the crew.'

'I will follow you.'

'Besides,' added the Canadian, 'if I am caught, I shall defend myself and get killed.'

'We will die together, friend Ned.'

I had made up my mind to anything. The Canadian left me. I went up on the platform, where I could scarcely stand against the waves. The sky was threatening, but as land lay there in those thick mists, we must fly. We must not lose a day nor an hour.

I went down to the saloon both fearing and wishing to meet Captain Nemo, both wanting and not wanting to see him. What could I say to him? Could I hide from him the involuntary horror he inspired me with? No! It was better not to find myself face to face with him! Better to forget him! And yet –

What a long day was the last I had to pass on board the *Nautilus*! I remained alone. Ned Land and Conseil avoided me, so as not to betray us by talking.

At 6 p.m. I dined, but without appetite. I forced myself to eat notwithstanding my repugnance, wishing to keep up my strength.

At half-past six Ned Land entered my room. He said to me:

'We shall not see each other again before our departure. At ten o'clock the moon will not yet be up. We shall take advantage of the darkness. Come to the boat. Conseil and I will be waiting for you there.'

Then the Canadian went out without giving me time to answer.

I wished to verify the direction of the *Nautilus*. I went to the saloon. We were going NNE with frightful speed, at a depth of twenty-five fathoms.

I looked for the last time at all the natural marvels and riches of art collected in this museum, in this unrivalled collection destined one day to perish in the depths of the sea with the man who had made it. I wished to take a supreme impression of it in my mind. I remained thus for an hour, bathed in the light of the luminous ceiling, and passing in review the shining treasures in their glass cases. Then I went back to my room.

There I put on my solid sea-garments. I collected my notes together and placed them carefully about me. My heart beat loudly. I could not check its pulsations. Certainly my agitation would have betrayed me to Captain Nemo.

What was he doing at that moment? I listened at the door of his room. I heard a noise of footsteps: Captain Nemo was there. He had not gone to bed. At every movement that he made I thought he was going to appear and ask me why I wanted to escape! I was constantly on the alert. My imagination magnified everything. This impression became so poignant that I asked myself if I had not better enter the captain's room, see him face to face, dare him with look and gesture!

It was a madman's inspiration. I restrained myself happily, and lay down on my bed to stay the agitation of my body. My nerves gradually grew calmer, but in my excited brain I passed in review my whole existence on board this *Nautilus*, all the happy or unfortunate incidents that had occurred since my disappearance from the *Abraham Lincoln*, the submarine hunts, Torres Straits, the Papuan savages, the stranding, the coral cemetery, the Suez tunnel, Santorin Island, the Cretan plunger, Vigo Bay, Atlantis, the ice-bank, the South Pole, the imprisonment in ice, the fight with the squids, the *Vengeur*, and that horrible scene of the sunken ship and her crew! All these events passed through my mind like the background to a scene at the theatre. Then Captain Nemo grew out of all proportion in this strange medium. He was no longer a man like me, but the genius of the sea. It was then half-past nine. I held my head in my hands to prevent it bursting. I closed my eyes, and was determined to think no more. Another half-hour to wait! Another half-hour's nightmare would drive me mad!

At that moment I heard the vague chords of the organ, a sad harmony under an indefinable melody, veritable wails of a soul that wished to break all terrestrial ties. I listened with all my senses, hardly breathing, plunged, like Captain Nemo, in one of those musical ecstasies which took him beyond the limits of this world.

Then a sudden thought terrified me. Captain Nemo had left his room. He was in the saloon that I was obliged to cross in my flight. There I should meet him for the last time. He would see me, perhaps speak to me. A gesture from him could annihilate me, a single word could chain me to his vessel.

Ten o'clock was on the point of striking. The moment had come to leave my room and rejoin my companions.

I could not hesitate even should Captain Nemo stand before me. I opened my door with precaution, and yet it seemed to make a fearful noise. Perhaps that noise only existed in my imagination.

I felt my way along the dark waist of the *Nautilus*,

stopping at every step to suppress the beatings of my heart.

I reached the corner door of the saloon and opened it softly. The saloon was quite dark. The tones of the organ were feebly sounding. Captain Nemo was there. He did not see me. I think that in a full light he would not have perceived me, he was so absorbed.

I dragged myself over the carpet, avoiding the least contact, lest the noise should betray my presence. It took me five minutes to reach the door into the library.

I was going to open it when a sigh from Captain Nemo nailed me to the place. I understood that he had got up. I even saw him, for some rays from the lighted library reached the saloon. He came towards me with folded arms, silent, gliding rather than walking, like a ghost. His oppressed chest heaved with sobs, and I heard him murmur these words – the last I heard:

'Almighty God! Enough! Enough!'

Was it remorse that was escaping thus from the conscience of that man?

Desperate, I rushed into the library, went up the central staircase, and, following the upper waist, reached the boat through the opening that had already given passage to my two companions.

'Let us go! Let us go!' I cried.

'At once,' answered the Canadian.

The orifice in the plates of the *Nautilus* was first shut and bolted by means of a wrench that Ned Land had provided himself with. The opening in the boat was also closed, and the Canadian began to take out the screws that still fastened us to the submarine vessel.

Suddenly a noise was heard in the interior. Voices answered one another quickly. What was the matter? Had they discovered our flight? I felt Ned Land glide a dagger into my hand.

'Yes!' I murmured. 'We shall know how to die!'

The Canadian had stopped in his work. But one word, twenty times repeated, a terrible word, revealed to me the cause of the agitation on board the *Nautilus*. It was not we the crew were anxious about.

'The Maëlstrom! The Maëlstrom!' they were crying.

The Maëlstrom! Could a more frightful word in a more frightful situation have sounded in our ears? Were we then on the most dangerous part of the Norwegian shore? Was the *Nautilus* being dragged into a gulf at the very moment our boat was preparing to leave its side?

It is well known that at the tide the pent-up waters between the Feroë and Loffoden Islands rush out with irresistible violence. They form a whirlpool from which no ship could ever escape. From every point of the horizon rush monstrous waves. They form the gulf justly called 'Navel of the Ocean', of which the power of attraction extends for a distance of ten miles. There not only vessels but whales and bears from the boreal region are sucked up.

It was there that the *Nautilus* had been voluntarily or involuntarily run by its captain. It was describing a spiral, the circumference of which was lessening by degrees. Like it, the boat fastened to it was whirled round with giddy speed. I felt it. I felt the sick sensation that succeeds a long-continued movement of gyration. We were horror-stricken with suspended circulation, annihilated by nervous influence, covered with cold sweat like that of death! What noise surrounded our fragile boat! What roaring, which echo repeated at a distance of several miles! What an uproar was that of the water breaking on the sharp rocks at the bottom, where the hardest bodies are broken, where the trunks of trees are worn away!

What a situation! We were frightfully tossed about. The *Nautilus* defended itself like a human being. Its steel muscles cracked. Sometimes it stood upright, and we with it!

'We must hold on and screw down the bolts again,' said Ned Land. 'We may still be saved by keeping to the *Nautilus* –'

He had not finished speaking when a crash took place. The screws were torn out, and the boat, torn from its groove, sprang like a stone from a sling into the midst of the whirlpool.

My head struck on its iron framework, and with the violent shock I lost all consciousness.

17

CONCLUSION

So ended this voyage under the sea. What happened during that night, how the boat escaped the formidable eddies of the Maëlstrom, how Ned Land, Conseil, and I got out of the gulf, I have no idea. But when I came to myself I was lying in the hut of a fisherman of the Loffoden Isles. My two companions, safe and sound, were by my side pressing my hands. We shook hands heartily.

At this moment we cannot think of going back to France. Means of communication between the north of Norway and the south are rare. I am, therefore, obliged to wait for the steamer that runs twice a month to Cape North.

It is here, therefore, amidst the honest folk who have taken us in, that I revise the account of these adventures. It is exact. Not a fact has been omitted, not a detail exaggerated. It is a faithful narrative of an incredible expedition in an element inaccessible to man, and to which progress will one day open up a road.

Shall I be believed? I do not know. After all, it matters little. All I can now affirm is my right to speak of the seas under which, in less than ten months, I journeyed

twenty thousand leagues during that submarine tour of
the world that has revealed so many marvels of the
Pacific, the Indian Ocean, Red Sea, Mediterranean,
Atlantic, and the austral and boreal seas!

But what has become of the *Nautilus*? Has it resisted
the pressure of the Maëlstrom? Is Captain Nemo still
alive? Is he still pursuing his frightful retaliations under
the ocean, or did he stop before that last hecatomb?
Will the waves one day bring the manuscript that contains the whole history of his life? Shall I know at last the
name of the man? Will the ship that has disappeared tell
us by its nationality the nationality of Captain Nemo?

I hope so. I also hope that his powerful machine has
conquered the sea in its most terrible gulf, and that the
Nautilus has survived where so many other ships have
perished! If it is so, if Captain Nemo still inhabits the
ocean, his adopted country, may hatred be appeased in
his savage heart! May the contemplation of so many
marvels extinguish in him the desire of vengeance! May
the judge disappear, and the *savant* continue his peaceful
exploration of the sea! If his destiny is strange, it is
sublime also. Have I not experienced it myself? Have
I not lived ten months of this unnatural life? Two men
only have a right to answer the question asked in the
Ecclesiastes 6,000 years ago, 'That which is far off and
exceeding deep, who can find it out?' These two men are
Captain Nemo and I.

Dragon's Rock

Other books by Tim Bowler

Midget
River Boy
Shadows

Dragon's Rock

Tim Bowler

Oxford University Press

Oxford   New York   Toronto

Oxford University Press, Great Clarendon Street, Oxford OX2 6DP

Oxford New York
Athens Auckland Bangkok Bogotá Buenos Aires Calcutta
Cape Town Chennai Dar es Salaam Delhi Florence Hong Kong Istanbul
Karachi Kuala Lumpur Madrid Melbourne Mexico City Mumbai
Nairobi Paris São Paulo Singapore Taipei Tokyo Toronto Warsaw

and associated companies in
Berlin Ibadan

Oxford is a trade mark of Oxford University Press

500 454006 First published 1995
First published in this paperback edition 1999

British Library Cataloguing in Publication Data
Data available

Cover illustration by Sam Hadley

ISBN 0 19 275036 4

Printed in Great Britain by Cox & Wyman Ltd, Reading, Berkshire

For my Mother and Father

'That only which we have within, can we see without. If we meet no gods, it is because we harbour none.'

RALPH WALDO EMERSON

1

That day it came for him again.

He remembered leaning back and resting, and rocking to the motion of the train. And closing his eyes.

The next moment it was upon him, racing like an angry fire through the landscape of his sleep. He ran, gasping for air in the stifling heat of its breath, but it was no good. He was already starting to weaken, starting to give up. And he could feel it drawing closer, closer, roaring its fury after him. Any moment now it would appear, any moment now he would have to face it and suffer for the wrong he sensed he had done it. Any moment now he would—

'The next station will be Exeter St Davids. Exeter St Davids the next station. Thank you.'

He blinked his eyes open, unsure for a moment whether he was still dreaming.

But there was no dragon before him. Only a man watching him over the top of his newspaper.

'Are you all right, lad?'

'What . . . what do—?'

'You were moaning while you were asleep.'

He looked out of the window at the fields rushing past.

'I'm all right, it's just . . . just—'

'A bad dream maybe.'

'Yes,' he said quickly. 'A bad dream. And something . . . '

He stared over the wintry land as far as the horizon.

Something I've got to put right.

He closed his eyes once more, but this time resisted sleep. Sleep had become a place of fear, a place where the dragon hunted him; and so it had been since that first fateful visit

1

six years ago. But now he had a chance, to go back and put things right, and start to live again. And perhaps then the dragon would let him be.

He opened his eyes again, ignored the man's quizzical glance and looked up at the sky, and for a while found his mind drifting away from the dragon. To the farm, the fields, the forest, his nervousness about seeing Toby again; but most of all to the things that had haunted him since that visit. The things he had seen but would never forget.

And one in particular, though he'd glimpsed it for but a second.

The face of a frightened woman.

The knife flashed and Toby smiled as he often did when he was whittling and found he'd poked his tongue out. But then whittling needs concentration, he decided, and you can't concentrate without poking your tongue out.

Chip, chip, chip.

The bits flew down on the grass, and he smiled again. There was always something reassuring about the feel of wood. He glanced at the sheep-dog curled at his feet.

Feigning sleep probably but he knew Flash would only need a sniff of action to be up and bounding. For a moment he stopped whittling and watched the slow movement of the stomach, in and out, regular and relaxed, as though nothing were really wrong after all. As if to remind him of reality, he heard his father call.

'Toby!'

He looked over his shoulder towards the paddock fence.

'Here!'

'What are you doing?'

'Whittling.'

'Is Flash with you?'

He wished Dad wouldn't keep asking, even if it was for the best of reasons.

'Yes!'

2

He heard his father thrust something into the shed, then close the door and clip the latch. A moment later he appeared round the corner, his arms bare despite the December chill.

'Good, I thought he might have . . . you know—'

'He's been with me for the last hour.'

As though sensing they were talking about him, Flash rolled over on his back, looking from one to the other. Dad bent down and ran his hand through the fur.

'You think I'm being over-cautious, don't you? But you know what he's like for running off.' He nodded towards the western fields. 'Specially that way. We can't take any chances. I saw her on our land again this morning when I was out. She was watching him.'

'Gordon saw her yesterday.'

'So we've got to be careful. You ready?'

'Suppose so.'

'Come on, it won't be that bad and you promised you'd try. We'd better get going. We don't want to be late.'

Yes, we do, Toby thought, but he followed Dad through the gate and down the muddy path to the house.

'Do it for your mum and me,' Dad said, stopping by the door. 'I mean, you wouldn't like it if you were stuck at a boarding-school in England while we were away in Hong Kong. You wouldn't want to spend Christmas on your own.'

'But you said they'd have paid for him to go out to Hong Kong for Christmas.'

'They gave him the choice. Said if he wanted, they'd pay for him to fly out, otherwise he could stay with us since we'd offered to put him up.'

'So why isn't he going out there?'

'Because he particularly wanted to come here. He said so.'

'But why?'

'I don't know.' Dad looked at him tetchily. 'Look, we've been through all this.'

3

Mum's face appeared round the door.

'Where's Flash? Is he with you?'

As though in reply the dog bounded into the house and through to the kitchen. Dad watched for a moment, then reached inside the door for his coat.

'Right, Toby.'

Totnes Station had a deserted air. Toby looked up and down the platforms but apart from Dad and himself, there was no one to be seen. The little café was shut, the waiting-room was empty, there were no sounds of movement or voices; it might have been a ghost station, waiting for a spectral train that would never come.

He frowned.

This train would come.

He looked down the track and to his relief saw no sign of it. A pied wagtail flitted over the station fence and ran along the track for a few yards before flying off again. He pulled his coat collar up and burrowed his chin deeper.

'Half-past three,' said Dad. 'Train's late.'

Toby glanced up and saw the sky already darkening. Let it be late, he thought, let it never come, let it go somewhere else. Then he heard the tinkling in the rails.

He cocked his head to one side and listened, wondering whether Dad had heard it too. A door banged behind them and a station official strode past them to the edge of the platform.

' 'Nother cold day,' said Dad.

The man peered down the line for a few seconds, but eventually managed a nod.

'We'll have a white Christmas yet.'

There was the train; he could see it now, a huge, hateful serpent snaking its way towards them until finally the engine and the first of the carriages swept past the platform. He glared at it, wishing it would rattle on to Plymouth without stopping.

4

But it slowly came to a halt; and now all he could pray for was that no one would get off. But that was certainly too much to hope.

Dad started forward.

'There he is.'

A door had opened and a small figure was climbing down.

Toby stared, trying to remember the picture in his mind of six years ago. The hair was longer, but it was still the same revolting blond, and even from here he could see the pale, unhealthy-looking skin. And the glasses were even more ridiculous than the last ones he had.

Dad bustled ahead.

'Benjamin! Welcome! Toby, get that suitcase.'

Toby was still studying Benjamin and he found he liked what he saw even less than last time. He's still got that funny way of looking past you, he thought, not meeting your eyes properly, and—

'Toby! Suitcase!'

Benjamin's lip quivered.

'It's all right, I can—'

Toby reached up and took the suitcase.

'No problem.'

'Thank you,' said Benjamin.

They set off down the platform, Toby hanging back slightly and watching with amusement as Benjamin struggled to keep up with Dad's vigorous pace.

'How's boarding-school?' he heard Dad say.

'Not very nice. Did . . . did you have to wait long?'

'Couple of minutes.'

'Ten!' Toby called.

He ignored the backward glance from his father and continued to study Benjamin.

It was pathetic.

He was out of breath already, panting and gasping like on a cross-country run, and he wasn't even carrying his suitcase. The prospect of Christmas and two weeks of Benjamin looked bleaker than ever.

They had reached the exit now and, as Toby expected, there was an interminable wait while Benjamin looked for his ticket, first trying this pocket, then that, before eventually finding it stuffed inside his handkerchief. But at last they were out of the station and heading up the road.

Even that was too good to be true. They hadn't gone ten yards before Benjamin stopped.

'Haven't you got . . . ?'

Dad looked round.

'Something wrong?'

'I just thought . . . maybe you'd have a car with you.'

Toby rolled his eyes. Fifteen miles from home and he thinks we're travelling on foot; this is going to be even worse than last time. Dad nodded up the road.

'We've got a car. See?'

'Isn't that a Land Rover?'

Toby saw the first sign of frustration on Dad's face, but the voice resolutely betrayed none of it.

'That's right, a Land Rover. Seen better days too, but it'll get us home. Right, Toby?'

'Nothing posh in our family.'

'Of course not.' Benjamin nodded quickly, as though anxious to show agreement.

Dad walked over to the driver's door and started to unlock it. Benjamin turned to Toby.

'Your father—'

'What about him?'

'He . . . he looks different.'

'Lost some hair probably.'

Benjamin's eyes slanted away towards the sky.

'He was nice to me last time. He gave me a ride on the tractor.'

Toby looked at the face before him, the wispy curls of hair blowing girlishly round it, and wondered what he'd done to deserve seeing this every day for the next two weeks. It certainly hadn't improved with time, he decided;

it was still a baby-face, a weak face, a nothing face. A face he could do without.

He ran ahead, pulled open the side door of the Land Rover and climbed in, dragging the suitcase after him. Dad was already in the driver's seat.

'Toby, push that case to the side, can you? Benjamin can't get in. And squeeze up.'

'I can go in the back.'

'Not with all the fencing stuff, you can't.'

'I can! I can climb over the top.'

'Do as you're told.'

He moved reluctantly to the right and pulled the suitcase away from the opening. Dad leaned across him.

'Right, Benjamin, jump in.'

Some jump, Toby thought, watching Benjamin cautiously lift one leg in, slide his body after it until he was sitting almost hunched up on the seat, then with equal caution lift the other leg in and close the door. Dad started the engine, swung the Land Rover round and they headed off up the road.

The sky had darkened further and as they pulled out of Totnes, Toby leant back and gazed upwards at the dusky islands of cloud, listening uninterestedly to Dad's attempts at conversation; asking Benjamin about the journey, why he didn't like school, how his parents would manage Christmas without him.

They're lucky, Toby thought. They're probably glad they haven't got him. And we're stuck with him instead.

The fields were soon racing past and Totnes behind them. It was good to be heading home to a warm house, even if they did have an unwanted guest with them. Dad seemed finally to have run out of questions, and since Benjamin asked none of his own, the journey was becoming slightly more bearable. At last they were off the main road and cutting along the old familiar lane towards the farm.

Dad, looking more and more at ease the closer they drew to home, caught Benjamin's eye and nodded out of the window. 'See that line of poplars, Benjamin?'

Benjamin stared blankly ahead and Toby chuckled. But Dad heard.

'No need for that, Toby. We weren't all born in the country.' He pointed over the field. 'See those trees, Benjamin?'

Benjamin nodded.

'They're called poplars. Now just beyond, you should see some buildings. Got them?'

'Yes, sir.'

' 'S all right, none of that "sir" rubbish. I don't get any airs and graces from Toby, so I don't expect any from you. Anyway, see the buildings?'

'Yes.'

'That's the farm next to ours.'

'The one with the geese?'

'You've got a good memory after six years. What else can you remember?'

Toby saw the lips quiver again in that annoying way.

'I remember lots of things,' said Benjamin. 'Lots of things. I . . . '

The pallid eyes assumed an inward look and Benjamin's voice trailed away as though it had never been.

Toby stared. This boy was weird; even weirder than last time. They drove on in silence and he found himself thinking about Flash again, wishing he'd locked the dog up before leaving. But perhaps Mum had him indoors, or Gordon was with him, or—

He leaned forward, impatient to get home and make sure all was well. Dad pointed again.

'Remember that, Benjamin?'

Benjamin squinted out of the window.

'The oak tree?'

'There you are, Toby, he does know a bit about trees.'

Benjamin took off his glasses and wiped them nervously.

'I only remember the oak tree because you told me about it last time I came.'

8

'Did I?'

'Yes. You were standing by it, and you were wearing a dark blue pullover—a big woolly one—with a funny pattern—'

'The things you remember.'

'—And you told me it's the old oak that guards the house whenever you're away.'

'Did I say that?'

'Yes. You had a hat on, too, a funny flat one.'

'I can't let you stay with us if you're going to be rude about what I wear.'

Benjamin flushed.

'I . . . I didn't mean to—'

Dad winked at him.

'I'm only pulling your leg. You can make as many jokes as you want about my appearance. Everyone else does.'

Benjamin carefully replaced his glasses and seemed on the point of answering; then, without a word, he turned suddenly and stared out over the field. Toby watched and frowned, wondering what could possibly have attracted Benjamin's attention out there. Probably nothing at all, he decided, or nothing of any interest. But he noticed that Benjamin had started almost imperceptibly to shake.

He ignored Benjamin and looked about him; there was something far more important to think about and he wouldn't be happy until he was home and everything was all right. They were through the farm entrance now and bumping along past the orchard towards the house; too early to feel anxiety, he knew, but he felt it just the same and wished Dad would drive faster. They entered the yard, pulled up outside the door and Dad switched off the engine.

And Toby's anxiety grew.

Inevitably Benjamin was taking his time getting out.

'Come on,' said Toby. 'We haven't got all day.'

'Give him a chance,' said Dad. 'And don't forget to take his case in.'

Benjamin climbed clumsily out. Dad laughed.

'Don't worry about Toby. He's always a man in a hurry. He's probably forgotten to make your bed or something.'

Toby was already out of the Land Rover and running towards the house.

'Toby!' Dad called after him. 'Suitcase!'

Toby whirled round and saw Benjamin smiling shyly at him.

'I can . . . get it.'

'No bother,' he said huffily, ran back and grabbed the case, and raced towards the house so fast that he almost barged into Mum coming out.

'Careful, Toby,' she said and quickly stepped past him. 'Now, where is he, where is he? Benjamin!'

Toby stopped to look, despite his impatience, and immediately wished he hadn't. Benjamin was gazing up at her, a simpering smile round his lips, and she was smiling back, her arm round his shoulder as though she actually liked him.

'It's lovely to see you again,' she said. 'We've been so looking forward to having you with us for Christmas. Six years has been too long.'

She drew him towards the house, her arm still round his shoulder.

'We'll have lots to talk about and lots of things for you to do.'

Toby recognized the tone of her voice: it was the one she used when she spoke to animals or little children; which seemed appropriate here, he thought grimly. Anyway, Benjamin was obviously enjoying it. But this wasn't the time to stand around.

He dashed into the house. From the oven came the tempting smell of baking bread and he saw three loaves already on the kitchen table, each one prickly with sunflower seeds. The clock in the hall chimed reassuringly. Everything seemed normal.

But everything was not normal. He knew that. He

10

dropped the suitcase, ran to the window and scanned the yard, listening intently. Behind him he heard Mum and Benjamin come in.

'You remember Gordon?' she was saying. 'Toby's brother?'

'Yes, he's got a big brown coat.'

She laughed.

'Well, he did have. Anyway, he's nineteen now. He works on the farm with us. He should be around somewhere.'

Gordon! Toby stroked his chin. Maybe that was it. Then he heard Dad call from outside.

'Has anyone seen . . . ?'

But his father's voice died away. And as it did so, Toby saw the bulky figure of his brother at the far end of the paddock, walking towards the house.

Carrying something in his arms.

2

Toby sat on the paddock fence, kicking his legs back and forth, glad the darkness had come. He hated crying; it made him feel he was weak and childish, like Benjamin.

Benjamin. Stupid Benjamin. He could imagine Benjamin crying; he almost wanted to see Benjamin crying. He heard footsteps behind him but didn't need to turn to see who it was.

'Come inside, Toby,' said Dad. 'You've got to eat.'

He ran his eyes over the silver birch, its trunk shiny in the moonlight. Dad touched his shoulder.

'Let's have a walk at least.'

He climbed off the fence and followed Dad away from the house, and they walked in silence for a few minutes. The evening air was growing colder. Dad stopped to light his pipe, eyeing Toby over the flame of the match.

'I know how you feel. It's tough losing a dog. It's like losing a friend.' He shook the match and blew out a cloud of smoke. 'Reminds me of old Socks.'

'Socks?'

'Didn't I tell you about Socks? He was my dog when I was a kid. Sheep-dog, same as Flash. Bit bigger maybe. I lost him when I was fourteen.'

'Why Socks?'

'Can't you guess? He had these funny white bits at the bottom of his legs, like a pair of socks.'

'Two pairs for a dog.'

'Right. Two pairs.'

'Did he die the same way as Flash?'

'In a trap? No, thank God, least I hope not. I don't really

12

know how he died. There were some gypsies camping near the farm and they took a fancy to him. When they moved on, he moved on too.'

'Did you see them take him?'

Dad thumbed his pipe.

'Not as such but I always reckoned he went with 'em. He was just like Flash, too sociable for his own good.'

Toby looked down.

'But we know who did this.'

'Maybe we do, but we can't prove anything.'

'We can. It could only be her. Gordon said it wasn't a normal trap, it was some horrible thing cobbled together, and if it hadn't been so huge, it probably wouldn't have killed Flash outright when he—' he shuddered, '—when he put his nose in to sniff it. And Gordon saw her standing over it. How much more proof do you need?'

Dad shook his head.

'Technically, the police could say she was just looking. And there's no hard evidence. The trap's gone, Gordon said. He's just been back to look for it.'

''Cause she took it, that's why. To cover up. You know it's her.'

Dad turned back towards the house.

'It still won't stand up as proof. Come on, let's join the others. We've got a guest to look after.'

Toby felt his fists tighten.

Supper should have been a joyous event: his favourite rolls, crusty brown and speckled, and a tantalizing smell of herbs and vegetables from the soup in the tureen. And Christmas to look forward to.

But there was no joy tonight. And for some reason, despite the fire, the room felt curiously chill.

The others took their normal places, Dad at the head, Mum at the foot, and Gordon opposite. To his annoyance, he saw a place laid to his left.

13

'We're putting you there, Benjamin,' said Mum. 'Next to Toby.'

'Thank you,' said Benjamin.

'So you can give Toby a kick,' said Gordon, 'when he slurps his soup.'

'Very funny,' said Toby.

He glanced at Benjamin and to his surprise saw he had his eyes closed. He looked at Mum.

'What's he doing? Praying or something?'

'Ssh!' Mum put a finger to her lips, and quietly reached for the tureen. At the sound of the lid moving, Benjamin's eyes opened.

'Oh.' He looked startled. 'We've . . . we've started.'

'No, we haven't,' said Mum. 'Pass me your bowl.'

Benjamin studied it for a moment before holding it out.

'You had these last time. I remember the pattern.'

'That's right.' She filled the bowl and handed it back. 'Not as many though. We've broken a few since then.'

'He's got a good memory,' said Dad. 'Remembers all kinds of things.'

Gordon held out his bowl.

'Shame he's not staying during school time. He could help Toby with his homework. When Toby does homework, that is. Thanks, Mum.'

Toby ignored the leg pull and turned to Benjamin.

'What were you doing just now?' he said bluntly.

Benjamin's lip trembled again.

'What—?'

'You had your eyes closed. What were you doing?'

Mum touched him on the arm.

'Let Benjamin get started on his soup.'

Toby heard Dad clear his throat and knew a reprimand was coming. But Benjamin spoke first.

'I didn't know I had my eyes closed.' He looked from face to face. 'I just—'

'You don't need to explain anything,' said Mum. She glanced at Toby. 'Let's just eat, shall we?'

14

'Good idea,' said Gordon.

Toby kept his eyes from the others, sensing their disapproval. They started eating and for some time nobody spoke, then, to his annoyance, he heard Benjamin's voice again.

'Who's that lady?'

He looked up angrily and caught Gordon's eye; but his brother casually dipped a piece of bread in his soup.

'What lady's that, Benjamin?'

'The lady I saw in the field as we were coming into the farm.'

Toby played with his spoon, making patterns in the soup.

'Sure you didn't have your eyes closed?' he said.

'Don't be rude, Toby,' said Dad. 'Eat your soup.'

You don't eat soup, he thought rebelliously, you drink it. But this wasn't the time to answer back. He reached for another roll and let the others talk on.

'She's got a very nice face,' said Benjamin. 'Who is she?'

Toby saw his parents exchange glances.

'Some lady out walking,' said Mum.

Dad nodded.

'Must have been. Obviously wasn't her.'

'Who?' said Benjamin. 'Obviously wasn't who?'

Again they exchanged glances; but it was Gordon who spoke.

'The Wild Woman.'

Benjamin sat up, his face twitching.

'Who's the Wild Woman?'

Dad cleared his throat again.

'Just a vagrant. Turns up from time to time. Bit unusual.' He took another roll and reached for the butter. 'Best to keep out of her way if you see her.'

Toby almost snorted. It was pointless Dad trying to sound casual when he was such a hopeless actor. He wondered whether Benjamin had sensed what he was not being told.

'What does she look like?' said Benjamin.

'You'll know her,' said Gordon. 'She's not called the Wild Woman for nothing.'

'Don't frighten him,' said Mum. 'Benjamin, you probably won't see her and if you do, one of us'll be with you. Let's leave it now.'

But Benjamin's face was alive with questions.

'Where does the Wild Woman live?'

'Nowhere special,' said Gordon. 'Like Dad says, she's a vagrant. But they do say she's got some kind of a . . . lair.'

Toby listened sullenly. Now it was Gordon trying to sound casual, and he was no more convincing than Dad.

Benjamin's eyes misted.

'What's it like? Her lair.'

'Don't even know there is a lair,' said Gordon. 'That's just what people say.'

'Is it a ruined house at the top of a valley? With a rock down below?'

Gordon stared at him.

'How do you know that?'

Benjamin's eyes misted further and the lids half-closed, as though to block out all distraction from his thoughts.

'I've been there,' he said softly. 'What's it called?'

Toby leaned close to Benjamin's ear, meaning to shout and startle him from his reverie; but he found he could only whisper.

'Dragon's Rock.'

After the meal Mum stood up.

'Right, who wants tea? Benjamin?'

Toby looked across and wondered whether Benjamin had heard; the opacity in the eyes was still there and he hadn't spoken for the rest of the meal. But he stirred suddenly and even smiled.

'Have you got any of that hot chocolate you had last time? In the red jar, on the shelf by the cooker.'

She laughed.

'Yes, want some?'

'Yes, please.'

'Toby?'

'Tea, please. In the black jar, on the shelf by the sink.'

He regretted his words at once; there was only one person he wanted to hurt, and it wasn't Mum.

'Sorry,' he said quickly.

'Make yourself useful and clear away these things.'

'I can help,' said Benjamin.

'Thank you. Later on we can go and decorate the Christmas tree. Tea for everybody else?'

'Yes, please,' said Gordon.

Dad was poking the fire and merely nodded. Toby watched him for a moment, wondering why no one had mentioned the strange chill in the room. He stacked the empty bowls on top of each other and followed Mum through to the kitchen, then, as she prepared the drinks, he walked back and forth, bringing the supper things through.

Each time he entered the dining-room the coldness seemed to have deepened.

Gordon and Dad were by the fireside, talking farm business. Benjamin had obviously forgotten his offer to help and was wandering about the room, gazing, it seemed, at nothing in particular.

Back in the kitchen he found Mum washing up.

'The dining-room's cold,' he said.

'Put some more logs on the fire, then. Dry the tureen first, can you, and make some space for the other things.'

He reached for it, glad to have something to do.

'Mum, why's Benjamin . . . I mean—?'

'Why's he the way he is?' She shook her head. 'Why are you the way you are?'

'But he's weird.'

She stopped washing up for a moment.

'You can't see the world through his eyes. You've got to be patient when people don't act the way you do.'

17

He rubbed hard at the tureen.

'I just don't like him. I don't like him at all. There's something creepy about him.'

'What you mean is, you don't understand him. But you must try. He's a guest in our house. He probably finds it just as difficult to understand you, or any of us. We lead a very different life to him.' She smiled. 'I think you can safely say that tureen is done.'

He put it down and reached for a plate.

'No,' she said. 'Take the tea through. It's brewed. I'll bring Benjamin's hot chocolate. I can finish the drying later.'

The fire was roaring now and the dining-room felt slightly warmer. Benjamin still wandered about, his eyes staring as before, though at what, Toby could only guess. Dad looked up from the fireside.

'Gordon wants to go out tomorrow and check over some of the fencing, in case there's any damage after the gale last week, and he thought it might be nice to give Benjamin a ride on the tractor at the same time. Show him some of the farm again.'

'Right.'

Gordon kicked off his slippers and stretched.

'Suppose you'll be tagging along. If you're not too busy whittling or something.'

Toby said nothing. It wasn't that he minded Gordon making fun of him, but no one seemed to be thinking about Flash any more. He watched Benjamin furtively; nothing had been right since he arrived, and now here he was, drifting about the room, acting funny.

As if to contradict him, Benjamin stopped by the window.

'I'd love to go out on the tractor tomorrow,' he said.

'Fine,' said Gordon. 'Let's hope it doesn't tip down on us.'

Benjamin's face clouded.

'Do tractors do that?'

Gordon laughed.

'I mean the rain. Let's hope the rain doesn't tip down on us. Or the snow for that matter. Looks like we might be in for a bit.'

Toby shivered and moved closer to the fire. Then Benjamin spoke again.

'Why do you light the fire when it's so hot in here?'

Toby looked round and saw Benjamin's cheeks flickering like flames.

'Hot?' he scoffed. 'How can you say you're hot?'

He heard Mum's voice behind him.

'You're probably tired, Benjamin. You've had a long journey and it wasn't the happiest of arrivals.'

'I am a bit,' he said.

'Well, why don't you turn in? Come on, I haven't shown you where everything is in your room. We can do the Christmas tree tomorrow.'

'I thought I was going to have some hot chocolate.'

She held up the mug she was holding and he smiled.

'Thank you.' He walked up to her and took it. 'That lady in the field—I saw her last time I came. I wish I knew why she's so frightened.'

And without another word, he walked past her and up the stairs.

Toby watched Mum follow, then turned and looked over the room. Dad had lit his pipe and Gordon was reading the newspaper, and both seemed contented enough and unperturbed by Benjamin's latest remark.

But the room still felt cold.

He walked through to the kitchen and opened the back door, and gazed out over the yard towards the paddock. The place where Flash loved to play.

There would be no stars tonight.

Benjamin woke in the early hours, sweating from the nightmare of the dragon, and for a few seconds of anguish he lost all memory of where he was. He threw out an arm in panic and it brushed back the curtain a few inches; and he saw the slumberous fields stretching away into the darkness.

Recollection returned, and with it some relief. But for the first time the suspicion arose within him that the dragon had ceased to be a figment of his sleep; that it was now no fiction, no falsehood, no illusion, but had somehow broken the fetters of his mind and was even at this moment prowling through the night.

3

'Jump on!' shouted Gordon, looking down from the tractor.

Toby gave a curt nod to Benjamin, standing awkwardly in the mud, his new boots already dirty.

'You first.'

Benjamin stepped forward, hesitantly searching for handholds.

'Here.' Gordon reached down. 'Put your feet there, that's right, and pull yourself up on this.' Benjamin climbed slowly up. 'Toby? Come on!'

Toby jumped on as nonchalantly as he could manage, noting the look of admiration from Benjamin.

'Show-off,' said Gordon.

He started the engine and pulled out of the yard onto the track. Toby settled back, glad that the roar of the engine gave him an excuse not to talk.

Gordon was pointing things out to Benjamin, who was leaning close to hear. Toby watched for a few moments, wishing Benjamin wouldn't keep nodding his head as Gordon spoke, then an idea occurred to him and he touched Benjamin on the shoulder.

'How old are you?' he shouted.

Benjamin turned. 'Fourteen.' He paused, as though frightened to offend. 'How old are you?'

'Nearly fifteen.'

Gordon laughed. 'Nearly fifteen!'

'Well, I am!'

'You're fourteen, same as Benjamin. You're not fifteen till you're fifteen.'

'Shut up!'

But Gordon only laughed again.

The tractor was bouncing now that the ground was more uneven and Gordon leaned forward to concentrate on the driving.

Toby shivered, the chill of the breeze adding to the frosty crispness of the morning. Then he noticed Benjamin stroking something in his hand.

'What's that?'

Benjamin flushed.

'You mean . . . ' He held out his hand with some reluctance. 'You mean this?'

'A stone? Is that all it is? I thought it was something important, the way you were stroking it.'

Benjamin's mouth quivered again.

'I found it last time I came.'

'Let me see it.'

'Well, I—'

'Come on!'

'It's only a stone.'

'So let me see it!'

Toby checked to make sure Gordon was leaning too far forward to see or hear, then snatched the stone; and now that he'd seen Benjamin's reluctance to hand it over, he decided to hold on to it as long as possible.

'What do you keep stroking it for?'

'I just do.'

'So where did you find it?'

Benjamin's eyes were fixed on the stone.

'At Dragon's Rock,' he said.

Toby tried to ignore the apprehension he always felt at the mention of Dragon's Rock and to enjoy instead the anxiety in Benjamin's undeviating stare, not to mention the curious beauty of the stone itself. He was beginning to see why Benjamin liked it: it was a strange violet colour, long and slim and tapering at one end, and while the sides felt smooth and almost silky, the base was flat and sharp against his finger. He pondered the contrast, as he let the stone play over his fingers.

So smooth and so sharp.

One side to soothe, and one side to cut.

He looked up and saw Benjamin's eyes still on the stone; and suddenly he found himself fighting the desire to drop it. Accidentally on purpose, of course.

But perhaps not yet.

He tossed it in the air a couple of times, noting with satisfaction the consternation on Benjamin's face, then he closed his fist round it and pretended to throw it away.

Consternation turned to panic. He grinned and, before Benjamin could call out and alert Gordon, opened his hand to reveal the stone still there.

'Give it back,' said Benjamin.

Toby glanced at Gordon again. But all was well: he was still leaning forward and hadn't heard anything. He tried to think of an excuse for keeping the stone longer.

'You still haven't told me why you stroke it.'

The tractor rode a bump in the field and Benjamin put a hand behind his back to steady himself.

'I just do.'

And before Toby had time to think, he grabbed the stone and thrust it in his pocket.

Toby watched suspiciously, almost wishing he'd never seen the stone. But as they jolted down the field, an idea started to form in his mind.

The tractor ride went on too long and Toby was soon bored and ready to jump off. Tractor rides were only a novelty for townies. He cast an eye over Gordon's huge shoulders, the thick black hair only partially covering the somewhat elephantine ears that everyone joked about, no one more so than Gordon himself. Unable to resist, he reached out and flicked one of them.

Gordon didn't bother to look round.

'Watch it, Toby!' he called. 'Or you'll be sitting on a cow-pat.'

'How d'you know it wasn't Benjamin?'

'Benjamin's got manners.'

'I've got manners.'

'First I've heard of it.'

They were close to the bottom fence now and he could see the rows of young larch that Dad had planted along to the right. The final stretch was the bumpiest of all but at last they were there. He jumped straight down and ran up the field, glad to be moving.

Gordon's voice rang out.

'Hoy! Toby! Grab some of the stuff, will you?'

He ran back and stood by the tractor, blowing his hands.

'Bring this.' Gordon handed him the old bucket-bag they used for carrying tools and tramped over to the fence with the wire under his arm. Toby followed and stood by while his brother bent over one of the posts.

A huge raven wheeled overhead only a few feet from them, and glided away over the larch trees. Toby watched until it disappeared from view.

'Not much wrong here,' said Gordon, straightening up.

'Dad was right then, about you fussing over nothing.'

'He only says that 'cause he's got other jobs he wants me to get on with. But I still reckon some bits of the fencing need looking at after the gale.'

'We going then?'

'No, I've got a bit of work to do here. You and Benjamin can buzz off for a while.' He looked round suddenly. 'Hang on, where's he got to?'

Toby scanned the field, then pointed.

A hundred yards away, Benjamin stood gazing over the fence towards the lower ground to the south.

'He's really peculiar,' he said.

'Doesn't mean any harm,' said Gordon. 'Give him a chance. We weren't all born the same.'

'Just as well. We could be like you.'

24

'No, I'm serious. You've got to be patient. He's away from his mum and dad.'

'It's not that.'

'What then?'

'I don't know.' Toby shrugged. 'I just don't like him, I suppose.'

Benjamin was coming back, apparently out of breath already, then, a few yards from them, he stopped, took off his glasses and pointed with them to where he had been standing.

'Where's that mist come from?'

Toby gave a start, both surprised and slightly disappointed that he hadn't spotted the grey cloud rolling up from the low ground towards them. Gordon stared at it too.

'Funny, I could have sworn that wasn't there a minute ago.'

Toby watched, uneasily: there was something about this mist that seemed unusual, and he was sure it hadn't been there when they arrived. He wondered how fast mist could travel.

Gordon dipped into the bucket-bag.

'Mist or no mist, I've got to sort out this fence. You two can disappear but don't go too far.'

'Where do you want to go?' said Benjamin.

'How should I know?' said Toby, turning away.

He wandered along the western fence, not looking to see whether Benjamin had followed but aware from the sound of laboured breathing that he was somewhere behind. No need to slow down or stop. He turned north and carried on as far as the plantation.

Benjamin caught him up breathlessly.

'I remember these trees, but they've grown a lot since last time. What are they called?'

'Sitka. Dad's little hobby. We'll probably need it, the way farming's going at the moment. He's got some larch too, back near the tractor. You wouldn't recognize 'em.'

25

'Sitka.' Benjamin's brow wrinkled. 'I remember, you told me last time.'

'*I* told you?'

'Yes, you were standing here—well, not here, over that way a bit—and you had a green jacket on. With a Manchester United badge on it.'

'Mum's thrown that away.'

'Oh.'

'It was falling apart. Anyway, I support Spurs now. Come on.'

He could see Benjamin wanted to rest, but mischief prompted him to move on, to see how much the boy could take. He pushed ahead between the rows of sitka, running his hand along the spiny branches, then after a few minutes he stopped and listened for the sound of breathing or the tramp of feet in the undergrowth behind him. Hearing neither, he turned.

Benjamin was some way behind, his head low, and walking more slowly than ever.

'Benjamin!' he shouted. 'You coming or what?'

Benjamin looked up, then, to Toby's amazement, raced towards him, half-stumbling over the uneven ground.

'What's the matter now?' he called, but Benjamin rushed straight past. Toby ran after him and grabbed him by the arm.

'What's up? Where are you going?'

Benjamin stared ahead, gulping in breath.

'That fence.' He pointed to the end of the plantation. 'What's on the other side?'

'Trees, more land.'

'But further on.'

Toby frowned. 'Dragon's Rock.'

So that was it, this thing about Dragon's Rock. Benjamin walked closer to the fence, still staring beyond it towards the trees.

'Maybe that's where the nice lady comes from.'

Toby snorted.

26

'There's only one person who hangs round Dragon's Rock, and she's—' He broke off. 'I'm going back to the tractor,' he said, and stomped off through the plantation.

Nice lady, nice lady. He was starting to hate Benjamin, not just dislike him. He thought of Flash and the soft fur he'd touched and cried over. And the woman he knew had caused his pain.

And now Benjamin.

Gordon was waiting for him by the tractor.

'Where's Benjamin?'

He nodded back towards the sitka plantation.

'In there somewhere.'

'You shouldn't have taken him up that way. You know why. You'd better go back and find him.'

But there was no need.

Benjamin had emerged from the rows of sitka and was picking his way slowly back, his eyes cast down to the ground, his hands passing back and forth a tiny object.

And as Toby watched, the idea came back to his mind.

The raven passed overhead a second time.

4

The floorboard creaked and Toby held his breath while he waited for the silence to settle; then gradually the quietness of the night crept round him again and he inched his way forward.

The darkness was no problem: the moon cast a cool light through the landing window and brightened the floor ahead. Down in the hall he heard the soft chime of the clock.

One o'clock.

He felt a chill round his neck and fastened the top button of his pyjamas, momentarily wondering why he was doing this. But doubts were brief; Benjamin deserved it and that was reason enough. Besides, he told himself, it was only for fun.

Benjamin's door was ajar, and that made things easier. He pushed it slowly.

And drew breath.

But it was only the glow of the moon on Benjamin's face that gave the eerie impression that he was awake. He crept forward and bent over the bed; Benjamin was lying on his back, a moon-halo round his head, weird and slightly unnerving. He glanced at the window, wishing the curtains had been drawn right across and that the moon were not so bright. The face below him looked harmless enough, yet there was still something unsettling about it. The mouth was open and the breathing so quiet it was hard to believe Benjamin was alive; only the slight movement of the chest betrayed it. He remembered watching Flash sleep.

The eyelids started to flicker.

Dreaming, he thought. He remembered Gordon saying

that when you blinked a lot it meant you were dreaming. Suddenly Benjamin moaned.

He took a step back, certain that someone in the house must have heard.

But no one stirred and Benjamin rolled over the other way. He waited a moment longer, then put his mind on what he had come to do. Benjamin's clothes lay on the seat at the foot of the bed, neatly folded, unlike his own. He crept over and felt through the pockets.

Nothing there. He looked round the room and saw the suitcase lying flat on the floor in the corner, tiptoed to it and bent down. To his relief the catches did not click as he opened it.

But the suitcase was empty.

Another moan from the bed made him look round. Benjamin had rolled back and was facing his way again; the eyelids still flickered and now from the mouth there came a strange, wordless murmuring.

Then he saw what he had come for.

In Benjamin's hand.

He stared in dismay. This was something he had never expected. Benjamin had pushed the sheets down slightly, and as Toby watched, he saw the hands move together and apart, together and apart, as though feeling along a string of beads.

But there were no beads.

Only the stone.

He watched, with a mixture of frustration and disbelief. It seemed impossible that Benjamin could sleep and yet pass the stone from hand to hand without dropping it.

Footsteps sounded outside the door.

Benjamin shifted restlessly, as though he had heard. Toby shrank back, trying to keep to the shadier part of the room in case Benjamin woke up. The footsteps made their way down to the bathroom. He listened, once again holding his breath. It sounded like Gordon, but he couldn't be sure.

For what seemed a long time he heard nothing, then the

footsteps returned, a door closed and silence fell once more. He looked quickly back at Benjamin. It was now or never.

For a moment something made him hesitate: the silent room, the shadows, the moon on the face; he didn't know. But the dare he had imposed upon himself was stronger.

Before he knew it, he had plucked the stone from Benjamin's fingers and was back at the door. With any luck he'd be able to slip out before Benjamin saw him. But, in spite of himself, he cast a quick glance back.

To his surprise, all was as before.

No change of position, no eyes upon him, no voice calling his name. Benjamin had not woken up.

And the hands passed back and forth an imaginary stone.

In the morning Benjamin was gone.

Toby kept quiet at the breakfast table and let the others argue it out.

'He must have been early,' Dad said. 'Gordon or I would have seen him if he'd gone out after six. I don't like this at all. It's very dark these mornings, he doesn't know his way about and he's a bit helpless.'

'But where would he go?' said Mum.

Gordon downed his tea.

'Toby took him up the sitka plantation yesterday.'

Toby saw Dad's mouth tighten.

'What did you go up there for, for God's sake?'

He shrugged. 'I don't know, just did.'

'How close to Dragon's Rock did you go?'

'Not very.'

'Close enough to see the buildings?'

'I'm not that stupid.'

'Over the boundary fence?'

'No.'

Dad frowned at him, then went over and started to lay

30

the fire. 'You're not being very helpful. Now think. Did he say anything or do anything that might give us a clue? Was he worried about anything? Interested in anything?'

Images started to mingle in Toby's mind: the mist below the fence, the raven; Benjamin staring.

'He seemed sort of worked up about Dragon's Rock. Wondered if it was the place where that "nice lady" lives.'

Dad dropped the kindling.

'Come on, Gordon.'

Toby jumped up. 'Can I come?'

'Not if we're going near Dragon's Rock.'

'More eyes the better, Dad,' said Gordon.

'All right, but no running off.'

'Promise.'

Mum hurried with them to the door.

'I'll stay here in case he wanders back on his own.'

The fields were bright and silvery with frost as the sun rose above them, fiery and gold. Toby jumped into the Land Rover and shivered on the cold seat; Dad climbed in the other side, slammed the door and started the engine. Gordon's face appeared at the window.

'I'll take the tractor down to the bottom fence. He might have gone down that way and had a fall or something. And there was a mist there yesterday. Meet you at the plantation.'

'Right,' said Dad. 'Let's go.'

5

Her face was hidden and she was bent over the ground, sorting with a billhook through a pile of long sticks she must have just cut from the forest nearby.

Benjamin crouched behind the fence at the top of the plantation, trying to keep out of sight just in case; then she turned slightly and he caught a glimpse of her face.

He relaxed.

It was all right after all. He'd been worried that it might have been the Wild Woman rather than the lady he'd seen the day he arrived, and for that brief moment, six years ago. So he hadn't been imagining it; she did exist. And now he had found her again, though he'd come out looking for something else.

She looked up suddenly and saw him.

He stiffened. 'I—'

At once she dropped the sticks and rushed away towards the trees.

'Wait!' he shouted.

She didn't turn, didn't stop.

'Wait!'

He climbed the fence and ran after her.

'I'm not going to hurt you!'

She hurried on, not looking back. He caught up with her but still she didn't slow down or look at him.

'Why are you frightened?' he said.

She flashed a glance at him, no more; but enough for him to catch the strange beauty of her eyes.

'You can't be scared of me,' he said. 'Nobody's ever scared of me.'

She stopped suddenly and peered at him hard, as though searching for some deception.

'What are you scared of?' he said.

Her eyes left him and darted about her. He followed them, trying to find a clue among the trees, bushes, and fields. A question rose in his mind, though why it came, he didn't know.

'Is it the Wild Woman you're scared of?'

Her eyes fixed on him again. 'What do you know about the Wild Woman?'

Her voice startled him: he had expected something hesitant, but this was deep and attractive. He tried, without much success, to make his own deep and attractive too.

'I only know what Toby's family told me. So it is the Wild Woman you're frightened of?'

She looked away again.

'Everybody's frightened of the Wild Woman. No one more so than me.'

'Is she so terrible?'

'Ask your friends. Ask anyone round here. They'll tell you what she's like.'

'But why are you more frightened of her than anyone else?'

'I'm her prisoner.'

She turned from him again, this time back to where she had left the sticks. He followed, glad that she seemed to trust him enough to speak; but surprised at what she had said. He remembered his purpose in coming out and wondered whether this meeting might be a part of that purpose. A part he had not foreseen.

'What's your name?' he said.

'Ione.'

She didn't ask his.

'Mine's Benjamin,' he said.

She reached the sticks and started to gather them, and he bent down to help. But she waved him aside.

'I don't need any favours.'

33

There was no anger in her voice; no sharpness.

Only pride.

But it was a tired pride, a pride he sensed had been tested, perhaps many times.

'What are the sticks for?' he said. 'To make a fire?'

'To make a cage. My cage.'

He stood back, unsure what to do or say. She seemed so capable, yet so vulnerable, and she said such strange things. He tried to guess how old she was but even that was hard to tell: older than Mum certainly, or Toby's mum, but not all shrivelled up like Aunty Maud.

The more he thought about her, the more mysterious she became.

'Why do you have to make a cage for yourself?'

She stood up, her arms clasped round the sticks.

'The Wild Woman forces me. I told you, I'm her prisoner. She's got a halter round my neck.'

'I can't see one.'

'No one can see it. But it's always there.'

'Can't you run away somewhere she can't get you?'

She gazed down the field, then, still holding the sticks, walked to the fence and looked over one of the sitka, its branches laced with gossamer.

'If the spider spins a strong web, you never escape.'

'But can't you go where there isn't a web?'

She set off back towards the trees.

'Not if it covers the whole world.'

He followed again, more and more drawn to her.

'Why haven't Toby's family seen you?'

'Nobody sees me.'

'But I see you.'

'You're different.'

Her face had lost its earlier agitation, but fear still hovered over the features like a shadow. He wondered what she meant about him being different.

'Why don't other people see you?' he said. 'Do you hide from them?'

She didn't answer. But he remembered how she ran away when she first saw him.

'Why do you hide?' he said. 'Please tell me.'

She threw him another glance, as brief as before.

'I'm an empath,' she said.

'An . . . empath?' He stared at her. 'What's an empath?'

She walked for a while in silence and he began to think she was not going to answer; then she began to speak.

'Some people have to live apart. They're too sensitive. They have too much empathy with the suffering of others. They feel the pain of the world as though it's their own, and it's too much to bear.'

'And are you . . . sensitive like that?'

She stopped and faced him.

'Go back to your friends. You shouldn't be out here.' She looked him over. 'You haven't even got a coat on.'

'I don't need one. I feel hot. Anyway, you haven't got a coat on either.'

Strange that he hadn't noticed it before. He had been so fascinated by her features that he hadn't realized she was wearing no coat. And what clothes she had were ragged: a tattered jumper, an equally tattered skirt, an apron made from what looked like sacking, and an old pair of worn-out boots.

Yet in a curious way, these things only highlighted the strange dignity in her face.

She said nothing in reply.

'Ione?' he said. It felt odd saying her name when he had only known her for a few minutes. 'What's the Wild Woman doing to you?'

'Destroying me,' she said. She nodded in the direction of the farm. 'Go back to your friends and don't come here again.'

'But I've got to. I've got to find the stone and put it back on the rock.'

'What stone?'

'When I was eight we came to stay at the farm. My

parents and Toby's parents all went to the same school and they're friends. Toby and I had to go out and play together. We came to the sitka plantation and Toby ran off, on purpose, and left me to find my own way home.'

He remembered Toby's face, scowling at him all through that first visit; just as it seemed to have scowled at him ever since.

'Toby hates me,' he said. 'I tried to get back by going through the forest but I got lost and found myself at this big rock. Down in a valley.'

He paused.

'It had some jagged bits and I put my feet on them. I don't know why but I just felt I wanted to climb it, to see if I could get to the top. I found a stone there, inside a little hole. It fitted perfectly, like a key.'

She said nothing but he sensed she was listening and went on.

'I took it. I collect stones and this was a lovely violet-coloured one. But I didn't show it to anyone. I kept it secret. I sort of knew I'd done something wrong. And that's when the nightmares started.'

A robin fluttered down to the ground, the brightness of its chest in cheerful contrast to the grey of the morning. Grasping the sticks tightly under one arm, she held out the billhook towards it. He waited for it to fly off.

To his surprise it hopped straight onto the blade, up her arm to the shoulder and down onto the sticks. She watched it for a moment, then looked at him again.

'What nightmares?' she said.

He took his eye from the robin and looked away over the fields.

'About a dragon,' he said. 'It's so scary. Ever since I took the stone, I've been having these nightmares. It's always the same one. I even had it on the train coming here. Mum and Dad have been worried sick about me. I know I should have come back before now to return the stone. But we've moved about so much, it hasn't been possible, and anyway,

I didn't want to have to put up with Toby again. And . . . and I suppose I sort of hoped the nightmares would go away and I could keep the stone. But they've just got worse.'

'What happens in the nightmare?'

'I'm being chased by this huge dragon, and it's getting closer and closer and closer, and any moment it's going to catch me. I can hear it roaring and feel its breath, but I never see its face. I always wake up just before I see it.' He found himself searching the landscape. 'And now I've got this feeling it's more than just a dream.'

'What do you mean?' she said.

He turned back to her and saw the robin still perched on the sticks.

'Toby's family told me the rock's called Dragon's Rock. I didn't know that before. And . . . ' He hesitated, unsure of whether he should tell her more. But she was still watching him, and seemed concerned about what he was saying. 'And I've just got this feeling the dragon's real. I can feel it, somewhere close, somewhere really close. But I can't see it and I'm frightened. And . . . and I feel so hot all the time.' He looked at her sharply. 'You haven't got a coat on. Is that 'cause you feel hot too?'

She turned towards the trees and the robin flew off.

'Go home,' she said. 'And when you find the stone, give it back to the rock.'

'But I might not find it.'

'Maybe your friend's taken it.'

He pondered this, remembering Toby's malicious interest in the stone during the tractor ride. He'd been thinking he must have dropped it, but Toby . . .

It was certainly possible.

She had started to walk away again, back to the forest, to her hidden life, her fears, her cage. Her empathy with the world. And he knew that this time she would not let him follow. But one problem still bothered him, though why he felt she might be able to explain it was a mystery to him.

Perhaps because she hadn't answered his last question.

'Ione, why do I feel hot all the time?'

She stopped and half-turned towards him.

'Because the dragon's angry,' she said.

'So there is a dragon!' He stepped forward eagerly. 'But where is it? What does it look like?'

She motioned him back.

'You must find that out for yourself.'

'But is it my fault?' he said, searching her face. 'That it's angry, I mean.'

She looked him over for a few moments, as though trying to decide whether to respond; then slowly nodded. And before he could speak again, she walked quickly on and disappeared among the trees.

From below the plantation he heard the sound of the Land Rover.

6

Benjamin slept through the rest of the morning.

When he came downstairs in the early afternoon, Toby noticed he was withdrawn and uncommunicative. Not that he cared. For him Benjamin was a source of nothing but contempt: not a word about why he'd gone running out, just a lot of rubbish about meeting the 'nice lady'.

There was only one woman roaming these parts.

And everyone knew what she was like.

He remembered the drive that morning across the frosty landscape, the strange mist creeping up from the lower fields as they scoured the ground; and how he'd spotted her, just for a second, through the back of the Land Rover as they headed for home with Benjamin, her face dark against the sky.

And how the darkness remained, even after she'd turned away.

Lunch was a depressing affair, and it didn't help to see the others trying to act natural, as though nothing were wrong. Presumably he was meant to do the same.

Well, he wouldn't. Benjamin was a liar and running away was just a sympathy act to get attention, which obviously had worked. He heard his name mentioned and saw Dad looking at him.

'We thought you might like to take Benjamin round with you this afternoon.'

It didn't take much in the way of brains to work out why. But the prospect of an afternoon with Benjamin was too much. He tried to think of a way out. 'I'm not really going anywhere. I was going to finish some whittling.'

'Yes, but . . . you know . . . ' He heard a touch of exasperation in Dad's voice. 'You could take him round a bit, show him some of your secret haunts.'

'What secret haunts?'

'Well, places you go to get away from us lot.'

He could see there was no point in arguing, as Dad's mind was obviously made up.

Suddenly Benjamin spoke.

'Maybe we could go back to that field. The one you found me in.'

Toby looked round for reactions but the others were clearly determined to appear normal. Dad even put a napkin to his mouth, something he never did.

'Back to Skinny Sam?' he said. 'Well, I'd prefer it if you went somewhere—'

'Skinny Sam?' Benjamin leaned forward. 'Who's Skinny Sam?'

Gordon laughed.

'Skinny Sam's the field. Thought you knew. We give all our fields names. Skinny Sam's the one I took you to yesterday, just below the sitka. Where Toby and Dad found you this morning.'

'But why Skinny Sam?'

'Can't you guess?'

'Because it's skinny?'

Toby sighed. Bravo. And he could guess the next question.

'What do you call the other fields?'

Spot on. Ten out of ten.

Dad reached for his tobacco pouch.

'Paddy's Pasture.' He pointed with his pipe out of the window. 'That's the one out there. Then you've got Norman's Nook, Dawny's Dip, Ivan's Meadow, Lizzie's Hollow.'

'Molly the Twist,' said Gordon. 'Long Louis, Big Willy.'

'Big Willy?' Benjamin tittered. 'Have you really got a field called Big Willy?'

'What's wrong with that?' said Toby.

But the others were laughing too and nobody took any notice of him.

'It's sort of a funny shape,' explained Gordon. 'If you know what I mean.'

Mum began to collect the plates.

'The fields had other names when we moved here but we decided to give them our own private ones.'

'What for?' said Benjamin.

'We didn't like the old ones. Each field's got its own personality. So we made up our own names, based on eccentric characters we've known over the years and what each field's like.'

'Mucky Meg,' offered Gordon.

Benjamin looked round at him.

'Mucky Meg?'

'Where Mum lost her boots.'

Benjamin's face clouded again.

'It's very muddy,' said Toby testily. 'And Mum's name's Meg.'

He wondered how much longer they were going to humour the idiot, with his pathetic questions and nervous nodding gestures. And the movements, seemingly unconscious, of the fingers.

Those he liked least of all.

He remembered the way the fingers had moved as the moonlight played on the face; as he waited and watched in the night. And he felt a sudden urge to run upstairs and check under his pillow.

Benjamin gazed dreamily out of the window.

'This land, it's . . . it's so strange now.'

'Strange?' said Mum. 'In what way?'

'It was different last time.' Benjamin frowned. 'It seemed all velvety then but now it's—'

He stopped, and seemed to be searching for the right word.

'It's what?' said Mum.

'Sort of scaly,' he said finally. The wispy hair fell across his face and he pushed it back.

'Scaly!' said Mum. 'I've not heard it called that before.'

'It's like a dragon's body,' said Benjamin. 'A big dragon, lying asleep. But starting to wake up.'

She laughed. 'The things you think of. Anyway, what about doing the Christmas tree? We could—' She broke off suddenly. 'Are you all right, Benjamin?'

Benjamin was suddenly breathing heavily.

'I'm . . . so hot,' he said.

She rested a hand on his arm.

'You've been up half the night, running about the fields without a coat on. You've probably picked up something.'

'I'm still ever so tired.'

'Well, why don't you go back to bed for the afternoon? I'll come and wake you in time for supper.'

'Can I?'

'Of course. We'll see if you still feel hot when you wake up. Come on.'

Toby glared after them as they left the room, and heard his thoughts mimic Benjamin's voice.

I'm . . . so hot. I'm still ever so tired.

Only Benjamin could feel hot when it was freezing cold, and if he was tired, that was his fault.

And scaly! Like a dragon's body!

'What a twit,' he muttered and walked out into the yard. The animals stirred restlessly around him.

Benjamin did not appear for supper.

But he was there. Toby could see from the others' faces that even from upstairs Benjamin could intrude upon everyone's thoughts.

After supper they took their tea through to the living-room. Toby sat at the end of the sofa, watching the flames from the fire flicker round the wall. For some reason he still felt cold and the room seemed dark, despite the glow from the hearth and the big lamp in the corner. He stood up and switched on the main light. Dad blinked and rubbed his eyes.

'Turn that off. I was dozing.'

'Sorry,' he said and switched it off again.

'I'll pop up and see how Benjamin is,' said Mum.

He listened to the sound of her footsteps on the stairs, then above his head as she walked across the landing. All of a sudden the room seemed darker, colder. He threw another log on the fire and stretched towards it, listening to the steady crackle of burning wood.

Footsteps sounded on the stair again, then Mum burst into the room.

'Quick! Benjamin's rolling about the bed. Mumbling something. I can't wake him.'

The others rushed on ahead, and Toby hurried after them. But at the top of the stairs he stopped.

Through the open door of Benjamin's room he could hear Mum's voice, coaxing, encouraging. He waited a few seconds to make sure no one was coming out, then turned towards his own room.

It was no good; he had to see the stone, had to make sure it was still there. He didn't know why it mattered so much, or why he had to check it now. But that was the way it was. He pushed open the door.

And stood back in disbelief.

The wardrobe doors were open and the drawers had been pulled out from the chest and desk. His jacket had been thrown over the chair and he knew he had left it hanging on the door.

Benjamin.

It could only be Benjamin. So obsessed that he hadn't even bothered to tidy up and pretend he hadn't been there. And there was only one thing he could have been looking for. He ran to the bed and lifted the pillow.

The stone seemed to stare up at him accusingly.

He heard footsteps outside and hurriedly replaced the

pillow. A moment later Mum appeared in the doorway. He shifted from one foot to the other, disconcerted by her expression.

'Is Benjamin all right?' he said.

She walked slowly into the room, looking about her.

'What was Benjamin trying to find in here?'

'I don't know. Has he woken up?'

'What was he looking for?'

'How do you know he's been in here?'

'He just told me.'

'Well, he must have told you what he was looking for, then.'

'He said it's a secret but I have a feeling you know what it is.'

Gordon's voice boomed out from down the corridor.

'Mum, can you come back?'

She looked at him hard for a moment, but then turned and left. He followed surlily, hearing now from Benjamin's room the voice he had come to despise. He stopped in the doorway and looked in.

Dad and Gordon stood by the window; Mum sat on the bed, leaning forward; and Benjamin was holding her hand.

'A big dragon,' he was saying, 'a great big dragon . . . '

Toby stepped in and Benjamin looked up. And the two of them stared at each other without speaking.

'Toby,' said Mum, 'did you put the guard across the fire before you came up?'

'No.'

'Can you go down and do it now?'

He lingered, unwilling to stay, yet more unwilling to go back to the strange chill of the living-room.

'What's all this stuff about a dragon?' he said.

'Never mind,' she said. 'It's a nightmare Benjamin keeps having.'

'About a dragon?'

'Yes, a big dragon. Now will you go and sort out the fire?'

He looked at Gordon and Dad, wishing one of them

would say something to keep him there, but neither spoke. He made his way slowly back to the living-room.

A shiver ran through him as he entered, though he didn't know why. He stood close to the door, watching the shadows above the fire ripple over the wall like barley swaying in a field. This was stupid, he told himself; he'd lived in the house all his life and never felt scared before. He walked to the centre of the room.

It was all Benjamin's fault. Ever since he'd turned up, things hadn't been right, and here he was again pretending he was having some crazy nightmare about a dragon, just to get more attention. The others were stupid to take him so seriously. He walked closer to the fire but the warmth did not increase.

Steps sounded on the stairs again and the others came back in, fortunately without Benjamin. He waited to see whether anyone would say something about the change in the atmosphere.

Gordon stood over the fire and rubbed his hands; Dad threw himself in the armchair.

'Right, Toby,' he said. 'What was Benjamin looking for in your room?'

'I don't know.'

'So why would he go and hunt through your things?'

'Don't ask me.'

He saw Mum walking round the room, looking about her.

'What's up, Mum?' said Gordon.

'I thought I heard something.'

She stopped walking and looked at Toby.

'Toby, if you have taken something of Benjamin's—'

'I haven't.'

'If you have,' she said firmly, 'you must give it back.'

She listened again. Dad sat up.

'What is it?'

'I'm sure I heard something.'

'The animals?'

'Sssh!'

Talking ceased and now Toby began to feel the unearthly stillness in the house, broken only by the crackle of the fire and the occasional squeak of the chair springs as Dad shifted his weight. Something clipped the windowpane: a branch from the apple tree perhaps, caught in the breeze, but Toby jumped all the same. Now, more than ever, he wanted someone to say something, anything, just to break the silence. He wanted someone to put the main light on.

But no one spoke and no one moved.

The glow from the lamp seemed weird and wan and oddly interwoven with the tiny figures of shadow thrown up from the fire onto the wall. And as Toby watched them, he felt the darkness and coldness deepen around him, and the certainty came that this silent room now housed a sinister intelligence.

A spark flew from the fire and landed on the carpet. Gordon reached down and flicked it onto the tiles.

The back door clicked and footsteps sounded on the gravel.

Running.

Dad jumped up.

'Quick!' he said and ran out of the room, closely followed by Gordon. Toby made for the door too.

But Mum barred his way.

'Toby, there's nothing you want to tell me, is there?'

He bit his lip, then shook his head.

'No, Mum,' he said, and raced past her towards the back door.

7

Benjamin heard them calling.

But he took no notice and ran on down the slushy path by the paddock as far as the gate. Only then did he stop and listen for sounds of pursuit.

Toby's father was still shouting after him, but there were no footsteps yet. Probably they would take the Land Rover like last time. He climbed the gate and ran across the field.

The voices grew more distant and eventually died away. He slowed down and tried to decide which way to go. Last night he had run without thinking, and found his way to Skinny Sam and the sitka plantation more by accident than skill.

Tonight must be different.

Tonight he had to go further, to continue the search, not just for the stone this time, because he was starting to have a suspicion about who might have that, but for the other things that had haunted him for the last six years.

He looked about him, wishing there were more moonlight to see by. Yet curiously there was some light: a light he had seen last night as he raced over the fields, a strange luminosity that seemed to issue from the ground itself. As though the soil were breathing, like the body of an animal.

Sleeping.

But restless.

He walked on, treading carefully, anxious not to disturb this terrifying beast. He was feeling hot again, and he knew it wasn't fever but the suffocating closeness that had afflicted him since his first trip to Devon. Thoughts of the dragon began to pour through his mind again, and as he looked over the land, he began to sense a new, bestial form.

He came to a fence, climbed over it and found himself among gorse and long grass. Nothing here seemed familiar. He tried to remember the way he had to go, but the distant memory in his mind was only of the destination.

He looked towards what he thought was the south. If this was the right way, Skinny Sam and the plantation must be below him somewhere to the left. He tried to remember the name of the field he had just crossed.

Mucky Meg.

That was it, the muddy one. He remembered Toby's scornful expression when he'd explained why they called it that. But this wasn't the time to think of Toby. He had to keep his wits about him if he was to find what he was looking for.

And avoid the person he feared.

He thought of what the others had said about the Wild Woman, and what Ione had said; and he found himself looking about him as he walked.

Ione.

If only he could speak to her again. There was something so fascinating, so mysterious about her, so—

He stopped suddenly, convinced he was being watched.

He didn't know why he thought that. Maybe it was the inner sense he had come to rely on over the years. But in the silent landscape of bushes and long grass, he sensed an attentive presence.

A whine cut through the night.

He tensed, wondering what it was, and where.

The ground still exuded a ghostly light, and the bushes and hillocks and swaying grass seemed sombre and hostile. He looked over his shoulder, trying to work out where the farm was. And he realized he was lost.

The whine came again, closer. He looked quickly about

him, straining to catch a moving shape among the shadowy forms.

There, to the left. Or maybe—

He turned and scanned the dark clumps of gorse, and his boot sank into a patch of slush. The whine came again, and with it a scurrying sound.

Then silence.

He was more frightened than ever now. Frightened of going on and frightened of going back. And frightened of this glistening land on which he stood.

His other boot was sinking too. He pulled them both out and forced himself to walk on. There was nothing else for it. He had to find the place again, even if he couldn't complete the task he had come back to fulfil.

He plodded on, hoping he was heading west, and gradually the ground became firmer, though still it was unfamiliar. He had been hoping to cut across north of the sitka plantation and perhaps come upon something he remembered, but there was nothing here that he recognized. Certainly he hadn't come this way last night when he ran out and groped his way up from Skinny Sam, or that first time all those years ago.

But perhaps he had come this way: parts of it felt peculiarly familiar, as though the land were a huge serpent that had simply changed its skin. He came to a fence and climbed over and the moment he did so, he knew he had been here before.

He found himself thinking of Ione again, and wondered where she was right now. Sleeping safe, he hoped, even though she was in a cage. He walked a little faster, trying to blot from his mind the thought of the other person who roamed these lands.

This person wouldn't be sleeping, of that he was sure. Probably she never slept; probably she roamed through the nights like a phantom, maybe even watching him this very minute. She wouldn't fear the world like Ione; it was obviously the world that feared her.

He stopped at another patch of gorse, breathing hard. He had never liked exercise, even walking, and always had his leg pulled by the other boys when they had games. He picked his way through the gorse and bracken, and the ground started to soften again. He stared about him, trying to decide which way to go next.

And the landscape seemed to stare back, as though waiting to see what he would do.

Turn right, he told himself. Try north. If that's where north is.

Immediately the land felt more comfortable: there were fewer bushes and shrubs here, and the ground seemed firmer. After a while he saw trees ahead. The land was climbing too, leaving behind the flat, slushy ground he had come through. He walked on for a few minutes, then tripped and fell, face-down, into a small hollow.

Spitting earth from his mouth, he scrambled to the farther edge and looked out. And to his surprise found that the ground fell away into a small valley.

Stretching round the top he saw trees moving against the sky. Beyond them, the skeleton of a house.

The roofless shell that housed no one but had dwelt in his mind ever since he first saw it six years ago.

And below the house, at the bottom of the valley: the rock.

He gazed at it, memories pouring back. Somehow, now that he was here, he felt unwilling to approach. He looked about, searching for danger, then cautiously made his way down. A few feet away, he stopped: it seemed smaller than he remembered, though it was still twice his size. But he had been smaller when he first came, he thought, so perhaps that was the reason.

Then, as he stood there, a feeling of its vastness came back, a feeling that the rock was but an acorn, yet he could sense an oak. He wanted to touch it, but didn't dare.

He walked round it, studying it from all sides, searching in the darkness for the features he had seen in his memory.

And as he walked, it seemed that the rock grew and grew until it dominated the valley.

He heard a rustling sound up the slope.

But all he saw was the ruin rising above him.

He moved closer to the rock and now he saw that, like the ground, it too had a luminosity. And as he drew closer still, he began to feel the heat, just as he had felt it that first time, and ever since, no matter where he was. Yet here it was more intense, more enticing, more frightening.

Unable to resist any longer, he reached out and touched the surface. Surprisingly it was cool, but as he moved his palm upwards, the body of the rock grew hotter. He paused, allowing the strange energy to run through his arm and into his body; and the little stone came back to his mind.

What made him look up the slope again he didn't know. It wasn't a sound or scent or movement in the corner of his eye. But with a sureness that tensed his whole body, he knew someone was near.

He backed away from the rock and crouched behind a bush, searching anxiously about him. Nothing seemed different but the valley had begun to emanate a new presence.

He heard the snap of a twig, then the soft sucking sound of footsteps in wet ground. He stiffened, trying to gauge where they were coming from. But it was impossible. One moment they seemed to be behind him, then to his right, then to his left.

Finally he saw.

A woman was standing by the rock. He didn't know how she had come, whether down the slope from the ruin, or by some other way. But he knew enough.

It was the person he dreaded most in all the world.

As though sensing him, she twisted and stared towards the bush. He held his breath, fighting the urge to call out. Her features were hidden in the darkness but he felt the power in her face, the strength in her body.

51

She began to circle the rock, running her hand over the surface, just as he had done only moments ago. He watched and shuddered. Her body seemed as lithe as a cat, as strong as a bear, and it oozed menace. He thought of Ione, gentle, frightened Ione, and knew she would be powerless against this woman.

This woman could do anything she wanted. The dread of discovery churned his stomach into a knot of fear. With that dread came the conviction that she knew he was there, that she was playing with him, letting him suffer before catching him.

And she would catch him. He knew he could not outrun her.

And what she would do with him he did not dare to think.

But it was not the strength of her body that frightened him most. It was the dark power that swirled about her like a river, a power he knew was harnessed to the rock. A power that now harnessed him.

The whine he had heard earlier split the silence again.

The woman took her hand from the rock and sniffed the air, then, to his relief, began to climb the slope towards the ruin.

He edged round, ready to run.

At once she turned and looked back towards him.

He froze, certain that now he had been seen. She stood motionless, still staring towards the bush behind which he crouched, and for a moment he saw the gleam of an eye in that dark, featureless face. Then she turned back up the slope and disappeared among the trees.

The moment she was gone, he buried himself in flight.

He had never run like this before, even when he escaped from the farm. Heat still licked about him. His head started to spin. He knew he had to keep calm or he would never find the way back.

But his mind was racing too. And as he ran he thought of the Wild Woman. Maybe she was close behind him. Maybe she didn't go back to the ruin. Maybe she turned right at the top of the valley.

She could reappear any moment.

Behind. In front.

Anywhere.

And she would kill him.

With one hand. Or just a look.

He plunged into a brook and out the other side, dimly aware that he hadn't passed it on the way out. A fence appeared before him. He scrambled over it and found himself among trees. Gasping for breath, he drew up, trying to force himself to think of where he was.

But his mind would not think. His mind said 'run'.

The whine broke through the night again. He whirled round, expecting to see the Wild Woman's eyes burning into his own.

He saw no face, no eyes. Only the grizzled countenances of trees. Yet he felt her presence, everywhere.

The whine came again.

He tore into the forest. Branches seemed to swing out, clutching, clasping, clinging. He broke through them, his glasses almost falling from his eyes. Now he saw her face, staring from every tree, every tussock, every rock, and from the spectral darkness that seeped around him like a cloud.

He started to shout, and shout, and shout.

A figure loomed in front of him.

8

'I found him at the bottom end of the forest,' said Gordon.

He looked wearily at Benjamin, fast asleep in the corner of the kitchen by the stove.

'He was out of his mind, shouting his head off. Just as well probably, I might not have found him otherwise. He didn't know what was going on. I called his name and he bolted the other way. I had to run and catch him.'

Toby looked at his parents, both still in their coats like Gordon and himself, and just as bleary-eyed; and he wondered how popular Benjamin was now. Dad glanced balefully at his watch.

'Three o'bloody clock in the morning, and two nights in a row. What's he up to, for God's sake?' He looked at Gordon. 'Did he say anything about what he'd been doing?'

'Don't think he even recognized me. He was scared out of his mind. I just bundled him into the Land Rover.'

Mum sighed.

'I'm really bothered about this. I hate to think of him wandering round Dragon's Rock.'

Toby fumbled with his gloves, still wondering when somebody would mention the chilly atmosphere in the house. Maybe the others had hoped it would go away while they were out looking for Benjamin, but they must have noticed it; it was even worse than yesterday.

And it had spread.

He glowered at the floor. All this had happened since Benjamin came to stay: the coldness in the house, all the talk about the nice lady he claimed he'd seen, and dragons, and running off.

And the stone.

And Flash, dear old Flash. He thought of the dog as he'd been before Benjamin came, healthy and sleek, lying on the grass, ready for work or fun. Then as Gordon had found him, the fur ruffled and pricked where the crows had been.

And the eyes. Toby gulped. He remembered the eyes.

Dad yawned.

'Whatever's going on, we'll have to have a talk with Benjamin, when he's had some rest. Talking of which—'

'Dad?' said Toby. 'What are we going to do about the house?'

It was obvious the others were avoiding the matter for some reason, so he would have to bring it up himself.

'What's wrong with the house?' said Dad.

'You know what I mean. It's cold.'

'We've still got to sleep.'

'But there's a . . . funny atmosphere as well.'

'I'm too tired to notice anything at the moment.'

Gordon rubbed his eyes.

'Sleep in my room if you want, Toby. I can probably put up with your snoring for what's left of the night.'

'No, thanks.'

'Sure, Toby?' said Dad. 'Sounds like a good idea, if you're worried.'

'I'm not worried. It's OK. No problem.'

He looked quickly away; this wasn't the time to show anyone he was frightened. And now he was puzzled too. They must have noticed the atmosphere; it couldn't just be him.

'What about Benjamin?' said Mum. 'If anyone needs company, he does. If only to keep an eye on him.'

'No need to worry about Benjamin,' said Gordon. He nodded towards the stove. 'He's out for the count.'

Dad stood up.

'Let's get some sleep. We'll see how Benjamin is at breakfast and try and get him to tell us what he was up to.'

'It might be an idea to get him away from the farm for a

few hours,' said Mum. 'Give him a change of scene.'

'I've got to go into Totnes,' said Gordon.

'Fine,' said Dad. 'Take the boys with you. Now let's go to bed.'

'And Toby,' said Mum, 'you're to come to our room if you feel frightened.'

'I'm not frightened.'

'No, of course you're not.'

Gordon walked over to the stove where Benjamin was slumped in the chair, still fast asleep.

'Might as well carry him. He's not going to wake up.'

They hung up their coats and Dad led the way out of the room, Toby following, Mum close behind and Gordon at the rear, the sleeping Benjamin in his arms. For Toby the relative cheer of the kitchen vanished as they entered the hall and the chill he had felt seeping into the kitchen enveloped him like a fog. He shivered and found himself wanting to look round at Mum and Gordon; but he kept his eyes on Dad's back and walked on, across the hall and up the stairs.

And as he climbed, he felt the coldness move with him.

Dad stopped at the top of the stairs and the others crowded round him.

'You're still looking worried, Toby,' he said. 'Want me to leave the landing light on?'

Toby tried to look unconcerned.

'Don't mind. Could do.'

'Leave it on,' said Gordon. 'I'll put Benjamin to bed. Toby, come into my room if you change your mind.'

'Or ours,' said Mum. 'And leave your bedside light on if you want to.'

'I'm OK, Mum. I told you.'

'All right,' she said and kissed him. 'Goodnight, then.'

'Goodnight.'

He entered his room, switched on the light, and closed the door behind him. And as he'd feared, the coldness slid after him.

He sat on the bed, knowing he would not sleep, and that he had several hours to endure before it would be light enough to go out and do what he had decided he must do. It would have been better done now, in the darkness, away from prying eyes, but the darkness was too frightening, especially outside on his own, even among the fields he knew so well.

He looked about him, wondering how familiar things could possibly have become so threatening since Benjamin came.

Benjamin, bloody Benjamin.

For a moment fear fell back as anger rose within him. He held on to it, determined not to lose it, and tried to think what to do for the next few hours. The urge to reach under the pillow was strong but he checked himself; somehow he knew that the presence in the house and in this very room was linked to that tiny thing he had prized, but which now weighed like a colossal burden upon him. He reached instead for the stump he'd found the week before Benjamin came.

Benjamin. Anger. Hold on to it.

He rummaged in the drawer of the cabinet and pulled out his favourite whittling knife.

Hold on to the anger. Use it.

He turned the stump and examined it, remembering the dog's glee on finding it at the foot of the privet. Dear old Flash. More anger flooded in and he struck out with the knife. Before long chips were flying over the floor.

'Some kind of reptile, that's what you'll be.'

He plucked away a couple of strands with his blade and took a shaving from the curved top.

'Hang on, we'll leave you as you are up here. Then you can be holding something in your mouth.'

He trimmed the lower part of the stump and gradually it took shape: a slender body, curving upwards from the belly, the head back, and some large object in its mouth.

'Your prey,' he said. 'What'll it be?'

He pondered this for a while, idly stroking the wood with the flat of the blade.

'You can be a dragon,' he said suddenly. 'Seeing as Benjamin keeps having nightmares about a dragon, or so he says. And your prey . . . '

He smiled; he knew what the prey would be.

Now the blade was rasping over the wood, chipping, shaping, refining. He smiled again: no one else would recognize the prey, but he would always know what it was. He glared round the room at the unseen presence.

'You haven't stopped me whittling, whatever you are. You haven't—'

A wailing call sounded in the night. He clutched the dragon to him and listened. A moment later it came again, an eerie, plaintive cry, just outside the window. Gripping the dragon tightly, he turned off the light and peered out.

At first all was blackness outside and he could see nothing; then, little by little, the darkness softened. Just below him, on one of the new fence posts, was a large black shape. It seemed somehow hooded or arched over, its back flexed into a curve so perfect it seemed sculptured in stillness; then it twisted its head and two eyes flashed up at him.

It was a cat.

But that made him feel no better. There weren't any cats round here. None on the farm because of Mum's allergy, and the nearest local cat was over at Brambles Farm and much too decrepit to drag itself here.

And this was no ordinary stray. There was something about the way it moved its head, the way it crouched and twisted its body, the way it looked up, aware of him.

Suddenly it tensed. The eyes blinked, the back lengthened, it reared on its haunches, its head high; and once more the call broke the silence of the night.

He started to open the window.

'I don't think I like the look of you.'

Unhurriedly the creature stretched out its paws and

clawed the edge of the post, then the long shape tightened and quivered, the face turned, and the eyes glinted up at him again.

The next moment it was gone.

He fastened the window again and sat on the edge of the bed, thinking of the cat, and the chill in the house, and what he had to do. And as he sat and shivered and trembled, he gazed out of the window at the slow, cold lightening of the sky.

9

At dawn, he was out.

No need to tell anyone anything.

Just get it over and done with.

He ran round the house, hoping no one had heard him leave. The curtains were drawn but he doubted whether anyone had slept well. And Dad and Gordon were always up early.

No time to waste. The breeze was bracing but he was glad of it; it forced away the hunger for sleep. And the sky was reassuringly bright and clear after the shadowy turmoil of the night. He noticed that the coldness of the house had followed him.

Never mind that now, he thought. First things first. He stole round the side of the house, listening for sounds behind Gordon's window. But all was silent. He crept over to the shrubbery fence, looked up at his own window, then down at the posts.

That was the one, third from the end. He walked over and examined it but there was no sign of fur or scratch marks, not that he'd expected any. The animal was probably miles away by now. He turned back towards the yard.

And gave a start.

Up in the silver birch was a large black form. But it was not a cat.

It was a raven.

Or rather, *the* raven: he knew it was the one he'd spotted at Skinny Sam the time they took Benjamin out in the tractor. He'd seen plenty of ravens up on the moor but never in this part of Devon before. But that wasn't the only reason why he recognized it.

This raven was awesomely large.

He walked across the yard, leaned on the paddock gate and looked up at the bird sitting motionless above him.

'There's something about you I don't trust,' he murmured.

As though it had understood him, the bird flapped off the branch and swung away over Long Louis. He watched it disappear, then hurried down the path towards Mucky Meg.

Nothing else matters so long as it's done.

He pulled the overcoat tight around him and knotted the scarf a second time. The sky seemed to be losing its brightness already and suddenly looked grey and menacing; and the air was growing colder still. He heard a gruff croaking sound behind him and looked back at the house.

There was the raven again, this time waddling round the rim of the chimney. He walked quickly on down the track until he reached the gate into Mucky Meg. The wood was damp but he climbed astride and sat there to look out over the field. But the field was no longer there to see.

It had been swallowed in mist.

His mouth dropped open and he stared about him.

To the left, Long Louis was still clear and so were the fields to the south-east, but the whole of the forest to the west was gone, even the tops of the trees. He looked north towards the lane: that was clear, and he could see all the way along the hedge to the end, and into Big Willy. He gazed back at Mucky Meg and saw smudges of mist rolling in bulbous clouds from the south and west like an incoming tide.

But the job still had to be done. He jumped down from the gate into the slush. The mist'll even help, he thought, and reached into his pocket.

Cruk! Cruk! Cruk!

Startled, he looked up.

A hundred feet up he saw the raven soaring. After a while it stopped and hung there, directly above him, spiralling in the currents, then it swooped down over the field again and vanished in the mist. He glared after it and pulled out the stone.

It seemed to sparkle in the light and felt warm in his hand. He played with it for a moment, stroking the sides, then running his finger over the hardness of the base.

'Two-faced,' he said. 'That's what you are. One side nice and smooth. The other side you'll cut me.'

He tossed and caught it a couple of times.

'And there's been nothing but trouble since he brought you.'

He gazed out at the misty visage of Mucky Meg, closed his fingers round the stone and crooked his arm back for the throw.

Cruk! Cruk! Cruk!

Again the black speck appeared, soaring and circling, in and out of the mist. He relaxed his arm; there was something unsettling about this bird, and not just the fact that it was so big. He threw his arm back again.

Cruk! Cruk! Cruk!

Again the gruff call, this time far above him. He flashed his eyes upwards, searching angrily. At first he saw only sky, then he glimpsed it, plunging down over the poplars beyond Ivan's Meadow.

'Leave me alone!' he shouted. 'You . . . you bloody raven!'

He looked at the stone again, still sitting innocently in his hand.

'What is it about you? You're like . . . ' He tried to remember the story Mr Wilkins had read out in class about King Arthur. But it was no good: he'd never paid much attention to anything Mr Wilkins said, or any of the other teachers for that matter. He gazed desperately out over Mucky Meg.

This shouldn't be a problem. It should be easy. And

Mucky Meg was the perfect place: the one field with mud so deep he could guarantee no one would ever find the stone again.

One good throw and it's done, he told himself.

One good throw.

That's all.

In his mind he saw the stone fly over the field in a great arc and fall into the slush. Buried forever, in mist and mud.

But it was no use.

Holding it more tightly than ever, he turned, climbed the gate once more, and trudged back towards the house.

Benjamin stared down at his undrunk tea.

'I'm so hot,' he said, wiping his face. 'So hot.'

Toby watched him across the kitchen table.

Hot, hot, hot, he thought. Stupid idiot. Even his tea's gone cold. And he's slept through the whole morning yet again.

Mum drew up a chair next to Benjamin but Toby doubted even she'd get any sense out of him. He noticed Dad and Gordon had stayed out with the animals; probably they'd decided it was best to leave the talking to Mum. Or maybe they were just fed up with the whole thing.

The chill now seeped through the whole house. But still no one had mentioned it.

Benjamin's eyes rolled round the room.

'It's like . . . breath,' he said. 'Hot breath.'

'Well, I'm cold,' said Toby.

Mum frowned at him and took one of Benjamin's hands.

'Benjamin, you don't have to tell us anything if you really don't want to. But you must understand, we've been worried about you. Wandering about on your own. Up at Dragon's Rock. In the dark.'

Benjamin stared vacantly ahead and his lips moved, the words just audible.

'I had to . . . try and find it.'

'Find what?' said Mum.

His eyes fixed on Toby.

'What I lost.'

The back door opened, and Dad and Gordon came in.

'Getting nippy out there,' said Dad. 'And the mist's up to the top of Mucky Meg.'

Gordon thrust his hands over the stove.

'How are you, Benjamin? Better?'

'He's hot,' said Toby.

'Maybe he's got a fever,' said Gordon.

'Do you want us to take you to the doctor?' said Mum.

Benjamin dreamily wiped his face again.

'I don't want to go to the doctor. I haven't got a fever. I just feel hot. Like there's a huge—'

'A huge what?' said Mum.

Toby watched the changing expressions on Benjamin's face and a recollection came from the day before: of the nightmare, and the sculpture lying on his bed.

'A huge dragon,' he said suddenly.

'Yes!' Benjamin's eyes were on him again. 'A huge dragon.'

'But where?' said Mum. 'Where do you see this dragon?'

'I don't see it, but I feel it. Here.' Benjamin spread his arms about him. 'Underneath us. We're standing on it.'

'Funny looking dragon,' said Toby. 'Looks more like a stone floor to me.'

'You lads better eat,' said Dad. 'It's half twelve.'

Mum stood up and reached for the frying pan.

'It's eggs or eggs. No grumbling, all right?'

'I'll help,' said Gordon.

She heated some fat, then cut some slices of bread and laid them under the grill. Gordon handed her the eggs, one at a time, and she broke them into the pan.

'Great team,' he said.

She chuckled and Toby could see Gordon's cheerfulness was doing some good.

'Fried bread, Toby?' she said.

'Yes, please.'

'Cut me a piece, will you? Benjamin?'

'Yes, please.'

'Cut a piece for Benjamin too.'

Toby took the bread knife, cut two large slices, and handed them to her. Out of the corner of his eye, he saw Benjamin walk over to the window where Dad was standing.

'What do you use Skinny Sam for?'

'Cattle. Not right now, of course. They're all inside.'

'Have you got lots?'

Dad grunted.

'Not any more. That's why we're giving sheep a try. Not that they're doing any better. Specially now we've got to get another dog.'

'But why haven't you got so many cattle any more?'

'Don't get me going on that subject.'

Gordon called over his shoulder from the stove.

'Disease, Benjamin. We used to have loads of cattle but things have got a bit tough lately.'

Lately? thought Toby. They've been tough for the last six years. And it started after Benjamin first came to stay.

'We've had disease several years running,' said Dad. 'Just about finished us. We're still trying to rebuild the herd.'

Mum walked over to the table with the first of the eggs.

'So no Christmas presents for anyone this year. Boys, get started, as you're going into Totnes.'

Gordon sat down at the table.

'Another year without Christmas presents. Well, at least we're used to it.' He caught Benjamin's eye and winked. 'She's only joking. By the way, Toby, funny looking bit of whittling in your room. What's it meant to be?'

Toby took his knife and fork with elaborate unconcern.

'Nothing special,' he said. 'Just a dragon.'

10

Gordon swung the Land Rover into an empty space in the top car park at Totnes and switched off the engine.

'OK, I've got several things to get. You two can—'

'Why's it called Dragon's Rock?' said Benjamin suddenly.

Gordon looked him over tolerantly and didn't seem taken aback by the abruptness of the question, or the fact that it was the first thing Benjamin had said since breakfast.

'Don't know. Don't think anyone does. I remember a load of people talking about it in the pub once. None of them knew either.'

'Somebody must know.'

'Maybe. They're not that bothered round our way. Everybody keeps clear of the place, case they bump into you-know-who. Nobody I know goes there.'

'Except Benjamin,' said Toby. 'And sheep.'

'Sheep?' said Benjamin.

Gordon nodded.

'Funny thing. If any of the sheep go missing, we generally find 'em round Dragon's Rock. Don't know why. But that's why we're so careful about fencing.'

Benjamin thought of the haunting mystery of the place; its beauty, its danger.

'What did the ruin use to be?'

'Don't really know. Farmhouse probably. It's been a ruin for donkey's years.'

'Who lived there?'

'No idea. Before my time. But they reckon the locals drove 'em out.'

'What for?'

Gordon opened the door and jumped out.

'Witchcraft,' he said and strode over to the ticket machine.

Toby saw Benjamin look his way and quickly jumped out, too, before the next question came. Luckily Gordon was soon back.

'Right, you two, I've got loads of places to go. Meet back here at half five. And don't—'

But again Benjamin interrupted him.

'Does the Wild Woman live at Dragon's Rock?'

And again, Gordon seemed unruffled.

'Nobody knows. She's been seen in lots of places. There are loads of stories about her. They say she eats beetles, slugs, birds, rabbits—'

'Hedgehogs,' said Toby.

'Don't know about hedgehogs.'

'She does, they all say she does.'

Gordon shrugged.

'Maybe. Some of the locals leave food out for her so she won't put a spell on their farms. They reckon she's the one who's sent all the bad luck these last few years.'

'Have other people had bad luck, then?' said Benjamin.

'Oh, yeah, it's not just us. Everybody's had trouble.'

'She's behind it,' said Toby. 'Everybody knows she's behind it. She's a witch, she's evil, she's really evil. They reckon she can take the form of animals and birds.'

'Come off it,' said Gordon.

'She can. I know she can.'

He remembered the raven wheeling overhead; the cat on the post, watching him.

'I know she can,' he said.

And Benjamin thought of the woman he had seen in the night, the tall woman, swathed in power; and of Ione, her slave, caught in that power, caught in a cage of fear, in a web she could not break.

Suffering the pain of the world.

'Do you leave food out for the Wild Woman?' he said.

67

Gordon shook his head.

'Dad won't allow it. But we've seen her after dark, drinking from the outside tap.'

'And looking in the bins,' said Toby.

'That was a tramp.'

'It was her, it was definitely her.'

Gordon gave Toby's scarf a playful tug; then his face grew serious.

'I'll tell you one thing about Dragon's Rock. Some people say they've seen smoke coming out of the ground either side of it. Like a dragon's nostrils, someone said. So maybe there is a dragon there. Maybe it's got a lair underneath the rock.'

'You never told me about the smoke,' said Toby.

Gordon chuckled.

'See you later.'

Toby wandered down towards the Narrows, not bothering to look behind to see whether Benjamin had followed, and fighting the urge to sleep which, despite the coldness still clinging to him, was starting to grow worse.

Gordon had already clumped off.

All this talk about Dragon's Rock and the Wild Woman. Of course, Benjamin had started it, as usual, but the surprising thing was that even Gordon didn't seem to understand how evil she was.

He frowned.

Maybe Benjamin was in league with the Wild Woman and all these questions were just to fool them. After all, he kept running away to Dragon's Rock, and he was the one who brought the stone to the farm in the first place; and it was then that the horrible cold presence arrived.

He plodded on through the Narrows and down to the square. Totnes was packed, presumably with late Christmas shoppers, he thought, looking morosely at them. He'd never felt less like Christmas in his life, and right now he could have done with some peace and quiet, to think things through. As though to taunt him further, a busker nearby started to play 'Silent Night' on an accordion.

He stomped on down the hill.

Everyone knows the Wild Woman's evil, he thought. Everyone knows she can take any form she likes. She was inside that raven, inside that cat, I know it.

He stopped suddenly.

She's inside Benjamin. She must be. That would explain everything. Benjamin's in her power.

He turned suspiciously.

But Benjamin was nowhere to be seen.

Benjamin didn't know how he came to be outside the bookshop. He remembered Gordon leaving them at the car park and Toby walking on ahead, clearly not wanting company.

At least, not *his* company.

He remembered darkness falling as he meandered about the town, passing several bookshops and not noticing much about any of them; yet feeling led by a strange compulsion. Then he was staring through a window at rows of books, and the image of a face forming in the glass.

At first he thought it was someone's reflection, but when he checked to see, he found there was no one behind him. He turned back and saw the image still there. Slowly it defined itself.

Ione.

Her beautiful, unmistakable features. But almost at once it started to fade.

'No!'

He reached forward and clutched at the glass. A man shouted from inside the shop.

'Hoy! Stop that!'

He stepped back, still peering at the window, and to his surprise found that where the image had been, his eye had fallen on a book. He read the title aloud.

'*Dragons in Landscape and Legend*.'

He dashed inside. The shopkeeper looked him over mistrustfully.

'What's up with you, then? Messing about with the glass.'

'I'm sorry, I . . . ' He squeezed past the man to the display stand by the window. 'I didn't mean . . . I just . . . '

The shopkeeper muttered something but asked no further questions. Benjamin reached eagerly for the book and opened it.

But his heart sank at once.

There was no message here. This book was far too difficult. It was much thicker than it had looked from outside, the writing was small, the paragraphs were long, it was full of maps and diagrams, and it cost far more money than he had, even if he'd wanted to buy it.

But there was no point in buying it anyway.

It would take a lifetime to read, and even then he wouldn't understand it. It was a work of scholarship for experts.

Not for him.

But the image he had seen stayed in his mind. He stared down at the book, certain that there must be something here.

On an impulse he closed his eyes, slammed the book shut, opened it at random and placed his finger blindly down one of the pages; then he opened his eyes and read the passage his finger had chosen.

' . . . and special thanks to my wife Dorothy for all her help and encouragement during the writing of this book, for typing up the manuscript and . . . '

He closed the book impatiently and tried again, this time keeping his eyes shut for some time, even after his finger had found a place on a new page.

'Give me a message,' he murmured, and opened his eyes again.

Almost in disbelief he found his finger on the blank backing sheet of one of the maps.

He stared out of the window. Soon he would have to go back and meet the others but he knew he couldn't leave yet. Out of the corner of his eye he sensed the shopkeeper watching. He turned his back to him and looked at the book.

One last try. One last try.

He screwed his eyes tight and held the book firmly closed; then, holding his breath, he opened it, stabbed his finger onto the page, opened his eyes and read.

' . . . of the theory that currents of power known as dragon paths run through the land. These are said to be especially powerful at certain points such as old church sites, mounds or standing stones in remote hills or valleys. It is from these key points that the dragon power is thought to flow over the landscape.'

He looked up, trembling.

Standing stones. Remote valleys.

Dragon power.

He read on.

'It is believed by some that the ancients understood and manipulated the dragon power for their own purposes, and that this power can still be invoked by persons sensitive to it, especially where the current is strongest.'

Power that can still be invoked, especially where the current is strongest. Already there had been witchcraft on that spot, if what Gordon said was true; then all the bad luck the farms had been having.

He wondered about the little stone he had found and lost.

Nearly half-past five. The shop would be closing and he'd have to get back to the car park. But he knew he had to read a little more.

'Whether the power was and is invoked for positive or negative ends is difficult to say. Perhaps the answer is both. But it is interesting to note how the symbolism of the

71

dragon has changed over the centuries. Whereas formerly the dragon was a symbol of life, fertility and harmony, now it has largely become a symbol of evil.'

He thought of the Wild Woman up at Dragon's Rock. And Ione, caught in a cage, a halter round her neck. Being slowly destroyed.

He had to help her escape.

Somehow.

He heard a sharp knock on the window close by and saw Toby scowling at him from the other side. Over his shoulder he heard the carping voice of the shopkeeper again.

'What is it about my window?'

He turned and saw the man standing there, hands on hips.

'If it's not you hitting the damn thing, it's your friend!'

Benjamin looked once more at Toby's face, then closed the book and replaced it on the stand.

'He's not my friend,' he said.

'I don't like the look of this,' said Gordon.

Toby came to with a start, suddenly aware that he had been secretly watching Benjamin all the way home to the exclusion of all else.

'What's wrong?' he said.

'See for yourself.'

The road before them had disappeared in mist.

'How far are we from home?' said Toby.

Gordon looked round, eyebrows raised.

'You been asleep or something?'

Toby shrugged. 'Sort of.'

'We're just down from the entrance.' He stared into the gloom. 'Darkness and mist together. Great, just what we need.'

'The lights don't seem to be doing much good,' said Benjamin.

Gordon leaned closer to the windscreen.

'We'll have to take it really slow. If you see anything, shout. I'm not bothered about the hedge but I don't want to bash into the oak.'

They edged their way into the mist, Gordon craning forward, his hands tight round the steering-wheel. Toby strained his eyes to see some familiar shape to guide them, but all he saw was billowing clouds. He noticed Benjamin staring at the floor, lost in thought.

'You might try and help, Benjamin.'

No answer.

'You listening, Benjamin? I said you might try and help.'

Benjamin looked up suddenly.

'You'll be glad when I'm gone, won't you?' he said.

Gordon sounded the horn.

'Cut the bickering, you two and—Christ!' He swerved suddenly. Toby heard something graze the side of the Land Rover.

'What was that?'

'The oak. We've gone past the entrance. I'll have to reverse. Keep your eyes peeled.'

'OK.'

They started to back and Toby narrowed his eyes, searching for a sight of the entrance; he knew it could only be a few yards away. There was a sudden jolt and the Land Rover stopped. He looked at Gordon.

'What happened?'

'We just found the oak. Didn't you see it?'

'Sorry.'

'Don't worry, I didn't either. We'll try and get round it.'

Gordon wrestled with the gear lever for a moment before finding first gear again. The Land Rover rumbled ahead a few yards.

'Now then.' Gordon twisted the wheel. 'Sing out if you see anything. You too, Benjamin.'

'What? What did . . . ?' Benjamin blinked as though he had just woken from a deep sleep.

'Never mind.' Gordon gritted his teeth and slipped the Land Rover into reverse again. 'Eyes skinned, everybody.'

They crept backwards, more slowly than before.

'There's the oak!' shouted Toby.

'Take your word for it,' said Gordon. 'Can you see the entrance?'

'No.'

Gordon leaned over Benjamin and opened the side window.

'It's got to be about here. Let's try it.'

He pushed the lever into first gear and turned the wheel; the Land Rover bumped round to the left and met no resistance.

They were through.

Toby felt the motion steady as Gordon found the centre of the track. Any moment now they should reach the back end of the shrubbery. He looked for signs of the fence but the ground was starting to feel uneven and he began to suspect Gordon had lost the track.

There was another jolt, this time in front.

'Blast!' said Gordon.

Toby leaned forward.

'What've we hit?'

'Shrubbery fence probably. Hang on.'

He jumped out of the Land Rover and wandered round to the front. Toby noticed uneasily how quickly his brother vanished from view, but fortunately he reappeared almost at once.

'Yep,' he said, slamming the door. 'It was the shrubbery fence.'

'Bust?'

'Well and truly. Can't do anything about it now.'

He reversed back onto the track, then drove on towards the unseen house.

To Toby's disgust, Benjamin seemed to have no interest at all in what was happening and was simply staring at the floor, as though nothing mattered but his own inner world.

The urge to reach out and hit him became almost irresistible.

He grew more certain than ever that Benjamin was in the power of the Wild Woman.

'We should be round the house by now,' said Gordon. 'Ah, we're in the yard. I can hear the gravel. We've made it.' He braked and switched off the engine. 'Can anyone see the house?'

Toby took his eyes from Benjamin and peered through the window. It was hard to believe that mist could be so thick. He, too, had heard the reassuring sound of gravel under the wheels and knew that the house was only yards away.

But he saw no sign of it at all.

'Come on,' said Gordon. 'Mum'll be worrying. We can find the way now.'

He jumped out and hurried towards where the house lay. Toby looked scornfully at Benjamin.

'You going to just sit there, then?'

Their eyes met, and Toby found himself wondering who was really watching him behind that faraway stare.

'I'm going in,' he said and, without waiting for Benjamin to move, climbed over him, jumped onto the gravel and plunged towards the house. Even here, only yards from home, he felt a wave of insecurity at the density of the mist, and the way it seemed to swirl about him.

Yet again he thought of the raven and the cat; and Benjamin's eyes.

The wall felt pleasantly solid under his hands and a moment later he saw the kitchen light to his right, then the open door.

A light touch on his shoulder made him jump.

But it was only Benjamin.

He shrugged away, surprised and a little angry that he hadn't heard Benjamin following across the gravel, and made for the light of the doorway. Gordon appeared in the entrance and gazed out into the mist.

'We're over here!' Toby called.

Gordon waited until they had reached the door.

'It wasn't you I was looking for,' he said, and gazed out again.

'What's wrong?' said Toby.

Gordon frowned.

'There's nobody here.'

11

At nine o'clock Gordon picked up the big lamp and beckoned Toby towards the back door.

'You and Benjamin stay here. I don't want you wandering off in this mist. I'll go out and see if I can find anything. Might as well look in on the cattle first.'

'But you know they're not there. They'd have heard us shouting.'

'Maybe, but I'll have a look. Got to start somewhere. Anyway, like I said, you two stay put.'

Toby hesitated.

'Gordon?'

'Um?'

'Do you reckon the house is haunted?'

'What do you mean?'

Toby looked about him.

'It's so cold.'

He didn't say that the coldness had followed him to Totnes and back.

Gordon shrugged.

'What do you expect, a heat wave? It's Christmas Eve tomorrow, case you'd forgotten. I'm more bothered about Mum and Dad. They'd have left a note if they were planning on being out for any length of time.'

Toby nodded towards the stove where Benjamin sat, still lost in his thoughts, and lowered his voice.

'What are we going to do about him?'

'Not much we can do,' said Gordon, also in a low voice, 'but for God's sake, keep an eye on him. The last thing we want is him running off again.'

'He's getting worse,' said Toby. He saw Gordon raise his eyebrows and quickly added, 'And I'm not just saying that 'cause I don't like him.'

'Maybe. Anyway, don't let him out of your sight.' Gordon reached for the door. 'See you later.'

Toby watched him vanish in the mist and immediately wished he hadn't gone. He closed the door and turned to find Benjamin standing before him.

'Where's my stone?'

The voice was different: not whining or hesitant or shy. Almost bold.

'Where's my stone?'

He tried to look indifferent. 'Don't know what you mean.'

'You do. You took it. Where is it?'

Toby glared back, expecting Benjamin to drop his eyes, but to his surprise the gaze did not waver. He faked a yawn.

'I haven't got it.'

'Well, where have you hidden it?'

'Why all this fuss about a stone? There are hundreds of stones. I could easily find you a better one. And yours isn't that good anyway.'

'So you have got it!'

Toby silently cursed himself. But all was not lost; he hadn't actually admitted anything, and even if he did admit having the stone, he could still keep it. After all, it was only Benjamin's, and he could handle Benjamin.

'I haven't got your stupid stone,' he said. 'And even if I did have it, I don't see why I should give it to you. It doesn't belong to you.'

Without warning Benjamin jumped. Momentarily taken aback, Toby fell to the floor, Benjamin's squirming body on top of him.

'Give it back!' shouted Benjamin, raining punches down. 'Give it back!'

Toby twisted his head to avoid the fists but quickly

realized there was no danger. Benjamin was no fighter and there was no power behind the blows. He waited, choosing his moment, then rolled over, pinning Benjamin easily beneath him.

'You can't have your stone.'

'You have got it!'

'What if I have?'

He jumped up.

'You don't deserve to have it back. You've been nothing but trouble. Running off and making us all go and look for you. And all the stupid things you keep saying.'

Benjamin climbed slowly to his feet, eyes downcast, body shaking. Toby watched warily, waiting for another charge. Then Benjamin looked up.

Toby narrowed his eyes, determined not to be out-stared, determined to show in his gaze all the anger he felt. And he searched Benjamin's eyes for a similar rage.

But he saw no rage.

Only despair.

He gulped. He had not expected despair. He had expected anger, wanted anger even, to match his own and relieve his guilt. He stepped forward, unsure what he wanted to do.

'Benjamin, I—'

But Benjamin turned, threw open the door and raced out into the mist.

Toby ran to the threshold, Gordon's words of warning flooding ominously back. From somewhere in the yard he heard the sound of running feet.

Cautiously he edged down the steps and away from the house, which almost at once receded in the mist. The footsteps sounded further away now, but he could tell where they were heading.

He stumbled across the yard until his hands touched the paddock fence, felt along it to the end and plunged down the track towards Mucky Meg.

Cruk! Cruk! Cruk!

The raucous cry sounded overhead and he looked up; but saw only mist swirling. He fumbled on, straining to see something he knew.

Cruk! Cruk! Cruk!

Again he looked up, and again saw nothing but mist.

The sound of footsteps had ceased.

He felt the gate under his hand, climbed up and swung his leg over the top, and listened. At first he heard nothing, then, after a moment, the squelch of footsteps somewhere in Mucky Meg.

He jumped off the gate onto the muddy ground.

'Benjamin!'

The footsteps stopped.

'Benjamin! Come back!'

For a while there was silence; then a voice, nervous, suspicious.

'What do you want?'

'Where are you?'

'What do you want?'

'Come back to the farm.'

More silence; then the voice returned.

'What for?'

He tried to gauge the direction of the voice. It had come from somewhere to the right, or so he thought, but there was no sign of Benjamin. He tried again.

'There's no point in running away. We've got to stick together.'

Cruk! Cruk! Cruk!

The gruff call came again, high above him.

'Benjamin?'

'Leave me alone.'

'Come back.'

'What for? You don't want me here. Nobody wants me here.'

Toby thought of what Gordon would say if Benjamin wasn't back on his return and took a deep breath.

'We . . . do want you here,' he said, certain that Benjamin

would feel the lie as much as he did. Benjamin didn't speak; and that was sufficient answer.

He moved as quietly as he could towards where he had last heard the voice.

'So where are you going?' he called.

'What do you care?'

The voice had moved. More to the left.

He changed direction and crept closer, crouching low to the ground. He knew the answer to the next question but it was worth asking it just to get another bearing on the voice.

'Are you going to Dragon's Rock?'

'Maybe.'

Now it was dead ahead, and close. He stopped, anxious not to give himself away by the sound of his footsteps. He'd have to make sure his voice didn't sound too loud when he spoke again. Fortunately Benjamin spoke first, without prompting.

'You don't want me here. And you won't give me back my stone.'

There was the figure, blurred but recognizable. But Benjamin saw him at the same time.

'Leave me alone!' he shouted and bolted into the mist.

'Benjamin! Wait!'

He started forward but the mist folded round him like a cloak. He heard the spatter of mud as Benjamin sped away.

'Benjamin! Benjamin!'

He began to run after him.

But another sound had come. A new, frightening sound, this time above him. He looked up, his neck prickling.

The next moment the raven burst upon him.

12

Benjamin could not run for long.

The hotness he had felt for so long still hung about him, as did the breathing presence in the land. He remembered what the book had said about dragon power flowing over the landscape; and in the boggy ground of Mucky Meg, surrounded by mist, he began to feel a sense of smallness, as though he were but a parasite on the body of a huge, quivering monster.

Toby's shouts had stopped with a strange abruptness. He listened to be sure there were no footsteps in pursuit, then tried to think which way to go.

He had to keep his wits about him, he knew that. No mad running or all would be lost. He peered round at the clouds of mist: here and there they receded and he could see slushy ground stretching away for a few yards, but such patches were rare; he knew there would be little or no warning if he met anything.

Or anyone.

He stared into the mist, searching in vain for encouraging shapes.

The heat grew more oppressive and he stepped forward. It felt better to be moving, even with the tingling under his feet, and so far he was fairly sure of his direction.

He hadn't come to a fence so he must still be in Mucky Meg, and he was certain he'd run westward after leaving Toby. So that way he should either come to the sitka plantation or, if he'd strayed too far south, to the top of Skinny Sam.

Yet again he thought of Ione. Somehow he had to help

her escape from the Wild Woman. And if the Wild Woman came—

He clenched his fists and pushed forward. The heat was growing more intense, more stifling; he tried to inhale more slowly but the air seemed to choke him. He tripped and rolled onto his side in the mud.

'Idiot,' he said. 'Concentrate.'

He scrambled to his feet, his trousers now sodden and clinging to his legs, and struggled on. The ground started to feel firmer and he wondered if the fence were near. But no fence appeared. He stopped and listened.

All around him was a deep rumbling sound. He knelt down and put his head to the ground. And now he heard it more clearly: an endless, oceanic roar, like the respiration of a huge beast stirring.

He walked on, yearning for a glimpse of the fence, and his foot brushed against something hard. He bent down and felt his hand touch a tiny mound with some kind of root on top, or maybe a young tree. He walked on and found another, then another.

This didn't make sense. He hadn't come to a fence so he must still be in Mucky Meg, but he had been walking for some time and should have reached the edge of the field by now. Or perhaps he'd crossed the fence without realizing it. Somehow the mist seemed to cloud memory as well as sight.

The roaring sound around him grew more powerful.

He carried on, praying that the fence would appear. It did not, but a gap opened in the mist, not wide but enough of a clearance to see a patch of grass. He hurried forward, trying not to run. He could make out bushes now, and a line of small trees he'd not seen before, young ones with protective fencing round them, not like the spiny sitka spruce above Skinny Sam. And there was the fence.

He breathed out with relief. Nothing looked familiar but at least he'd come to the edge of the field, whether it was Mucky Meg or not. He climbed over the fence and slipped between the rows of trees, wondering what they were, and where he was.

Behind him the fence vanished as the passage in the mist closed.

He forced himself on, the mist still billowing around him but slightly more patchy than it had been. To his right he glimpsed a small clump of nettles and further ahead what seemed to be a line of tall conifers. He stumbled towards them, following another slender passage in the mist.

They weren't conifers; he could see that now that he was drawing nearer. They were some other kind of tree, though he didn't know which. No doubt Toby would know.

He stopped again.

Toby.

It would have been nice to be friends with Toby. He looked back the way he had come, and for a moment wondered where Toby was.

Toby threw himself to the side.

Too late.

A stinging pain like a knife blade stabbed into his temple.

He fell back, crying out. Before he could recover, the black shape was at his face.

Fluttering, jabbing.

He gulped in breath, flailed his arms.

Cruk! Cruk! Cruk!

The raven's wings brushed his face, its beak darting like a shower of arrows. Pricks of pain stung his cheeks and brow.

He ducked his head, trying to keep his eyes from the bird's beak, and thrashed his arms round his head. The jabs started on his legs, stomach, arms.

He drew his knees up and pressed his face down. The fluttering seemed all around him now, as though ten birds or more were attacking him.

The jabs started on his head. He struck out and felt his

arm smack against the body of the bird. The fluttering moved back to his legs. He cuffed downwards with his palm and hit the bird again.

Cruk! Cruk!

The jabbing ceased suddenly. He crouched over into a ball and waited, quivering. A moment later he felt a wing brush his hair as the bird flew away.

He stayed hunched over, breathing hard, his body still shaking, his head throbbing where the beak had done its work. And he was frightened, really frightened; but at least the bird had gone. Slowly he raised his head.

Instantly the beak skewered into his cheek.

Pain shot through him again. Now the fluttering was louder, fiercer, the jabbing harder, deeper, and only round his eyes. He threw his head back and rolled it from side to side, but the wings still beat over him, the feet of the raven almost in his mouth. He swept his arm across his face and brushed the bird to the left.

In a flash it was back over his eyes.

He thrust his arm up and pushed the bird to the other side. It clung to the hand and pecked at the palm.

'Get off! Get off!'

He shook his arm but still the bird hung there.

'Get off!'

He drove his other arm down, forced the bird off and kicked up. The action threw him on his back but he felt one foot connect.

The black shape soared up and was gone.

He struggled to his feet and looked about him. The mist still closed in on all sides, faceless, formless, fearsomely chill. He was so cold now, so cold, so frightened. For some reason he found himself wondering where Benjamin was.

Cruk! Cruk! Cruk!

There it was again, the loathsome call croaking through the mist. He crouched, his arms across his face, ready for the attack.

But none came.

Keeping his arms raised, he turned and swept his eyes about him. And as always, saw nothing but mist.

Cruk! Cruk! Cruk!

The call was further away now and receding but he kept his arms across his face and continued to turn and scan the cold, vaporous wall. Still he saw only mist, but even that was better than the hideous bird. He ventured a step forward, his arms still high, karate-style. The ground felt fairly hard so he took another step, and another. His left foot sank into slush.

He pulled it out and it made a large slurp, and for the first time he felt some relief. There was always something reassuring about Mucky Meg. He thought of the times he had played here, giggling at the rude sounds he could make in the mud.

Cruk! Cruk! Cruk!

The sound was barely audible now and he decided he was probably safe; but still he kept his arms raised, as he tried to work out what to do.

It shouldn't be too difficult to get back to the farmhouse. All he had to do was walk until he reached some part of the hedge or fence and follow that until he came to the north gate. There was nothing he could do about Benjamin now. It would be more sensible to get back to the house, even if he did have to face the music.

Besides, Benjamin might have returned. He certainly wouldn't be able to find his way to Dragon's Rock in this mist, and Mum and Dad should be home by now. He lowered his arms and stepped forward.

And the beak drove into his face.

He whirled round, his arm out, but the bird was coming from below, aiming for his throat. He pulled his hand back.

But he was not quick enough.

The beak plunged into his neck like a dart. He staggered, thrashing wildly, and saw the bird close in on his face.

With a shout, he turned and stumbled into the mist.

He felt the bird light on his shoulder, the wings swish

round his ears, the beak stab at his eyes. He shook his head, cried out, but the stabbing went on, and on, and on. He tripped and fell to the ground, and curled up, sobbing, his face pressed into the mud as he waited for the fluttering presence to return.

To his surprise it did not. And to his inexpressible relief he heard a footstep in the mud nearby. Almost choking with joy he rolled over.

And saw the Wild Woman standing there.

13

Gordon groped through the mist, trying to follow the sprawling beam from the lamp. At least the cattle sheds should be easy enough to find, though it was hard to believe they could be so near to the house and yet remain hidden from view.

Not that he expected to find Mum and Dad there, but it was worth checking. He crunched over the gravel in the yard, the sound of his steps sharp against the eerie silence, and flashed the beam to where the first shed should be.

'Come on, you bugger. Where are you?'

A second later he walked into it.

'Damn!'

He stepped back, slightly shaken, and shone the lamp ahead. Dimly it picked up the contours of the shed wall. He walked slowly forward and put his hand against it; it was moist and cool, but somewhat comforting. He carefully felt his way along until he came to the entrance, then, still holding the wall, he stabbed the beam into the shed.

All well with the cattle but no sign of Mum and Dad. He fumbled along to the second shed, but they were not there either.

The sheep, then.

He felt his way back along the wall as far as the gate into Big Willy and flashed the beam over the ground beyond.

Boot tracks.

Two sets, one smaller than the other, heading into the field. So that was what had happened: they'd gone out to the sheep and got caught in the mist. He climbed over the gate and started to follow the prints.

Just as well the ground in Big Willy was good and soft, though nothing like as slushy as Mucky Meg; but at least the prints were clear to see. He bent low as he walked, scanning the ground under the focus of the beam. And as he walked, he began to guess where they were going.

And why.

He frowned. If only Dad hadn't been so stubborn and insisted on moving the sheep to Big Willy: the one field where the fencing still needed to be checked over after the gale. He cupped his hands round his mouth.

'Dad! Mum!'

He listened, straining for a response, but heard nothing: no answering call, no sound of sheep even; only a strange, soughless silence. He hurried on after the footsteps. It was more important to find Mum and Dad than the animals, and they must have gone to check the fence first. Certainly the prints seemed to be leading that way, unless the mist had distorted his sense of direction.

On and on they went, Dad's to the left and slightly in front of Mum's, as though he were striding ahead. Here was the fence now and, as expected, there was a break. It was easy to see where the sheep had forced their way through. He searched the ground with the lamp, looking for signs that Mum and Dad had turned back. They surely wouldn't continue; it would be much more sensible to wait for the mist to clear before trying to find the animals. Besides, heading in this direction was never a good idea, whatever the weather conditions.

But the footprints did continue. And just up to the right he spotted something new. Something disturbing.

A third set of footprints tracking the others towards Dragon's Rock.

Benjamin heard the voice and stood rigid.

'Help me!' it called. 'Help me!'

'Ione!' he shouted and rushed forward. 'Where are you?'

'Help me!'

He gaped at the bulging clouds all around him, smothering even the tenuous passage he had followed since the fence.

'Where are you?'

There was no answer.

He blundered on and saw the outline of another fence. And on the other side, the figure.

'Ione!'

He stumbled towards it, filled with wonder at how she could have seen him so clearly. But that didn't matter; he had found her and everything would be all right now. Everything would—

He stopped suddenly.

'Ione?'

But the figure was gone.

He slumped to the ground.

'You were here,' he groaned. 'I heard your voice. I saw you. I know you were here.'

He tried to picture her face and found he could only remember her eyes. He'd never seen such beautiful eyes. And he knew he wouldn't rest until he'd seen them again. He stood up.

'I'll help you,' he said. 'I'll help you. I'll kill anyone who tries to hurt you.'

He climbed over the fence.

'Even the Wild Woman,' he said, and walked on into the mist.

Toby knew she had come for him.

She had power. He felt it rippling about her like the chilling presence that surrounded him, in the house, in his room, and now here amid the darkness and the mist, a power that reached inside him and held him like a hand of ice. And he knew that this woman was the architect of that darkness and that mist, and of the deep despair swelling within him. He wanted to jump up and run but his body felt like a dead thing, a sack of bones and flesh no longer his but hers. He felt his mouth open to shout.

But no sound came.

She was moving closer now. He heard the squelch of her boots again in the slush, saw the grotesque body lean towards him. Then her face sharpened into focus.

He recoiled.

Not from the hideousness of it; he had seen that before, though from a distance. But only now was he close enough to see where the real terror came from.

Her eyes.

Suddenly he was on his feet.

Running.

Mist clung to him like a bag over his face. He heard his breath pounding against it.

The face emerged from the mist.

Dead ahead.

He blundered to the left, panting, his feet plunging deep in the mud.

It appeared again. Still ahead.

He turned and stumbled back the way he had come.

Again it took shape.

Always before him.

He staggered to a halt and stared, praying that the face was a trick, that it would fade into the gloom. Then the eyes moved, and beneath them, uncoiling like a serpent, the body thickened and closed upon him once more.

This time he did not run. He knew now it was useless. But he also knew that somehow he had to resist. He heard a growl deep in the woman's throat, saw the mouth twitch into an obscene leer, like the smile of a dog.

He ran at her, fists clenched.

'Leave me alone, you bloody witch!'

He threw out a punch. But it never connected.

A hand squeezed the breath from his throat and forced him back. He struggled but the grip only tightened. The other hand started to claw his body. Wriggling with revulsion he tried to squirm free. Then suddenly he understood.

The stone. She's come for the stone.

But there was no time to think. Both hands were round his throat now, holding him in a vice that wrung all resistance from him. Then her eyes bore into his.

And that was the worst of all.

More than the jabbing beak of her demon-bird, more than anything she could ever do to his body, this was the worst. He saw himself suddenly, as though through her, a helpless bundle of fears, trembling, yearning, begging her eyes to release him.

But they did not release him.

Instead they spoke, with a dark inner growl he instantly comprehended. One word. One question. For the one thing this woman wanted from him.

Where? The eyes said, Where?

And as they drove down into him like a torrent, searching his mind for the answer, he felt deep within him the frail bubble of his secret stir and strain upward towards her, longing to give itself to her so that he could be free. But even as it rose, floating on the current of her will, he felt another part of him awake, a part he did not know existed, a part that reached out and snatched the bubble back.

He prayed that the defiance had shown in his face.

Her eyes blazed on, driving deeper into him until he no longer knew whether she had torn the secret from him or not.

Then she threw him to the ground and was gone.

14

Gordon burst into the house.

'Toby! I've found out where they've gone. They've—'

The silence of the house fell over him. He stood still, listening.

'Toby? Benjamin?'

Damn them!

They must be outside, and he could imagine at least one likely reason: they'd had an argument, Toby would have spoken his mind and Benjamin would have run off. Simple as that. It was plausible enough.

He quickly checked the house to make sure it was empty, then tore a piece of paper from the pad by the phone, scribbled a note and propped it up in the middle of the table.

'Right,' he said, and threw open the back door.

Outside the mist seemed thicker than ever.

'Toby! Benjamin!'

Still nothing, and that was bad. They must be some distance from the house if they couldn't hear him. But the boys would have to wait. He still had to try and find Mum and Dad. He thought of the third set of footprints following theirs towards Dragon's Rock, and shuddered.

But at least he had some clues.

'Come on,' he said. 'Move yourself.'

He cautiously made his way through the mist towards where he had left the Land Rover. At least that hadn't moved. He ran his hand over the bonnet and along the door; it was cold but pleasantly familiar and welcoming. He climbed in.

The dashboard and instruments relaxed him further:

everything in its place, everything as it should be. He started the engine and switched on the headlamps, but all they showed was an eddy of mist. He flicked onto main beam. As expected, that was worse, and he dipped them again.

'Ah well. Have to guess the way.'

He looked over his shoulder to where the house lay, now gobbled up by the mist, and pushed the gear lever into reverse.

'Careful now. Slowly, slowly.'

He eased up the clutch pedal and the Land Rover moved backwards. 'Not too fast. Left hand down. Stop!'

He slumped back in the seat. This was going to be even harder than he'd imagined. For a moment he toyed with the idea of walking, but quickly dismissed it. He'd need the Land Rover if he found the others and besides, he knew he'd feel safer with its solid bulk around him, despite the problems of driving through the mist. He thought over the various routes to Dragon's Rock.

No use heading over the fields. He might find his way down to Skinny Sam but he'd never navigate the Land Rover through the trees beyond the sitka plantation. The track along the top of Mucky Meg could be worse. Even if he did dodge the trees, the ground was so treacherous and uneven he could only envisage a blind, frantic journey, the Land Rover bucking and barging through the hollows, maybe crashing and leaving him stranded in the murky environs of Dragon's Rock.

And there was no warning of the little valley; the trees ended and the ground fell straightaway. He shivered at the prospect.

The road, then.

Take it slow, one thing at a time. Swing the old bus into the centre of the track and stay there. Get past the house, left out of the farm and down the lane as far as the road. Left again and carry on till you reach the old track up to the ruin.

If it's still there, and if it's passable. It must be a long time since anyone used it.

It was hard to believe that the old ruin he had avoided since the day the family moved here had ever been lived in.

He peered about him.

With the mist as thick as this, the bends in the road near the Dragon's Rock entrance would be almost invisible. He stared along the beam. Two, three feet, it seemed, before it died away.

'Come on,' he said. 'Bite the bullet.'

He tried to gauge where the centre of the yard would be, pushed the lever into first gear and eased in the clutch. The Land Rover edged forward into the gloom and almost immediately bumped and reared. He braked sharply, opened the door and bent close to the ground.

He'd driven up the rockery.

This was hopeless; he hadn't even found his way out of the yard and he was off course.

Yet again he peered about him. But there was nothing to see: no house, no fence, no cattle sheds, no track. He slammed the door and started to reverse. Almost at once the Land Rover crunched into something.

He cursed and braked again. But at least he didn't need to look this time to see what he had hit. Too bad. The paddock fence would have to wait. He must have turned the wheel too far. He stared in front and tried to work out where to aim next.

Straight ahead. Give it about twenty yards, then right.

Slowly, slowly, he told himself, as the Land Rover slid forward again. He felt the left side of the vehicle lift. It had to be the rockery but he wasn't going to stop this time. He turned the wheel a fraction to the right and a moment later the Land Rover thumped down again.

So much for the rockery. He thought of the next obstacle to negotiate.

The side of the house.

'Keep left, keep left.'

Better to shave the outside of the cattle shed than crash into the house. The crackle of gravel under the wheels was gone and he knew he must be somewhere near the corner of the house. He slowed down, trying to guess when he would be past and free to turn right along the orchard.

The front of the Land Rover plunged into a spongy mass. Shoots spattered against the windscreen like tiny fists. He braked again.

'Think we've gone a bit too far.'

He pulled back from the hedge and swung the Land Rover round to the right.

'Hang on, not full lock. Stay close.'

Better to let the left side of the Land Rover brush the hedge on the way down the track; at least that way he should stay on course. The motion was bumpier but he expected that, being on the edge of the track, and trying to fumble down the centre would be more risky; he could easily skew off to the right and hit one of the apple trees.

He brought the Land Rover closer to the hedge until he could hear the scratching and scraping against the side, and see the branches ahead dancing in the beam before the Land Rover nosed them away. The mist was growing thicker as he quarried a path through it towards the end of the track. Before much longer he should come to the farm entrance. But the windscreen was moistening and every so often the Land Rover bounced away towards the centre of the track, making him jerk the wheel back.

He switched on the wipers, leaned forward and tried to follow the beam. But all he saw was a pale fan-shape where the hedge ran to the left, and that was fading. If he lost sight of the hedge, he would have to stop.

But he couldn't stop. He had to get to Dragon's Rock. Somehow.

To his relief, the mist fell back a few yards and he found he could see further along the track.

'About time too,' he muttered. The prospect of crawling at five miles an hour all the way to Dragon's Rock had been lowering his spirits, but now it looked as though the mist was clearing after all. He thought of Mum and Dad again, changed gear and put on speed. There was no time to waste.

The shape came at him so quickly he remembered little: his own scream; a rushed recognition; a flash of guilt. That he had been over-confident, that he was going too fast; that the mist was still dangerous.

That he should have thought of the oak.

He heard the crash. But nothing more.

15

Benjamin pressed himself against the broken-down wall of the outhouse, shaking from exhaustion, and looked at his watch.

To his surprise he saw it was three in the morning.

How long, he wondered, had he been stumbling about in the mist. It was hard to believe that it had been so many hours. But at least he had reached the first outhouse. He remembered there had been three, each one crumbly and abandoned, when he came here all those years ago, so this time he must have come in from the east and avoided the little valley. He felt his way round the outside of the building.

Somewhere nearby Ione must be hiding; he could sense her and he was sure she must sense him. But she would be frightened. He knew she would be frightened.

Just as he was.

He looked about him, searching for the Wild Woman's face.

At least the mist hid him as it hid her, though he had the disconcerting feeling that she had created it and was not affected by it at all. He was feeling hotter and hotter, and the roaring sound was still with him, louder than ever. It did not feel evil, but it felt powerful; as though the land itself were yawning as it woke from an unsettled sleep.

He thought of the dragon again.

'Come on,' he said aloud. 'You can't stay here.'

He had to find Ione, had to rescue her. He might have lost the stone and made the dragon angry, as Ione had said, but he could still do some good. And he knew where he had to go: the one place his instinct told him not to go, but the one place that might hold the key.

He tried to push his fear aside.

'Don't chicken out now. For God's sake, don't chicken out now.'

He had to find the courage to look for her, despite the danger of being caught by the Wild Woman. If he could only find Ione first, alone, there was a chance. Not that he knew how he was going to persuade her to leave this place and come back with him to the world. Maybe she wouldn't come. Maybe she'd refuse.

Then he would stay. And they'd face the Wild Woman together.

He waited a moment longer, wiping the sweat from his face and listening to the unending roar; then he slipped away from the outhouse. Somewhere in this direction, if he remembered correctly, there should be another outhouse. He scurried forward, arms outstretched.

Please, he said silently, please let me—

He barged into something and stepped back, a little dazed. But he knew his prayer had been answered.

He'd reached the next outhouse.

He felt his way round it, struggling to catch a recognizable shape. Somewhere here, perhaps only inches away, he'd meet the person he sought. Or the one he dreaded.

He ran into the mist again, praying as before that he would come to the next outhouse. But this time he did not. He drew up quickly, glancing tensely about him. Perhaps he hadn't come in from the east after all, perhaps he was going the other way, back towards the farm; or perhaps he'd just missed the third outhouse. He took off his glasses, wiped them and put them back on.

Walk on, he decided, and stepped forward.

To his amazement, the mist fell away as though a curtain had been drawn back, and he found himself in a moonlit clearing.

Before him was the ruined house, standing stiff and gaunt like a sentinel over the valley from whose belly the rock rose, wrapped in mystery.

He looked back and saw the mist gliding like a moat.

Courage, he told himself. For Ione's sake.

This wasn't the time to give in. He had to try and save her before the Wild Woman destroyed her. It might be too late already.

But he tried not to think of that possibility.

He ran forward and pushed himself against the side of the house, glancing feverishly about him. Nothing stirred in the darkness.

Courage. For Ione's sake.

He looked along the wall of the ruin and memories flooded back, more now from the smell of the place than from what his eyes remembered. But then, he had not been inside when he was eight; he had come to Dragon's Rock from another direction, taken the stone and run up the slope and away, past this place, hurrying home with his prize.

And his guilt.

But now he was here again, touching its shell, smelling its decay, feeling its pain. And this time he would go in.

He crept along to the first glassless window and looked in. All was dark inside but gradually his eyes made out the shape of an old fireplace forlornly standing on the far side.

An empty room, nothing more. Perhaps a living-room once.

But a dead room now.

He heard an owl call and glanced over his shoulder.

Courage, courage. Don't run away.

He stole to the next window. Another empty room, also with a fireplace; perhaps a dining-room or kitchen once. He tiptoed round the back of the house but there were no windows on this side. He looked up and saw moonlight brightening what was left of the roof. And to his surprise he found himself wishing Toby were here.

Toby would have plenty of courage.

He crept round the house, peeping in all the windows but there was no sign that anybody had been here for a very long time. At last he came to the opening that had once held the front door.

From inside came an odour of damp and mould. He peered round and saw a dark hallway, the ceiling still intact, unlike some of the rooms where the roof had caved in above and left them exposed. At the end of the hall he saw the outline of a stairway.

Anybody living here would use one of the downstairs rooms where there was a ceiling for shelter, he decided. They wouldn't use the upstairs as there was hardly any roof. So there was no point in going up.

He gritted his teeth and walked towards the stairs.

His mind was racing with fear now. He tried to relax, tried to tell himself there was nothing to be afraid of upstairs, and that he was just going to look for clues. He braced himself and ran up.

But all was well: half of the upstairs was open to the sky and what roof remained was rotten; there was nobody up here. He turned to walk back down.

And tensed.

Down below was a large stone slab, part of the old flagstone floor. Innocent enough, it seemed, yet from where he stood, he could see as the moonlight caught it that it was not snug and square like the others.

Someone at some time had moved it.

He walked slowly down, telling himself that there was nothing to worry about, that whoever had moved it and not replaced it properly probably did so years ago and was long gone; that it was hardly worth bothering to check it over.

He bent down and, with an effort, pulled the slab to the side.

Underneath was a tunnel leading down below the house. Just big enough for a man.

Or a woman.

He stared at it and at the choice that now faced him: to run or to confront. Sweating with fear, he lowered himself down.

His feet soon touched the ground, and he sat down for a moment and peered up at the floor just above him; then, after a moment's thought, he reached up and pulled the slab back.

Darkness enveloped him at once.

He lowered his head and crawled forward, following a tunnel he could not see but which felt strangely hard and bony wherever he touched it. It was twisting downwards, that much was clear, away from the house, away from the air, and into a realm he could not foresee. He wondered who built this tunnel, who used it.

And where that person was.

Now he could see an eerie glimmer reaching up towards him, illuminating the sides of the tunnel so that it looked like a giant worm sliding down into the earth. And with that impression came another, stranger still: that the body of the worm had ribs. Then, as he looked more closely, he saw why.

The walls and ceiling were covered with a curious latticework, a crisscross ornamentation of sticks woven to a wattle skin. He stared at it, remembering the sticks he had seen Ione with that day, sticks just like these. But those had been for a cage, she said; a cage she was being forced to make.

He looked over his shoulder, wondering again who roamed this place.

The jailer or the slave?

The roaring had grown louder. He crawled on, closer and closer to the light, and the more he did so, the more the roar intensified. He stopped again, trying to discover the source of the sound. One moment it seemed all around him; the next, inside his head. He remembered a time in church when the choir had sung a long 'Amen' that seemed to go on for ever. This sounded like an 'Amen' too, and it really did go on for ever.

But he was not in church now.

And he was feeling hotter, hotter, hotter.

The tunnel dipped and came to an end. And to his amazement he found himself standing in a vast underground cave.

He stared round in wonder. The light came from a candle pushed in the earth and by its glow he saw boxes and crates and old plastic bags thrown together in a corner. What was in them he could not tell. In the middle of the cave was a small bed made from coarse bits of timber, roughly nailed together; no mattress or pillow or sheets, just hard boards and a large old blanket thrown over.

Stuck in the ground on the far side of the bed was a long knife.

He walked nervously past it and saw, beneath an overhang in the rock, the remains of a fire. Cautiously he bent over the cinders and looked up. Two slender shafts reached towards the ground above, clear, he presumed, or the fire wouldn't work. Then he remembered what Gordon had said about people seeing smoke coming from around the rock, thinking it was from the dragon's nostrils. But if the smoke came from here—

He wheeled round.

The cave must be directly beneath the rock.

He glanced about him, again wondering about this place. It could be Ione's cell. That was possible. He'd seen the sticks. But it could be the Wild Woman's lair. And Ione could be dead.

Then he saw the markings on the ceiling.

Deep, clear markings, scratched there, he knew, by the same hand that had gouged the tunnel, covering the roof of the cave with a huge fearsome shape.

The face of a dragon.

The roar seemed to split his head, the heat to smother him. He staggered back and kicked the knife so that it quivered in the ground. The next moment he was stumbling for the tunnel.

He had to get out. Back to the surface. Ione wasn't here and he had to help her, if she was still alive. And this was a terrifying place.

He scrambled up the tunnel as fast as he could, breathing harder and harder in his desperation to reach the top. But as he drew near, he heard a sound he had been dreading.

The sound of the slab moving above him.

16

Toby lost all track of time, all track of reality. As in a macabre dream, he floundered in the sea of his hatred, struggling to find relief.

There was none.

He was running, falling, running, falling, finding only mist and mud and madness, and longing for revenge. Then he was lying in the mud, his body shivering like the string of a hideous instrument, plucked and left to vibrate out of tune by some malicious, discarnate being.

Don't give in, he told himself.

Don't let her win.

He stood up and plunged into the mist, not knowing where he was going, aware only that he must move, must find his way back to the house. He felt dangerously cold and knew panic was still near.

Cruk! Cruk! Cruk!

He ducked at once, hands over his face.

No attack came; but he had thought that before. He pushed on, head lowered, shoulders hunched.

Keep walking, keep walking.

His feet made the familiar sucking sound as he pulled them out of the mud and he tried to think which part of Mucky Meg had slush as deep as this. But there were many parts of the field it could be. He stopped and looked around him.

This was stupid: he only had to keep walking straight until he came to the border of the field. If he was heading away from the gate along the top of the field, he should end up at the hedgerow on the west side, just below the forest;

and if he was going south, he would end up at Skinny Sam. Maybe he was already heading towards the gate.

He frowned. Or east. Or round in circles.

As if to taunt him, he saw bootprints in the mud, cutting off to the right. He placed his foot inside the nearest one.

A perfect fit.

'Damn!' he said. Then he spotted tractor marks nearby, trac-tracks as Gordon called them, running off into the mist. He bent over and studied them.

'Please take me to the gate. Please.'

At first they were easy enough to follow, then the mud hardened and he lost them for a few yards. He bent closer to the ground and spotted more trac-tracks further on, heading in the same direction, scrambled after them and a moment later saw the outline of the hedge to the right.

It was the north side of the field after all. He hurried along the hedge and almost at once came upon the gate. Looking cautiously about him, he climbed over and edged his way towards where the farmhouse lay, still hidden in the mist.

The paddock fence was not yet in view but he could just make out the dusky shape of the hedgerows on either side. The mist seemed to be clearing slightly but it was still dark and cold. He tried to think of what he would say. Gordon should be back by now, hopefully with Mum and Dad; maybe Benjamin too.

First of all, own up about the stone. If Benjamin's there, go and get it and give it back to him in front of everybody. Then tell them about the Wild Woman.

And if Benjamin's not there—

He stopped, frowning.

I'll just have to face the music.

But despite his good intentions, he felt hatred rising again. Hatred for Benjamin, for the Wild Woman, for the stone.

He caught the scent of newly-treated wood and the paddock fence appeared; he reached out and ran his hand down the overlapping timbers as he made his way towards the yard. The mist was definitely clearing, yet even here on familiar ground he sensed danger. He walked on, more slowly, and saw the silver birch before him and ahead, a speck of light.

The kitchen.

It couldn't be anything else, though the light was very faint. He left the fence, following the light now, and felt gravel under his feet. Then the house took form before him.

He was right: it was the kitchen, and the only room that seemed to have any light. He opened the back door and stepped in.

The moment he entered he knew something was wrong.

The light was on but cast no welcoming glow over the room, nor was the remnant warmth from the deserted stove sufficient to counter the creeping chill that had made itself his companion.

'Anybody here?' he shouted.

All was silent.

He walked to the hall door and opened it. Everywhere was dark. He switched on the light by the door; from inside the bulb came a faint whir, and a taper of light slid grudgingly out. He hesitated, then walked through to the living-room and switched on the lights there.

It too was cheerless and chill, the half-dressed Christmas tree no match for the air of dejection that permeated the house. No fire burned in the grate and all the radiators were cold.

He saw a face and jumped back.

Then relaxed.

It was his own, caught in the mirror.

'Clothes,' he muttered. 'Be practical. Clothes first, then light the fire.'

He wondered dully when he last slept and how long it would be before he could sleep again. If only he could curl up in bed right now and forget all this, and wake up tomorrow and find everything all right again.

But he knew there would be no sleep tonight.

He walked back to the foot of the stairs. Above him the landing seemed sombre and forbidding. Somehow he didn't want to go up, though he knew he would have to some time to fetch the stone. He pulled open the hall cupboard and dug through the jackets and coats. There was the battered anorak, an old friend of many escapades. Just as well he hadn't let Mum throw it away. He slipped it on, saw Gordon's old duffle coat and pulled that on too.

But he was still shivering.

He wished one of the others would come back, even Benjamin. Because although no one had answered him, he had a disquieting feeling that the house was not empty.

He walked back to the kitchen, usually such a happy place but now unwelcoming and cold, and his eye fell on the clock.

Four thirty! He stared at it. It couldn't possibly be four thirty. He'd only run out a short while ago.

Then he saw the note on the table.

A huge printed scrawl, clearly done in a great hurry but immediately recognizable as Gordon's.

TOBY/BENJAMIN
GONE TO DRAGON'S ROCK. DON'T FOLLOW. STAY AT HOME.
IF NOT BACK BY BREAKFAST, CALL POLICE.
GORDON.

He read the note twice.

Stay at home: the last thing he wanted to do, but it made sense. And there was something he had to collect; something he could no longer avoid.

He walked through to the foot of the stairs and looked up. The stillness of the house seemed to touch him like clammy skin and the landing looked dark and uninviting, the scant power from the lights somehow adding to the unseen menace he felt everywhere. He put a foot on the bottom step.

From upstairs came a scuffling sound.

17

When Gordon came to, all he saw was a blur. His head throbbed, his chest pounded; he felt pain in what seemed to be every part of his body. He tried to remember what had happened.

But memory was a blur too. A haze, a mist.

Mist.

The thought came more strongly.

Mist.

Something about mist.

'Mist . . . ' He heard a voice, his voice, mumbling the thought aloud. 'Mist . . . '

He sat up abruptly.

The pain in his head checked him at once. He clapped a hand to his brow and felt what could only be blood. Moving more cautiously, he stretched forward again, searching for something he knew, something that would tell him where he was. He felt a hard, sharp object under his fingers.

Glass.

A piece of glass, like a cube. A new image pushed its way into his mind, and with it came a third.

'Tree,' he said dreamily. 'There was a tree.'

His body sagged in the seat, aching for rest, but he forced himself to stay upright, despite the pain.

'Mist . . . glass . . . tree,' he said. 'Mist . . . glass . . . tree.'

The pain was growing worse.

'Mist-glass-tree. Mist-glass-tree.'

It was better saying it briskly, almost like the rhymes Mum used to teach them.

More images flooded in.

Mum. Rhymes.

'I had a . . . ' he started drowsily, 'I had a . . . little . . . a little . . . '

The throbbing in his head felt like hammer blows now, but he stumbled on through the rhyme.

' . . . a little nut tree. Nothing . . . would it bear.'

The words were coming, falteringly. He went on, moaning with the pain.

'But a silver nutmeg. And a . . . golden pear.'

This was stupid, chanting a nursery rhyme. He should be trying to work out where he was and what to do.

'The King of Spain's daughter,' he went on, but the rhyme was fading. 'The King of Spain's daughter . . . ' The blur over his eyes deepened, then inspiration came and he hurried on to the end.

'The King of Spain's daughter . . . came to visit me . . . and all for the sake of . . . my little nut tree.'

Tree.

The image was back and it was stronger than the others.

Nut tree. Birch tree. Oak tree.

Suddenly he remembered. And with remembrance came a chaos of pictures. Toby, Benjamin, Mum and Dad, tracks in the mud.

The accident.

He breathed slowly out; at least he was thinking again. But he knew he was badly hurt, and that if he moved too sharply, it could be serious. If only the concussion would clear so that he could see. He tried to focus his eyes but the blur was still there.

'Try moving your hands,' he said aloud.

That was all right, as long as he wasn't too vigorous. He lifted his left hand, held it close to his face and tried to read the digits on his watch.

That was no good; it looked like four something, which couldn't be right. He'd gone out around nine and couldn't possibly have been stuck here that long. But then, he was no longer sure of anything at the moment. He tried the watch again but this time the figures eluded him completely. His sight was getting worse and so was the pain.

He reached tentatively forward and traced round the shattered edge of the windscreen. Some of the glass seemed to be intact but there was a large gap where his head must have struck.

'Have to get that fixed,' he said. 'First job when I'm out of hospital.'

He stretched further forward and his chest touched the steering-wheel. Pain seared through him at once and he stiffened, groaning. It was easy to work out where the injuries had come from. Just as well he hadn't been going fast; but there'd be yet another lecture from Dad on seat belts. He ran his hand round until he found the ignition.

'Now then, battery,' he said. 'Let's see what you're made of.'

Somehow the engine struggled into life. He tried the headlamps, without success.

'Ah well. Can't see anyway.'

He thought of the others and tried the horn, but that, too, had ceased to work.

'Too bad,' he said. 'Just have to shout at pedestrians.'

He wondered why he was being so flippant. Perhaps because he could feel consciousness trying to leave him. Or because he was frightened it would never return.

This was doomed to failure, he told himself. If he had any brains, he'd sit here and wait for someone to find him. But he thrust that train of thought aside. He knew he had to get back to the house to call for an ambulance, and maybe the police, if the others still weren't back.

He pushed the gear lever into reverse.

'If we swing round on full lock, we should be facing the house.'

At least there should be room round the farm entrance to turn without hitting anything behind him, as long as he

111

didn't go back too far. He edged the Land Rover backwards, the wheel hard down, and felt the vehicle cross the centre of the track.

'Easy, easy. Now straighten up.'

He found first gear and slowly let up the clutch pedal.

'Left a bit, we're bumping. We're off line.'

He adjusted the steering-wheel. That was better; the Land Rover was running more evenly. He tried to think of how he was going to find his way past the house.

'Safer to get out and walk,' he said. But he knew his body could not walk. Indeed, it was weakening by the second.

'Keep it slow,' he said. 'Really slow. Stop if you don't feel right.'

The Land Rover juddered on towards the farm and he leaned forward, straining to see some familiar outline. And as he did so, he felt the first flecks of snow upon his face.

18

Benjamin held his breath.

He knew he had heard the slab move but now, no matter how hard he listened, all he heard was the deep roar, resounding in the tunnel. Then another sound came, just above him, round the corner.

Someone scrambling towards him.

He stared into the darkness, uncertain what to do. It could be Ione. There was just a chance. But perhaps—

He looked frantically about him. But he knew there was only one place to hide.

As quickly and quietly as he could, he crawled back down to the cave, ran over to the bed and eased himself under, the blanket brushing his face as he did so. He felt dust in his nostrils and a pebble hard against his cheek. But before he could move it, he sensed someone standing behind him.

He waited, shaking, his legs drawn up to his chest, his heartbeat so loud he felt sure she must hear it. He was certain now that it was the Wild Woman, though she was still hidden from view. Holding himself rigid, he stared towards the base of the opposite wall, at the knife stuck in the ground.

She had stopped, somewhere behind him.

He was going to scream. He knew it. Any moment now he was going to scream and give himself away. But he dare not scream. He dare not move or even breathe.

Somehow he felt she knew he was here. Perhaps she had already bent down at the other side of the bed; perhaps even at this moment she was looking at him.

Don't turn round.

Stay still.

Don't scream.

The urge to turn his head grew stronger. She must have heard his breathing by now, must have bent down, must be watching him. Any moment a hand would seize him from behind.

He heard her move round the foot of the bed towards the knife and stop again, but still he could not see her feet. Again he held his breath, his eyes fixed on the bright blade of the knife. Suddenly there was a new danger.

Sneezing.

Dust always made him sneeze. And already he could feel—

He opened his mouth and tried not to breathe through his nose; and, to his relief, the tickle in his nostrils went.

She moved again and for the first time he sensed in the corner of his eye the vague outline of her feet. In a moment she would bend down and see him.

She must know I'm here. She must. She'll have seen the slab's been moved. She's probably seen me under the bed.

She'll kill me.

A hand reached down and grasped the knife. But the face did not appear below the edge of the bed. And she straightened up again. He tried to imagine what she was doing: fingering the blade maybe, thinking of him, caught here, in her power.

Suddenly she turned and he heard her striding back towards the tunnel.

And she was gone.

He waited a few seconds, then quickly crawled out from under the bed. There was no time to waste. He knew what he had to do, no matter how dangerous it was. She had a knife and it might be for Ione. Somehow he had to follow her.

Without getting caught.

He crept up the tunnel, peering ahead to make sure she wasn't waiting for him. But she hadn't stopped. He heard

114

the slab moved aside and replaced, crawled forward, waited a short while, then forced it aside and wriggled out, praying she wouldn't be standing over him.

She was not.

Through the doorway of the ruin he caught a glimpse of her back as she vanished into the nearest outhouse; the one he hadn't found on the way out because of the mist.

Mist!

He looked about him. The mist was gone. And it was snowing.

But the night could still shield him.

He slipped through the door and ran for the cover of the nearest tree. To his right, below the sharp cut of the brow, he saw Dragon's Rock, bright and mysterious, down in the base of the valley. He reached the tree and threw himself against it, then, keeping low, stole across the clearing towards the outhouse.

Like the ruin, it had no door, and there was no light to be seen through the opening. But he heard a voice: a man's voice, angry, confused.

'I've told you, we don't know anything about this bloody stone.'

Toby's father! He gasped. The tone was unmistakable. He crept forward, wondering what it meant, and whether Toby's mother could be in there too. At that moment he heard her speak.

'We're not hiding anything from you. I promise we're not.' The voice was softer, calmer, but there was fear in it. 'If we knew where it was, we'd tell you. You must untie us.'

He stiffened.

They were tied up. And the Wild Woman had a knife. He inched closer as Toby's father spoke again.

'Look, for God's sake, killing us won't do any good. We can't help you. We don't know anything about—' The voice rose suddenly. 'Don't touch her!'

From inside came a scream.

115

19

Toby looked warily up the stairs, listening again for the scuffling sound. But all was still.

Slowly, stealthily, he began to climb.

Never in his life had he felt so frightened. Each step seemed louder than the last, as though the boards themselves wanted to creak and betray him. Upstairs an ominous silence had fallen, as though whatever stalked the rooms had heard his approach and was waiting in readiness, perhaps watching him even now from some hidden corner as he ascended the stairs.

He reached the top, switched on the light and peered along the landing, then back down the banisters to what seemed the relative safety of the hall.

And the silence seemed to deepen.

For a while he stood there, stroking the banister rail where it curved round the top of the stairs and stretched along the landing towards his room. The wood was cool and shiny. He squeezed it hard and tried to stop the shaking in his hand, but it was no use; he could no more stop it moving than stop his stomach churning or the hairs on his neck rising. Yet he squeezed the wood even so, until his hand hurt.

There had been no further sounds.

He listened and listened, almost wanting to hear something, but the house was like a tomb. Running his hand along the banister rail, he tiptoed towards his room. The door was half-open but he could see the foot of the bed and his school bag on the floor. He stopped outside and listened again.

If the thing was inside his room, it would have heard him and be waiting there in the darkness; unless it had crept out and was behind him. He looked quickly over his shoulder.

But there was no sign of danger.

He stared back through the gap into his room, then pushed the door fully back. It swung inwards with a soft brush of the carpet and he surveyed the familiar shapes: bed, chair, dartboard, the desk he pretended to do his homework on.

All seemed reassuringly normal.

The next moment claws ripped into his hand.

He cried out in pain, whirled round and hit his elbow on the edge of the door. The claws released him and he took a step back, darting his eyes about the room.

But nowhere could he see the creature that had attacked him. He raised the hand to his lips; it was bleeding, throbbing, trembling more than ever. He shook it hard, feverishly scanning the room.

Somewhere in here the creature was lurking, watching him for certain, waiting to pounce again. He took another step back, still facing the room. Behind him he felt the edge of the door and cowered against it, glad that at least his back was protected.

Then he saw the eyes, coldly watching him from the corner.

He stared back, remembering the Wild Woman's eyes, and the body of the creature took shape.

It was the cat he had seen on the post.

Suddenly it jumped. He braced himself, but it had not sprung at him; it had bounded onto the bed and was scratching at the pillow with its claws.

He knew now what the cat wanted. And he knew how much he hated this animal, hated its unnatural presence in the house, the way it had attacked him, the way it was coolly picking its way through his room.

It had come from her. Like the raven. Like all evil things. Like Benjamin.

117

The pillow rolled back and the cat bent to sniff what it had come for.

Toby jumped.

The cat looked up and he caught a flash of its eyes; but only for a second. The next moment he had grasped it by the neck and twisted it on its side. The claws whipped round at once and he felt them tear into his hand. He squeezed the neck tight and threw the animal to the ground.

It lay still, momentarily stunned. Without hesitation he stamped on its head.

Trembling, he stood back from the corpse. His hand was still hurting but at least he knew what had made the noise. And now it was dead. That was one thing the Wild Woman wouldn't get back.

He picked up the stone and it felt warm and comforting. And to his surprise he saw it was glowing. He let it roll from side to side over his palm. And still it glowed, like a crystal.

'What are you?' he said.

He'd thought the stone was an evil thing, part of the malignant power in the house.

'Maybe you are evil,' he said, answering his thought. 'Maybe you're just pretending to be nice and friendly.'

He closed his hand round it and glared down at the corpse. 'Well, you're dead anyway.'

He heard an eerie cry behind him and spun round.

And saw two more eyes watching him from the doorway.

This cat did not wait but bounded straight at his face.

He raised an arm to protect himself. Claws tore his hand again, the same spot as before. He shouted and hit out. The cat slipped over his shoulder but clung to him somehow. He struck out again. It fell to the ground and darted under the bed.

Before he could move, it shot out again and sank its teeth into his shin. He kicked out and tried to shake it off. It clung on, biting, scratching, squealing. He kicked again but still it clung to the shin, and the pain was starting to tell. He kicked harder, over-balanced himself and fell back against the door, slamming it shut.

Madness and terror swept through his brain. He kicked harder, more frantically, but still the cat held on and the biting and scratching grew worse. He reached down to try and prise the animal away. The claws and teeth drove his hand back at once.

Suddenly the answer came.

Instantly he turned and kicked the wall, using the animal's body to cushion the blow. The cat yelped and Toby felt the first moment of satisfaction. He kicked again; it held on as tightly as ever but he could feel he had hurt it. He drew his foot back and kicked the wall again as hard as he could.

The cat stopped biting and scratching but somehow clung on still.

'Stay there, then,' he snarled, and kicked the wall again.

This time there was a loud squeal, and the body of the cat slithered onto the floor.

He knew he had killed it. But without a second thought he stamped on its head.

Shaking more than ever, he leaned against the wall. The wounds from the raven and the cats now smarted viciously. At his feet lay the two cats, so alike it was hard to remember which one he had killed first. He wondered how they had found their way into the house.

With something of a shock, he realized he was still holding the stone.

The new cry froze him to the spot. High, hateful, unearthly, this time outside the room. He squeezed the stone tight and listened.

It came again, this time longer, higher, louder. As though summoning other forces.

And summoning him.

He faced the enemy hidden behind the door.

'But I've got what you want.'

He pushed the stone into his pocket.

'And you won't get it or me without a fight.'

He opened the door a fraction and peeped out.

A gallery of eyes met him.

He shuddered and tried to move back, but the pressure of the eyes seemed to stab him into stillness. Cats covered the stairs, their black bodies undulating like sinewy, silken waves, their eyes glaring unwinkingly at him as one.

And he knew it was one eye that watched him. A single eye, from a single enemy. An enemy with many bodies.

He watched, mesmerized by the subtly moving darkness of the stairway and the soundless approach of the cats. Somehow he had to think. He knew he couldn't stay here. He had to escape and find the others. The window was much too high and there was nothing to climb down. If he'd had some rope or long enough sheets, it might have been possible. There was nothing else for it.

He would have to go down the stairs.

But the sight of the cats filled him with terror.

He tried to work out how many there were. Twenty, thirty, forty; hard to tell. It made no difference. Wherever he looked, he saw cats.

All with the same hunter's eyes.

He thought of the claws on his body, tearing, scratching, gouging; but he knew the cats had come for more than that. They moved closer, not hurrying, as though they knew they had him in their power. Many had reached the top of the stairs and were only feet from the door. Others followed, as far down the stairs as he could see before the banister rail cut them from view.

How many there might be downstairs he could only guess.

Closer and closer they came, the nearest animals low over the floor. He opened the door wider and flailed his arms.

'Go away!'

None of the cats stopped and the leader bared its teeth.

He shrank back, desperately trying to think of a means of escape. The landing now rolled with dark, slinking bodies. He shot a glance over the rail: the stairs too seemed to writhe and swell, some of the cats climbing on the backs of others on their way to the top. But for a moment it looked as though the base of the stairs might just be clear.

But jumping was out of the question. He'd sprain an ankle or break a leg for sure, and the cats would finish him off easily. Then, in a flash, the idea came. It was fraught with risk and if it failed, he knew he would be finished. He glanced quickly towards the rail, wishing he could have craned over to see whether more cats were coming through from the hall.

But he no longer dared take his eyes from the creatures that had come to destroy him.

It was time to act. For better or worse.

He took a step forward and made as if to kick the leading cat.

At the same moment, it jumped.

He saw, as though in slow motion, the coiled body uncurl into a shining shaft, claws outstretched and thrusting for his face. He saw his elbow rise to block, his right hand punch down.

The cat fell to the side.

At once it tensed for a second spring. Bodies across the landing twitched and flexed, ready to jump too.

With a wild shout he leapt astride the banister rail and pushed himself down.

Face-forward he torpedoed towards the ground.

In the mad rushing flight he saw cats jump up, squealing. He twisted his face from them and clung on. The hall loomed towards him.

Clear of cats.

The ground punched into him and he found himself rolling across the floor. He scrambled to his feet, stumbled through to the kitchen and slammed the door behind him.

Claws started scratching on the other side.

He raced out into the yard. To his surprise the mist was gone, the sky was starting to lighten in the east, and it was snowing hard.

By the silver birch he saw the Land Rover, parked askew, and a small figure peering through the window.

'Benjamin!' he bellowed.

Benjamin looked round and beckoned frantically.

'Toby! Toby! Quick!'

Toby ran across and saw Gordon's body slumped across the passenger seat.

'What's happened?'

'I don't know about Gordon. He's not dead, he's still breathing. But . . . but . . . it's the Wild Woman.'

Benjamin was gasping for air.

'She's got your mum and dad. She's got a knife. She—'

Toby grabbed him.

'Where are they?'

'Dragon's Rock. One of the outhouses. Tied up. The Wild Woman. She thinks . . . she thinks—'

Toby shook him.

'What? Speak, for God's sake!'

'She thinks they know where the stone is. I heard your mum scream. The Wild Woman . . . she might have . . . ' His voice trailed away.

Toby stared at him, a feeling of unreality unfolding in his mind and adding to the madness already there. It couldn't be true. Mum and Dad couldn't be dead. They couldn't possibly be. They'd be back soon. Any moment now probably.

And Gordon would wake up, and the cats and raven would go away, and everything would be all right again, and—

He lifted his face to the sky and shrieked.

'I'll get you, Wild Woman! I'll get you!'

He dug furiously into his pocket.

'Here's the bloody stone!' He clapped it into Benjamin's hand. 'Come on!'

'But what are you going to do?' said Benjamin.

Toby pulled open the driver's door.

'Kill her.'

20

'You sure you know how to do this?' said Benjamin.

'Shut up! See if you can help Gordon.'

Toby fumbled with the ignition key and managed to make the engine turn over. But it wouldn't fire.

'Try the choke,' said Benjamin.

'I was going to.' Toby looked helplessly about him.

'Over there.'

'I know that!'

'You pull it out.'

'I said shut up!'

He pulled the choke out and tried again. Still the engine wouldn't fire. Suddenly he stiffened.

In the wing mirror was the face of a cat.

Desperately he tried the engine again, and again.

'You'll flood it,' said Benjamin. 'Try half choke.'

'How come you know so much about it?'

He didn't listen for an answer. In the mirror he could see cats pouring into the yard behind them. He felt panic rising again, mingled with despair at the knowledge that all was lost, and that even if he did start the Land Rover, he wouldn't know how to drive it, despite his boasts to Benjamin.

Into the turmoil of his mind came a quiet voice.

'I'll drive if you like.'

'You?' He was about to scoff but something in Benjamin's face stopped him. 'You know how to drive?'

Benjamin nodded. Toby saw more cats in the mirror and hurriedly made up his mind.

'Move across. Quick.'

He eased himself over Gordon's unconscious body and made room for Benjamin.

Benjamin seated himself at the steering-wheel and reached for the ignition key.

'Maybe you didn't press the accelerator when you turned the key.'

'Can we just go?' snapped Toby. He saw more cats creeping into view in the wing mirror on the other side; Benjamin obviously hadn't spotted them yet, but he would as soon as he looked in the mirror. The engine burst into life.

'Sounds all right,' said Benjamin.

'Go on, then!' shouted Toby.

'Which way?'

'Straight ahead!'

The Land Rover rumbled forward. Toby looked in the wing mirror and saw cats surging after them, fanning out in a huge black arc, in contrast to the snowy surface of the ground.

Overhead he saw a dark shape, whirling.

He put a hand on Gordon's shoulder, wishing he knew what to do to help him. But at least his brother was still alive. He glanced at Benjamin and saw him leaning forward, his face set in concentration, hands tight round the wheel. Snow billowed in through the broken windscreen.

'Which way?' said Benjamin. 'Down to Skinny Sam?'

'No, straight on.'

It was no use going through Mucky Meg. He'd have to get out to open the gate, the cats were still close, and they might get bogged down in the mud. The road was out of the question: they'd have to turn round and drive back towards the cats.

'We'll go through the forest,' he said.

'Will the Land Rover get through?'

Toby didn't know. He only knew that the ground would be treacherous and hard to see with the trees packed so

125

closely together; and that there would be no warning of the valley below the ruin.

If they made it that far.

'We'll soon find out,' he muttered.

He checked overhead and saw the odious form, arrogantly spiralling, and behind them, the rolling black wake of cats; and wondered why Benjamin had said nothing about them. Perhaps he hadn't looked in the mirror or above him.

They plunged on down the track, past the gate and around the north-west tip of Mucky Meg. In another minute they would be among the trees.

He looked about him again.

The cats had fallen behind but the bird still wheeled above them, as though marking their position. He clenched his fists and leaned forward. Somewhere ahead was the Wild Woman. And a test he had to face. A test of strength and will.

He closed his eyes tight and thought, Kill, kill, kill.

Benjamin was watching the trees through the onrush of snow and knew they would have to choose a path soon. He looked at Toby for guidance and saw him with his eyes tightly shut.

Yet the anger flowed about him more than ever.

He thought miserably of Ione. Probably the Wild Woman had killed her, just like she'd killed Toby's parents. And he realized that he too had his anger.

'Toby,' he said. 'I want to kill the Wild Woman too.'

Toby opened his eyes, and they were glazed, hard, dangerous. Benjamin nodded ahead.

'Which way?'

'Keep to the right of that big tree. We'll come to the valley from the east. The forest's not so dense there.'

The track ended and all at once they were surrounded by trees. The ground became a tossing sea over which the Land Rover plunged and reared like a dinghy.

'Keep to the right!' shouted Toby.

They twisted past the big tree, Gordon's body bouncing with the vicious new motion.

'Which way now?' said Benjamin. 'We'll never get through that gap.'

'Left. See if you can cut back later.'

Benjamin wrestled with the steering-wheel.

'It's getting hard to steer.'

Toby said nothing. He was looking out of the window for cats. There was no sign of them, but he could still see the black speck above them as it broke into view through the gaps in the treetops.

'I'm cutting back now,' said Benjamin, turning the wheel without waiting for Toby to agree. He'd seen a gap to the right that looked familiar.

But he was wrong; he hadn't been here before. The gap ran a few yards, then opened into a small clearing. He braked to a halt.

'What are you stopping for?' said Toby.

Already he could see the bird dropping towards them.

'Trying to work out which way to go,' said Benjamin.

'Straight on! Quick! Don't stop here!'

Benjamin drove on into the trees, realizing it was best not to argue. Toby's face had darkened and his fists were pounding his thighs as he stared forward, searching the forest.

'There!' he shouted suddenly. 'Go past that tree. But be careful. We're close to the valley.'

The engine started to splutter.

'No!' said Benjamin. 'Don't die on me.'

'Look out!' shouted Toby.

The trees fell away. Round to the right were the outhouses and the ruin. Below them, the valley.

'Brake!' he yelled. 'Quick!'

Benjamin drove his foot at the pedal and missed. At the same moment, the bonnet rose and fell.

And hung there, swaying like a seesaw.

The Land Rover had mounted the verge at the top of the

valley and was stuck, the front wheels clear of the ground sloping down to the rock. The engine had stalled.

Toby glowered at him.

'You idiot! I need the Land Rover for what I've got to do.'

But Benjamin didn't hear him. He was gazing down in rapturous relief at the rock.

Ione was standing there looking up at him, her face as unforgettable and beautiful as ever, even from this distance. He sighed. So she was not dead after all.

Toby's voice cut in, fierce, determined.

'There she is. Let's get her.'

Benjamin whirled round. 'But that's my friend!'

'That's the Wild Woman. Come on. We'll have to manage without the Land Rover.'

'Wait a minute. You . . . you—'

But Toby wasn't listening.

'She used a knife. So can we. There's one in the bag behind you. Pass it to me.'

But Benjamin was scrambling for the door, the Land Rover rocking as his weight moved.

'Hey!' shouted Toby. 'What are you doing?'

Benjamin jumped out and raced down the slope towards the rock.

'Wait!' shouted Toby. 'Come—'

But there was no time to finish his words. The black shape screamed in from the sky through the gap in the windscreen. The next moment he was fighting for his life.

This time the anger of the bird was worse, the beak greedier for his eyes. He struck out, blindly, wildly. Still it fluttered round his face.

'Get off! Get off!'

He ducked his head. The stabbing started on his neck, ear, cheek. Somehow he forced the bird back through the windscreen. Shielding his eyes he looked out.

It waited, hovering over the bonnet. He raised his arm, ready for the next attack; then froze.

128

A cat had jumped onto the bonnet.

He looked out and the ground seemed to be moving all around him. There were cats everywhere, far more than he'd seen at the house, as though they could multiply at will. And this time he knew they would be quick. They had let him escape once; they would not do so again.

A second cat jumped onto the bonnet. The raven still hovered, a few feet above them, but they took no notice of it.

Only of him.

A score of cats waited, poised to spring onto the bonnet.

'Damn you, Wild Woman,' he murmured. 'Damn you.'

She'd done this. Killed his parents, ruined his life. He'd come to kill her and she was going to kill him. He thought of her down by the rock. Laughing at him, probably. As for Benjamin . . .

Stupid Benjamin. Thinking she's his friend. She'll probably kill him too.

Two more cats bounded onto the bonnet. And in that second, the plan formed. It was as mad and risky as the last one but there was no time to weigh the pros and cons. He knew he would have to act at once. Gritting his teeth, he edged himself towards the opening in the windscreen.

'Come on, then, kitties,' he said. 'Let's have a party.'

And slowly, slowly, he stretched forward towards them.

'So who are you?' said Benjamin. 'Tell me who you are?'

She stood by the rock, her face somehow more beautiful than ever amidst the falling snow.

'Who do you want me to be?'

'You can't be Ione *and* the Wild Woman. You can't be—'

'Both good and evil?' She ran her hand over the rock. 'We're all good and evil. What matters is which is stronger.'

He said nothing, no longer knowing what to believe. She watched him for a moment and seemed uncertain whether to speak further. Then she leaned forward.

'You must put the stone back. The things the ancients left us shouldn't be interfered with.'

He moved back from her.

'How do you know I've got it?'

She straightened up again and he relaxed slightly.

'I can sense it,' she said. 'Just like I sensed when it was coming back. I knew the farm had something to do with it. Then you told me how you took the stone and lost it. So I went dowsing for it. I felt sure I could find out where it was. Then yesterday I saw footprints leading to Dragon's Rock.'

Her eyes darkened.

'I thought it was more people coming to get me, so I followed, to keep track of where they were. But the mist came down, I got frightened and lost my way. Then I saw your friend in the field.'

Colour drained from her face.

'I could see he knew where the stone was. I could hear it calling for me from inside him. But he was full of hate. I tried to pluck up courage to ask him where it was, tell him to give it back, tell him it was no good to him. But he ran at me. It was all I could do to hold him off.'

She took a deep breath.

'I was terrified of him. He has so much hatred. It's like a coldness deep inside him. It spreads outwards, over everything, like the mist. It's worse with him than all the others.'

Despite himself, Benjamin took a step towards her again.

'What others?' he said.

She shivered.

'There've been lots. And now someone's found the tunnel to my cave. I dug it when they started hunting for me and it's kept me safe. But now I've seen footsteps inside. I can never hide there again.'

He looked at her, unsure what to tell her, what to ask her, what to do. Unsure of what she was.

'Why have you stayed here?' he said. 'Because of the rock?'

She shook her head.

'Because of the ruin.'

'The ruin?'

She looked up at it, the snow moistening her face.

'It was my family home. My ancestors found the stone in the rock and learnt its secret, but the locals mistrusted them, accused them of witchcraft and drove them out. Generations later my parents came back and tried to squat there, but they were driven out too. I was three years old.'

She shivered again. He studied her face, searching for the Wild Woman in the features. But the Wild Woman was not there. He remembered the figure he had seen standing by the rock, exactly where Ione now stood, and how it had terrified him. But the face had been obscured and it had been night-time; and perhaps his fears had done the rest.

But the knife and the scream: those things he hadn't imagined. He tried to keep his voice steady.

'Why did you kill Toby's parents?'

'Kill them?' She looked at him in surprise. 'I haven't killed them. I could never kill anyone. After I escaped from the boy in the field and found my way back to the ruin, I heard people approaching. I couldn't see them because the mist was still thick. But I remembered the footprints and thought they must be coming for me, like all the others.'

She wiped her face with her sleeve.

'They didn't talk and that made me suspicious, then they started looking round the outhouses. By that time I was sure they were after me. I picked up a stick to protect myself in case they saw me, then they came out. I panicked and hit them over the head. Knocked them both out.'

Images crowded into Benjamin's mind: of mist and darkness and unseen enemies; and a petrified woman. But still he did not know what to believe.

'I didn't mean to hurt them,' she said. 'I just wanted to knock them out and run away. Then I recognized them from the farm.'

She wiped her face again.

'I wanted to tell them I didn't kill their dog. And I thought they might know something about the stone. So before they came round, I tied them up. In case they hurt me.'

She paused to take in a quick breath.

'They didn't know anything about the stone. They said they'd come out looking for sheep. I went to untie them, then realized I'd thrown away the stick and didn't have any protection if they attacked me, so I went and got my knife. They thought I was going to kill them. When I bent down to cut the woman free, she screamed. She must have thought I was going to stab her.'

She shuddered.

'I cut the rope and ran off, and left her to untie him. They're probably back at the farm by now.'

Benjamin felt a sick premonition.

'Ione,' he said, 'Toby's come to kill you. It's my fault. He thinks you killed his mum and dad. I must tell him.'

'There's no point.' She looked at him wearily. 'What can you tell him?'

'That you haven't killed his mum and dad.'

'It makes no difference. His mind was made up long ago about me.'

'But he wants—'

'He wants to see the Wild Woman dead.' She stared at the ground, now bright with snow. 'And I do too.'

He moved closer, his hand on the stone in his pocket.

'But you're not the Wild Woman,' he said. 'You're Ione.'

'That's not what he sees. That's not what the world sees. I told you, I'm in a cage and the Wild Woman's my jailer. She's got a halter round my neck and she's destroying me. Why should I feel any love for her?'

He stared at the face he had only ever seen as beautiful.

'But I don't see the Wild Woman.'

'You're different. I told you that before.'

'But why do the others see the Wild Woman? Why does Toby?'

132

She turned to face the Land Rover at the top of the valley. 'When your mind's full of hate, you see demons everywhere.'

'Demons,' said Toby. 'That's what you are. Let's see what you can do.'

The cats on the bonnet hissed.

'Not enough of you,' he said. 'Not enough to get me.'

He watched the bodies slinking over the ground, brushing against the side of the Land Rover.

'Come on, little demons. Join your friends.'

As if in answer, three cats jumped up onto the bonnet.

'Still not enough to get me.'

The nearest cats moved closer, their eyes fixed upon him. The raven wheeled upwards but still circled the Land Rover. He looked anxiously over the side. If the cats on the bonnet jumped first, the plan wouldn't work.

Gordon moaned suddenly but did not open his eyes. Toby noticed snow on his brother's hair and shoulders where it had driven through the gap in the windscreen. It was strange to see Gordon helpless. He tried not to think of what the cats would do to him if they had the chance.

He leaned further over the bonnet towards the nearest cats. They crouched lower, watching malevolently.

'You can't handle me,' he said. 'Not on your own. You need help. Much more help. You need—'

Two more cats jumped onto the bonnet, then a third, a fourth, a fifth. The Land Rover tipped towards the front, but still wouldn't budge further.

'Not enough,' he said. 'We need more of you up here, loads more. Then we'll really have some fun. We'll—'

Before he could finish, the ground seemed to rise like a huge black wing as the rest of the cats jumped. The bonnet dipped under their weight and with a suddenness he had not expected, the Land Rover plunged down the slope.

* * *

'My time's come,' she said, looking quickly at him. 'It's up to you to look after the dragon now.'

Benjamin stared at her.

'But—'

'Put the stone back. You don't need it. Just put it back and the land'll have a chance.' She glanced up the slope again. 'And remember me.'

There was no time to answer. He had seen the Land Rover hurtling down.

She turned to face it, her back to the rock.

'You're the steward now,' she said.

The Land Rover thundered towards her. And suddenly he realized she was not going to move.

He ran forward, screaming.

'Ione! Get out of the way!'

21

Later, after the ambulance had left to take Gordon to hospital, they wandered down to the paddock fence. The snow had ceased to fall and the ground was smooth and soft but it was clear from the sky that there would be more showers later. The Land Rover stood by the silver birch, just as they had left it, both doors open, and much the worse for wear.

They hadn't spoken since the rock. But now Benjamin knew he had to ask.

'Why?' he said.

Toby didn't answer straightaway. He was watching his parents through the window of the kitchen and wondering at the bizarreness of everything: the house nice and warm again, Mum and Dad safely back, no cats or raven, no dead bodies in his room.

'Why what?' he said vaguely.

'Why did you swerve at the last minute?'

Toby traced a finger through the snow on top of the fence. This was odd too: talking to Benjamin. But for some reason it didn't seem so bad now.

He thought back to what he'd seen: the Land Rover charging down, cats jumping and sliding from the bonnet, the Wild Woman braced against the rock, gazing up at him as he gripped the wheel, yearning to kill.

'Something in her face,' he said. 'I don't know. She could have escaped, easily. Run to the side, behind the rock.' He frowned. 'But she didn't move. She just stood there. Then looked up at the sky, like she wanted to make it easy for me.'

He looked away.

'She was going to let me kill her. And I couldn't do it.'

Benjamin too thought back. But his picture was different. He remembered Ione, standing by the rock; the Land Rover swerving and rolling up the other slope; the snow blinding him as he ran.

And holding Toby, telling him it was all right.

Then turning, to find Ione gone.

Mum passed round the mugs of hot chocolate and switched on the Christmas tree lights.

'She didn't hurt us, Toby. Just this bump here where she knocked me out.'

Dad was stoking the fire.

'I've got one, too.' He touched a spot on his head and winced. 'I'll say one thing for that woman, she can pack a punch.'

'It wasn't a punch,' said Benjamin, before he could stop himself. 'She used a stick.'

They all looked round at him.

'How do you know?' said Toby.

Benjamin looked down, hoping they wouldn't question him further.

'Whatever it was,' said Dad, 'it damn well hurt. Still, we're all right now. I'm only sorry it's mucked up Christmas a bit. We'll have to see how Gordon is before we get going on presents and things.'

'But how did you get caught?' said Toby.

'Stupid really. Went out about half five and found the sheep had got out of Big Willy. Yes, yes, I know I should've listened to Gordon and checked the fence straight after the gale. Anyway, they got out and we set off to look for them. And down came the mist.'

'It was awful,' said Mum. 'I've never known a mist like it. We couldn't even see each other. We had to hold hands.'

'I didn't mind that bit,' said Dad.

Toby gave him an impatient glance.

'But what happened?'

'Got totally lost,' said Dad, 'that's what happened. Blundered about for hours, worrying about you lot wondering where we were, and whether you'd got back from Totnes OK. Couldn't see a thing. In the end we huddled under a tree and waited. Waste of time moving. Must have been midnight before it started to clear a bit.'

'Much later than that,' said Mum. 'I remember telling you it was nearly one and that was some time before we left the tree.'

'Maybe.' Dad took a sip of hot chocolate. 'Anyway, we wandered round again for ages and ages, and somehow or other ended up at one of the outhouses above Dragon's Rock. The mist was still too thick to get anywhere, so we went inside to see if it was clean enough to shelter in, but it was filthy. We came out and that was that. Crack on the head. When we came to, we found ourselves tied up.'

'But what did she want with you?' said Toby.

'It wasn't easy to understand her. She's got a funny way of talking. Some kind of a lisp and a really rough voice. And I'll tell you, she's even uglier close up.'

'And more frightening,' said Mum. 'I was really scared of her.'

Dad nodded.

'Anyway, she started going on about Flash. Something about him turning up at Dragon's Rock all the time and the only reason we kept seeing him with her was 'cause she was bringing him back to the farm, or so she claimed. Well, at least we know now where he used to go when he ran off. If it's true.'

'But why would he want to go up to Dragon's Rock?' said Toby.

'You know what a funny place it is, specially for sheep turning up there.'

'But there was something else,' said Mum. 'She said something about animals and birds being drawn to her.

137

About how Flash took a liking to her and kept trying to follow her.'

Benjamin remembered the robin hopping onto Ione's arm, and he held on to the image: so bright and clear in his mind, but so different from the picture the others were creating.

Dad sniffed. 'I didn't believe a word of that rubbish.'

'So was that all she wanted?' said Toby.

'She went on a bit about how she didn't kill Flash. Said she found him caught in the trap and was bending over to see if he was alive when Gordon appeared. She ran off but reckoned we maybe thought the trap belonged to her.'

'We did.'

'Well, she said it didn't, and it wasn't an animal trap but a man-trap someone had made to catch her. She reckoned she'd found lots of them over the years and said she'd buried them so they wouldn't be a danger to anyone else. I took all that stuff with a pinch of salt. Oh, and there was another thing. She seemed to think someone from our farm might have taken a stone of hers or something.'

Toby saw Mum's eyes rest on him for a moment. Dad threw a log on the fire.

'Lot of fuss about a bloody stone. Anyway, we told her we didn't know anything about it. Said we'd come out looking for sheep, and she let us go.'

'We still haven't found the sheep,' said Mum.

'I'll take another look after I've drunk this.' Dad's face grew stern. 'Now then, you two, I want to know what you were playing at taking the Land Rover out, specially with Gordon seriously hurt.'

Toby and Benjamin looked at each other.

'Well?' said Dad.

To Toby's surprise, Benjamin answered.

'It was my fault. I was up at Dragon's Rock. I heard you in the outhouse with Ione.'

'Who?' said Toby.

Benjamin looked at him.

'The Wild Woman.'

'What did you hear?' said Mum.

'I heard you scream. I thought she was going to kill you.'

'So did I. But she was only reaching down to cut the rope.'

'I ran back and got Toby. That's why we took the Land Rover. We wanted to try and save you.'

Save them? Toby thought. He remembered the despair, the anger, the sense of hopelessness; the feeling that they were already dead. And that his world had died with them.

It hadn't been about saving.

It had been about killing.

He wondered how much Benjamin would tell them; how much he himself would tell them.

'And who did the driving?' said Dad.

'I did,' said Benjamin.

'*You?*' Dad raised his eyebrows. 'Who taught you to drive?'

'Dad did. I kept pestering him to teach me and in the end he gave in. He used to take me out in the van and let me practise on some waste land.'

Dad drained his chocolate and looked from one to the other.

'Well, your motives were good enough, but I don't want you doing anything like that again. If you were worried, you should have called the police.' He reached for his pipe. 'Anyway, it doesn't look as though the Wild Woman'll be bothering us any more. Or anyone else for that matter.'

Benjamin sat up.

'What's happened to her?'

'She's gone, or so it appears. Been seen heading for the moor with a big pack on her back. I've just had a phone call from Brambles.'

'The next farm,' Mum explained to Benjamin. 'They're one of the farms that always leave food out for her.'

'She didn't touch it apparently,' said Dad. 'Went straight past and across the fields. In a hurry, they said. Didn't stop,

139

didn't look back. Funny, I'd have thought she'd have taken the food if she had a journey in front of her.'

Benjamin thought back to that first meeting above the plantation: the wintry sky, the early morning stillness, Ione gathering sticks; refusing his assistance.

'She's got her pride,' he said.

The others were looking at him again. He turned away, not wanting to talk, and into his mind came another picture of her, a picture of her face as he had seen it in the window pane. And he wondered yet again what she really was.

A frightening woman or just a frightened one?

Good or evil? Or good and evil?

We're all good and evil, she'd said. What matters is which is stronger. And he thought, maybe it's only evil that sees evil, and good that sees good.

Toby's father stood up.

'Right,' he said, 'I've got things to do.'

But Toby stopped him.

'Have you and Mum been up to my room since you got back?'

' 'Course we have. First place we looked for you.'

'So you must have seen the . . . you know—'

'Seen the what?'

Toby saw only puzzlement on Dad's face; he looked over at Mum and found the same. And his own puzzlement deepened. He thought of the desperate fight, so fresh in his mind and so real: the claws, the teeth, the rippling bodies, the crunch of the skull under his foot. The weight of the animals on the bonnet.

'Cats,' he said. 'Everywhere. Over the landing, down the stairs. So many of them. I killed two. You must have—'

Mum and Dad looked more confused than ever. He turned frantically to Benjamin.

'You must have seen them! When we drove off, they were following. And up at the rock. You . . . you must have—'

Benjamin shook his head.

'The raven, then!' said Toby. 'Didn't you—?'

But he could see Benjamin knew nothing.

'More likely a crow,' said Dad. 'Don't get ravens round here. Up on the moor, round the coast. That's the place for ravens.'

'It was a raven! It attacked me. Look at my face.'

'Do I have to?'

'Dad!'

Dad studied him in mock seriousness.

'Ugly as ever. What's the problem?'

Toby angrily rolled up his trouser legs and held out his hands.

But there was not a single scratch mark.

Mum watched with unconcealed amusement.

'You don't seem to have come to too much harm. Whatever it was attacked you.'

Dad laughed.

'What with Benjamin's dragon and your cats—'

'And raven!'

'And raven, we're turning into a flipping zoo.' He looked at his watch. 'I'm off. I'll give the hospital a buzz in a couple of hours. See how Gordon's doing.'

Toby sat in silence for some time after Mum and Dad had left the room. Then he turned to Benjamin.

'Why doesn't anyone believe me?'

Benjamin looked at Toby's face and it seemed somehow different. He remembered something Ione had said about seeing demons everywhere when your mind's full of hate. But Toby didn't seem full of hate now. Perhaps there might even be a chance they could be friends one day. He hesitated.

'If you believe in my dragon, I'll believe in your demons.'

'Demons?'

Toby thought back.

Demons.

He had called them that, just before they jumped on the

141

bonnet and sent the Land Rover down the slope. Strange that Benjamin should use the word.

But lots of things were strange now.

He nodded slowly.

'I'll believe in your dragon.'

22

They set off together across the fields, walking in unaccustomed harmony. Neither spoke, yet for once there was no strain, no anger, no awkwardness. It had snowed again during lunch but obligingly stopped as they slipped quietly out of the house.

It hadn't seemed necessary for either of them to mention where they were going, even to each other. It had simply been understood between them.

To Benjamin, this was doubly strange. Firstly because he could never have foreseen any alliance with Toby, slender or otherwise, and secondly because he had always intended to take the stone back alone.

He knew he should have put it back earlier when he was with Ione. But things had happened so quickly: the Land Rover rushing down the slope, Toby trembling in the driver's seat, fighting tears, his foot pressed hard on the brake; Ione disappearing. The time had not been right.

But now it was right. And he was not alone after all.

They passed the gate at the top of Mucky Meg and wandered down the track, the snow already deep under their boots. He looked around him, trying to remember the features of the landscape he had known.

But he could not.

Everything was different now, as though the snow had altered not just the fields and hills but the whole vista of his life.

He looked at Toby, a few feet in front.

Certainly Toby was different.

And Toby felt different, though he didn't know why. He

had looked for the bird and the cats the moment he left the house. He had looked for the Wild Woman in dark places.

But he knew they had all gone; left his life forever. And the house was warm again. As for Benjamin . . .

He listened to the sound of Benjamin's boots in the snow behind him.

Benjamin was still a mystery.

But not an enemy. Not any more.

All the demons were gone now.

They stood at the top of the valley and looked down at the rock, rising solitary and proud from the snowy ground. Toby spoke for the first time.

'Is this where the dragon is?'

Benjamin spread his arms.

'It's everywhere, but this is where it's strongest.'

'How do you know?'

'I can hear its roar, feel its breath. That's why I've felt so hot all the time. Since I took the stone.'

He paused, unsure whether to risk derision, but for once Toby's face held no contempt. It was worth a gamble.

'The dragon was angry with me,' he said.

Surprisingly Toby didn't laugh, and when he spoke, his voice was unusually subdued.

'My demons are gone now. Do you think your dragon's gone too?'

Benjamin shook his head.

'My dragon will never go.'

They wandered down towards the rock, sliding in places where the snow made the slope more difficult. Half-way down Toby stopped and pointed up at the ruin.

'Look!'

Benjamin looked up eagerly, hoping for a second that it might be Ione.

But it was only sheep.

So they had come here after all.

Toby had already turned back to the rock.

'We'll deal with the sheep later. Dad'll have to get help from Brambles. They've got a couple of good dogs up there. Come on.'

They walked to the base of the valley and up to the rock. And to Benjamin it seemed to grow more immense, more awesome, more frightening than ever.

'What've we got to do, then?' said Toby.

Benjamin reached into his pocket and pulled out the stone.

'We've got to put this back.'

He held it tight for a moment, aware of the keenness of both their eyes upon it, then, not quite knowing why, he held it out.

'You do it.'

The confusion in Toby's face was almost comical, and he wondered somewhat mischievously whether it stemmed from shock at being offered the stone or anxiety at not knowing where it went.

Perhaps both.

Toby took the stone and studied it for a moment.

'I never thought of this but—' He held it up. 'Look, it's a miniature Dragon's Rock.'

Benjamin stared in amazement, wondering why he had never noticed the resemblance himself. But Toby was right. And the likeness was unnerving.

'So where does it go?' said Toby.

'I'll show you.'

He walked round the rock and tried to remember the spots where he had placed his feet.

'Have I got to climb it?' said Toby.

'It's a bit slippery. Maybe I should—'

'I can do it. Hold the stone while I go up.'

Toby cast his eye over the rock.

'No problem,' he said and expertly began to climb.

Benjamin watched, trying not to feel envious, and thinking back to his own climb all those years ago; a

145

climb he never should have made, a climb that had caused pain to others, and to the land.

And here was someone else putting it right. But perhaps there was some purpose in that.

He heard Toby call down.

'There's a little notch in the top. Is that where it goes?'

'Yes, but it must never come out again.'

Toby reached down.

'I won't take it out. Here, let's have it.'

Benjamin stared for the last time at the stone and suddenly it felt heavy in his hand, far beyond its normal weight; something too heavy to carry much longer.

'Take it,' he said. 'Quickly.'

Toby closed his hand round it and reached over the top of the rock. Benjamin turned away, unable to watch.

Toby jumped down again.

'But where's the dragon?' he said.

Benjamin looked up at the rock, then around the valley.

'It's here. In this place and all over the land.'

'And is it still angry with you?'

'No.'

'How do you know?'

'I don't feel hot any more. And . . . and the roar's not like it was. It's peaceful now, a sort of purring sound.'

Toby looked about him with a hint of his old impatience.

'Well, I can't see any dragon, or hear one. And I've been feeling cold.' He thought for a moment. 'Funny though, I don't feel cold now.' Then he chuckled. 'I reckon you're making it up about the dragon.'

'Like your demons? Your cats and raven?'

'They were real.'

Toby started to walk back up the slope.

'Come on, I'm knackered. I haven't slept the last two nights and we've got to tell Dad about the sheep. And it is Christmas Eve, remember.'

Christmas Eve!

Benjamin shook his head. He'd forgotten about

146

Christmas altogether. They took a few steps up the hill, then stopped for a last look at the rock.

'You did promise you'd believe in the dragon,' said Benjamin.

'I know,' said Toby. 'But I can't see it. You sure it's there?'

Benjamin nodded.

'It's there,' he said softly. 'I know it's there.'

And as he gazed towards the rock, it seemed to him suddenly that the snowy floor turned blue like a deep, still pool; and into that pool the rock fell, shattering the stillness and sending waves up and over him and away in all directions, as far as he could see. In that moment, unbearably fleeting, unutterably beautiful, he looked into the dragon's eye.

Toby saw only a rock.

And a valley.

And a small boy, crying.

'Come on, Benjamin,' he said.

Benjamin looked round, and the briefest of smiles passed between them. They set off back up the slope.

And Benjamin saw that the blue had melted into the white again, or maybe the white had melted into the blue; it didn't seem to matter which. All things would melt away in the end, he decided, like the snow now falling once again.

At least the dragon could rest in its lair and the land would have a chance, as Ione had wanted. He wondered what she meant about him being the steward.

'Benjamin! Come on!'

He'd fallen behind already. A few yards up the slope he saw Toby waiting for him. He stopped, breathing hard, expecting some impatient gibe. Toby bent down, scooped up some snow and with great deliberateness patted it into a snowball, looking Benjamin over playfully, as though choosing his spot. Then he flung his arm back and, with a great shout, hurled the snowball high over the valley.

Neither looked to see where it landed.

They had already turned for home.

Other Books by Tim Bowler

Shadows
ISBN 0 19 271802 9

Jamie's father keeps driving him on to win, to become a world squash champion. But Jamie can't take it any more and is desperate to get away.

Then he finds a girl hiding in his shed, and in helping her to escape from the danger that is pursuing her, he is at last able to deal with his own problems.

He realizes he can't run away for ever. He has to come out of the shadows and face up to his father, whatever the cost.

River Boy
Winner of the Carnegie Medal
ISBN 0 19 275035 6

Grandpa is dying. He can barely move his hands any more but, stubborn as ever, refuses to stay in hospital. He's determined to finish one last painting, 'River Boy' before he goes.

At first Jess can't understand his refusal to let go, but then she, too, becomes involved in the mysterious painting. And when she meets the river boy himself, she finds she is suddenly caught up in a challenge of her own that she must complete — before it's too late . . .

Midget
ISBN 0 19 275037 2

Midget doesn't have much going for him. He's fifteen years old, three foot tall, and puny as anything. He's trapped in a useless, twitching body he can't control, tortured by Seb, his cruel older brother, and can only communicate in grunts and gestures.

But Midget knows one thing — sailing. He dreams of sailing his own boat, and showing Seb a thing or two. Everyone says it'll take a miracle, but that's when Midget starts to realize that even miracles are possible. It's just that sometimes they hurt people who get in the way . . .

'a masterly handling of suspense and cold trickling horror'.
Sunday Telegraph